FOREVER FAMILY

GINNY STERLING

INTRODUCTION

A change of station is in your future, Flyboy...
Elliott '*Copperhead*' Trent's life is filled with adventure and distance, creating a very lonely existence. An untimely death of a friend brings to the spotlight a chance he never imagined. He's willing to defy the miles that separate him from the broken family – making an offer he never imagined.

Prepare to take flight, ready or not!
Sarah's world shatters with the loss of her husband, finding solace in the unwavering support of her best friend, Elliott. With four lively children and a whirlwind of chaos, the late-night calls, heartfelt letters, and scattered visits solidify their bond as they conquer the challenges of time zones and missed milestones.

Can a brave pilot's unwavering devotion to a friend and a new family be enough to overcome the obstacles they face?

Wow! I was finally able to get into this series and wow! Wow! WOW! It's starts with tragedy and there's almost tragedy near the end and then this amazing band of brothers pull through for each other. There's also an amazing love story woven throughout. Each of these men, egotistical, loud, cocky and wonderful have hearts of gold and their own personal demons to overcome. I can't wait to binge on the rest. Flyboys here I come.

This was amazing story about how 2 pen pals complete a cross the world ended up falling in love and getting married. A beautiful and wonderful book. Was hard to put down. Now got to read the others.

What a beautiful, fun, and thrilling sweet Romance. I loved all of the humor, quirky characters, and daring moments as a firefighter. There were so many cute inside joke moments that stick in your head and make you fall even more in love with this book. I can't believe I hadn't read any of Ginny's books before now and now I need to read ALL of them!!!

FLYBOYS
Family tree
Ginny Sterling

THUMPER
(Jackson Sloan)
m. Harley Petersen
Samantha
m. Toby Sharon

ALPO
(Hunter Petersen)
m. Glory Madison
Twins
Madison   Michael
m. Emmett Wilkes   m. Penelope Walters
Father is Colin Wilkes in HH Remember Love

ACE
(Bryan MacKenzie)
m. Jessica Logan
(Wolverine)
Neil

ROMEO
(Lee Tarrant)
m. Dixie Lancaster
India
Lee's brother is Micah Tarrant in HH Remember Peace

ARMADILLO
(Cody Fuller)
m. Delilah Chaplin
Luke   Abbs   Duke
m. Nicolette Saxon   Beth   Eric
CJ   Faith

VALKYRIE
(Aeron Saxon)
m. Marisol Jenkins
Toby   Caspar   Nicolette
m. Samantha   m. Luke
Sloan   Fuller

FIREFLY
(Sutton Grainger)
m. Melody Green
Betsy   Liberty
m. Johnny Macks
Betsy's father is at Mr. Clark.
Aunts are Karen & Emily Marks

REAPER
(Ryan Merrick)
m. Sophie Lane
Ben   Ruby
m. Rose Griffin   m. Michael Griffin
Father is John Griffin in
HH Remember Home

HOT CAKES
(Jace Sorensen)
m. Karen Marks
Claire
m. Esteban Martinez
Father is Julie Martinez in
HH Remember Patience

VAPOR
(Matthew Barlow)
m. Jana Sorensen
Julian
m. Charlotte Reed
Father is Daniel Reed in
HH Remember Wishes

CABOOSE
(Nick Evans)
m. Ivy Quinn
(Maiden)
Quinn
m. Lexi Tarrant
Father is Micah Tarrant (HH
Peace) & niece to Romeo

X-RAY
(John Masden)
m. Emily Marks
Lisette
Sister to Karen Marks & aunt to
Johnny Marks

HANDSY
(Mike Wheeling)
m. Meredith Bailey
d. Aaron   Gwen

HOUDINI
(Gage Walters)
m. Abby York
Penelope (Peppy)
m. Michael Petersen

GHOST
(Jax Cunningham)
m. Mary West
Jolie
m. Braysen Mitchell
Father is Everett Mitchell
in HH Remember Faith

MAESTRO
(Alex Wilcox)
m. Everly Briscoe
Caleb
Caleb's mother is Mallory
Duncan

RICOCHET
(Killian Briscoe)
m. Destiny Richards
Cate   Dillon

SPARKY
(Austin Calder)
m. Giselle Beck
Grant   Wendy

PARADOX
(Joshua Parr)
m. Mallory Duncan
Caleb
Caleb's father is Alex Wilcox

RIPTIDE
(Andrew Carter)
m. Megan Josephs
Drew   Emmaline   Twins
Laura   Jacob   Faith &
Hope

Created in Canva by Abby Butler

FLYBOYS
Family tree
Ginny Sterling

COPPERHEAD
(Elliott Trent)

m. Sarah James

Morgan   Leslie
Bethany
Henry
Colton
Josie

OUTFIELD
(Pete Walker)

m. Sunny Heing

Hope

INFERNO
(Max Carpenter)

m. Elara Cole

Ember

PIRANHA
(Stephanie Ely)

m. Joey Charlton
(Scarecrow)

BUBBLES
(Derek Thorne)

m. Toni Baird

CAVALIER
(Lance Grant)

m. Toni Malone

INSPIRATIONAL SONG LIST FOR THE BOOK

Song list to get my head in the 'right place' for this story - and boy - did it help! There was so much intensity in a few of the moments... and if you know the songs? I think you'll see what scenes each 'fell' into. This was a fun addition I wanted to share with you to give you that much MORE when you read the story.

A New Day Has Come – Celine Dion
It's Always Been You – Caleb Hearn
Little Wonders – Rob Thomas
Photograph – Ed Sheeran

This one has been on my radar for a while...

Ginny Sterling Newsletter
(You get a free book!)

PREFACE

Trigger warning… because you know me. I would rather err on the side of caution for anyone that could be bothered by content.

This book has a few episodes that deal with:

- Death of a spouse referred to - not described.
- Dealing with long-distance relationships
- A new step-parent in the mix
- childbirth
- Post op pregnancy
- Mildly crude language and innuendo (… *but no cursing!*)

And as always… a Happily Ever After.

CHAPTER 1

SARAH

Several years ago...

THE BELL RANG over her head, causing everyone in the classroom to stand up in a hurry, all of them more than ready to exit the building. Today was final exams, and it really didn't matter if she didn't pass at this point. There was no changing the outcome – she would still graduate no matter what. That was a comforting thought and took a little stress off her already strained thoughts that bounced around in her mind.

Only to feel someone grab her left arm while someone else hooked her by the right arm's elbow. Not panicking, she knew exactly who the dynamic duo was on either side of her.

David and Elliott.

"Sooo?" Elliott drawled knowingly, dipping his head playfully toward her. "Are you taking down the valedictorian –

ahem – Me! Or shall we just settle for second place now, my friend?"

Sarah laughed easily and met his arrogant grin, knowing it was all in friendship, and there was zero malice in his words. She and Elliott had been friends for years, growing up down the street from each other.

"Don't try poaching my girl," David teased as the trio walked down the hallway, arm-in-arm.

"You can have your girl if she's actually your girl...?"

"Guys, not this again..."

"Can't be married at the Academy, which is the only reason I'm going to let you have my Sarah," Elliott grinned, winking at her playfully. "If I wasn't going then..." He let his words hang in a mock threat that only made both her and David roll their eyes.

Elliott could be such a flirt sometimes – and it was empty taunts.

"Then nothing," David retorted, kissing her on the cheek and causing her to laugh once again as the two guys reached across her, pushing at each other's shoulders playfully.

David was her high school sweetheart – and Elliott's friend on the football team. The two were inseparable during practices, and the trio was always hanging out when they could except on Fridays when she and David went out on a date.

Elliott practically avoided dating like the plague, and it was rare that he had plans with anyone. In fact, the second he was accepted into the Air Force Academy, he dropped his brand-new girlfriend like a hot rock. They'd gone out once, but either he wasn't interested, or the Academy meant that much to him.

As they got to the parking lot where David's car sat, Sarah hopped up onto the trunk, perching there as the three of them just hung out together talking. They'd done this several times, but this time, it was bittersweet in a way she never expected.

They were going in three different directions.

Elliott was leaving Thursday for Colorado. David was going to be attending the police academy in Tyler to become a police officer like his father. Sarah had landed a cushy job as a teller in Yonder at the bank, planning on trying to take a year for herself, saving up for college. Her parents didn't have savings set aside, and while her grades were good, the grants and scholarships she earned for college would barely cover her books… forget the tuition.

No, college would come later… one day, she mused, listening to them talk.

"Are you all packed and ready to go?"

"I can't take much," Elliott admitted. "Most everything I have is staying here, and I told my mom to give it to my aunt's kids. I mean, the Air Force provides just about everything I could need…" he shrugged and smiled. "Except a photo of the three of us."

"Dude! Yes, we've gotta get a picture."

"Hey! You – yeah, you – come here, kiddo," David hollered at one of the other students getting ready to walk home. "Can you take our picture?"

Sarah handed David her cell phone to use as a camera – and then posed in between the two men, smiling. She felt David's arm around her waist, and Elliott leaned in close, crossing his arms over his chest, as she put an arm around each of their shoulders.

"Guys, we cannot lose track of each other," she began nervously, her voice quiet as she smiled at the camera – only for David to collect it a moment later. "You guys are the best, and we have to promise to keep in touch."

"We will," Elliott said quietly, turning to look at her with those gentle brown eyes that reminded her of a Tootsie Roll.

"I think if we try hard enough, we can keep this friendship going."

"I'm not letting you get away from me," David boasted, wrestling around playfully before hugging her. "You are stuck with me, Sarah."

"And you both are stuck with me."

"Let's go with 'voluntarily attached'…"

"Friends?"

"Family…"

"Always," she smiled at him, realizing that the three close friends were indeed parting and going separate ways much too soon. "Let's grab a burger tonight or…"

"I can't," Elliott grimaced. "I've got to get some things together and help Mom clean out my stuff. Four years is a long time, and she's going to rent my room to help pay the bills."

"I'll watch out for her," Sarah immediately promised, touching his hand. "I know it's been tough since your dad died…"

"Yeah, it's not been the same, and I appreciate that. That actually takes a load off of my mind because it's been really bad lately…"

"We can get together Monday night," David offered.

"Can't," Elliott repeated, chuckling as they rolled their eyes in unison.

"Tuesday?"

"Nope."

"Wednesday?" Sarah asked, feeling her heart hammer in her chest in awareness. "You are leaving Thursday, and I can't have my best friend taking off without a proper goodbye…"

"I know," Elliott smiled sheepishly and shrugged before pushing on David's shoulder. "Besides, with this big lug in the way – you'll never even miss me."

"I won't let her," David grinned, and she smiled know-ingly, looking up at him. "You might be running away, but a real man is going to step up to the plate and handle Sarah."

"Where's he at?"

"Funny, brother… very funny," David laughed – and hugged Elliott, causing Sarah's eyes to sting with tears as she realized they were saying 'goodbye' right now without any warning. "Try not to get kicked out and keep that mouth shut, okay? We'll watch out for your mom – I swear it."

"Thank you," Elliott said gruffly and looked at Sarah, who immediately held open her arms, hugging him tightly. She held onto him and heard him take a deep breath.

"You are going to be amazing," she whispered in a hushed voice. "They are so lucky to have you – just come back and visit when you can."

"I'm gonna miss you."

"You'll always have a place here."

"Promise?"

"I swear it, my friend."

"Hey, hey, enough of that, or I might get jealous…" David interrupted easily, causing Elliott and Sarah to look at each other, grinning.

"I don't date guys with a coppertop," she quipped, using one of the first insults that the duo had thrown at each other as kids, ruffling his hair.

"And I don't date flat-chested, whiny girls," Elliott joked, but his voice was thick as he looked at them. "Look at us getting sappy – sheesh. This is the best thing in the world for me, and we all know it."

"And everyone is so proud of you," Sarah volunteered, laying a hand on his shoulder again as he nodded.

"Take care of my best friend."

"Always have and always will."

And with that, Elliott was gone.

He turned and walked away toward his car that had a 'For Sale' sign in the back glass, and out of their lives for an unknown length of time.

THREE YEARS LATER...

"IS HE HERE YET?" Sarah exclaimed excitedly as the door to the small room she had been primping in opened, and Elliott slipped inside. Her breath caught in her chest as she smiled at him, barely holding back tears, rushing over to him, hugging him tightly in his dress uniform.

"Hey there... who said you got to wear white?" he teased emotionally, chuckling at her as he wiped his own glassy eyes – and she swatted at him.

"You twerp! You know better than that, and why are you wearing more bling than the bride?"

"Don't hate the player, hate the game..."

"Gosh, I've missed you," she laughed joyfully, hugging him again.

"Missed you too – now I've only got the weekend in town, and David looks ready to puke," Elliott chuckled. "Are you really ready to be a police officer's wife? It's the handcuffs, isn't it? I knew it. I just knew it. Pretending to be meek, but really a freak."

"Oh my gosh," she chuckled, blushing wildly. "When did you become such a troll?"

"I've always been one... you just chose to ignore it because of my stunning looks, red hair, and this sexy uniform."

"You do look nice... and it's not really red, but copper like a penny."

"You look incredible... Mrs. David James," he said softly, taking her hands in his and leaning back from her to admire her wedding dress as he smiled proudly. "I'm so glad I am getting to walk you down the aisle. It kinda seems fitting, doesn't it?"

"That my best friend in the entire universe stepped in when my father couldn't?" she said tearfully, smiling up at him. Her father had passed away six months ago unexpectedly, and Elliott had called immediately when he heard the news, relaying his sympathies. "It's everything to me - and I'm so happy you could be here."

"I wouldn't miss this for the world."

Sarah laid a hand on his cheek and looked at him as he leaned down, kissed her forehead affectionately, and smiled at her. He nodded emotionally and then held out his arm to her as she looped hers, resting her hand on his forearm.

"You two are so good together – and I'm really happy for you both."

"Once you get stationed at a base and settled down – then we are going to come up, visit, and find you a Mrs. Trent to call your very own..."

"Oh gosh, no," he chuckled. "Let me live vicariously through you two lovebirds. I can't see myself settling down anytime soon or anyone putting up with me for very long."

"Hmm – that's true," Sarah mused dramatically, pursing her lips, causing Elliott to laugh aloud as he grinned at her. "Shall we?"

"Run away together and make David work for it?" Elliott teased. "You'd be sick of me in no time, and I can't have the police after me."

"Oh my gosh, I would be sooooo sick of you," she retorted as he laid a hand on his chest, pretending to be wounded by her words. "Let's go – and just for your information? You are surrounded by officers, so be on your best behavior."

"… Moi?"

"Don't give me that innocent look…"

"I'm really happy for you," Elliott repeated gently, hugging her once more before they entered the sanctuary as they turned to each other. He pulled her veil down over her face, fluffing it for her as she simultaneously smoothed his lapel and straightened his tie.

She looked up at him – and swallowed, feeling so many things at once as he spoke again, his voice thick with emotion. The two of them turned as the doors opened – and the music began playing, announcing the bride had arrived.

"David had better understand just how lucky he is – or I'll be sure to tell him."

She glanced up at Elliott, grinning tearfully, and then looked at her future, David. She could feel herself choking up emotionally the second her eyes met his as he stood there proudly at the altar in his uniform.

"I think he knows…" she breathed.

"I know he does, Sarah… people would have to be blind if they couldn't see that he loves you. Congratulations, my friend."

"Thank you, Elliott."

They walked forward together, entering the sanctuary. Today, her best friend was going to fill in for her father, walking her down the aisle. She couldn't picture this moment any differently and they had been through so much, all of them. Elliott had his life and was leaving her behind… and she was marrying her high school sweetheart – David.

One year later…

· · ·

Sᴀʀᴀʜ ᴡᴀs ᴇxʜᴀᴜsᴛᴇᴅ and lying in the hospital bed, holding their son, as David proudly hugged and shook hands with everyone that came to visit them at the hospital, almost protectively.

Her husband was standing at the door, greeting people, allowing them a quick peek before corralling them away. Uniform after uniform, officer after officer, a sea of black polyester seemed to pass the doorway all congratulating the young couple that just had their first child, and saw her husband's face light up – as he exclaimed something, hugging Elliott, who had just arrived.

The two men she loved most— well, three now, she thought, looking at her son, were there within reach – and she couldn't be happier. David and Elliott were grinning at each other, clapping the other on the back, before her best friend turned to look at her.

"Hey little mama…" Elliott began quietly, grinning proudly as he came to the side of the hospital bed. She reached for him, taking his hand in hers, as he leaned down to kiss her hair easily. "How are you feeling – and how's this little man?"

"We are both worn out," she admitted ruefully and turned to look at the infant as he gave a little grunt before sighing. "I had no idea you could love someone so much, so fast…"

"He's beautiful, Sarah."

"Isn't he, though?" she beamed, smiling up at him. "Morgan, meet your Uncle Elliott, sweetie. Isn't he beautiful, Elliott? When did you get into town?"

"About two hours ago. I went and saw Mom, then came by your house, and one of your neighbors told me you'd gone into labor…"

"You really need to get a cell phone," she chided, laughing tiredly.

"Maybe I will," he hedged evasively and then shrugged,

before giving her a sideways glance... and smiled. "It's just one more thing to keep up with on my way to flight school."

"You got in?" she exclaimed excitedly, seeing David hugging the chief of police who was retiring soon. "I'm so proud of you!"

"I did. I couldn't believe it – and it was harder than I imagined because there was a lot of competition, but yeah. I'm reporting to flight school in a few days."

"So soon?"

"Yup."

"I was hoping you would stay for a while..."

"I'll be in town – but you need to sleep while you can and focus on this little guy," Elliott said softly, reaching out to touch the infant's cheek. "He's really beautiful, Sarah."

"I can't believe I'm a mom... I mean, just look at us," she smiled tearfully, feeling exhaustion sweeping over her. "Who would have thought that those knobbly-kneed kids that rode bikes together would end up like this – and still friends after all these years?"

"You'll never shake me, remember?"

"I remember," she smiled as he leaned down to kiss the top of her head again.

"Get some rest and put your personal security guard on duty. Try to take care of yourself, okay? I'll swing back by before I fly out. I promise."

"I took your mom a crockpot full of stew, some corn-bread, and some canned goods right before I went into labor," she began and looked at him. "She's getting along okay but misses you terribly."

"I know. She's got a new tenant that is helping pay the bills, and I keep trying to send her money, but she won't take it."

"That infamous Trent pride?"

"Very much so, I'm afraid."

"Get grocery store gift cards or just order online and ship it directly to her, then she can't refuse it."

"Hey, that's a good idea…"

"Smart, beautiful, and your best friend."

"Well, two out of three…" he teased as she swatted at him, causing him to laugh. "Rest, Sarah – and let me go take your husband's ego down a notch so he can get that big head of his back through the door."

She smiled tiredly as he left the room.

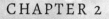

CHAPTER 2

COPPERHEAD

Ghazni, Afghanistan
Several years later...

ELLIOTT TRIED NOT to stare and buried that feeling of foreboding deep within his soul as he entered the barracks. Afghanistan was sure a lot different than Robins Air Force Base in Georgia, where he'd been stationed briefly. It was humid and warm there, and you could hitch a ride with the fellas off-base to get a burger or take a bus in town if you wanted to get away... but here?

There was nothing.

He wasn't a snob in the slightest nor spoiled... but this?

This was really bad. He went from having a room he shared with another pilot to what looked like a rundown military installation out of some horror flick. The rectangular windows high above your head, the yellowed and heavily painted cinder block walls, the lockers, the fluorescent lights on the ceiling and the bunks.

Okay, maybe he was a snob at a certain level – because the bunks had seen better days. Some footlockers had stickers that had been peeled off, and another sticker slapped over them. There were lockers on the wall near one pilot, bins for their dirty clothing, and in the distance, he could see a shower room that looked like something you'd find in a high school gym.

"' Sup Rookies…"

"You've got your choice of 'suites,' fellas…" a man with golden-brown hair began and winked at a skinny guy nearby with spiky blackish hair, obviously making fun of their reaction to their new accommodations.

"The Presidential and Governor's suites are those two bunks over there…"

"I'll take the penthouse," Elliott interrupted, striding forward and selecting one of the empty bunks with sheets folded and waiting on the end of the bed.

"Oh, I like him…"

"Downright sassy, I tell ya'…"

"This place is a dump…"

"Hey! Hey!" the dark-haired skinny man protested theatrically. "It's a quality dump… and don't you ever forget it. Think of it more like a pigsty or a run-down trailer park in hell - if you shared a single room with sixteen other bumpkins from around the globe, located under a broiler."

"Pretentious, aren't they Sparky?"

"Right, Paradox? I was just thinking that…"

Several of the others stood up and walked over, shaking hands as each of them introduced themselves, including the duo.

"Ignore those two," a man with blond hair smirked and pointed at Paradox, who laid a hand on his chest and looked offended, causing Sparky to laugh as he gave everyone the finger. "I'm Ricochet, and the only one you've really gotta worry about here is me."

"Oh yeah?" Elliott grinned, liking the way the man subtly challenged him. "And why is that?"

"'Cause in the skies, I'm everywhere…"

"So you can't fly or stay focused – gotcha…"

Ricochet's mouth dropped open in shock at the quick rebuttal, and two seconds later, he threw back his head, laughing along with several others nearby.

"He's got you there, Ricochet."

"Thanks a lot, Reaper…"

"Anytime."

"I like you, Trent," the man grinned. "What's your call sign?"

"Copperhead."

"Copperhead… or Coppertop like the battery?" - and Ricochet started to put an arm around Elliott's neck, to wrestle him down like he was about to rub his knuckles on the top of his head, only for Elliott to step sideways quickly… reaching out and shoving his arm away - HARD.

"Do it, and it will be the last time you use that hand," Elliott snapped – and then groaned as soon as he saw the rank pinned to the man's shirt. He hated people testing him to see if he had a temper to go with his red hair and had gotten in a few fights over the years. He never really got mad about anything and was pretty easygoing.

A smart mouth? Definitely…

Anger issues? Never…

Dang it! First day here, and I just threatened a senior officer… greaaaat.

"…Sir," he finished lamely.

"Relax, Copperhead," Reaper said quietly from his bunk,

looking up from his notebook in his lap. "Welcome, and a few housekeeping issues for all of you, newbies."

The arrogant man didn't even get up or bother to look interested. Whatever he was working on had priority over anything else, and this was his supposed squadron leader?

"First off, relax. Things are a little different out here, and the only time you need to really bring your 'A' game is in the war room when discussing the next mission – or when we are in the air."

No one said a thing as the man continued speaking like his word was law.

"Second rule – you have a wingman – protect each other, no matter what. Third and most important – we are a team," and Reaper paused for a moment, looking at each one of them.

Elliott saw Ricochet nod; Paradox acknowledged the same. Sparky gave two thumbs up, whereas some of the others simply exchanged looks and nodded or smiled in awareness.

"We help each other, and no one drags the others down. It's hard enough being away from friends and family. So, if any of you are planning on dragging down morale or being the 'anchor' of the group? - I suggest you get ready to swim because I will cut your 'line' before I let any of these men drown... Am I clear?"

The man's voice was nonchalant as the softly spoken threat was made boldly to all of them right before he cleared his throat, adjusted the binder in his lap, and smirked.

"Have fun and welcome to Ghazni," Reaper finished simply – and went back to whatever he was doing.

Hours later, after being shown where the commissary, the exchange, the post office, the clinic, and the gym were located– they finally ended the 'tour' at the communications room. There were a few rows of what looked like cubicles that housed computers, some phones that had seen better days, and a few worn-out chairs.

"Don't knock it – we've got more than the grunts on the other side of the fence," Ricochet admitted. "Rumor has it that they have assigned computer times because they are down to one terminal. Not sure what happened to the others. I don't know if it was logistics, if they destroyed them... or what. But yeah, we have access to write home whenever we want here – and that metal thing in the corner?"

He pointed at an old Westbend commercial coffee maker.

"That beast makes the best coffee, hands down. If you are the first one in, you make the brew, if you empty it? Make another pot – please. I cannot tell you how frustrating it is to pour a cup only for it to be empty."

Elliott chuckled in awareness. Nothing changed. He had that happen to him several times at the Academy where he went to fill his coffee mug and it was either all grounds, empty, or burnt on the bottom.

Not holding back, he took a seat and logged in to write home.

> *Hey Mom,*
>
> *Hope all is well – I just got settled here and am glad to report that it's a lot nicer than I thought it would be. The food is great, the town is so pretty, and I really love the weather.*
>
> *Please stop worrying and just take care of yourself. I know things are hard sometimes, but you really need to relax and let me help sometimes, okay? No one expects you to work yourself to death to pay the bills – especially when I have nothing to spend my money on except you. Ha ha ha.*
>
> *Please, let me help. Dad would want it that way.*
>
> *Love,*
>
> *Elliott*

He sighed, hating that he was so blatantly lying to his mother, but there was no way he could tell her how much he hated this place already. She was already worried, scouring the news, and questioning everything, and she was doing so badly. Her clothing hung from her, and she wasn't eating as much.

Frowning, he opened another window and placed an order on Amazon for several nutritional items to be shipped to her – a daily vitamin, Ensure, some candy bars, bags of peanuts, some protein-laced cookies, and then things for the house.

Sarah was right— again. She always was, always looked out for him, and was probably the best person he'd ever met in his life besides David. He never imagined his detention partner and football buddy would end up being someone he considered a brother – and he felt blessed.

Smiling, he went to email the duo with an update on how he was doing. It had been several hectic months, and he tried to reach out when he could. Writing, visiting, or calling the James family just to stay in touch with his best friends.

Hey Sarah and David,

Hope all is well – and congratulations AGAIN. Y'all do know how babies are made, don't you? Sheesh. Every time I turn around, Sarah is pregnant.

David, seriously dude, give her a break.

Sarah – that will be fifty bucks or a homemade dinner next time I'm in town.

How's Morgan? Tell my buddy that Uncle Elliott mailed him some dinosaurs and that I love him. I sent Leslie a pink, soft little dolly that she can cuddle with.

And yes, Mama – no button eyes. I promise!

I can't believe you are about to deliver baby number three already – you've been married four years, so I guess they've been blissful ones? I can't say that I'm jealous because I'm loving the AF and the adventure. I can't say where I am, but maybe I can call sometime. We'll see.

Thanks for checking on Mom – and I finally took your advice. I sent her a bunch of boxes of stuff to snack on and eat. I can't tell you how much it means to me to have y'all helping out.

Give the kiddos a hug from me, and take care of yourselves, okay?

Your friend,
Elliott

CHAPTER 3

SARAH
Tyler, Texas
Almost two years later...

"Coming!" Sarah called out from the kitchen and heard the cartoons in the living room, practically picturing it in her head. Not one of them was going to move while re-runs of Blue's Clues were on the screen. Nope. All three children would be staring slack-jawed at the blue animated doggie and singing about the mail with Steve, the host of the show, and she heard the knock again.

"I'm coming!" she hollered, rolling her eyes. "I swear if this is some joke or you are selling something," she muttered, yanking her floured hands out of the dough she had been kneading to make rolls for supper and marching toward the front door in frustration. She had flour everywhere on the front of her shirt and would need to wipe down the door handle just as soon as she shooed off the solicitor.

Yanking it open, she hesitated in confusion.

"Chief Griffin? What's g-going on?" she stammered – and then covered her mouth with the floured hands in horror as she saw the answer in his eyes. "No..."

"May I come in, Mrs. James?" he said quietly. "Can we talk for a moment away from the children... please?"

Sarah stared at him, unable to speak or move as something within her was screaming out in pain and awareness. Something was seriously wrong, and that little hopeful voice that always looked to the bright side of things was suddenly being brutally assaulted, mugged, and snuffed out by every mental demon ever known.

That light within her was flickering and dying as Chief Griffin walked into the house, shutting the door behind him, and took hold of her arm – pulling her away from the living room where the children were still parked in front of the television.

"Mrs. James... Sarah..."

"Where's my h-husband?" she asked in a broken voice she didn't recognize, strangling on the words as her world collapsed around her, brick by brick.

"There's been an accident..."

Sarah closed her eyes in resignation as she listened to the chief of police speak softly to her as they sat at the kitchen table.

Elliott,
I got your email and can you call me?
I can't...
Just call me please – it's an emergency.

I need help,
Sarah

IT WAS ALMOST three in the morning. The children were sleeping in the bed with her, and there was so much confusion, chaos, and lack of comprehension of what was going on that it was heartbreaking.

They were so little, and life was so unfair, she thought brokenly as she smoothed back the hair on Leslie's little head where she and her sister were both sucking their thumbs for comfort.

Morgan was eerily quiet and simply left the room to go get his old teddy bear that was hidden away in his toy box. He hadn't slept with that bear in two years but needed it now.

It was like that fragile bubble of happiness had popped, leaving them all flailing to hang on to whatever they could – and she had reached for Elliott, needing her friend for comfort.

She hadn't seen him in a year since his mother had passed away from pancreatic cancer. That had been so hard to tell him what happened, and she had been there for him during the funeral, never imagining that the shoe would be on the other foot so soon.

Her cell phone rang, and she closed her eyes as she slid her thumb across the screen to answer it.

"Sarah? Sarah, what's wrong? I got your email and…"

Bless him, she thought idly, hearing the concern in his voice and feeling her heart break all over again as she wept, unable to speak for several moments.

"Sarah, talk to me… what's going on? I'm starting to panic and…"

"David is... dead," she warbled, her voice strangling over the words she never thought she would have to utter aloud.

"Whaaaat?"

"David is..."

"No, I heard that – what happened? When? How? Were you with him? Where are the children? Are they okay?" the rapid-fire concern in his voice was touching as she tried to pull herself together.

"Elliott, there was a high-speed chase and..." she broke down again, weeping bitterly in her hands and leaving the room where the children were sleeping as to keep from waking them again.

"Okay," he interrupted gently, his own voice thick with tears. "Stop. Listen to me, okay? You don't have to talk, and it's okay to cry – heck, I'm about to – but I want you to know I'm here for you and always will be, my friend."

"I don't know what to do, Elliott. I'm just... lost," she sobbed. "There is paperwork, the children won't quit asking questions, and I don't know what to tell people. There are the funeral arrangements to be made and..."

"Shhh..." he croaked thickly in the earpiece, obviously trying to calm her down. "I'm on my way. I'm going to hang up the phone and go talk to my boss right now. I'll catch the next flight."

"I'm so s-sorry t-to ha-have to tell you..."

"Sarah, we've always had each other's back - and this is no different. David wouldn't want you beating yourself up," Elliott said brokenly, and she could hear tears in his own voice now. "He'd make some stupid crack, tell us both to 'suck it up,' or 'quit bawling like a bunch of babies'..."

She didn't think it was possible to laugh and cry at the same time – but hearing his words, she did just that, and it was an awful snorting sound that made her laugh even harder. Maybe she was losing her mind or slipping a little too far into that terrifying abyss that seemed to be dragging her down mentally.

"Twenty-six, a widow, and pregnant..."

"You're pregnant again? Sheesh, woman..."

Both laughed tearfully, knowing the inside joke the trio shared, and her laughter turned into pathetic wails of despair as she covered her mouth, bawling horrifically to the point she couldn't talk.

"Sarah, my timer is going on my phone card. Breathe. Take a deep breath and just breathe. I'll be there in fifteen hours, okay? It's going to be all right – repeat after me: It's going to be all right," he instructed in a rushed voice, sounding almost desperate.

"It's going to be okay," she whispered dutifully, tears still streaming down her face as she sat there.

"That's right – and breathe. Just get through the next twenty-four hours, and I'll see you tomorrow night. Okay?"

"Okay," she began and heard the call disconnect as she held out the phone. Nothing mattered anymore. She felt like she was in a daze of hurt, feeling bereft, her mind adrift in pain and loss. Numbly, she set the phone down beside her on the couch and buried her face in her hands.

... And she still had flour on her.

ELLIOTT SHOWED up on the front stoop almost seventeen hours after he'd hung up on the phone, looking exhausted, red-eyed, and had obviously been crying as well. She opened the front door and took one look at him, and that fragile shell collapsed once again as she began weeping, immediately embracing him in a hug, just needing to hold on to something familiar to keep from falling apart.

Her friend cursed softly, hugged her tightly, and they

stood there, both crying, standing in the doorway of the house for several minutes until it began to reach her that he was talking to her.

"… You sit down, and I'm going to make the kids something to eat. I want you to rest for a bit and we'll talk," he was saying brokenly, causing her to look at the children.

Sure enough, they were watching cartoons again. Leslie and Bethany's diapers were sagging pathetically on them as she realized that they were all wearing the same clothing from yesterday. She had flour still on her shirt, under her fingernails, and…

"I'm a wreck," she admitted painfully, staring at him. "Mentally, physically, and emotionally a disaster."

"I think it's allowed," he smiled sadly. "Go change clothes, wash your face, and I'll make something for dinner. Then we'll tackle the kids and…"

"The funeral arrangements and… the chief said to call him about…" she stammered, lost once more, as the tidal wave of what saying 'goodbye' would entail.

"Tomorrow, Sarah," he interrupted firmly. "Today we're grieving, picking up the pieces, and tomorrow will be soon enough to make plans. Now, go take five minutes for yourself, and let me help."

She had no clue how long she was hiding in the bathroom, crying, but when she came out, the children were fed, changed, and tucked into bed – which only compounded what she was feeling. Not only was she a widow at a young age with three, soon-to-be-four, children, but she was a bad mother for neglecting her little ones, who had to be confused and grieving too.

Elliott took one look at her despondent face, sighed, and nodded, pulling her into his arms as she broke down for the millionth time in the last forty-eight hours. They sat down on the couch together, putting a throw pillow on his lap and holding her - brushing her hair from her face while she wept bitterly until she finally fell asleep.

THE NEXT FEW days were a blur of activity, heartbreak, and emptiness. Thank God that Elliot was there to be her rock because she wasn't sure how she could have handled any of this alone. The trio of close friends was now a duo – and like a stool missing a leg, everything was ready to topple with a breeze.

He stood by her side at the funeral, staring straight ahead with this broken expression on his face while he held Leslie in one arm and held Morgan's hand with the other. Sarah carried baby Bethany who was asleep on her shoulder and felt like she had no more tears to weep.

It was a beautiful service full of honor – and she appreciated Police Chief Griffin and his wife coming to pay their respects to the family. The flag draping David's casket was folded and given to her, which she would put in a frame with one of his badges and a photograph of her husband so the children could see it.

Everything seemed so surreal like she was watching all of this on television, yet it was happening to her. The bank manager, her boss, came by to pay his respects, and everyone seemed to love David, reaching out to the young family wanting to help, except she had no clue what to say, what to ask for.

That evening, it was much the same.

Elliott picked up drive-thru, getting the children Happy Meals, and knew he had to be just as exhausted as she was – yet her friend never stopped. Instead of him sleeping on the couch, he insisted she lie down there, and they spent hours talking about different moments in high school that they shared, memories of David, until she finally fell asleep.

It was nearly dawn when Elliott woke her, slipping off of the sofa, jostling her from where she had been resting, and gently rubbing her arm, crouching down in front of her exhausted face.

"Hey, I'm so sorry to wake you, but I've got to catch my flight back," he said softly, his voice full of regret. "You are one of the strongest women I know – and you'll be okay. Take things one day at a time and focus on the children."

"You're leaving?"

"I have to report in, and it takes a long time to get back overseas."

"I don't want you to leave."

"I'll be back to visit when I can."

"But…"

"Sarah, you're scared, and I understand. This is all different, but it will be okay. One day at a time," Elliott paused and then attempted a smile. "I've got pizza set up to be delivered for you this evening at five – and diapers are on the way for the kids. Focus on the small things and try not to cry. We need to get Morgan talking, so I've got a dinosaur-shaped teddy bear coming for him. He doesn't understand, and he's old enough to comprehend something is seriously wrong."

Elliott sighed heavily, clearing his throat.

"The girls don't and won't understand for years. They are too young. We'll have to help them remember David. You need to eat, see a doctor, and take care of yourself for the baby. Please don't make me come back and bury my other best friend, Sarah…" he said raggedly, his dark eyes watching her. "I've got to go because I don't have a choice – but I really need to know you are okay."

"I hate this so much," she whispered in sheer exhaustion and numbness.

"I hate this is happening to you, to us, but David wouldn't want you giving up. He would want you to fight and take care of yourself – and the kiddos, and you know I'm right."

"I hate that too," she admitted and felt a smile touch her lips for the first time in days as he chuckled tearfully. "Be careful out there, and you are always welcome on the couch – and you know that. You don't need an invitation to visit. You're like family."

"Well, I sure don't want you visiting Afghanistan – and you won't be welcomed by me if you show up there," he retorted and hugged her quickly as she got to her feet. "But I do want you to take things day by day. Email me every day before you go to bed, so I don't worry – and tell me if you need anything, Sarah. Now, lock the door behind me and try to lie back down."

She followed him to the front door and saw the taxi waiting outside. Just as she was about to shut it behind him – he turned and leaned in, looking at her pointedly.

"One day at a time – and no one expects you to be perfect, but I do expect to see you again. You got me?"

His dark eyes held hers, and she nodded.

"I'm not giving up," she promised.

"I know you aren't because you aren't a quitter. You are a fighter, and it will be okay someday."

"I'm glad you have that much faith in me – because I'm really struggling."

"Hang on," he urged softly and nodded. "Let me know if you need help. Promise me you'll tell me."

"I promise."

"Good girl," he said quickly as the taxi honked. "I've gotta go."

"Be safe, Elliott."

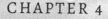

CHAPTER 4

COPPERHEAD
Afghanistan
Six months later...

TIME WAS PASSING BY MUCH TOO QUICKLY, and Elliott realized that he was having a tough time in his own private hell, mourning the loss of his friend. Things were so hard because each night, he would lie there in his bunk and picture the three of them laughing, cutting up, or fooling around as kids.

They had been very close, and it had never really surprised him that David and Sarah had hit it off. He couldn't have imagined a better couple, and couldn't fathom how short that fragile happiness could be.

Her emails were always the same.

I'm fine... this is what numb feels like I guess?

The kids are doing well, should I be upset about that?

Just making it day by day... you?

I miss him.

Why did this happen, Elliott?

He couldn't answer any of those questions – but knowing Sarah, it was not that she was really requesting an answer so much as rather it was just trying to get it off her chest. Perhaps that was what he was doing too when he wrote her?

Dear Sarah,

Things are quiet here – much too quiet sometimes. I'm really glad to hear that the kids are doing well. I sent a book for each of the children. It was pleasantly surprising to see that they have some cute books for the little tykes.

Bethany's is supposed to have little crinkle pages and furry ones so she can touch them – it's a sensory book for learning. Does Leslie like baby dolls still – or would she prefer Barbie stuff? At what age do little girls get into Barbies?

I found a new book series that Morgan might like, and I was chuckling as I read the description. It's called Captain Underpants, and this kid goes on adventures. I don't think it's above his grade level... he's seven now, right?

(bad uncle, I know)

How are you doing? How's your pregnancy progressing? You never say anything much, and your emails are so short. I tried calling, but I'm guessing you were at work. The emails are still coming, so that gives me hope that you are okay.

Keep plugging away each day... you're a survivor.

Write when you can, okay?

Elliott

⚜

IT WAS NEARLY three days before he heard back from her.

> Dear Elliott,
>
> I saw I missed your call, and I know you are reaching out as a friend – but this is the hardest thing I've ever done, you know? Keep writing and don't stop, even if I seem like I'm snapping, short, or don't say much, because knowing I have someone out there on my side is helping me get through this.
>
> Forgive me if I ramble, but I don't know what to say anymore.
>
> I feel broken, lost, and like a new person is taking over my world. I recognize the face in the mirror, but the person IN that face scares me because she's empty and just going through the motions.
>
> I want to laugh. I want to smile,but I feel like it's just gone within me. I put on a face with everyone at work and with my own children because no one wants to know what is really going on inside my head.
>
> So I'm fine.
>
> I'm just great.
>
> Getting by, day-by-day, right?
>
> Thank you for being so kind to the kids. They love the books, the toys, and the diapers, gifts and treats are always welcomed. In fact, every time Amazon delivers to the house, there's a race to get to the box because they know it's from 'Uncle Elliott'... maybe you should send a little less? I don't want to 'train' the children like that – do you? Remember how we were when we heard the ice cream truck growing up?
>
> I should probably go try to get some rest. The baby has been keeping me awake a lot, and trying to keep up with life, home-work, laundry, and work is all taking its toll.
>
> Thanks for always checking on me.

Sarah

Elliott hesitated, glancing around the computer room to see some of the other guys were concentrating on their own emails or activities online. Some of them played computer games, a few would shop, and most of the time, they would email or reach out to family or loved ones.

Yet he had no one except Sarah and her family – and even that felt like it was growing distant to a point. It was hard because time, life, and the universe had a way of changing people, and he missed the old versions of themselves.

He didn't even realize it until he read her email that he was stuck in the same quagmire as she was – he missed laughter, missed smiling, and didn't know how to get it back either.

Instead of feeling invigorated that he was out here doing the job he loved and hanging out with his teammates – he felt almost stuck. Like he was trapped in a room, blinded, and knew she was in another room needing help or support, but couldn't get to her or see what she needed.

And it was hard.

Dear Sarah,

Maybe it's because we've known each other for twenty years that I realized you are being evasive or flat-out lying. I'm not doing so hot, so I assume you aren't either, and you are trying to keep it from me so that I don't worry. That would be a classic 'Sarah-move' on your part – and one that I've seen before.

I'm glad the kids like getting stuff in the mail, and honestly - If seeing the Amazon truck pull up distracts them, then I don't really mind. It's not so much conditioning but wanting to make sure that someone is thinking of them and cares. You are pulling double duty, covering all the bases for both mother and father right now. This is the least I can do to help my best friend.

So let me BE that best friend... okay?

Don't take that from me because I need it – and on that note, I was thinking about doing a short visit. Would you mind if I borrowed the couch again? If not, it's no biggie. I can get a hotel room, but I would like to hang out and treat you all to dinner or something.

Maybe I can take Morgan out to get some school clothes or whatever you need. Do you need maternity clothes? What about baby stuff?

I'm going to see what dates are available, so let's talk soon – okay?

Elliott

Getting up from his seat, he went to check the calendar that they all used to keep their vacation time straight. It was hard mentally to put in for vacation only to get it denied because someone else was out. Sure enough, there was a spot open in a few weeks that would allow him three days in Texas.

"Going somewhere?" a voice said behind him – and he winced. It was the scrawny guy with the smart mouth, Sparky and his new wingman. Turning and looking over his shoulder, he gave him a droll look and let the calendar page drop.

"I'm checking when the next fumigation for pests is scheduled – and it's not soon enough."

"Ouch, you know you might actually hurt someone's feelings with that mouth of yours, Copperhead..."

"How do you think I got the name?"

"Ya' might be a snake in the grass...?"

"Careful there..." Elliott warned softly.

"Or you might have a high tolerance for all the BS going

on around you, but when you've reached your limit – you strike," Sparky grinned knowingly and pointed at the calendar. "Where ya' going?"

"None of your business."

"But it could be," the man quipped... actually following him as Elliott left the office to head toward the barracks. He had duty tomorrow and would be working all day long, but today, he intended to burn off a little energy and frustration at the gym just to keep from thinking of everything going on back home.

"Don't you have someone else to pester?"

"Huh, Reaper said the same thing and told me to go find Paradox."

"Great suggestions – do it."

"But I like you, Big Red..." Sparky grinned as Elliott turned around to glare at him. "I like you a lot – and I see how I used to be lingering inside of you – and wanted to give you the same pep talk that I got."

"Oh gee, can we? How about we sing songs and braid each other's hair too?" he smarted and then hesitated at the cheerful man standing there looking at him unfazed. "I'm not you – go away."

"Not now," Sparky replied quietly, and something in his voice caused Elliott to pause. "I know how hard it is out here, how hard it can be to think there is nothing... or to feel lonely or empty."

"I'm not gay, kid..."

Sparky burst out laughing and wagged his finger in Elliott's face.

"You are a funny one... wow, I did not see that coming. I just got married, you, dweeb. I'm trying to get my backside outta here so I can go home with my wife in a few months," the skinny man said, holding up his hand and showing off his wedding ring. "Look, Big Red..."

"Quit calling me that…"

"You're wallowing in the mental quicksand that I was stuck in – find someone to talk to, someone to reach out to, and find something to spark an interest in your head so you don't drown in that depression."

"You know nothing about me…"

"You're right, I don't – but I do recognize the signs, and I thought I'd talk to you about it. So, Big Red, where are ya' going for vacation?"

"Texas."

"Ooooh," Sparky said gleefully. "Me too – where are you going?"

"Look, Beanpole. I'm from Tyler and going home to…"

"Really? You're not funning me? I'm looking at houses online right now and working with a realtor. I want me and my girl to have a place to go when we both get out – and it's in Tyler."

Elliott cursed and looked away, causing Sparky to laugh again knowingly. Then, to his utter shock and surprise, the lean man put an arm around his shoulders and began walking, pulling him along.

"Let me tell you about Flyboys and the team out there…"

HOURS LATER, he checked his email and saw there was no reply yet from Sarah and wondered if it would take several days for her to reach out again as Sparky's words wrapped around him, weaving in and out of his head.

Typing, he surprised himself and hoped Sarah could forgive him for what he was about to do.

> *Dear Sarah,*
> *Look, you might hear from a stranger, but know that it's*

okay. These people come very highly recommended, and please don't be upset. I'm trying to help where I can from a distance, but if it hasn't dawned on you yet – it sure has been lingering in my mind. You need someone to help you when the baby comes – because the children are too small to stay alone.

I'm coming to visit in a few weeks, so maybe everything will kind of fall into place – but if not, something has to give somewhere, right?

Always your friend,
Elliott

Clicking send, he quickly opened another window and began another email – to a perfect stranger based on a recommendation from his wingman, who was a very weird, outgoing guy.

Firefly,

You don't know me – but you come highly recommended from Sparky... and I have a friend in Tyler who is in desperate need of help within the next few weeks to maybe a month.

Sarah is a single mom (a widow) with three children and is pregnant with her fourth child and due soon. My concern is when she does go into labor, there will be no one to watch out for the kids while she goes to the hospital. She needs a helping hand from someone we can trust – and Sparky kept saying to reach out to you.

I cannot help her from here – and they are like family.

Please reply and let me know if you talk to her, because I need to make sure she has the help she needs.

Thank you,
Elliott 'Copperhead' Trent

He paused for several minutes before finally clicking send. He didn't want to upset Sarah about asking for help from strangers, but the more he thought about it – the more worried he got.

Growing up, he was a 'latch-key' kid himself. His parents divorced, and his mother worked two jobs to make ends meet. His dad died young and that had been hard. He knew what it was like to come home to an empty house, to feed himself, and almost felt lucky that he didn't have any siblings he had to take care of but Morgan did.

Sarah's oldest child was probably learning how to change a diaper or how to help his mom. He knew Sarah had the children in daycare because she used to complain to David about the costs before...

Elliott swallowed.

They had to be struggling financially – yet she said nothing. Yeah, he was going to visit and not take 'no' for an answer.

CHAPTER 5

SARAH

SHE WAS busy making macaroni and cheese on the stove while cutting up hot dogs into bits to mix them in so the children would eat something filling and hesitated as a knock at the door was heard.

"I'll get it, Mom…" Morgan called out and that sense of déjà vu hit her like a ton of bricks.

"NO…" she yelped, remembering how she had been making David's favorite rolls for dinner and had been in the kitchen then – only to hear a woman's voice at the door.

"Hi, sweetie. Is your mama home?"

Dang it, she thought silently in frustration. Morgan had opened the door. How did you explain to your child that 'Mommy did not want to get served papers from a debt collector' and 'Mommy still had flashbacks of Chief Griffin standing there to tell her Daddy wasn't coming home'…

She sighed, wiped her hands, and walked into the living room to see a woman standing there on the stoop, talking to the children.

"I'm going to be a friend, and I'm here to meet your mama..."

"Can I help you?" Sarah said warily – only to see a bright smile on the woman's face as she smiled at her. She had bright pale orangish-red hair as a man walked up behind her holding a little girl in his arms. "Morgan, step back from the door."

"But Mom, they said they were friends..."

"We don't know them," Sarah said bluntly, moving forward to pull her son back and pushed him protectively behind her. "Who are you?"

"My name is Melody Grainger and this is my husband, Sutton. This little girl is Betsy, and I wanted to say 'hello' before we have a little chat."

"Chat about what?"

"When are you due?"

"I think we are getting off on the wrong foot, Mel..."

"I'm not a surrogate, not selling, and not..."

"Whoa, whoa, whoa..." the man laughed, interrupting her. "I assure you we don't need a surrogate – and I'm Firefly. You can call me Sutton, but I use my call sign all the time with everyone else. It just kinda becomes who you are. I'm Copperhead's newest buddy and now yours."

"Who?"

"Mel, are we at the right house?" he asked warily, looking at the woman as he juggled the little girl in his arm. She was struggling to get down and play, wanting to meet Leslie and Bethany, who were waving 'hello'.

"Sarah James, right?"

"Yes, but I don't know anyone named Copperhead or... Elliott?" she whispered in awareness, remembering how many times she'd called him Coppertop growing up. Was it him? "Wait – Elliott's call sign is Copperhead?"

"Yup, right house," Firefly grinned. "I'm gonna let my girl down – and she's probably going to race inside, so how about that chat? Melody, you want to do the honors or…"

"Sutton, you are something," the woman smiled as he set down the little girl, who darted inside, hugging Leslie like they were the best of friends.

"How long has it been for you?" Melody smiled at her knowingly. "I'm guessing things are still really fresh and raw emotionally… and I get that. It was so hard after Jordan passed, and it still hits me hard sometimes. I've been in your shoes, and you don't want to do this alone."

"What?" she whispered, feeling a lump in her throat as she realized the woman was referring to David's death.

"May we come in… please?"

Sarah stepped back, allowing the couple inside and saw Firefly get down onto the floor almost immediately, playing with the children. Melody laid a hand on her shoulder, guiding her away from the others, and she paused just as the macaroni was boiling over.

"Sit," Melody instructed softly. "I'll make it, and we can talk."

"I can…"

"Sit," the woman interrupted firmly – and looked at her feet. "Put those up on a chair because I still remember the swelling from nearly four years ago. Trust me, if you can listen and hear me out, this will all make sense, I promise."

Numbly, Sarah sat down and put her feet up as she was told, feeling the fight melt out of her as the children were laughing in the living room close by.

"So I got the news that my husband's jet crashed in Afghanistan when I was pregnant and delivered Betsy alone, afraid and scared to death of what would come next… but you have a friend that is looking out for you," Melody said soft, looking at her sideways from where she was stirring in the butter and packet of orangish powdered cheese. "You are lucky…"

"I don't exactly feel lucky right now," Sarah whispered painfully, hating that they were even having this discussion.

"No, I know. You feel lost, betrayed by the universe, scared, and alone, and I understand. I had my baby by myself, no one was there to help me along or tell me I was doing the right thing and then suddenly I got a letter."

"Okay…?" Sarah drawled. "Check the mail and it's all better? My husband comes back, or life resembles what it once used to look like?"

"I wish I could say that," Melody said softly, shaking her head. "Life will never be the same, but it does change and grow into something new."

"I was really partial to the 'old' version."

"I like you," Melody chuckled, grinning. "You've got spunk."

"I've got cankles, stretch marks, and bills out the wazoo, too…"

"Don't we all? Do you have a can of green peas? I can sneak something green in here for the kiddos…"

"Right behind you," Sarah began, watching the woman curiously. She seemed so normal, so happy, and so easy-going, and she wanted that comfortable life again. "How long has it been for you? When does the pain fade or go away?"

"Four years… and I'm not sure it ever goes away. You are more accepting; you'll always treasure the memories, but as time passes – then you make new ones."

Sarah remained silent, processing her words and recognizing the small glimmer of hope deep down inside. Someday, it would be easier; those memories would be there, but there would be more made as time passed... along with reminders of what David would miss.

Birthdays, graduations, so many firsts, and her days of sharing were now over, and she knew it. Being a mother was like jumping into the deep end for the long haul, no matter what. No guy would ever look at her because who would want to take care of four children, and she wouldn't want to remarry because it would never be something as wonderful as what she'd once had.

"You look deep in thought..." Melody said softly, putting the plates on the table for the children. "Ask me anything, and I'll share what I can – because it's a very hard experience to live through, and I know it."

She shook her head, unable to speak aloud her thoughts.

"Let me give you my phone number... and if you ever need anything – call. Believe it or not, we have a whole tight-knit group that would love to meet you and the children, but I think right now you might still be at the 'one-day-at-a-time' phase..." Melody smiled easily. "I don't want to overwhelm you, but just know you aren't alone."

Neither said a word for several moments before she sighed and pointed to her stomach. "I didn't have anyone when Betsy came, but I also didn't have children at the time. When your time comes, call me. The kids can play with Betsy, and you are welcome to drive out to the house to see our place..."

"Why are you doing this?" Sarah interrupted, her voice thick with emotion and gratitude, because it had dawned on her that she couldn't abandon her three other children to deliver one.

She had honestly considered staying home to try to deliver and dialing 9-1-1 as she got ready to push in order to minimize the time away. It was a horrific plan, but the only one she could scrounge together.

Leaving the kids with a neighbor wasn't an option. One neighbor had a massive dog that always barked, and the children were scared of it. On the other side of her house lived a pilot for UPS who was gone all the time.

She had no one close to rely on here in Tyler.

Melody smiled softly and touched her arm.

"We all know it takes a village. You are welcome in our homes, our inner circle, and our 'village'… because of Copperhead. He asked. We take care of each other, so we came. It's that simple."

"Because of… Elliott?"

"Yes. The team might change, modify, or leave, but those are our boys and always will be, right Firefly?"

"Oh dang… Betsy, your mama used my call sign. Hang on, gang – ol' Firefly might be in the doghouse in two seconds flat…"

Melody chuckled easily and surprisingly enough – so did Sarah. The man came around the corner, looked at his wife warily, and hesitated.

"What'd I do?"

"If Valkyrie asked for help with something, what would you do?"

"Help him… why? Did he call you? What's wrong, Mel?"

"No, he didn't – but <u>why</u> would you help him?"

"Because he's one of us, and we take care of our team – no matter what. We're flyboys," her husband said simply, looking at her curiously. "You know we all step up to take care of each other – which is why we are here. One of our flyboys asked for help for his girl, so here we are."

"I'm not his girl," Sarah hesitated. "We're friends and have been for a long time. He grew up with me. The way you said that implies something weird is there, and it's not. It's just Elliott. There's nothing there for either of us."

"You're his friend, so you're in," Firefly shrugged simply,

crossing his arms and leaning back against the door frame. "Is that why you called me in here, Mel – to prove a point? I'll have you know there are Lincoln Logs out there, and I haven't played with those since I was a boy at the children's home. Me, Betsy, and Morgan were building a cabin and…" he paused and then gave his wife a slow smile. "My girl is talking about her daddy. I gotta go."

Melody laughed softly and shook her head before looking at Sarah.

"That man spoils Betsy…"

"He doesn't care that she's from a previous marriage?"

"Not at all. He's got a big heart and is excited about our own that will be joining us in about seven months," and laid a hand on her lower stomach.

"Congratulations."

"Thank you. It's very different this time around, that's for sure. My husband is home, and it doesn't feel so overwhelming," she began and looked at Sarah. "So, I am telling you now, you are not alone… call me anytime, day or night, if you need something."

"Thank you," she sniffed tearfully, realizing that somehow, she had made a friend with someone who understood what she was dealing with – and it was all orchestrated by Elliott. Getting to her feet slowly, she looked at the other woman.

"Now, let's feed the little heathens and exchange information. Did I mention we have a massive garden and chickens – so I'm expecting you to come get some groceries for free, sister…"

Sarah did let out a little laugh this time as the woman hugged her.

"Welcome to Flyboys, hon… I'm so happy to meet you."

AFTER FEEDING THE CHILDREN, there was another knock at the door and a pizza arrived that Firefly had ordered on the sly, causing them all to laugh in awareness. The family stuck around for a few hours, just talking about anything and everything, while the children played after dinner.

Honestly, it was probably the best evening she had experienced in forever, and she was so grateful for it. As the clock chimed, everyone glanced at it, and Firefly stood.

"We're going to need to head out. I'm teaching in the morning, and my little missy needs to get to bed..."

Betsy immediately jumped up, tossing her arms in the air for her daddy – while she and Melody shared a pointed look before smiling. Melody got to her feet, picked up her purse, and nodded.

"Call or text me, okay – and if the girls are getting together, I'll let you know. There is nothing better than free babysitting..."

Sarah chuckled and promised to text her.

As they left, she tucked in the children after washing their faces and brushing their teeth before putting away the leftover pizza and picking up a few toys. After several minutes, she finally retired to her room and hesitated. She had only begun sleeping in here again two weeks ago, having spent the last several months sleeping on the couch, unable to bring herself to sleep in there alone. Pulling out her iPad, she emailed Elliott before playing one of her games or reading a book.

> *Dear Elliott,*
>
> *Or should I say 'Copperhead'?*
>
> *I feel like a bad friend for not understanding that you would get some cool call sign as a pilot. I guess I should have known after watching Top Gun. I guess this is me asking for more details about your world, Copperhead.*

And thank you.

I don't know how you did it, but I am truly grateful to have you on my side, even if it's a bajillion miles away. Firefly and his wife just left – and they are going to watch the children when I go into labor . I feel like such a weight is off my shoulders, and I am really grateful for our friendship.

My couch is always yours, and you know it.

I'm glad you are coming to visit.

Sarah

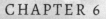

CHAPTER 6

COPPERHEAD

ELLIOTT SWALLOWED NERVOUSLY as the taxi came to a stop in front of the house – and he could already see the changes that had come from David's death. The lawn needed to be mowed, the bushes that lined the front of the house needed trimming, and he hadn't even made it inside yet.

It had been a few days since he'd heard from Sarah, then with his flight, there was a distinct gap in their communication, and the house looked quiet as he hefted up his bag, paid the driver, and walked up to the front door – only to see a little face peering out the window.

Leslie had grown, he thought warmly and then smiled as another face appeared beside her, followed by the muffled sounds of 'Uncle Elliott is here!' being hollered loudly by Morgan. The front door opened seconds later without him having to knock as he smiled at the children, seeing David in each of their faces.

"Hey, gang… do I get a hug?" he asked, immediately kneeling as he was tackled by three sets of arms… and heard an exhausted voice that he recognized.

Sarah.

"Y'all step back and let him inside," she began, and he looked up to see her standing there in a robe with rings under her eyes as she smiled wanly at him… holding an infant.

"You had the baby already?"

"Three weeks early… but yes."

"Jeez, Sarah," he began, getting to his feet and leaving his bag on the porch as he walked inside, taking her arm. "Sit down before you collapse – you look exhausted."

"Sweet talker," she mumbled and smiled at him. "I just got home late last night, and the first few weeks are always the toughest."

"I wouldn't know," he smiled, urging her to sit down again as Morgan was dragging his bag inside. "Leslie, can you get your mama the footstool? Bethany, get her the lap blanket, sweetie…" he instructed, taking over almost protectively. "Have you guys eaten, Morgan?"

"I could eat," Morgan shrugged, causing Elliott and Sarah to share a look. She rolled her eyes as he grinned in awareness. Growing boys had hollow stomachs and could always eat.

"They had breakfast about an hour ago."

"And you? Did you eat?"

"I had an egg."

"… An egg – and that's it?" Elliott frowned and hesitated, turning to look at the children who were carrying over the pillow and quilt for Sarah. "All right, gang – your bossy Uncle Elliott is here, and we're gonna take care of your mom.

Let's have her get some sleep and do a couple of things around the house to help out so she can take care of your new baby..." he hesitated and looked at Sarah.

"Brother," she volunteered. "Henry David James."

He smiled – and nodded approvingly. Henry was David's father's name, and it was fitting that she dubbed him that. It was probably what they had selected prior to David's passing away.

"Baby Henry needs all of our help, so we are going to do what family does best – annoy each other, work together, and take care of things while your mama does all the hard work... okay?"

The children looked at him in confusion, before looking at each other.

"Chores?" Elliott prompted. "You do your chores right?"

"Elliott..." Sarah began, and he stopped her, holding up a hand.

"Morgan, you are the man of the house – so you are with me," he continued, unfazed and not willing to let Sarah have a say. She was obviously trying to handle too much, and the kids needed to help out because she was not capable of doing it all, and it showed on her pale face. "Girls, I need your help with folding the clothes out of the dryer, picking up the trash, and we'll all do the dishes together – okay?"

"But mama does..."

"Leslie, your mama needs our help," he said gently and saw the little girl look at her mother in confusion. "We want to help her, right? And if we are doing things together, then we get to be the ones that decide what to have for dinner or if we should make muffins or..."

"We do?"

"Yes."

"Can I use my tea party set?"

"You sure can," he smiled as both girls looked at him with

wide eyes… and he heard a sniffle behind him. He looked over his shoulder at Sarah and saw her exhausted eyes glistening with gratitude. "You need to rest, my friend. I'm going to make you something to eat while you take care of Henry – and then I want you to take a nap."

"But you just got here…"

"And I'll be here a few days," he interrupted softly, smiling gently at her. "Lemme play 'house' for a day or two, and then you can kick me out."

They shared a smile as he got to his feet. He clapped his hands together, rubbing them excitedly, and smiled at the children.

"All right – who's ready to learn how to make scrambled eggs and toast?"

All three started jumping around him, following him into the kitchen, and he hesitated, seeing a few dishes in the sink and half a loaf of bread on the counter. Making himself at home, he got out three bowls, three forks, and a plate. Opening the fridge, he hesitated once more.

Groceries.

She needed groceries badly.

He didn't say a word but instead added it to a mental list of things to do while he was here. Opening the freezer, he saw there wasn't much more in there either and then peered in the pantry – only to find it in the same condition. There were several bags of beans, rice, and cans of tuna, but not much else, making him wonder what they ate most of the time.

"Uncle Elliott, can I crack the egg?"

"You sure can…"

"Can I put the raisins in?"

"In the scrambled eggs?" he chuckled at Bethany's bright smile as she clapped happily, practically giddy as she stood on a kitchen chair. "How about you put the cheese in?"

"Can I put raisins on the plates?"

"Now, that sounds like a great idea."

"What do you want me to do, Uncle Elliott?" Morgan asked, looking so grown up at the age of eight. The boy's eyes were soulful, like he'd seen too much and buried it deep to keep from processing what was going on around him.

"You, sir, are the biscuit man…" he invited, rubbing his hair affectionately. "I'll even show you how to put them in the oven – and how to take them out without burning yourself. It's one of the perks of being the eldest child, you know."

And the children set out to work, happily helping him in the kitchen as he did the dishes, setting the oven to preheat, and getting out a skillet. He made a large pot of coffee for himself and poured a glass of juice for Sarah, crooking his finger at Bethany.

"Can you take this to your mama without spilling it?"

She nodded, sending her brown curls bouncing on her shoulders, as she bit her lip and walked slowly into the living room.

"All right, is the first bowl of eggs mixed and ready?" he asked, as Leslie handed him one… and he smiled nervously. There was a piece of eggshell in the scrambled eggs that looked stirred, not whipped with a fork, and four raisins.

Someone really loved raisins.

Chuckling, he picked out the eggshell and whipped the bowl until they were slightly frothy – despite the raisins – and cooked the first omelet, laying a slice of cheese across the top. Once done, he cut it in half, made a smiley face with ketchup, and put two plates on the table.

"Second bowl?" he asked… and was handed another, worse than the first, making him chuckle in amusement as he shook his head. He was apparently getting raisins in his eggs when it finally got to his turn, and he could only imagine what the team would say if they were served this at the commissary back in Ghazni.

Serving Morgan, he picked up the third bowl and chuckled. More raisins, more shells. He strategically removed the shells, and made the third omelet, and put it on a plate with a biscuit before walking into the living room… and saw Sarah was sound asleep, the baby in her arms. He set the plate down, scooped her up, and felt her protest slightly as he carried the two of them back to the bedroom.

"Shhh…" he said quietly, laying her down on the bed. He saw her carefully adjust, laying the baby beside her on the bed, and heard her heavy sigh. She was exhausted. "Rest while the baby is sleeping. I've got the kids."

"I'm sorry… I'll get up…" she protested faintly.

"Sarah – sleep, please."

"Are you sure?"

"We'll talk later… just rest, okay?"

Elliott saw her slowly nod as her eyes closed again, fatigue written all over her face. He couldn't imagine what level of exhaustion came with having a baby, then coming home to take care of the children, the housework, and everything else, but she was managing somehow – barely.

He was really glad to be here for her.

Hours later, he was hauling in groceries with the children and saw her shocked face as she stood at the end of the hallway.

"What's all this?"

"Go back to bed, and I'll make dinner…" he ordered, smiling at her. "Rest while you can, and we've got this, right Morgan?"

"Yup!"

"Mommy, we went grocery shopping with Uncle Elliott…"

"We got more raisins…"

"And grapes…"

"And chicken nuggets shaped like dinosaurs…"

"Elliott," Sarah protested as he set down the bags in the kitchen and turned to go get some more out of the trunk of her station wagon that he'd borrowed. "I'll pay you back for this and…"

He stopped before her, pausing.

"You'll do no such thing," he admonished quietly so the children couldn't hear him. "If you want to help, then take care of yourself. Sleep, eat, and feed the baby because I sure cannot help with that."

She smiled hesitantly and looked past him as the kids were carrying one bag each.

"I bought some vitamin shakes for you," he said softly, looking at her with concern. "You've lost weight, and I'm worried about you. We'll talk later when they are asleep. I'm just keeping them busy and trying to wear them out so they rest tonight."

"I'm fine – I promise."

Elliott nodded and moved to go get some more grocery bags out of the car – and looking for the protein shakes he'd bought her. He still had a lot to do, and time was whittling away already much too fast for his liking.

CHAPTER 7

SARAH

'MORTIFIED' did not begin to touch on her feelings within the last forty-eight hours. When Melody and Firefly showed up to pick up the kids, they were fighting like hooligans, crying, and Bethany actually bit Morgan out of frustration because he was holding her doll over his head and threatening to color her eyebrows into one long line with a marker.

Then, to top it off, her water broke as they were going to the vehicle, which prompted several exclamations of 'Mama peed!' to be announced in front of several neighbors who were working in their yards.

Not her finest moment.

But all of that was nothing compared to having Elliott walk into her house and look at her like he'd seen a ghost. The concern was written all over his face, and she knew she looked like a semi had hit her. Everything was leaking on her body, weirdly puffy, sore like you wouldn't believe, and her hair hadn't been washed in three days.

The laundry was piling up, and Morgan asked if he could make lunch consisting of peanut butter and jelly sandwiches – and she agreed easily having no idea that he was going to use several plates, spoons, forks (for who knows what), along with a different knife for each sandwich. When she saw the sink full of dishes, her shoulders slumped, and she went to sit back down… exhausted.

Elliott looked so healthy, so tanned, and so happy to be there – and she felt like an absolute hormonal train wreck. He corralled the children, got them to help him in the kitchen, and she fell asleep holding the baby. She had allowed herself to close her eyes for just a moment only to feel arms slide under her as she was lifted off the couch.

Elliott picked her up – and carried her to her bed.

She didn't have the strength to argue or fight with him as she had been up most of the last forty-eight hours. If she wasn't feeding the baby, she was feeding the kids. Her body ached, her soul was tired, and this was just all tiptoeing on her breaking point that had been ravaged only months ago by David's death.

And her best friend was here, taking care of her and her children. She went to check on them and actually greeted him for the first time since his arrival, only to see that look of concern on his face again as he shooed her back off to bed.

Sarah lay back down with the baby – and fell asleep weeping, not knowing why.

It was several hours later when she heard a faint knock on her bedroom door. She had just finished breastfeeding Henry and changed his diaper, only to look up to see Elliott's arm sticking inside of the door, holding an Ensure chocolate shake as he wiggled it.

"Are you decent, or should I come back?"

"It's fine," she offered up and glanced at the clock. It was nearly ten o'clock and she had completely missed tucking in the children, having slept nearly four hours.

The bedroom door opened, he gave her a nervous look, bringing her the Ensure and hesitated.

"I want you to start with this – and I made dinner if you are up to it?"

"I've had a baby," she countered, smiling wanly at him. "I don't have the flu, nor am I contagious. I'm just exhausted from using every muscle in my body to spit out a watermelon and then watching three children destroy the house slowly."

"Let me get you a tray then – and you stay right here."

She watched him leave and then looked at the baby sleeping soundly beside her, those little breaths and the sweet way his eyelids would flutter.

"What are you dreaming of, little one?" she whispered, laying a hand on his tummy, always touched by the miracle of life. She loved children. It was just hard physically on the body, combined with feeding the baby every few hours.

Elliott walked back in, holding a plastic tray that had a small bean bag on the bottom to balance it on the lap. She had gotten it for Morgan so he could color in the station wagon last summer when they took him to the Aquarium in Dallas for the day.

He hesitated for a moment, leaning closely to put the tray on her lap despite her reaching for it.

"I can get it…"

"I've got it…"

And Sarah looked up, only to meet Elliott's eyes not far from her own. Neither moved, yet she saw his eyes widen slightly and knew her own had done the same thing, feeling a flare of awareness for her friend for the very first time as she took a moment to look at him.

Elliott had a very square jaw that had a dusting of growth on his beard that only seemed to highlight the angles and planes of his face. His dark brown eyes held hers just beneath his thick brow. His hair was closely cropped on the sides, but he'd always worn it a little longer on top, proudly, as if waving a dark auburn flag. But what caught her attention was the sprinkle of freckles just across the bridge of his nose.

Had he always been handsome – and she was just too blind to see it?

David, her brain whispered in painful awareness. What kind of monster ogled the nearest male in the vicinity like he was a piece of meat after losing her husband? Was she sick?

"Thank y-you," she stammered, not even bothering to look at the tray, immediately withdrawing and backing away slightly, giving him a wary smile. "This looks great and smells even better."

"It's homemade p-potato soup and grilled cheese," he said quietly, his voice tripping up like he used to do when he had to speak in front of the class. Why on earth was he nervous?

He just stood there awkwardly for a few moments and then moved to pull up a chair she had sitting in the corner where David used to hang his gun belt for the department. Her husband had joked that the spindles kept his belt from sliding off onto the floor.

"How are you doing?" Elliott began, his hands clasped together as he looked at the floor, his voice quiet. "The kids are in bed. I'm sorry I've been running around all afternoon, but I've only got a couple of days here."

"I'm sorry I haven't been much company," she replied, her voice just above a whisper as she looked away from him.

"You don't have to entertain me, Sarah. You've never had to – I'm just here to help while I can."

"I don't expect you to slave over the stove or do all the chores that I'm behind on…"

"I really don't mind – and the kids are so good."

That caused her to look up in surprise because they usually got frustrated with each other, fought like little hellions sometimes, or would pair up – ganging up on the singled-out child, and he chuckled.

"They are good," he smiled. "They just get bored and don't know what to do to help you. They're old enough to do small tasks, things my mother had me do around the house to help her. You don't have to be super-mom, you know."

"I'm not."

"Eat," he urged again, causing her to pick up the grilled cheese and dip it in the soup. "I left the skin on the potatoes to give you a little iron – and I picked up some steaks at the grocery store. I'll make a roast tomorrow and…"

Sarah choked slightly, swallowing the lump in her throat as she looked at him in surprise.

"You don't have to do that, Elliott."

"Maybe I want to earn my keep," he offered. "I'm borrowing the couch, which means I don't have to foot the bill for a hotel. I can be here when everyone wakes up and help put the kiddos to bed."

"You're my friend, and I would never…"

"I'm Uncle Elliott to the children, remember? And you are my friend – and friends take care of each other. Take another bite."

She chuckled softly and took another bite as he ordered, fighting back a smile.

"Now," he said a few moments later, looking at her harshly. "How are you really doing – and I want the truth."

"What do you mean?"

"I've visited you and David before – and that pantry has never been empty like it is now. I noticed you don't have

57

cable or internet, which means you are emailing me on your phone. The car had three bald tires on it and needed an alignment…"

"Had?" she interrupted, looking at him. "What do you mean 'had'?"

"I had tires put on it at Walmart and got the alignment taken care of while I took the kids grocery shopping in the store. Is it money? Are you depressed and need to talk to someone? You can tell me anything, and you've always been able to until now – so what changed?"

She pushed the tray away from her slightly and looked at the baby – just anything to keep her eyes from meeting his.

"Sarah?"

"I'm finished, and I think I'm tired."

"I've never known you to be scared of talking to me…"

"Yeah, well, I've also never been widowed at twenty-seven years old and had to handle everything on my own. Is that what you want to hear?" she snapped hotly, feeling tears sting her eyes. "You want to hear that daycare is horrifically expensive, and I make two dollars an hour too much to get food stamps? The pantry has a ton of beans, rice, and tuna in it because of the WIC program for mothers who are pregnant, but that benefit ends when the baby is six months old."

Elliott didn't say anything. He just let her get it out of her system.

"You want to know that I've had to cut corners every-where I can? I've sold all my jewelry except my wedding ring. I've had three garage sales in the past four months, grateful for the eighty or hundred dollars it brings me to help keep the lights on. That… that…" and her voice died off, unable to say anything else as she looked away from him. "That I thought about selling the house, but an apartment is even more expensive per month – and I couldn't cut off my health insurance at work because of the baby. I'm not sure what else to do or where else I can cut things."

"You could talk to me," he said quietly. "You don't have to let things be this hard for you. If I needed lunch money at school, you gave it to me. If you needed something, I gave it to you. Why would any of that change when you are still my best friend?"

Her eyes met his dark ones.

"I never thought this would be so hard, Elliott," she confessed, hating the warble in her voice. "I know David is gone, and I should be grateful that the children are not screaming and crying wretchedly… but it's so hard to handle a family of three, soon to be four, on one income – and I'm scared."

"Of what?"

"How will the children be taken care of if I have to get a second job," she swallowed nervously. "I don't mind, but I'm so afraid that they will open the front door to a stranger or hurt themselves, and I don't want to leave them alone in the evenings…"

"So don't," he said simply.

"It's not that easy…"

"Yes, it is," he countered, interrupting her. "You could let me help you and shoulder some of the burden until you are back on your feet."

"No, I can't…" she said in a pained whisper. "I won't use you or take advantage of your friendship. You've always been there for me, and I won't do anything to jeopardize what we have."

"You aren't jeopardizing anything – and I understand what you are saying, but don't be too proud, okay? I won't press this matter right now, but if you feel yourself slipping - stretch out your hand, and I will take it. I'm not going to let you fall when I am perfectly capable of holding you up."

Neither said a word, and the silence hung between them as she finally spoke.

"Thank you for offering."

"The offer is always there."

"I appreciate that."

"I'm getting ready to turn in for the night because Morgan warned me that Bethany likes to put her finger in your mouth when you are asleep…" Elliott began, grinning lopsided at her – and Sarah chuckled, nodding.

"It's true. I think she was a dentist in a previous life because she thinks it's funny to touch your teeth or tongue. It makes her giggle."

"Good to know," he laughed softly. "I'll face the back of the couch to protect my poor teeth."

He got up and put the chair back in the corner of the room before looking at her once again.

"Finish eating," he began and hesitated. "I'll bring you a few fresh diapers for Baby Henry and will come back to retrieve the tray after I get a quick shower and brush my teeth if that's okay."

"Make yourself at home," she acknowledged. "There's a plastic laundry hamper in the tub to hold the toys – and the good shampoo is under the sink. I started putting it away when the girls decided to wash their dolls. You know how they say, 'if the child is quiet, they are up to something'… well, it's true."

"So screaming, laughing, crying, or talking isn't a bad thing? I need to watch out for the silence?"

"The silence is deadly…"

Both shared a glance and chuckled in awareness right before he left the room. She heard him in the distance, entering the bathroom and sighed. It was sweet of Elliott to offer to help, but she couldn't take advantage of his generosity and kindness. It would kill her if he ever thought she was mooching off of him or if it strained their friendship.

Hearing Henry make a grunting sound, she picked up her bowl and hurriedly began to shove in the potato soup, knowing that the baby would be stirring soon for yet another feeding.

CHAPTER 8

COPPERHEAD

ELLIOTT LET the water run over him in the shower; his eyes closed as he stood there helplessly lost in his own thoughts. He had known deep down inside that Sarah was struggling, but her refusal to reach out to him was just like a slap in the face. He'd always wanted what was best for her, even if it had been falling in love with someone else.

He cursed softly and grabbed the bar of soap, not wanting to use 'her good shampoo.' Lathering it up in his hands like he did back in Ghazni, he scrubbed his head almost vigorously – just needing to be alone for a moment to sort through everything bouncing around in his mind.

That look…

Swallowing, Elliott drew in a ragged breath and shook his head, keeping his eyes closed as he dunked his traitorous head under the water, wanting to wash away the unsolicited thoughts beating within him.

She was in a fragile state right now, exhausted and emotionally worn out after David's death seven months ago.

"You're an idiot…" he whispered aloud to himself and turned off the water, grabbing a towel.

TEN MINUTES LATER, he was putting the tray from her room on the counter, feeling like the biggest fool in the world, as he looked down on her sleeping form curled against the infant. She was a mother, had four children, was his friend's wife— ah, widow, and his best friend from childhood.

Entering the kitchen, he braced his fists on the edge of the counter, sighing heavily and letting his head hang in awareness of how hopeless all of this felt. He needed to be the bigger man and be a friend. Leaving the dishes, he moved to the living room and laid down on the couch, facing the back after having been warned about Bethany's little fingers.

Yanking the throw over his shoulders, he angrily shoved at the pillow as if to soften it and took out his silent, hidden frustrations, before settling down and closing his eyes.

Trying not to focus on those thoughts in his head.

ELLIOTT HEARD the hushed little giggle and fought back a smile of awareness. Instead, he lay there on the couch and listened to the children talking to each other.

"Do it…"

"What if he gets mad…"

"Uncle Elliott never gets mad or angry…"

"I saw him cry one time…"

"Me too…"

"It was when he had to put up with two annoying girls…"

"Morgan! Be nice. Mama told you to…"

"Mama is asleep, and you better not wake her up tattling on me…"

"I won't…"

"Do you think my doll clothes will fit Baby Henry?"

"Henry is a boy… your doll clothes are pink."

"Boys can wear pink…"

"Who says?"

"Mama said that I can wear whatever makes me happy inside…"

"You think Henry is going to tell you he wants to wear a pink frilly dress and ruffled diaper?"

"They are nicer than your stupid dinosaurs, you big-doody head…"

Interesting, Elliott thought, fighting back a laugh. Leslie has a bit of sass and spirit to her, giving it back to her brother. Playing along and pretending he was asleep, he felt something touch his ear and fidgeted slightly like he was close to waking up before settling back down.

"Bethany! You almost woke him up!"

"Morgan, be nice…"

"Are you going to put your finger up his nose? I'm telling you that you can touch the brain…"

… And heard the telltale giggle again only seconds before he cracked open an eye and grabbed the closest child, which happened to be Morgan. The boy was leaning across the back of the couch, surprising Elliott because he never heard him climb up and slither across there.

"Rawwwwrrr…." Elliott growled, hearing the girls shriek in delight as they ran and wrestled Morgan to the ground, taking the sheets and pillow with him. Tickling him, he heard Morgan laughing emphatically before letting him go.

"You are a sneaky thing, aren't you?"

"Maybe…" Morgan replied proudly, grinning, and he saw the loose tooth in the front of the boy's mouth.

"Just a heads-up up," Elliott smiled tenderly at him, seeing so much of Sarah in the boy's face. "Girls are annoying until you hit about fifteen or sixteen, and then they become magical beings to you… but you never tell them how you really feel, okay? It can hurt their feelings or confuse them – and boys do wear pink sometimes."

"Don't take their side."

"I'm not picking sides; I'm just telling you how the world works."

"You don't wear pink."

"Because I have red hair," Elliott replied easily, propping his arms on his knees where he sat on the floor with the boy. "I don't wear much green either. People ask me where I stash my Keebler Elf cookies. Apparently, red hair makes you an elf or a leprechaun to a lot of people."

"No pot of gold, Uncle Elliott?" Morgan grinned.

"If there was one, I lost it long, long ago, kiddo… are you hungry? We have a big day planned, and we're doing manly stuff."

Morgan's eyes got wide.

"We are?"

"Yup, and I'm going to need a helper."

"I'm hungry, Uncle Elliott…" Leslie volunteered, peeking around the corner just as Sarah was emerging from the bedroom and met her smile.

"Hey, Sleeping Beauty," he teased and winced as the little girls started laughing, talking about how Sleeping Beauty had blonde hair.

"That's just my mama, and she has brown hair, Uncle Elliott," Leslie admonished him, laughing and covering her mouth with her tiny hand. "Sleeping Beauty wears a pink dress, and when she dances with the prince, it turns blue with magic…"

"Oh man," Elliott grinned, seeing Sarah roll her eyes. "My mistake."

"Well good morning, everyone," Sarah muttered, chuckling. "I've probably got about an hour of peace while Henry sleeps, so how about I fix everyone some…"

"How about," Elliott countered, interrupting her, as she put the baby in the bassinet and looked up at him in surprise. "You take advantage of that hour for yourself. Get a shower, relax, and we can make breakfast for you – right, Morgan?"

Morgan jumped in surprise and then nodded.

"Men stuff."

"See?" Elliott grinned and bumped his hand against the little boys as if they were conspiring. "Men stuff."

"But what about me…" Leslie said, coming out of her room and moving to tackle him. He grunted playfully, leaning back onto the floor as both Leslie and Bethany hopped on him. He looked upward, between his knees where he lay on the floor under the children, and saw Sarah watching him only to see her expression drop.

"What do you say, Morgan? I think we are better off as a team, don't you?"

"So long as there are no raisins in my food."

"But I like raisins," Bethany whispered, her lower lip wobbling precariously.

"Then you can have my raisins and Morgan's," he interjected quickly. "Sarah, I'm going to make some coffee – would you like some?"

"… Sure," she said quietly, turning away.

"Okay, team, someone get the pancake mix. Morgan, can you crack two eggs in a big bowl? Leslie, get the whisk, and Bethany, grab the raisins, honey. I'll be right back," he started and jumped to his feet following Sarah down the hallway –

shoving his hand into the bathroom door just before it closed.

"Careful..." he warned – and then pushed it open, looking at her only to see her look away from him. "What's wrong? Are you all right or..."

"Do I look so awful," she said quietly, looking at him with tears in her eyes. "I mean, I'm a hormonal mess, my boobs are leaking, and I smell like milk, sweat, and goodness knows what else... but..."

"Shhh," he said quietly, smoothing his hand down the side of her head and fighting back a smile. "I thought you might want a break, and I know I feel better when I get a shower. It was an offer from a friend. I've got the kids handled, and like you said, you have an hour. This isn't about looks – it's about taking care of your mental well-being. Get a nice long hot shower, and then come have coffee with me," he murmured. "We can watch the kids fight or..." And to his surprise, she laughed softly, shaking her head as she looked up at him.

"You're right," she whispered, nodding. "Thank you."

"Should I be a complete jerk and make you say that again?" he teased, feeling his spirits lift at just seeing her smile.

"You could ask but I don't know if I will admit it again."

"That's my girl..."

She put her hand on his chest, directly over his heart, and pushed him out of the bathroom pointedly. He heard her lock the door and turn on the water, turning back to the kitchen where there was silence.

Elliott cursed.

He raced toward the kitchen and saw that the entire box of Pioneer pancake mix was dumped into the bowl and on the floor. Bethany was trying to sweep it up with her hands, while Leslie was trying to use the dustpan by swishing it quickly back and forth, scattering the baking mix. Morgan was cracking eggs just as fast as he could and was on what looked like the fifth or sixth egg, and all three froze when he rounded the corner.

Taking a deep breath, he hesitated.

"Did you read the directions?" Elliott simply said, trying not to lose his cool and then looked at Leslie. "Can I show you an easier way to use that dustpan, missy?"

"You said a bad word," Leslie said nervously, her lip wobbling. "Are you mad at me?"

"No."

"I guess it's okay to say stuff like that," Morgan hesitated and then said the word quite loudly, almost as a dare – actually lifting an eyebrow to look at Elliott.

"You shouldn't say that."

"You're not my father."

And to his disbelief, Morgan didn't look away at all as he cursed once more to get his point across.

Elliott saw red.

Why you little... he thought silently as he hesitated, hearing Leslie whisper to Bethany as they stared at him wide-eyed, waiting.

"Ooooo... Uncle Elliott is turning mad."

Teaching moment, he kept thinking. *Don't whip him, don't scream or yell, this was bound to come up sooner or later. Might as well grab the bull by the horns since it's out of the pen and charging directly at me.*

He yanked open the cabinet under the sink and grabbed two bars of soap, scattering several other bars of Ivory onto the floor. Only to hear Morgan say that word again three more times, taunting and daring him. He pressed his lips together, fighting the urge to snap and yell in frustration. Instead, he shucked the wrappers off two bars of soap in record time, tossing both of them on the counter angrily.

And turned.

Both girls hugged each other, cowering, which only served to make him even madder as he looked at Morgan and pointed at the floor next to him.

"Come here."

"No."

"I said, 'come here'…"

"Make me…"

Oh, heaven help me, Elliott thought wildly as he leaned over, picked up the child under his arms, and heard Bethany yelp. He walked back over to the counter and set Morgan down like he was nothing – and blocked him from jumping down.

"You listen to me, young man," Elliott began, putting his finger in the little boy's face. "If you are the man of the house, you have to set an example for your sisters… and that is not done saying nasty words or having a potty mouth."

As Morgan opened his mouth to say something smart, Elliott grabbed a bar of soap and shoved it in the kid's mouth, only to see the horror and disgust on his face as he backed away, trying to spit it out.

"I'm not your dad," Elliott said simply, not backing down. "But I am your uncle and your friend. I'm not too proud to admit when I've made a mistake. If you say something nasty, you get your mouth washed out with soap. That's how my mother did it when I was your age, and she would do it now if she was still alive. So, that's your bar, and this one is mine."

And put the bar of Ivory soap in his mouth, glaring at the boy as they stared at each other. Elliott gagged slightly and saw Morgan do the same as neither moved, waiting.

"WHAT IS GOING ON IN HERE?"

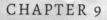

CHAPTER 9

SARAH

SARAH GOT out of the shower, dressed in a clean gown and robe, putting her wet hair back in a ponytail. As she headed toward the kitchen, expecting to smell coffee or pancakes, she realized it was silent or almost silent.

"… how my mother did it when I was your age, and she would do it now if she was still alive. So, that's your bar, and this one is mine."

As she rounded the corner, she stopped and surveyed the carnage in disbelief. There was some sort of whitish powder mix all over the floor, and both girls. Eggshells were every-where, along with big clear trails of egg-goo along the table. She could see several yolks perched in the bowl, but what got her attention most was that both girls were staring at Elliott and Morgan in something akin to fascination and shock, neither moving, while the two boys were glaring at each other – with soap in their mouths.

"WHAT IS GOING ON IN HERE?" she snapped hotly, yet neither male moved. It was like they were in a contest of wills, and her son had no idea what he was up against. Elliott was pretty stubborn when he put his mind to it.

Looking at her daughters, Leslie and Bethany came flying over, talking rapid-fire and nearly in tears.

"Oh, Mama, Uncle Elliott said a bad word…"

"Morgan said Uncle Elliott couldn't tell him what to do…"

"Said he wasn't Daddy…"

"Uncle Elliott's face got really mad and red…"

"He made my brother eat soap…"

"Morgan said a bad word lots of times…"

"What did he say?" Sarah asked curiously as neither male would look away from the other – only to see Leslie nearly in tears.

"I don't wanna eat soap, Mama…" she wailed plaintively. "If Morgan makes Uncle Elliott mad, is he going to spank him?"

"No."

"Is he going to go away like Daddy did?"

Sarah felt those words like a stab in the heart – and nearly fell over from where she had been kneeling.

"Your Daddy didn't want to go away, honey. If he could be here, he would, and he would probably do the same thing as Uncle Elliott because he didn't like people using bad words around him either."

Sarah looked at Elliott as he was removing the bar of soap from his mouth – and Morgan's. Both were ignoring her, still measuring each other up, which made her wonder exactly what happened while she was in the shower.

"You're right," Elliott said quietly. "Your dad was a great

man, and no one will ever replace him. Not you - and certainly not me – but you and I will always be family because we choose to be. Your mother has been my best friend for twenty years now, and I would do anything to make sure she is happy. Can you say the same, young man?"

"Yes," Morgan said quietly, glancing at her and looking back at Elliott warily. "Are you going to tell her what happened? What I said?"

"Do I need to – or can this be settled among us fellas?"

"I can be done and I'm sorry."

"Then so can I – and we won't repeat that word."

"No, sir."

"Hug?" Elliott asked, causing her to swallow in awareness as Morgan hugged him tightly and sniffled, whispering something to him. She didn't know what he'd said, but she could hear Elliott's response. "Shh, we're good. I love you, buddy - and I always will."

She watched the two of them for a few moments as Elliott wiped away Morgan's tears. The two nodded to each other, whispering something before laughing softly. They were having a moment, and it was precious to watch from the sidelines.

Getting to her feet, she smiled at the girls.

"Why don't you both get your dolls and we'll change everyone's diaper when Henry wakes up? I'm really hungry and think we might be able to fix this mess into something delicious."

"With raisins?" Bethany volunteered and Sarah heard Elliott chuckle as the two of them looked at each other in the small kitchen.

"I'll take raisins in mine," Elliott volunteered. "Bethany, can you fix me up when it's time to add them?"

"Oh yes," she exclaimed, looking almost starry-eyed.

"Go get your dolls," Sarah urged softly, and both

disappeared.

"Why don't you make sure they behave and tell them that you aren't in any trouble, so your sisters don't worry," Elliott said quietly to Morgan, helping the boy down from the counter. "But I think I'll leave our bars of soap there – just in case either of us need them again."

Morgan shivered in disgust, looked at him curiously, and then ran off – leaving the two of them alone.

"Hi," Elliott said simply, looking at her and putting his hands on the counter behind him. "How was your shower?"

"What exactly happened here, Elliott?"

"We've got it all handled," he shrugged simply and smiled. "You don't want me to break my word to Morgan, do you?"

"It looks like a tornado hit the house… and what you said about David," she whispered painfully, realizing that something had been said aloud by one of them.

"Please don't, Sarah," he said simply, looking away. "Morgan was letting off steam and needed to have a safe place to do it. Words are only words – and I need him to know that…"

"What?" she interrupted hoarsely, looking at him.

"That I'm not trying to take his dad's place," Elliott whispered painfully, not looking at her still. "We've been friends forever, and I don't want the children to ever look at me like a threat. I want to help, not make things worse."

"Oh…"

It was painful to think that she had been imagining Elliott in a slightly different role than friendship – and he wasn't interested in the least bit. Maybe she had picked up things between them wrong, maybe it was her hormones, or perhaps she was desperately lonely and grasping at any hint of friendship, wanting to warp it into something else.

Elliott sighed and pushed away from the counter,

handing her the massive bowl of raw ingredients, and hesitated.

"Think you can do something with that... mess?" he asked quietly, still not meeting her eyes, and she felt like something was 'off' between them. "I'll clean up the floor and table."

"Thank you."

"That's what friends are for, right?" he shrugged evasively before kneeling down to clean up the mess.

She watched him silently, unsure what to say and wondering if his feelings had been hurt by the children. Sometimes, they could be so innocently brutal without meaning to be. Like Leslie had told her that her stomach was floppy after she had given birth to Bethany, and that had been a blow to the ego, yet true.

Yet, something was different in the house – and between them. She wondered if maybe the children had picked up on it, imagining things or if maybe she was seeing what she had ignored for years, a tiny voice said from deep within, causing her to turn away in dismay, alarm, and fearful recognition.

After eating breakfast with everyone, Sarah heard the baby make a whimper of protest and knew her free time with the children had come to an end. Little Henry was making his presence known once more, and she felt her breasts tighten in awareness that it was time to feed him. Just that cry, that sound, would cause her milk to flow, and she had always had an easy time feeding the children.

Getting up from her seat, she moved to pick up the baby, and met Elliott's eyes as he froze, his eyes glancing downward before looking away. She looked down and saw a small circle on her robe had soaked through – and sighed heavily in awareness.

"I'm sorry," she instantly apologized for making him uncomfortable and then started to walk off down the hallway toward her bedroom to feed Henry – only to feel him touch her arm.

He stood there, not looking at her, his head bent, yet he was close and spoke softly for her alone.

"It doesn't bother me," he breathed. "Can I get you anything to help make you comfortable while you take care of Henry? I'm going to take the children outside to play so this can be a peaceful moment for you – and maybe you can sneak in a nap, too."

Sarah looked at him, touched by the simplicity of his words and thoughtfulness, trying to ignore the flutter in her chest. This was nothing. They were only friends... right?

"Could I have some hot tea? I've got everything else in my room beside the bed that I could need in a little tote."

"I'll bring it to you," he began, nodding... and looking so terribly alone. As he started to move away, she reached for him this time – grabbing his elbow and saw his eyes fly up to meet hers.

His warm dark gaze held hers, and neither moved until she finally spoke.

"Thank you... for being you."

AN HOUR LATER, she heard the lawnmower going and got up to peek outside. She saw Elliott was rolling a ball toward Leslie and Bethany was picking weeds, trying to give them to him. He obligingly tucked a dandelion behind his ear and was grinning at the children. Morgan was running the lawnmower, which shocked her when she realized that Elliott was right.

Morgan was growing up.

He looked back at Morgan and hesitated, saying something to Bethany – and then moved to help Morgan as he rocked the mower over a clump of grass. She could hear the mower threatening to choke before it started up again. Morgan gave Elliott a thumbs up – and went back to mowing the backyard happily.

And saw Elliott kneel before the girls, pointing.

Both of her daughters turned and waved 'hello' – making her smile as she realized that he must have spotted her at the window. Bethany put another dandelion behind his other ear, creating two bright yellow circles on either side of his head, as he smiled, waving at her.

She waved back and let the blinds drop, moving to go take that nap that he'd offered and recognizing that he was giving her a much-needed break. When he was gone, there would be plenty of things she would need to handle, but for now?

She just appreciated this so much.

Lying down beside Henry, she closed her eyes.

SOMETIME LATER, she heard a noise and lifted her head to see her bedroom door opening slowly.

"Shhh…"

"I'm shushing, Uncle Elliott…"

"Do we have it all?"

"I has my stuff…"

"I have mine - and it's *have*, not has, Bethany…"

"Leslie?"

"I have it…"

"Okay, then let's sneak in and set up quietly before we wake your mama for her surprise," Elliott said, not bothering to whisper, and she fought back a smile. He was prepping her for whatever the children had planned so she had time to brace herself. She kept her eyes closed and lay on her side on the bed; her covers pulled up to her waist.

Hearing the children moving around the room on the side of the bed, she was awfully curious about what was going on – yet remained still, listening.

"Okay, now let's get this set up…"

"Do we need raisins?"

"Not this time, Bethany, but if your mama wants them for dessert – you can get her some of your raisins."

"M'kay…"

"Can I pour the tea?"

"Shhh…"

"Mama cuts them in half, not like this."

"Just because it's different doesn't mean it will taste bad."

"I don't think she likes this."

"Well, if she doesn't, then we can split it and make something else."

"But…"

"What's wrong?"

"I don't think she likes that."

"Really?"

She could hear the indecision in their voices – including Elliott's – and made a big show of stretching, yawning, and pretending to wake up slowly.

"Shhh…"

"You woke her!"

"Everybody get really still…"

"SHUSH, Leslie!"

"You shush, you big poopy head…"

"Hey kids, we don't say that…"

"Oh no, I don't want the soap…"

Sarah couldn't fight the chuckle that escaped her and heard Elliott smother a laugh. Turning over, she looked at the children and hesitated. They were each carrying a different colored rose for her, and Morgan had a small cup of water in his other hand. Elliott stood there with a bag looped over his arm and carrying a tray of food.

"What's this?"

"Surprise!" the children began, jumping up and down excitedly as Elliott shushed them softly. Henry, lying beside her, threw his little arms and feet into the air before settling back down into his nap. Morgan put the cup down and put his rose in the water. Leslie added hers and then Bethany as she sat up gingerly in the bed.

"My goodness," Sarah exclaimed softly, as the children hugged her one at a time. "I'm so surprised, and this is just wonderful. How did you manage all of this?"

"Uncle Elliott took us to get Happy Meals for lunch after we finished playing outside," Morgan volunteered, and Leslie clapped her hands happily, interrupting him.

"And there was a flowery place next door!" she gushed.

"It smelled good," Bethany volunteered. "I sniffed all the yellow flowers."

Sarah looked at Elliott, touched, and saw his easy smile as he asked her, "Are you hungry?"

"Yes."

"Sit up," he instructed and set a tray in her lap that held a burger and fries. "It's not exactly healthy, but it is hot."

The moment she sat up, Bethany and Leslie were already climbing onto the bed excitedly, just happy to be in Mom's bedroom. Morgan went around the bed and scrambled up to join them. She laughed, trying to hold onto the tray while guarding Henry's sleeping form protectively and heard Elliott doing the same.

"Watch the baby... hang on... careful guys..."

"Hi Mama..."

"Mommy, I told Uncle Elliott to make sure there was cheese on your burger..."

"Can I have a French fry?"

"Sure," Sarah chuckled, giving each of the children a fry and smiling at Elliott as he stood there watching them silently. For her, this was her whole world around her, and he'd given her a chance to enjoy a bit of it before reality interfered... but for him?

She wondered what was going through his mind and wished she could take a glimpse inside, just to know what he was thinking. She saw him watching, waiting, looking unsure of himself, and slightly protective as he hovered nearby when it hit her.

She wanted him to feel included, a part of her world and felt slightly guilty for wanting such a thing.

"Do you want to pull up a chair and sit with us?"

"I don't think I should," he said quietly, looking away. "I've got a few things to do before I fly out tomorrow night and..."

"Elliott, wait..."

"Just rest, Sarah," he replied quickly, leaving the room.

And her.

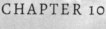

CHAPTER 10

SARAH

THE HOURS SEEMED to melt away, and the next thing she knew, Elliott was going over a few things with her before he left. He was extremely brusque and quiet about things, making a list and talking about it with her.

"Morgan is going to mow the lawn for you once a month, and I told him that I would pay him..."

"You don't have to do that," she countered immediately and saw him put up a hand defensively.

"This isn't up for negotiations or debate. He needs to have something to work toward, and it will give him a sense of pride. Ten or twenty bucks a month for helping his mom around the house is nothing – and everything. He's capable although, you might have to watch him."

Sarah nodded, listening, fascinated as he spoke.

"Leslie is going to empty the trashcan for you and unload

the dishwasher if it's full. She can put the plates and cups on the counter so she doesn't try climbing up there to do it. Bethany is going to gather the dirty clothes and put them in the hamper – plus pick up the toys. Her job is anything on the floor."

"Okay..." she drawled nervously, making her feel like a poor excuse for a mother or housewife.

"Don't get that look on your face," he said quickly before looking away. "They need to help – and if they don't do it, tell me. I made a bargain with the children, and they must pull their weight. Chores and being part of a team build character. It's no different in a family or at least to me, it's not."

"You don't have to..."

"And," he interrupted again pointedly, smiling faintly before looking at her. "The daycare bill is handled, so when you are ready to go back to work – you don't have to worry about the cost for Henry, Bethany, and Leslie attending. I spoke to the manager, and they have a bus program that will pick up Morgan at school, so you can get all the kids at one location at the end of the day."

"What?" she gasped, shocked. "Elliott, I don't understand. Why would you... how...?"

"Don't worry about it," he said, brushing it off automatically. "The daycare situation is handled. Now, are you going to be able to keep up with the bills if you don't have to worry about that?"

"I should be able to... I hope."

"Is there anything else I should know about? Anything else you want from me?"

His words hung in the air, and she hesitated because he could have phrased that in so many other ways instead of asking what she wanted from him.

Companionship?

Friendship?

Maybe something more? She thought silently and pushed it to the back of her mind quickly with a tidal wave of guilt.

"No, but…"

"Don't make a big deal about this," he said evasively, sighing heavily and scribbling down a few things. "I'm just helping a friend out, and it's nothing - remember? I have no one except you and the kids, so it's not like this is some mighty grand gesture. It's just two friends helping each other like we've always done."

She stared at him, slightly shocked at how standoffish he was being toward her. It hurt to think that maybe she'd stretched their friendship too far, and she was losing him. Maybe he was fed up after helping with the children for a few days because they could be a lot sometimes.

"Now," he said, getting up from the table and handing her a sheet of paper. "I've got to go. My cab should be here any second."

"What's this?" she whispered, accepting the paper from him.

"Groceries are being delivered on Friday, and they are paid for. The warranty on the tires is in the glovebox, and I got you a 'AAA' subscription so if you get stuck, they can help you. The membership card should be coming in the mail at some point. Diapers were ordered for Henry and should arrive in a week . Let me know when you get low, and I'll reorder…"

Sarah looked up at him, shocked – and saw he still wouldn't look at her. Rising to her feet, she stood before him, terrified she was losing her best friend by being helpless for a few days and getting back on her feet.

"Elliott," she whispered tearfully. "Please don't leave angry with me…"

His eyes shot up to hers as he finally looked at her – and

his eyes were devastated, full of emotion for a split second as he shrugged easily in that way she'd always known.

"I'm not angry. I'm just trying to help…" he began evasively, looking away once more as if he couldn't stand the sight of her.

"I feel like something is different between us and…"

"Sarah, don't," he interrupted hoarsely and slowly raised his eyes back to her. "Things do feel different, but I don't think we should be discussing it before I leave. I'm your friend," he whispered, his eyes searching hers. "I will always be your friend – and always on your side. That will never change, but we should step back for a moment before we say something that would alter it. Does that make sense? I'm here for you. That's all we need right now."

She nodded tearfully, afraid to speak, and saw him swallow silently as he looked at her, and then his hand reached up to brush a tear from her cheek.

"Time," he whispered almost sadly, his thumb caressing her cheek. "We need time… and it's just not our ally right now. I see the headlights in the driveway and need to go. I'll write to you when I get back and please tell me if you need anything – okay? Promise me…"

"I promise," she murmured and nodded. "Please be safe, Elliott."

She saw him give her a slight smile for a brief second before his hand dropped away, and he nodded. The temptation to say 'I can't lose you too' was there, and the unspoken words seemed to hang in the air as he stepped back from her, glancing at her once more.

"Lock the door behind me and get some rest."

And with that, he hefted up his bag like it was nothing and left without looking back.

CHAPTER 11

Hi Sarah,

I'm back on base and believe it or not – it's louder here than the kids running around playing in the house. Will you remind Morgan that before he mows the yard, he needs to make sure there is nothing in the grass? No toys or spoons...

Give Leslie and Bethany a hug for me – and I just ordered some raisins for the kids. The box should be there on Friday. They sure do like them, don't they?

I also sent you a little something.

How's Henry? When does he go for his first checkup? The only stuff I know about babies is what I've learned from you over the years (I'm an only child, remember?). So, I'm not sure what questions to ask, and things are strained right now. I don't want to cross a line with you – and you were right.

Things feel different.

Elliott

Hi Elliott,

The package came today – and you shouldn't have. The girls are so excited about the raisins, and you didn't tell me you sent a plush one for them, too. You should have seen their faces!

Morgan loves his dino-warrior, and I told him about checking the grass. I will probably join him because I'm paranoid. Henry is doing so well and growing like a weed. He had his one-week checkup and didn't lose any weight. Sometimes, newborns lose a few ounces or up to a pound, but he's doing great.

How are you?

Yes, things feel strained, and I don't know how to fix it.

Sarah

Dear Sarah,

Did your gift arrive?

You didn't say anything.

Elliott

Elliott,

Yes. It was very sweet, and very thoughtful, and I've never used bath bombs before. My mother used to get these little melting bubbles that had oil inside from Avon, but this was much different. This was decadent, almost sinful. It didn't seem like a gift between friends when I had flower petals floating in the tub. It was very personal, and I don't know what else to say.

Sarah

85

Sarah,

I'm glad you tried them – I wanted you to be able to relax, rest, and unwind, and thought it might make you feel nice.

I want to write more, but my head is spinning. I don't want things to get stuck in the filters, and I can't say some things without the email being held. I can't figure out how to get it out of my skull in an appropriate manner – or how to say it where I don't come off as a creep. I can't see your face, and you can't see mine, plus this is just a bunch of words.

Elliott

Elliott,

We're friends – you can always say what is on your mind...

Sarah

Sarah,

Fine, if it's so easy – go ahead.

What's on _your_ mind?

Elliott

Elliott,

I'm sorry it's been a week since I've written – and let me eat crow now. So maybe it's not that easy to get the thoughts out of your head and into an email. If I type my thoughts, when I go back and re-read it, I always end up deleting it because I feel like a fool. You are right. This is harder than it seems because I want to say more or ask questions, and I can't yet.

Better?
Sarah

Sarah,

I understand because I can't bring myself to talk about it either. I start, trying to carefully word it, and I'm struggling.

I'm just really having a tough time right now because I can't seem to escape work or distance myself from it so I can unwind. I wish I was there, sitting on the floor with the kids and having a cup of coffee with you.

I miss your smile.

Elliott

Sarah,

Did I cross a line? You haven't written in almost two weeks, and I'm worried.

Elliott

Dear Elliott,

Bear with me – I'm sorry.

The flu is tearing through the house, and all of us are sick. I've got a humidifier going in every room. The kids have been sleeping with me for a few days now because of how miserable everyone is. It's really taken us down – and I'm sorry I didn't write.

I took the children to the doctor, who gave them some cough syrup to help bring up everything. Henry is too small, and they said if he's sick much longer, they are going to admit him to the hospital.

I'm glad you aren't here to experience this – and I'm a wreck just thinking about it. The sheer lack of sleep, the insane number of tissues we've gone through, and how ill I am right now. I can't even think of what line you crossed because my brain isn't working right due to the fever. Gimme a few days, and I'll go back through my stuff.

I've got to get some chicken broth down and I'm back to sniffing Vicks VapoRub (can't even put it on because I'm feeding Henry). Have I mentioned I'm miserable and drowning in snot? How's that for a visual?

Welcome to Ground Zero of the plague – not fun.

Do. Not. Recommend!

Sarah

Elliott bought two calling cards at the commissary and immediately called Sarah before muster the next morning. They were having a meeting today to basically get yelled at for thirty minutes because Reilly was in a bad mood… again. He was heartily sick of the guy and secretly looking to see if he could transfer to a different duty station anywhere else in the world.

Sitting down, he glanced up to see Outfield using one of the computers and ignoring him. Picking up the phone, he punched in the number on the card, listened for a few and then dialed Sarah's phone number.

It rang three times, and she answered it, sounding so hoarse that he winced.

"Hello…?"

"Hey. How are you feeling?"

"Oh gosh, I cannot breavvve but the kids seemed to haff rounded the corner, so maybe I'll feel better soon... I hope."

He chuckled as he heard the nasally sound in her voice, affecting her speech. Poor thing sounded like she was completely stuffed up.

"Did you take something for it?"

"I can't," she croaked. "It all ends up in my breast milk..."

"Oh."

"I'm trying to do some herbal remedies, but I have to be careful. Too much onion gives Henry gas and an upset tummy. If I take Benadryl, he's drowsy, and it's just tough right now."

"We don't want that."

"Nope," she said quietly and hesitated. "Uh, Elliott...?

"Yes?"

"I haff to ask you something and it's going to come out wrong, but bear wiff me," she started, and he would have smiled at how stuffed up she sounded, but the tone of her voice made him worry. He felt his heart hammer in his chest in awareness that something was wrong.

"What's on your mind?"

"Can I borrow two hundred dollars?" she whispered, and he heard her sniffle, choke, and then begin coughing – before realizing she was crying. He really hated hearing her this sick and felt so bad for her. She'd had such a rough time since David's death. "I'm so sorry and I'll pay you back, but wiff the doctor's visits, the prescriptions, and not being able to go back to work just yet, it's taking a lot out of what I had set aside and..."

"You'll have it tomorrow," he said simply. "I'll set up the transfer right after we hang up."

"I'm so sorry, and I keep..."

"Sarah," he interrupted. "I told you to tell me if you need

something – and this is what I meant. You aren't paying me back when it's something freely given. Okay?"

"I hate asking for help…"

"You <u>never</u> ask," he chuckled. "I believe I've had to be the one to push myself on you every time, just trying to help where I can because I know it's tough."

"It's awful," she wept. "I feel like I'm choking on snot, keep coughing so hard, and… it's like nothing is going my way. I cannot get a break. Have I done something wrong? Crossed a line somewhere? I mean, does life get a little easier because I'm hanging onto a ledge…"

"Sarah, breathe…"

"I can't," she wailed. "I'll start hacking again if I breavvve…"

He chuckled knowingly as she coughed.

"All right – then listen to me because my calling card is counting down. It's okay. I promise everything is okay. I'm going to transfer some money to you and…"

He saw a hand appear in front of him, glancing up to see Outfield leaning over the cubicle with his hand extended, grinning obnoxiously.

"I'll take some money, ya' lovesick dork…"

Copperhead slapped his hand away – hard.

"It's going to be fine," he said to Sarah, trying not to snap at her. "I don't ever want you to feel bad about it – and I want you talking to me, telling me what is going on… okay?"

"O-Okay…" she sniffed.

"Now, rest. Take care of yourself and the children – and I'll call you in a few days."

"Thank you, Elliott."

"Always…"

"Oh, and Elliott?"

"Yeah?"

"I miss your smile, too…"

And the line went dead as the calling card ran out.

He sat there holding the phone to his ear, replaying her words and disbelieving of what he'd just heard. She missed his smile? Did that... could that mean something was there for her, too?

"Ow! Ya' big orange-haired jerk," Outfield snapped hotly. "I was joking – sorta – and you slapped my hand into the wood paneling. That smarts, you know!"

"Suck it up, Crybaby..."

"So, how many kids do you have with your girl? I didn't know you were a daddy," Outfield grinned. "So even leprechauns get their freak on, huh? Is that how you make four-leaf clovers or Lucky Charms..."

Copperhead shot out of his seat, leaning over the cubicle as Outfield laughed merrily, jumping away and just out of reach.

"Temper, temper, flyboy..."

"I don't have any children – and I'm a little big for a leprechaun," Elliott said slyly, looking at the other man. "Or at least that's what your mother says when I leave her bed in the morning throwing a few bills onto the nightstand..."

"Hey!" Outfield frowned. "Now that's not funny... you leave my mama out of this and don't make up stuff like that."

"Mind your own business then," Elliott said simply, sitting down and ignoring the other pilot while Outfield griped for a few moments before throwing up his hands in frustration and walking out of the room.

Elliott transferred money to Sarah and opened another window, wanting to do something to make her feel better and touching on the comment she'd made.

Sarah,

The transfer to your account should be there shortly. You'll probably receive an email about it – and don't say a thing or argue. I'm here and always have been for you, or at least I've tried to be a friend when you've needed one.

I hope you are feeling better soon – and I'm going to check the calendar to see if I can take a few more days in the next few months to come visit.

I think my favorite couch is lonely, and I know I miss it.
Elliott

CHAPTER 12

SARAH

STARING at the deposit notification that popped up on her phone, Sarah swallowed nervously, closing her eyes and thinking as Henry kneaded at her breast, feeding and making all sorts of snorting noises due to his poor little button nose that was so congested.

When David had died almost a year ago, she had felt so lost, so alone – and Elliott had been there, arriving as quickly as he could. He was always there for her. When she skinned her knee when she fell off a bicycle in middle school, he was there. During exams in classes they shared in high school, he was there. At her wedding, he was there, walking her down the aisle. Every time one of the babies was born – except for Henry and Bethany, Elliott was there or soon after.

Elliott was her best friend and always had been – even now. She was stumbling, and he was there beside her, offering a hand. He sent her a thousand dollars. That was why he'd said in his email not to argue with him.

He was voluntarily sending her a financial cushion, giving of himself without prompting, so she didn't have to ask again because he wanted to help, to be there for her. He was always there and not afraid to be a friend, even when David had been a part of her world. He had said he would always be her friend, be there for her – and literally put his money where his mouth was, and that rattled her deeply.

While she treasured their friendship, the thoughts that were starting to cross her mind and creeping out of the shadows of her soul were anything but friend-like. It was like she was seeing him for the first time, realizing just what she had before her, and terrified to do something to break the fragile bond between them.

David had once joked to her that if she ever divorced him, all she would need to do would be to turn around – and Elliott would snatch her up. Her husband had shown a jealous side at the beginning of their marriage despite no attraction being there. She and Elliott were friends – that was it. Once she and David started having children and building their family, the small little comments finally stopped about Elliott.

Sarah loved David but now he was gone.

She was a widow.

Those once-prophetic words were ringing true now – and Elliott was there, stepping forward. Their friendship was still there, no matter what, except now her dead husband's words rang in her mind because she was seeing Elliott differently and wondering if David had suspected more because he had seen it too.

Her husband had been everything to her, and now he was dead. That didn't change how she felt about him. She would always love him, but that lonely girl was now scared deep down inside, looking around her world with fresh eyes.

If this was during the caveman era, she would have naturally searched for a hunter to provide meat, protection, or fire for her family. During the 1700s, she would have been looking for another man to marry, to support her, and take in her children because she would have lost her property and holdings as it transferred to another male relative. If it were the 1800s, she would have been looking for someone to help tend to the crops and feed her family – but it wasn't. Times had changed, yet that natural instinct for a woman to want a protector for her family was still there in its most basic elements despite the fact that she was now the provider, the nurturer, supporting her family (barely) on her own. Those same urges to look for a strong mate at her side were still there.

And she was seeing Elliott in a completely different light.

She saw her friend in a light that David had once jealously painted him in. That thought alone was making her feel horrifically guilty in a way that couldn't be explained or voiced aloud.

Melody?!

Had Melody felt this way after her husband had died?

Sarah's eyes widened in shock as she remembered that Melody had been a widow and would probably be the only person who could understand what she was feeling. Grabbing her phone and checking on the children, she texted her.

> Hey Melody – it's Sarah James. Do you think maybe we can have coffee in a week or two once I shake this flu-bug? I'd love to talk, but don't want to expose anyone to this nightmare.

Hey girl! I would love to talk – and I appreciate the warning. I literally just made a massive pot of homemade chicken noodle soup with veggies from the garden. Want some? I've got bags of zucchini, squash, and tomatoes, too

That sounds wonderful.

I'll bring it, set it on the front porch, knock AND RUN!

Thank you.

Anytime, my friend – and yes! We are having coffee because I need adult conversation that doesn't revolve around my husband's trousers or his ability to procreate. Good gracious, he's so proud we're going to have a baby! Love him to pieces, but man, he can be a real *MAN* sometimes. Ha ha ha!

Sounds perfect.

I'll be there in about thirty minutes; be ready for the knock-and-run.

IT WAS NEARLY a week before Sarah had finally shaken her cold. The children were back to feeling better, and life was settling back down once again. In fact, today was the first day back to work, and it felt good to get out of the house once more. She embraced that rushed panic to get to the daycare despite traffic because it felt almost normal.

'Normal' she could handle.

'Normal' kept her busy where she couldn't focus on the flurry of unspoken questions within her head... and that sort of normal kept her from thinking about Elliott's eyes or the way he looked at her before he left.

Buckling the car seats, she gave Morgan a thumbs up just as her phone rang. Climbing into the driver's seat, she slid her finger across the screen answering it.

"Hey girl, it's Melody…"

"Oh hey!" Sarah started, smiling. "I was going to call you this weekend and see if you wanted to meet for coffee now that I think we are free from disease…"

Hearing her new friend's laughter, she chuckled.

"Actually, the reason I'm calling is because we're grilling tonight at Flyboys, and you all are welcome to join us. In fact, I believe Sutton's exact words were 'Get Betsy's new friends to come over because she wants to play dolls with someone, and I'm already sportin' pink toenail polish. I need help and my masculinity back' so, I am trying to give my husband a night with his buddies, and I could use the company."

"Are you sure? That's three mouths to feed. I can go home and whip up something to bring or…"

"Or you can just drive over now because we'll be feeding a small army once everyone arrives. There will probably be fifteen kids here, and they should all be exhausted by about seven or eight this evening – which means we get to watch something on television that isn't animated. Am I right?"

Sarah laughed knowingly, seeing Morgan and Leslie's excited smiles.

"I'm on the way," she agreed.

TWENTY MINUTES LATER, Sarah was pulling into the gravel parking lot of Flyboys on the far side of town and couldn't help but stare.

There were people everywhere!

Children were running around and kicking a ball down the runway toward the airplane hangar in the distance. At the opposite end of the runway were a ton of folding chairs, a grill, and two large metal barrels that had fires burning in them.

She saw Melody point at her in the distance as several women turned and started waving. Turning off the vehicle, feeling extremely intimidated, she knew it was too late to turn back. Unbuckling the children, they were scrambling to get out of the station wagon as she heard shrieks of laughter and high-pitched, childish greetings in the distance.

"Mama, can I go see Betsy?"

"Mama, my friend! My friend!"

"Betsy, o'er here! Hi-ya!"

Oh yes, she was losing control of the kids quickly, and saw Melody walking toward her, laughing and waving.

"Sutton is kicking the ball with the kids; if they want to go join in…"

"Are you sure this isn't too much?"

"Relax – you are among friends. We love getting together like this because the kids can play, we can all sit down and unwind, plus it's Friday night… remember being young and going out? Well, this is it – but adult-style."

"I should probably go with them…" Sarah began as they started running toward the runway, adjusting Henry's carrier on her arm where he was sleeping. "Morgan! Watch your sisters…"

"Hey," Melody said softly, laying a hand on her shoulder. "I'm telling you – they are completely safe here, Mama Bear. Even Karen's brother came out with his wife this weekend, needing a break. Johnny and Morgan are probably close to the same age and should hit it off great. Sutton is extremely protective of Betsy and will come to shut the front gates as soon as Houdini and Abby get here with Cessna so none of the kids can decide to go exploring."

Sarah chuckled and shook her head.

"That's a whole lot of names of people that I don't know and…"

"Nobody expects you to," Melody interrupted. "You are Copperhead's girl – therefore, you are one of us."

"You keep saying that," she rasped painfully, almost retreating mentally as that wave of guilt hit her hard. "I'm not Copperhead's girl and…"

"I didn't mean it like that, and no one is pressuring you – besides – your business is your own, and I mean that sincerely. One thing you'll find with us is there are a lot of assumptions sometimes because we want everyone to be just as happy as we are…"

Sarah nodded, swallowing back the lump in her throat as they started to walk toward the runway to join everyone – only to feel Melody stop her for a moment, looking at her with so much knowledge in her eyes.

"People mean the best, but no one knows what kind of guilt and turmoil you go through when you lose a spouse. It's hard to accept that you'll have to move on someday, but…"

"That's what I was going to talk to…" Sarah's voice broke as she choked, hesitating and taking a few steps backward. Melody put herself between the woman and the group behind them, her eyes kind as she smiled softly.

"I know," Melody whispered. "You don't have to say it because I know. Just believe me that someday you are going to have a moment where you realize that there is a future in front of you worth taking, and when you are ready, you'll take that chance."

Melody took her hand in hers, putting her other hand atop the two in understanding.

"Hear me when I tell you that it could be a week from

now, a month, a year, or a decade… but when you are ready, all of that guilt and fear won't be so overpowering or debilitating. You are alive, and there is no guilt or shame in that - nor in wanting to find happiness again."

"I don't know about that," she said hoarsely. "There's a lot of guilt, actually."

"A massive amount…" Melody agreed quickly.

"You too?"

"Oh yeah…"

"Do you ever feel like…"

"You don't even have to say it," Melody interrupted, smiling softly. "It does get better, I promise. Quit looking backward and stop digging your heels into place because you are afraid – that's when you get stuck. Start looking forward, embracing a future. Now, come sit with us and just listen and open yourself up to new things. It will change your life."

"Anyone ever tell you that you sound like a walking infomercial?"

"Flyboys will do that to you," she shrugged – and then laughed as she hugged Sarah. "C'mon, we've got plenty of seats, and Thumper is making brats this evening, a bunch of hot dogs, plus we've got enough potato salad and deviled eggs to give someone a heart attack."

As they walked forward, Sarah was suddenly enveloped in a sea of smiling faces.

CHAPTER 13

COPPERHEAD

THANKSGIVING WAS THREE WEEKS AWAY, and waiting for the time to pass was going to feel like forever. A few of the guys were going home for the holiday, and Elliott was only able to secure the second week of December for himself. That meant he had almost a month before he could go back to Tyler, and it had already been four months since he'd seen Sarah and the kids.

"Paradox? Are you okay?" Elliott asked, handing him a cup of coffee and taking a seat at one of the computers. He'd seen the other man get up early, disappearing into the stillness, realizing that he wanted to reach out to someone on the other side of the world, too.

"Yeah, just a rough night and missing home right now."

"I understand. Sometimes it just kinda hits you like a

sucker punch to the gut when you least expect it. I think we all have our secrets and our burdens to bear."

"Tell me about it," Paradox muttered in frustration, accepting the coffee from him and taking a sip.

"Can I ask a question?" Elliott said quietly, not looking at him. "Just between us – I don't need to listen to anyone else's mouth or opinions right now."

"Sure, what's up?"

"I'm thinking about doing something out of character – but for all the right reasons," he admitted, the idea hitting him like a ton of bricks about a week after Sarah had asked for help. He'd kept quiet, kept it to himself, yet that simple idea had taken hold, festering within his mind.

"Like what? Should I be worried?"

"Naw," Elliott chuckled nervously. "Trust me – you are completely safe, but... I'm thinking of asking a buddy's wife to marry me. Convenience, insurance, and to help her out after his death."

Paradox had been mid-sip on his coffee, got this weird look on his face, and literally sprayed Elliott and the computer in front of him in coffee as he did a spit-take. He barely got his eyes closed and pressed his lips together in a gut reaction to the hot coffee now scalding him in several spots on his face and neck. His T-shirt was splattered and marred with brown splotches of extremely hot fluids, causing him to utter several cuss words that would have resulted in that bar of soap being shoved in his mouth once again before he glared at Paradox.

"Really?" Elliott said drolly, giving him a flat stare. "You're kidding, right? That was not the reaction I was expecting, numb-nuts, and I guess I'll be showering a second time this morning."

"Marry?" Paradox rasped out painfully, coughing repeatedly as he got up to get paper towels to wipe down the monitor.

"I suppose it's a bad idea, huh?"

"Why?" Paradox asked bluntly, still sounding hoarse and hacking a few more times. "Marriage is forever."

"No, it's not. People get married and divorced all the time."

"It's s-supposed to be," the other man balked, eyes wide in surprise and staring at him like he'd grown another head.

It wasn't like he didn't think about what a mess this would be. He could only imagine how many red flags the school district would have if Morgan told his teacher that 'his mama married his uncle.' He wasn't an uncle by blood, but other people didn't know that – and Paradox's reaction only cemented his worries.

"That's why it's a sacrament," the man was still staring at him in shock.

"You know," Elliott began in frustration. "A hundred years ago, people got married out of need, and you wouldn't be judging me for helping out a widow back then, would you?"

"That's not the part I have the problem with," Paradox snapped almost angrily. "It's the divorce part, the convenience," he stressed. "Marriage is a commitment; when you take a wife, it's forever. If she has children from a previous relationship, they become your children. There's a lot to think about, and you don't just go into marriage lightly like you are…"

"You know what? Never mind. I just have known better than to ask you," Elliott said hotly, wishing he'd never brought it up. Of course, the man started bringing up religion and commitments. It wasn't that he wasn't religious, but Paradox put anyone on the team to shame. He was on his knees more than any other person he'd ever met.

"You asked me because you know I will give it to you

straight, brother," Paradox said simply, giving him a resolute stare. "Do you love her?"

"As a friend."

"Are there children?"

"Four of them."

"Whoa..." Paradox sat back and stared at Elliott with something that looked like admiration or respect – and he didn't expect to see that on the man's face. "And you are still thinking about marriage, knowing she has four children. She might not want a fifth child and..."

"Paradox," Elliott interrupted tersely, already touching on a nerve. He had always wanted a child of his own to raise... someday. It just felt like that 'someday' would never come, and that door was closing faster than he realized. A lot of women wanted someone close by, had families and ex-husbands, and it was getting harder to find someone to talk to... especially when he compared them to Sarah.

If he married Sarah, then he would be raising her children as his own, and Paradox was right. He didn't want to treat her like a broodmare. She was pregnant by David every time he'd spoken with the couple, and he wanted more from her. Marriage to someone should be something where you could share your hopes and dreams with your spouse. He wanted someone he could laugh with and celebrate the little things.

Elliott wanted a deeper relationship with his best friend.

"I like you. I trust you. Don't make me regret opening up to talk about this. It's not like it is a spur-of-the-moment decision. She's struggling, the whole family is, and I'm no hero. But I am single, stationed here, and she can milk my benefits as long as she needs to in order to get by. Life is not fair and way too hard for good people sometimes – and if signing my name on a piece of paper makes me feel better about myself, then so be it."

"If you do it, then don't be an additional burden by adding to her problems – don't look at divorce as a simple solution. It never is. You'll compound problems for her if this isn't serious for you both."

"I already know that."

"Then, if you think it will help both of you – all six... SIX... of you," Paradox stressed pointedly, reminding him that this was an entire family he was taking under his wing. "If it will help bring a family together, help the children heal, and you can still be friends, then be the person she needs."

Elliott looked at him in shock, realizing Paradox just agreed with him and what he was suggesting. The man was right. This wasn't just about marrying someone but also about committing to a family. He never expected the other pilot to agree with his thoughts in supporting someone who needed help – and a second chance.

"I have a problem with divorce because of my beliefs," Paradox began bluntly. "I never said that it wasn't necessary sometimes. If more harm comes from staying married to someone you don't love, an exit plan is the best option – but it's the last option."

"I know."

"I think there would be a long talk between Him and me," Paradox said openly, pointing upward, "before I deemed that to be the answer for me... because I'm no quitter – and you aren't either. There's always another battle, another strategy, another game to play, and we both know that."

"Thank you."

"Of course," Paradox grinned. "Congratulations... papa."

Oh jeez, Elliott thought silently, realizing that if he married Sarah, it wasn't just a family friend but stepping into the role of father that he'd told Morgan he wouldn't take. Uncle Elliott could not share Sarah's bed, nor could he kiss her in front of the children. It would confuse and muddy the waters even more.

Nodding abruptly, he practically ran from the room – opting to email or call Sarah another day. He needed time to think and clear his head. This was a life-altering decision he was contemplating for all of them, and that was _if_ she accepted.

And what would happen if she said 'no'?

Dear Sarah,

If you are all right with it, I would like to visit the second week of December. That is the next opening available for me to take some time off, and I thought maybe we could combine the two holidays.

Do you think perhaps we could go Christmas shopping for the children together? If I am coming to visit too much or am becoming a bother, just let me know.

Elliott

P.S. I'd like to discuss something with you in person.

It had taken Elliott almost a week to get up the nerve to send that email. He wanted it to be casual and unassuming, yet start the process of opening the door to a discussion that he must have played in his mind at least a thousand times during that week.

He had never been 'scared' or 'chicken' regarding anything in his life – but this was certainly terrifying. Clicking send on the email, he did not return to the communications room for almost four days afraid of her response.

And it was there.

Her email was sitting in his inbox, waiting.

Taking a deep breath, he clicked on it and braced himself

for the worst. He had already bought his plane ticket, had purchased a few little gifts here in the exchange, wanting to arrive with something for everyone, and…

He swallowed as he read.

> *Dear Elliott,*
>
> *You are always welcome – but I do appreciate the consideration you show toward me, too. I will reach out to Melody and Firefly to see if they mind babysitting while we go Christmas shopping, but you must promise we'll get hot cocoa or something festive while we are out. Please? Perhaps we could drive around and look at the Christmas lights one evening?*
>
> *I haven't felt very festive and honestly – I made tacos for Thanksgiving. Combining the holiday while you are visiting sounds fantastic. I'll pick up a turkey breast and all the trimmings next time I go to the grocery store.*
>
> *Getting your email brightened my day, and I can't wait to see you.*
>
> *Sarah*

Elliott blinked, let out his breath that he didn't realize he'd been holding, and leaned back in his chair before leaning forward again, resting his chin on his hands as he re-read her email.

His email brightened her day? She was wanting to go out shopping with the two of them… and invited him to get a hot cocoa? Like a date? His heart was hammering in his chest wildly as he stared at the screen, reading it once more, and then let out a shout of joy before shooting to his feet.

"You okay, buddy?" Inferno asked and then looked at Outfield. "That wasn't the chair with the buzzer, was it?"

"Nope," Outfield drawled, leaning toward Inferno, making it look like the two were conspiring while not taking his eyes off of Elliott. "Different chair – and you are supposed to be quiet about that, remember?"

Elliott grinned, unable to fight it, the joy bubbling inside him.

"I'm going to the exchange to do a little shopping."

"Uh, Copperhead? We're not due to get new junk for a few more days, remember? The shelves were pretty bare in there two days ago when I went to see if I could get a calling card. Dude, I'd wait and pick over the new stuff."

"I'll be fine," he smiled. "I'm buying a wedding ring."

"DO WHAT?" Both men exclaimed in unison, looking at each other in shock.

CHAPTER 14

COPPERHEAD

Several weeks later...
Tyler, Texas

"OH MAN, it's good to be home," Elliott whispered aloud, stretching as he stood up from his seat on the plane and grabbed his bag in the overhead compartment. Slinging it over his shoulder, he began the trek from the airplane gate down toward baggage claim, knowing he could grab a cab easily.

As he made his way toward the exit, he stopped at the gift shop and bought a small brick of fruitcake from the Corsicana bakery that was so popular here. His mother loved that fruitcake, and he always sent her one with pecans on top each year for Christmas when he was at the Academy.

Holding his bag, he couldn't help the smile on his face,

holding out hope that this visit would be everything he wished for and tried desperately to ignore that gnawing worry within his soul. He was afraid to push Sarah too hard, that the children would resent him, or that this would all end up being some massive mistake that couldn't be repaired.

And drew to a stop on the walkway, staring.

Sarah was standing there, her head bent as she glanced at her wristwatch before looking up – and she had never looked more beautiful at that moment. He would never forget this sight in his life. The sunlight was streaming in behind her, creating almost a halo. She was wearing a button-up blouse for the bank, her name badge, and a pair of deep blue slacks that had a pressed pleat along the front of each leg, giving the illusion that her legs were longer than he'd imagined, and he swallowed as she raised a hand in acknowledgment, waving.

He glanced around for a second, shook his head to wake himself up if he was dreaming, and saw her smile widen.

Slowly walking forward, every possible explanation ran through his mind trying to explain why or how she was here, greeting him. Maybe they had flown over the Bermuda Triangle, and he was now in some other dimension. Perhaps there was turbulence, and he'd knocked his head into the fuselage of the plane, sustaining a massive head wound, and was actually in a coma somewhere, dreaming of this moment. What if they pumped hallucinogens into the vents of the airplane?

"Hey," she said simply as he walked up to her, certain that he was in the middle of a hallucination – and poked her arm. She poked him back, chuckling. "Do you have anything else we need to grab off the carousel? How was your flight? And what is with the poking?"

"Um… it was good," he hedged and looked around. "Where are the kids? Are you really here? I mean, of course, you're here – but I didn't tell you when I was coming in or..."

"Should I go?" she teased, hooking her thumb over her shoulder. "The kids are at school and daycare. I got off work a little early. I can go if you want, but I thought maybe..."

"No!" he interrupted quickly, throwing his arms out like he was trying to corral her from leaving. "No, don't go. If I'm hallucinating or dreaming, it's fine. I mean, it's perfectly normal to have weird dreams about people you know, and if there's a unicorn or a vegetarian dragon, then I'm safe, right?"

"Are you okay?"

"I'm asking myself that same question repeatedly right now."

"I thought it would be nice to pick you up and grab lunch – but if this is all making you act weird or freak out, then we can skip it. I thought this would be something friends do when they haven't seen each other in a while," she paused, her brow furrowing as she looked away nervously. "Unless that's what you wanted to talk about... our friendship."

"Oh man - do I ever..." he breathed and heard her breath hitch. "I want to talk about a few things, and lunch would be great."

"Okay."

"Okay," he repeated numbly, still in shock that she had made the effort to pick him up without being prompted to... and was asking him out to lunch. They both stood there, neither moving, and finally, she pointed nervously at the door.

"Should we go?" she invited warily, smiling at him.

"Yeah."

They left the building together, his mind racing as he tried to figure out what exactly had happened to the person that he'd left here months ago to the woman standing before him. She looked almost like her old self, like she was accepting what had happened and getting back on her feet. Did that throw his plans out the window?

"What time do we need to get the kids?"

"Anytime," she said quietly and then cleared her throat nervously as she opened the driver's side door to her vehicle. "The latest I can pick them up is six this evening. So maybe we can have a cup of coffee after lunch and just talk."

"I really want to do that. Talk. I want to talk. We can do all the talking – and coffee is g-good," he stammered nervously and then gritted his teeth, feeling like a fool. Taking a seat in the passenger seat and throwing his bag in the hatchback before looking at her and realizing she was watching him, her head angled slightly to the side.

"Is something wrong?" she asked warily. "You keep saying you want to talk, but then you make it sound so mysterious."

"Let's go somewhere quiet for lunch."

"See? I mean, why can't you just answer me – unless it's about me?" she finished in a horrified whisper and looked at him as she put the keys in the ignition, letting them hang there.

It's 'go' time, Copperhead... he thought silently to himself, almost as if he was giving a mental pep talk before a treacherous flight. He was nervous, never expected to be greeted or confronted so quickly, and this wasn't in his plans. He thought he would return, hang out for a bit, then take her shopping after a day or two, and then have the talk...

"I want to talk about our friendship..." he began.

"I do, too."

"You do?"

"I miss us being friends, and things have been so strained," Sarah admitted, taking her seat in the car and looking away from him. "I can tell something is different, but I don't know how to put it into words. Something changed and I don't know if it's me, because of David's death, or the fact that you've seen me at my absolute worst this last year, but…"

"Sarah, things are different, and I know it's been hard… but that was what I wanted to talk about."

"I'll pay you back the money," she said softly, clenching her hands in her lap. "I'm trying to set it aside for you, and I was able to save a hundred dollars from my last…"

"S-Stop," he interrupted in a broken, garbled voice that was just above a whisper. "Please, just stop. It's not the money, it's everything."

"I'm so sorry, Elliott… I'm really trying…"

"Please stop apologizing because I feel even worse now having this talk."

"I don't want to damage our friendship. We've known each other…"

"Sarah, look at me," he begged quietly, realizing this was all falling apart and not going the way he planned at all. Her pained expression turned toward him, and he saw the glassy look in her eyes as she met his. "Give me your hand and just hear me out… please."

She unclenched her hands, and he saw a few faint crescent marks from where her fingernails had left an indention on the skin. Taking her hand in his, he swallowed and tried not to sigh as he recognized the feel of them. It was like coming home, and he'd held this hand so many times over the years as friends.

"I want to help," he began softly and had to look away from her worried gaze, afraid of what he would see in those depths. Instead, he focused on their hands, marveling at how different they were. His hands had scars, a few freckles, and lines across his knuckles looking masculine and bulky, whereas her hands looked feminine. She had long slim fingers, and her nails were painted with clear nail polish, making them shine.

"I've always wanted to help, to be there, and for us to be friends," he whispered, staring at how his thumb kept caressing the skin, and he felt helpless to stop it. He wanted to touch her and was getting distracted. He closed his eyes and swallowed, feeling so nervous. He would rather bail out of a jet with an iffy parachute and take a chance on injury than butcher this conversation.

"And I don't want to miss a chance for us to deepen our friendship, to grow together despite the distance. I never want you to worry or struggle again," he said softly and wasn't sure if her silence was a good thing – or very, very bad.

"I've thought about this for a while now, and I know you are probably going to think I'm crazy, but…" he hesitated and tugged at his collar with his free hand nervously. "Is it stuffy in here? I can hardly breathe."

He heard her nervous chuckle and opened his eyes to see her turning away, pressing the button on the driver's side door panel that rolled down his window. A gust of cool air gently filled the car, removing some of the perceived warmth, and he met her eyes.

"I want you to marry me," he whispered quietly, not looking away. "I want us to always be friends, to always help each other. I want to help raise your children, and it makes sense. I can provide insurance for the family, help with money, and…"

"You want to marry… me?" he heard the incredulous tone to her voice and felt something wither within him as he looked away from the shock in her eyes.

"I can provide so much help and support – and I've always admired you," he said softly. "It would be a marriage of convenience between us. I know your past, can help the children remember David's memory, and…"

"Yes," Sarah whispered, interrupting him… and he drew up his gaze toward hers, stunned at the quick acceptance from her. He expected it to be a fight, to have to talk her into things, and was taken aback by how easy it seemed to be.

"Really?"

"You are right," she said quietly, her face flushed and eyes downcast, almost looking as nervous as he felt. "It would help things, and we do get along well, so…"

"I think we would do well together."

"I know you would be good to me and the children – you already are."

"I swear it…" he said disbelievingly, realizing that she was actually agreeing to marry him like he'd hoped.

"This would be the best arrangement for me and…" she said, and he flinched, realizing that the affection he felt for her was very one-sided. It was an arrangement to her, but to him – this was everything. It was the chance to step out of David's shadow to seize the moment that had been so badly timed his entire life.

The day he received his acceptance letter to the Academy all those years ago was the day he was going to ask her to Prom and couldn't. He couldn't have ties at the Academy, and it wouldn't have been fair for her to wait four or five years for him to return.

Then she fell in love with David, who was available, and he stepped back, still treasuring her from afar. But now it was his chance, and he wasn't about to let this moment pass again. He could be happy with just companionship if she didn't love him. He just couldn't lose her again.

"When do you want to do this?" she asked quietly, looking away.

"After lunch?"

"I don't know if I can eat now," she admitted… and that part of him that had withered away earlier was quickly shriveling into dust.

"We can go now," he hedged… and hesitated. "Or do you want the children there to see us married?"

"I don't know if they should come because they might think it strange or odd that we are getting married."

"Um, we'll need to tell them at some point."

"At home, where we can answer questions without an audience."

"You don't have to do this if you don't want to," he hedged. "I would never force you to marry me – nor would I push myself on you. I know we are friends and…"

"Thank you," she smiled nervously. "I'm trying to move forward, but my baby steps feel like massive hurdles right now."

"Massive… hurdles?" he repeated numbly, feeling sick.

Marrying him was a hurdle?

"I'm trying to move forward and take steps to regain the person I felt like I once was, so yes… I think this is a good idea and gives us both a firm relationship and a sense of security."

"Ah… y-yeah."

Elliott winced as his voice croaked painfully.

He was the biggest fool in the world, and it was like someone had shined a spotlight on him while holding mirrors all around him. He had just asked the woman he adored to marry him. While she agreed - she might as well have told him she was never going to sleep with him.

Security and helping her had been the excuse he was going to use – and she'd latched onto that curveball, swung, and knocked it out of the park straight over the bleachers, and he was left holding his glove.

With his pants down.

In front of a stadium full of people laughing at him and pointing.

"If we are going to tell the kids later, I guess I'll just head to the courthouse, right?" she said quietly, still not looking at him – and he wasn't quite sure what else there was to say. He'd rehearsed this repeatedly in his mind for weeks now, ever since he bought the wedding rings, and now that the time was here?

Elliott was at a complete loss at the lack of enthusiasm. He couldn't even speak at that moment – he just nodded. This was so completely unromantic, so uninterested, and so disinterested that his heart ached. His hand came up to rub his chest as he sat there in the car, looking blindly out the front windshield, feeling adrift.

He couldn't tell you how long the drive was, where he was , or what landmarks they'd passed, but before he knew it – Sarah was putting the car in park, opening her door.

This was not how he planned on getting married.

She was in her work clothes, and he was in a T-shirt and jeans, having slept in them on the plane. There was even a small stain on the hem of his shirt where he'd dropped some-thing on him during one of his layovers yet she was out of the car and waiting.

Elliott slowly got out of the car, stretching, and hesitated, only to see that she was watching him with the same wari-ness in her eyes combined with something else.

Hope?

"Do you want to be my wife?" he asked openly before he could stop his brain from asking those specific words aloud... only to see her nervous smile as she held out a hand toward him.

"I don't think I could handle being anyone else's, Elliott..."

It wasn't 'I love you' – nor was he expecting that.

It certainly wasn't a statement with David at the center of it nor was she comparing him to her dead husband and his friend – thank goodness.

It was honest – brutally so – and not hiding the fact that mentally she was still having a tough time, but willing to accept him into her life because she trusted him.

He would never, ever betray that trust.

CHAPTER 15

SARAH

Sarah had been so excited to see Elliott when he arrived that she had immediately gone to the airport in order to wait for him. There was only one flight inbound from Kabul, Afghanistan that had routed through Dulles International Airport, and when she laid eyes upon him, she smiled.

Everything within her smiled.

This certainly wasn't the greeting she expected.

That was a pathetically underwhelming marriage proposal.

He looked nervous. She felt scared and honestly? There was a spot within her that seemed to flicker and glow at the idea of being attached to Elliott for life. They had always been friends, always got along, and he'd been there so much for her – mentally and emotionally – that this seemed like it would be an easy transition, but as they stood there on the sidewalk, looking at each other?

It was going to be one of the hardest things to do – accepting that she was moving on with her life.

"Do you want to be my wife?" he asked, his voice trembling and telling her that he was nervous… which meant that it was important to him. Good. She was so happy to realize that she wasn't the only one who was anxious and took this seriously.

"I don't think I could handle being anyone else's, Elliott," she admitted softly, smiling at him, and held out a hand toward him.

It was true.

In this whole universe, she couldn't imagine a greater blessing than being tied to her best friend for life. She couldn't change the past – nor would she want to. She loved David with everything in her, but there was also a love for her best friend, too, and she recognized it, honoring the differences while keenly aware that it was true.

She could never love anyone like David again – and if she was ever going to remarry, it would have to be someone she trusted, admired, and cared for.

Someone like Elliott.

Watching him look at her for a moment, before he nodded, opening the back hatch of the station wagon and immediately began to rifle through his canvas duffel bag for something. A moment later, she saw him shove something in his pocket as he held up his passport nervously.

"I might need a second form of identification," he stammered – and took her hand. Neither said a word as they walked forward to the courthouse, climbing the steps. Entering the building, she was barely cognizant of what direction they were walking or people passing her. It was like she was moving through a fog blindly and clinging to Elliott's hand – frightened.

Life was changing again. She was about to get thrown onto the rocks once more before being dragged back down to drown – or swim in a whole new ocean. Her ears felt like they were stuffed with cotton right now, and her heart was hammering wildly in her chest.

"Trent and James party...?" someone called out – and she felt Elliott tug her forward, meeting his eyes.

Oh gosh, his eyes, she thought and nearly wept.

His brown eyes were full of so many emotions as he looked at her – and took her other hand in his, infinitely tender, almost like he understood how hard this was and what it was taking for her to make this step.

"I've got you," he breathed softly in a hoarse, hushed voice and felt a wave of fear-laced hope wash over her as he stood before her, his eyes searching hers as he said his vows.

"I will always be here for you," he began.

Sarah realized he was going off script. That was not something that she and David had done during their wedding, and this felt right. She did not want to say the same words because it wasn't the same person, not the same marriage. This was new - and like Melody repeatedly said over the last several months, 'Someday you'll be ready, and you'll be able to embrace the change that seems so scary.'

Was this what she meant?

"I promise to care for you, protect you, provide for you and your children always," Elliott told her, his voice trembling almost as much as his hands. "I will raise your children as my own while sharing memories of the past that they deserve to know. You will never want for anything, and I'll do everything I can to make sure you are happy. I promise to make sure that there's a smile not only on your face but in your eyes..."

121

His voice cracked, full of emotion, as she let out a sob of awareness, touched that he could be so much more of a wonderful, giving person than the man she already knew. She had always thought he was a great guy, but this was over the top and acknowledging so many fears and worries she didn't know existed within her.

"And maybe someday that smile will be in your heart," he finished in a hushed voice, his eyes glassy with unshed tears and filled with hope.

"I promise to care for you," she whispered thickly, ignoring the tears on her cheeks as she made her vows straight from her soul. She had never lied to him, had never hidden how she felt about their friendship - and wouldn't start now.

"I never want you to look back or regret this chance you are giving us to move forward – and I recognize it for what it is. I would be honored to have you help me raise the children, proud to stand at your side, and will hold your hand through all the moments that shape the rest of our lives. I hope that I can put a smile on your face, in your eyes, and maybe someday in your heart," she finished nervously, using his own beautiful words, and saw him chuckle tearfully in awareness.

"Do you, Elliott Nicholas Trent, take Sarah Michelle Smith James as your wife?"

"I do."

"And you, Sarah Michelle Smith James, do you take Elliott Nicholas Trent as your husband?"

She saw Elliott stiffen as he braced himself and drew in his breath – waiting.

"I do," she whispered, not looking away from his eyes – seeing them sag in relief as a small laugh escaped her. Both of them were looking at each other, both either crying or near tears, and smiling in this unexpected moment they were sharing.

"Then I pronounce you husband and wife – you may kiss your bride."

Her eyes widened, and she saw his do the same, realizing neither had thought about this part of the marriage. A mental alarm started to sound as everything in her started to buckle.

That part of marriage wasn't something she had ever thought of or prepared for, nor something she could imagine with Elliott. When she thought of marriage, she thought of permanently attaching herself to another being and companionship. The intimacy between a man and wife hadn't even clicked in her head yet – but it was sure clicking now!

With David, he was so masculine, so aggressive with his wants and needs – and her brain shut down thinking that Elliott could someday push himself on her like that. She couldn't kiss him could she? This was her best friend, and she'd married him?!

Was he going to expect to sleep with her?

"No…" she whispered in a panic, snatching her hands back from him, and saw the flash of pain in his eyes. "I'm not ready…"

"No," he blurted out just as quickly toward the magistrate. "I'm sick, and I don't want to get her sick."

"Next!" The magistrate rolled his eyes, slammed down the gavel, and looked past them.

"C'mon," Elliott whispered, his voice achingly quiet as he took her arm and pulled her along beside him. "Let's get out of here."

She skittered along beside him, trying to keep up as he was rushing out of there, almost in an embarrassed panic. They were weaving through the hallways that seemed to be so crowded as another courtroom emptied, and he shoved the doorway to the courthouse open almost angrily, jogging down the steps.

"Elliott... wait..." she snapped tearfully, still nearly drowning in that overwhelming panic within her. Pulling her along just reinforced he was stronger than her, and she was having flashbacks of David pressing her for more – and nearly fell, tripping on the concrete steps.

He caught her immediately and paused; his face was exceedingly close to hers where he kept her from falling. She could see his eyes searching hers just before they dropped to her lips and then raised back up, looking apologetic.

"I'm sorry," he whispered, not holding back. "I'm so sorry. I know you didn't want to do this, but I promise I'm not some horrible monster. I would never..."

"I know," she interrupted hoarsely. "I'm sorry that I panicked. I know that deep down inside, we... ah... you and I, well - I can't help it – and that's not your fault."

He took her hand in his and placed it on his cheek, his eyes holding hers as they stood there. She felt him swallow and stared at him, knowing they were making a spectacle on the steps of the courthouse, but couldn't pull away.

"I'm always going to be your friend... it's just different," he began softly. "I won't push you for more than you are ready to give. I promise, Sarah."

"I'm sorry..." she breathed, feeling tears threaten once more – and saw him shake his head.

"No more apologies between us – especially for something you should never have to apologize for. You are my best friend and now my wife," he offered softly, holding her gaze. "You never have to apologize to me."

"But..."

"Let's get the kids and go to the house. How about we grab a pizza or something easy for dinner? I think I could use 'easy' right now – could you?" he smiled tearfully at her. "Please, relax. It's just me, okay?"

"I could use 'easy' too."

"Then let's do that – together," he told her softly, still holding her hand against his cheek, his thumb brushing gently across the skin. "An easy dinner between friends, preparing to field a billion questions from four smart children. We can talk alone tonight after they go to bed. Does that sound okay, Mrs. Trent?"

Sarah made a weird noise that was half-snort, half-sob, and half a hysterical giggle of fear as she looked at him, unsure if she was going to balk, cry, laugh, or run away.

"It's okay... I promise."

"I believe you," she admitted in a hushed whisper, searching his eyes. "Pizza, the kids, and lots of talking." She didn't want to comment on how tightly she was clenching his hand or how badly the other one was trembling as it lay on his cheek. They did not look away from each other. It was almost as if they were trying to see that person they trusted in the other's eyes – and struggling silently.

"Sounds like a perfect evening, my friend." He took her hand from his cheek and laid it on his chest, still holding it. "Take a deep breath for me," he urged softly and smiled. "... And again."

"I think my panic attack is over for the moment," she chuckled, feeling embarrassed.

"You're allowed to have them."

"We just got married. Us? Married – and you had a ring? Were you planning this for a while? How are you so cool and collected?"

"I just hide it better."

"You're nervous?"

"Terrified. I'm afraid that I'm going to cross a line and drive away my best friend," he admitted and released her hand, only to shift slightly and lace their fingers together as they stood side-by-side.

She looked at him and smiled tearfully.

"Thank you for sharing that with me."

"Thank you for not screaming or slapping me."

Both looked at each other – and then laughed once more like they were sharing a private joke, except the other knew how precariously close that event had been not moments ago.

"You're the best, Elliott," she whispered softly, and he rolled his eyes, smiling. "Even if I'm freaking out, I still think you are the best."

"I keep telling you that, and maybe one of these days you'll believe me."

She met his smile and nodded before looking away.

"Maybe..."

AN HOUR LATER, Sarah was being cross-examined by the children.

Morgan, Leslie, and Bethany sat on the couch while Henry slept in his glider, and the questions were flying. Elliott stood at her side, only speaking up when she looked at him, giving silent support and letting her take the reins.

"I don't understand. You married Uncle Elliott today?"

"Yes."

"Why?"

"Because he's my friend."

"I'm friends with lots of people. Does that mean I have to marry them someday?"

"No."

"Do we call you Aunt Mama now – or just Mama?"

"My name doesn't change, sweetie."

"Is he Uncle Daddy?"

"No, he's still the same person."

"Uncle Elliott is my new dad now?"

"That's weird."

"It doesn't sound right. I like Uncle Daddy…"

"Please don't call him Uncle Daddy," Sarah exclaimed, putting her hand on her forehead in despair. That sounded like some redneck episode of The Maury Povich Show, and there would be so many more questions from other people if they heard Bethany referring to her new husband as Uncle Daddy.

She looked at Elliott.

"How about we drop the 'uncle' since we are officially a family now, and you can just call me Elliott instead of 'Uncle Elliott'…?" he offered, smiling at Bethany.

Leslie raised her hand like she was at daycare.

"Yes, Leslie?" Elliott answered simply.

"How come you don't want us to call you 'Daddy'? Don't you like us?"

"I love you," he stressed softly, not looking away from the little girl. "I love all of you, but I'm not your daddy. Your daddy was a wonderful man, and I would never want to replace him. Instead, I would like the chance to earn whatever title you want to call me later on when you are ready."

"Like 'father' or 'papa'?" Bethany added excitedly.

"Sure," Elliott smiled, and Sarah felt her heart clench in awareness. He wasn't going to force or push his way into the family but rather just wanted to be a part of it, and she couldn't be more grateful. "If you want to call me something other than 'Elliott' someday – I would be honored."

"Am I your daughter now?"

"Oh, me too – am I your daughter, too?"

"By marriage – yes."

"Is my last name Trent now?" Morgan asked – as both

girls looked at him in shock because it hadn't dawned on them that their name could change.

"No," Elliott said gently. "Your last name is James because your father gave it to you. I gave your mother my last name when I married her."

"But we don't get it?" Bethany's voice warbled tearfully. "Why?"

"You can have it, or you can add it to your name when you are older – if that is what you choose to do," Elliott explained carefully, glancing at her. "But you will always be my 'little-raisin-girl' no matter what name you go by."

"Me too?" Leslie chimed in.

"Oh yes," he smiled. "I can't have one without the other - a pair of Raisinettes."

"Does that mean I have to listen to you?" Morgan interrupted, speaking over Elliott as he finished.

"Morgan," Sarah hissed aghast at the boy, realizing he was testing and pushing Elliott. She glanced at him to see if he was offended or upset, only to see a knowing smile on his face as he stared at Morgan.

"You and I are going to be close friends because we think a lot alike, Morgan," Elliott began. "Listening to someone is a sign of respect and courtesy, and I thought you listened to me before now. I would hope that you would listen to what I have to say because I would like to share moments, ideas, or thoughts with you all. After all, we are family – but," he paused dramatically and pointed at Sarah in almost a casual fashion as he stood there leaning against the console table that held some extra dishes and knickknacks hidden away.

"Your mother is the only person in this room that you must respect... period. Do you understand me or the reasoning behind it?" Elliott asked simply, not waiting for an answer as he continued. "There is not another person in this world that I will ever tolerate treating her badly, making her upset, or causing her to cry. She gave you the miracle of life, nurtured you as babies, and works hard to give you a home and put food on the table. So, while you don't have to like me or you feel like challenging what I say to you in this house – you will *never* question or ignore her."

Sarah stared at Elliott in surprise and gratitude as he laid down the law with the children in a way that they could understand – and effectively quelling any uprisings, arguments, or backtalk that was sure to come.

"Thank you," she said softly, looking at him – and saw the understanding in his face as he gave her a wink and nodded.

Leslie's hand shot upward once more, and Elliott chuckled.

"Yes, sweetie?" Sarah began and saw the little girl squirming nervously.

"Does that mean I have to share a room with Bethany, Morgan, and Henry? I don't think we'll all fit, and there isn't one for Uncle Elliott – ah – Elliott," Leslie corrected, glancing at him. "Are we going to put a bed in here so he can sleep? Where do we sit to watch cartoons? Is he going to have to make his bed every day? Am I supposed to? I don't want to share a room with Morgan and Henry. It's too much and…"

The little girl was getting in a tizzy, and Sarah heard Elliott clear his throat nervously as she glanced at him – only to see him looking away.

"Elliott is my husband," Sarah rasped painfully. "He will sleep in my room because he is my spouse now. Your bedrooms will not change, nor will anything else."

And Leslie's hand shot upward again.

"Yes, honey…" Sarah said, trying to be patient with the smart little girl.

"Are you going to have another baby? Where's that baby going to sleep?"

Sarah should have laughed at the dedication that her daughter had in NOT sharing a bedroom with anyone other than Bethany – however – she could see that the innocent question had caught the attention of Morgan and Bethany as well. All three sets of eyes looked at the two of them expectantly, waiting, and Sarah had no clue what to say.

"If your mother decides to have a baby in the future," Elliott said quietly from beside her. "Then it will be something that I'm sure she will tell you all right away. Currently, her hands are filled with four intelligent children who keep her on her toes."

"Are you still going away sometimes?" Bethany asked nervously.

"Yes," he said quietly, glancing at Sarah.

"Are you coming back?" the little girl asked quietly. "Or will the police come to the door again for Mama?"

Sarah staggered slightly, putting her hand over her mouth and felt Elliott's arm steady her as he stepped closer in support. Without thinking, she turned to him wanting to hide her emotions and the destruction such an innocent question created because Bethany had a right to know, to ask it. She buried her face against his shoulder and felt his hand touch her arm, rubbing it slightly in silent sympathy.

"Well," Elliott said quietly. "That's a big question for a little girl, so let me see if I can handle this one while your mama hugs me."

Sarah stiffened slightly, trying not to cry, and realized he was trying to make this innocent and brushing off her movement as a hug.

"When I go to work, sometimes it's for weeks or months, but I will always do my best to come home. Nothing will change in my visits. It will be just like before. I'll come here, bug you all, and then go back to work."

"So, no more police to make Mama cry?"

"If the police come to the door, you should absolutely get your mama because there is a problem. The police are here to help you – not to make your mother cry. That was a really bad moment, and the police thought so much of your daddy that they wanted to talk to your mom face-to-face," Elliott volunteered.

"And if you go away like my Daddy?" Leslie asked pointedly.

"It won't be the police at the door," Elliott said simply. "It will be the Air Force asking to speak with your mama – but that isn't going to happen for a very long time," he added trying to comfort the children as Sarah backed away slightly and wiped her face.

"Any more questions?" she said hoarsely, plastering a fake smile on her face.

"Can we get a pet?"

"No," Sarah said simply, and Morgan's eyes slid to Elliott.

"Can we get a pet?"

"What did your mother say?" Elliott asked simply, not moving.

"She said 'no,'" the little boy said begrudgingly, looking away.

"Then you have your answer – and her word is law in this house."

"Yes, sir."

The children sat there, again looking deep in thought, before Leslie's hand shot into the air once more, and she heard Elliott's amused chuckle.

"Yes, sweetie?"

"Can I have a hug?"

"You can have a hug anytime you want," Elliott said gently, kneeling as, surprisingly, all three children ran at him, and he flopped over onto the carpet, grunting playfully, letting them tackle him as he smiled at her.

Sarah nodded, realizing that the questioning was over – and they were accepting of him and this new role. The children were much too young when David died, except Morgan. She was not surprised he was testing and pushing back at Elliott; however, Elliott was taking it all in stride and trying to rekindle that bond with her son because he genuinely loved him – and was firm in honoring David's memory.

She couldn't ask for a better situation, no matter how hard this was.

"Let's have pizza," Elliott volunteered – and the kids started shouting 'pizza' as they ran for the kitchen table where they'd laid the boxes down. Henry threw his arms and legs in the air from the disturbance – and began crying.

Scooping up the baby, she kissed his cheek and looked at Elliott.

"Why don't you go eat – I'm going to be a few."

"I'll feed the kids and eat dinner with you," he countered easily. "Take your time."

"You don't mind?"

"Nothing's changed."

And they looked at each other.

"I think we both know better."

Without a word, Elliott stood up from the floor and headed toward the kitchen. She heard the kids exclaiming happily over which slice they wanted, who wanted a breadstick and who didn't, and bickering about their chairs at the table. She listened silently from the other room as they chatted and heard the easy conversation between them just like any other family.

There would always be a hole from David's death, but life went on – whether you were ready or not. They were each healing slowly, making their way, but hearing the children laughing, talking, and playing with Elliott was truly a blessing.

Sitting there, she listened to Henry smacking slightly as he made little grunts and noises, holding him against her and hesitating. Time was passing and the child she held in her arms was growing, ready to start on cereal.

Everything, everyone was moving forward at different paces including her. She'd taken the first steps in finding herself, a life she recognized, and trying to pull herself together by taking Elliott's hand in friendship – and accepting him as her husband.

Any other person would have thought her a fool for marrying someone, but this felt right. He was her rock, had been through so much with her, and was her best friend, even more so than David.

While she loved David, she had needed Elliott in her life too – he was another constant in her world that made her feel 'safe'. He said she was strong, but that wasn't the case. She was fragile, yet knowing someone was there to have her back was what gave her strength to handle everything.

"All right, kiddos, I'll handle the dishes tonight. Why don't you guys go wash your faces and get in your pajamas?" Elliott instructed from a distance, and she heard the kitchen faucet running as he filled the basin. She did the same thing sometimes. It was easier to just wash up the few dishes than to wait for the dishwasher to be full in order to run the load. Putting Henry on her shoulder, she burped the child and adjusted her clothing back.

Walking into the hallway, she checked on the children, before joining Elliott in the kitchen without a word. Opening the pantry, she got out a box of baby cereal and heard his voice behind her.

"Do you need any help? You've just got the one hand…"

"Moms become very good at doing things with one hand,"

she replied and hesitated, glancing at him. "But if you could unwrap the box, I'm going to try giving Henry a teensy bit of cereal to see if it helps keep him full a little longer."

"Just tell me what you need," Elliott offered quietly, unwrapping the box and pulling open the paper tab that would allow her to pour it into a bowl – which he quickly set beside the box.

"Thank you," she murmured.

"Anytime," he said simply, and turned back to wash off the dishes.

Sarah warmed up, in the microwave, some breastmilk that she had frozen and added a bit to the cereal to make it an extremely thin consistency. Putting Henry in his little seat, she carefully started to spoon it to him as he stared at her with wide-eyed amazement, making noises that sounded like he was saying, 'nom nom nom' while working his little tongue to swallow the different meal.

"I think he likes it," Elliott said softly from nearby as she looked up at him. He was looking at Henry with such a gentleness to his eyes that it was touching. She'd seen Elliott laugh, had seen him lose his temper, and had watched him cry in the past, but this was different, almost like there was a touch of envy or wistfulness to his expression.

"The cereal usually tastes sweet to a baby."

"Babies are miracles and so incredible..." he breathed with a slight smile touching his lips as he looked at her. "I see your eyes, but David's there too. It's like an incredible mixture of the two of you."

She looked at him, searched his face looking for something to latch onto, a trigger, some reason to draw a line or backpedal so she could retreat or pull back from a situation that felt a little overwhelming. David used to get jealous or would say something to rile her up, but as she searched Elliott's face. There was nothing except happiness.

He was truly happy for her, happy that he could see David in the child's face, and didn't feel threatened or jealous in the slightest. This felt so strange not having to defend or explain something, but rather seeing that there was acknowledgment and recognition - and it was okay. He was content just being here, a part of this moment.

"Babies *are* miracles," she whispered. "Each one is so different, too. I'm having to relearn everything each time. They are certainly their own little individuals."

"You're lucky."

"I don't feel so lucky some days."

"You've been through a lot," Elliott acknowledged quietly, looking at her. "But you are lucky because you have four amazing children that you will always share with David."

"Does that bother you?"

"Not at all. I'm glad you have a piece of him to hang onto."

She stared at him in amazement and gave him a nervous smile.

"Thank you," she whispered. "I really appreciate you saying that."

"I told you I'm not a monster or some horrible person. I know you've been through a lot, and I'm trying not to push too hard – I just hope you can find a tiny corner in your life for me someday."

"You've always been a part of my life and always will be."

"I think we both know that I meant differently," he mumbled – and turned away to finish washing the dishes. She sat there, holding the spoon for Henry, and realized for the first time that he was wanting more from her.

A lot more.

CHAPTER 16

SARAH

AFTER SARAH TUCKED the children in, she changed Henry's diaper and dawdled around as long as possible to avoid the inevitable – the marriage bed. Elliott seemed to be doing the same as her. She saw him straightening the couch cushions a second time, folding the throw for the recliner, and wiping down the kitchen table again.

This was ridiculous.

They were both avoiding each other, avoiding the conversation that needed to happen, and pointedly circling around the other person to avoid being in the same room or having the discussion altogether.

"Can we talk?" she finally said – and saw him hesitate as he wrung out a dishcloth… again.

"Sure."

"Maybe we can talk privately so the kids can't hear us?"

"You want to go into the garage? We can talk there."

"The garage?"

"Well, I, ah… um… we can talk out back or – oh heck, Sarah. Are you comfortable talking to me behind closed doors? I mean, I don't mind talking about things, but I didn't figure you wanted me anywhere near 'ground zero'."

"'Ground zero' is precisely where I think we should have this talk."

"Fine," he said simply – and dropped the rag into the sink, causing a bit of soapy water to splash upward. She followed him, realizing that he was on edge and starting to get a little snippy. There was a tension vibrating from him, a terseness to that single word he'd spoken and maybe that was what she needed to push her to say what needed to be said.

She marched off behind him, followed him to the bedroom, and shut the door behind her, only to see him standing there in the dim lamplight. His arms were crossed over his chest with his head bowed, not looking at her.

"Let's have it," he said simply.

"I think we need to talk…"

"That's what we are doing – yes."

"We need to talk about our sleeping arrangements."

"Not really much to say…"

"Yes, there is."

"You're my wife, and you already told the children I was sleeping here."

"Just sleeping though," she clarified – and saw his eyes raise to meet hers, not looking away.

"For now…" he said softly, and there was no doubt in her mind what he was referring to.

"Elliott…"

"Sarah…"

"If you think I'm going to just…" she started hotly, snapping at him - and he crossed the room toward her. Sarah

137

backed up immediately, stumbling in a hurry as she retreated. She stared at the intense look on his face, bumping into the wall behind her.

This was a side of him she had never seen – and felt a shiver of alarm ricochet through her as he put his hand on the wall beside her head and leaned forward into her personal space.

"Here's where we are going to talk and get things straight between us..." he whispered softly in her ear, his cheek almost touching hers as he leaned in close. "In here, when we are alone, you can say whatever you want to me behind that closed door. You can yell at me, fight me, push me around, and I don't mind - I'll still be here."

She tensed as she felt his nose brush against her cheek, almost in a caress.

"I'm whispering because I don't want the children to hear us arguing - ever," he continued, his breath tickling her ear.

"Elliott," she strangled out nervously. "I just..."

"I stepped into the shadows once for you... don't make the mistake of thinking that I'm strong enough to do it again," he breathed, and she nearly melted as he scraped his cheek against hers, his face close so he could whisper in her ear so the children wouldn't hear them. "I will stand behind you, support you, and I'm happy to let you take the lead, to do whatever you want, but..."

His words were driving her crazy, and combined with the sudden intensity between them; her heart was pounding in her chest as she listened silently.

"But don't think that I don't want more from you, Sarah," he murmured, his lips touching her jaw. "I can wait until you are ready, but I want you to know that I'm here. I want you to look at me like a husband or lover, not a dumb sidekick or a creep...."

"I d-don't..." she sputtered breathlessly and felt his hand

touch her waist as he stepped even closer to her. "I don't look at you like a sidekick or a creep."

"How do you look at me?"

"Like a friend... my friend..."

He grew still and drew in his breath audibly, where his face remained near her ear. She could hear him swallow, hear the hitch in his breathing, as she waited.

"Do you know why they call me Copperhead? Hmm?" he spoke, his voice infinitely soft and seductive at that moment, making her knees weak. When she didn't answer, he continued. "Because no one ever sees me, Sarah. No one sees the real me until it's too late. People don't notice me, they walk past me, they overlook me. Everyone does."

Sarah swallowed and made a little noise in her throat as his hand moved from the wall to cup the back of her neck, cradling her close to him.

"You have all sorts of people in this world," he whispered softly to her. His very stance so close to her, combined with his breath against her skin, was doing a number on her mind, body, and soul. "The braggarts, the ones that need the spotlight, and then there are the people like me... the ones that wait patiently for their turn – or for someone to hurt them unknowingly."

"Elliott..." she began, her hand finding his shoulder, clinging to him as he pressed her closer to him in an embrace.

"I wait, and I watch," he breathed quietly. "I've watched for a long time – and when I'm ready, I might let someone know I'm there with a slight warning..."

His lips touched her throat, kissing her softly.

"Oh, m-mercy..." she strangled in a choked quiet voice.

"But when someone gets too close, threatens me, or I see that the time is right to strike?" he whispered, his teeth grazing her jawline as he moved slowly away from her to meet her gaze in the dimly lit room. She saw his heated look, recognizing the passion in his eyes, and felt herself faltering as he leaned forward, holding himself still, his breath tickling her lips.

"I'll make my move."

He held himself there, cradling her in his arms and waiting.

"Well?" she whispered, unable to help herself, wanting to know what would come next… and anticipating it with every fiber of her being. "You think I'm scared of you?"

"I know you aren't," he smiled sadly, still holding back. "But you *are* scared – and I don't want that for you, ever."

"W-What?" she choked in confusion, her eyes meeting his.

"I'm not a monster, just a man," he began, still holding her close. "I want you to know I'm interested but willing to wait for you to see me differently. I know you are scared of being alone with another man – and I understand that, but I never want you to be frightened of me."

Her eyes searched his, her heart thumping like frightened rabbits in her chest. She could feel the muscles on him, holding her close, and knew he could take whatever he wanted, yet he wasn't forcing the issue. He cared - and it was in his eyes.

She felt hers burn with awareness and was about to say something when he spoke again.

"We've been friends for years, but let's try reaching for a bit more - one step at a time, together. I'm just like any other man and want companionship and intimacy between us. It's just tough right now because we have a past. Something I cannot change, nor would I," he said hoarsely, touching her jaw with his thumb. "Hold me," he urged in a faint whisper. "Hug me, touch me, kiss me… whatever you want - just let me be close as we grow comfortable together."

"Elliott…"

"I'm not expecting you to jump into bed with me," he interrupted tenderly. "But I will share your bed to sleep and would like to hold my wife close – if that's okay?"

She nodded tearfully, unsure what to say.

"I won't press you for more, but when you are ready," he whispered gently, his eyes holding hers. "I would love to have it all with you someday if you'll accept me."

"I… oh gosh," Sarah breathed, nearly whimpering and feeling so overwhelmed in this moment. She didn't want to hurt his feelings. "Do you know how this makes me feel inside? To know that I'm moving forward, that I've done the unthinkable? I've remarried, which is closing the door on my past, Elliott. I know he's gone, but this feels so final."

"I know – and I hate that you are having to go through all of this. We've always had each other's backs, but I cannot help you with reconciling your past in your mind. I can only wait and be patient."

They stood there, not looking away from each other, as he held her close… and then drew her into his arms, hugging her, just like he used to back when they were 'just friends' and David was still alive. She held him, unsure what to say or do, and felt his hand rubbing her back tenderly for comfort.

"Shhh… I've got you," he promised, holding her. "I'll always protect you, your children, our marriage, and our friendship. Please don't worry, and never be scared of any of this – don't be scared of me."

She nodded slightly against his shoulder, unsure what to say.

"Why don't you get ready for bed – and I will too. It will be morning soon enough, and the kids might have had time to think of more questions for us."

"Oh gosh," she laughed tearfully and leaned back to look at him. He was smiling tenderly at her, and she saw something flicker across his gaze. "What?"

"I have a request to make – and you are welcome to say 'No.'"

"What's that?"

"I would ask that we kiss each other good night each evening, because that is something spouses would do. Are you willing to try that - or is it too much, too soon?"

She looked at him, realizing he was putting himself out there, offering everything she could ever ask for, with almost nothing in return. He wasn't demanding a wedding night and wasn't pushing her for more. He just asked for a kiss good night and to accept him at her side, taking their time to grow beyond their friendship.

Sarah nodded slightly.

Elliott leaned down and barely brushed his lips against hers. The sensation made her heart stagger, her breath caught, and her fingers were digging into his side, clutching at him; yet it was only a soft, innocent kiss. His thumb brushed across her lower lip as he murmured simply, 'thank you' before releasing her.

He turned and picked up his bag, opening it and dragging out some running shorts and a T-shirt, before glancing up at her where she stood watching him.

"I'll sleep dressed, Sarah," he volunteered quietly. "Please don't worry."

And those simple words seemed to echo in the silence.

CHAPTER 17

COPPERHEAD

Elliott was going to Hell.

That was it.

What kind of man took his best friend's wife as his own after his death?

He had only had the best of intentions, wanting to help, having admired Sarah from far away, knowing that she loved David. He'd buried those feelings long ago – knowing it was hopeless. He had not been available to even entertain the idea because of him attending the Academy, then flight school, and had been content in her happiness.

Sarah had gotten married, moved on, and had a family.

And her family with David - was now his responsibility.

She married him, and he was stunned. He expected her to say 'no' deep down inside and had struggled with whether he should buy that ring he'd spotted at the exchange. He thought it was kind of fitting, and it touched him. The diamond had been tear-shaped, representing her loss, but the wedding band looked like a sunrise, framing the bottom of the diamond solitaire like it was the dawning of something new.

He was a romantic nitwit and had no clue how to handle any of this. A part of him wondered if it would ruin their friendship, kill the last remnants tying them together yet unbelievably,

Sarah agreed.

Elliott lay there in the bed, feeling like a charlatan, lacing his fingers across his chest in the darkness. His body was betraying him left and right like he was some boy who found his dad's magazine. His heart was beating wildly in his chest, his running shorts were much too tight, and the smell of her perfume was like a bolt of lightning that ran from his sinuses to his brain, striking his heart. Only a fool would think that this was going to be innocent.

And he was that big of a fool.

"My dang call sign should have been Jester or Moron or Idiot..." he muttered silently as he heard her brushing her teeth in the bathroom nearby. "I'm never going to get through this without..."

He drew in his breath quickly, keeping his panicked thoughts to himself as the bathroom door opened. Looking toward the bathroom, he swallowed – and choked on his own saliva. Coughing wildly, he heard her concern and closed his eyes to keep from seeing the swell of her chest in a simple nightgown that came to her knees.

That was it – he'd lost his ever-lovin' mind. When had a cotton, pleated, nursing nightgown ever been sexy to him? Yet, seeing that innocent look was more than anything he could have ever imagined – and he could imagine a staggering number of things right now as his brain ran rampant.

"Are you okay?" she asked softly.

"Yep," he rasped. "Drainage."

"Do you need some Benadryl or Claritin for allergies?"

"I'm good," he muttered, looking away and closing his eyes as he felt the bed sink nearby as she lay down far from him, quickly turning off the lamp on her side of the bed. Oh mercy, he thought wildly, swallowing.

Neither said a word, lying there in the silence.

He could hear her soft breathing – and the catch in it that quickened every once in a while, making him wonder what she was thinking. Looking slightly to his left, he could see the profile of her face beside him and saw her eyes staring sightlessly toward the ceiling.

"Are you okay?"

"Yes," she croaked out quietly and then hesitated. "No… maybe? No, I don't know."

"No?"

"I'm scared."

"Of what? I said I wouldn't touch you, and I meant it."

"I know," she admitted and then looked at him, her eyes glistening in the darkness as she looked so helpless and lost in that moment.

"Then what are you scared of?" he asked, confused, and waiting patiently for her to answer as the silence seemed to grow between them. He almost rolled away to turn on the lamp next to the bed, but this felt awkward enough already.

"Myself," she whispered, her voice sounding so pained and full of unshed tears. He was about to ask 'why' or what she meant when she continued speaking to him. "I'm scared because this is all so confusing. As much as you worry about things – I do too."

145

"What are you worried about?"

Her eyes searched his, and he saw her swallow nervously before shaking her head slightly. Everything in him wanted to reach out, to smooth her hair or touch her cheek. He wanted to take her hand in his, to hold it and promise her the moon, yet he remained infinitely still, thrumming with tension that was palpable between them. If he touched her lying in this bed, he was deathly afraid he would break his word.

"Nothing," she whispered, rolling away from him and curling into a ball. "Good night."

She seemed so tiny, so frail right now like she was shying away from the world and needed to hide. He promised to protect her. and the best way he could was to give her a safe place to hide, offering shelter.

"Good night, Sarah," he said quietly and heard a soft, muted whimper telling him that she was crying. This was not how he expected his wedding night to go. "It's going to be okay – I promise."

And she was silent.

EARLY THE NEXT MORNING, Elliott cracked open a bleary eye and noticed a bit of light streaming through the mini-blinds nearby. He glanced toward where Sarah had slept and saw her missing. Sitting up, he looked around the room and rubbed his eyes, exhausted.

He'd heard her weeping last night, felt the bed move every time she turned over or adjusted her position in the bed, as he lay there wide-awake and feeling like a heel. Getting to his feet, he stretched and heard the children in the distance talking, realizing they were already up.

Not bothering to change, he walked out of the bedroom

and down the hallway toward the living room and glanced in the kitchen to see Sarah there at the coffee maker pouring a cup. She's so beautiful, he thought, swallowing nervously, and walked up behind her.

"Good morning," he said hoarsely, and she turned quickly as if he scared her... only to see the rings under her eyes. "You didn't sleep much either, huh?"

"No," she admitted in a hushed voice, dropping her gaze. He immediately reached out, putting a finger under her chin and lifting her eyes to his.

"I promised that I wouldn't cross a line – and I won't," he offered again silently. "We've always been close as friends and..."

She made a slight noise and hesitated, her lips smiling sadly, almost in a grimace, as she didn't look away from him. Her eyes searched his as she stood there before him.

"Friends," she began hoarsely, "Friends don't have thoughts like mine."

Elliott didn't say a word – he couldn't. He stared at her in disbelief as she pulled back from him, looking away, and he immediately advanced.

"Wait..."

"I shouldn't have said anything..."

"Yes, you should have..."

"Morning Elliott," came Leslie's sing-song voice, followed by Bethany. "Morning, Uncle Daddy..."

And they both flinched.

"Please - just call me Elliott, Bethany," he said hoarsely, not looking away from Sarah as Morgan walked into the room, pushing past him and immediately climbing up on a stepstool to get three plastic bowls out of the cabinet.

"Cereal, Uncle Elliott?"

"Thanks," he said numbly toward Morgan. "I need to

speak with your Mom for a second and will be right back. Can you get the cereal out for everyone?"

"Yes, sir."

"Sarah?"

"It's okay, Elliott," she replied – and he wouldn't listen. It was not 'okay' with him. This was a mess and disturbing something big within him. He grasped her arm, pulling her out of the kitchen and tugging her toward their bedroom. The second they were inside, she yanked her arm away and looked at him.

"Finish your thoughts," he said bluntly. "Friends don't have thoughts like mine... what thoughts? What are you talking about?"

"We've crossed a line we can't come back from," she said almost in a panic, reaching for the doorknob and he put his hand on the door panel, blocking it.

"I don't want to come back from it."

"I'm scared – and you are pushing me..."

"I'm not pushing you - you volunteered that information..."

"What am I supposed to say?" she balked, panicking. "That I thought about you? That I thought about us? Together?"

"Yes!" he scrambled desperately, feeling a rush of emotion within him as he held his hands out before her, almost bodily begging for a chance. "Tell me what is going on in your head, in your mind. If you thought about me, then tell me..."

"I can't because..."

"Because why?"

"David..."

"David's dead," he said bluntly – and saw her flinch. "It's been over a year, and you are not," he continued softly. "You are not dead, neither are your children. I'm not dead. I want a chance, and we both deserve some sort of..."

"Hush," she hissed painfully, staring at him.

"I don't think so."

"I'm not having this conversation."

"Fine," he said bluntly, trying not to raise his voice but knew his temper was close to bubbling. This was too much, too emotional, and too big of a wound within him to just be something considered 'okay.' "But I want you to know that I think of you too – and do you want to know what I think about? Hmm?" he asked, not waiting for an answer. "I think about us holding hands, laughing, and talking together like we used to – but it's different now. I thought about rolling over and gathering you in my arms last night, just knowing I could hold you close. I wished desperately that you would turn to me for comfort instead of being scared to cross a line. I *want* you to cross it, Sarah. I want you to give us a chance to find some sort of happiness together."

He stood there, his chest heaving as he whispered those impassioned words to her in the stillness of the room, hearing the children in the distance.

"All I want is a chance to try to make you happy – because it would make me happy," he finished weakly, letting his hands fall and his shoulders slump in defeat. "I swear I'm not the monster, but I'm starting to think that maybe somehow, in your mind, I've been painted that way – and I'm sorry."

"Elliott…" she whispered softly, her voice full of the same agony he felt right now – and he didn't dare look at her, or he might shatter. This was a self-inflicted torture he never imagined or anticipated when he spoke with Paradox, and maybe this is what the other pilot was implying.

"Look," he interrupted painfully. "Let's just feed the kids and see if Firefly can watch them today. I want to get them stuff for Christmas – and then we can get it wrapped, and put it under the tree while I'm here. Just see if you can find it within you to put up with me for two more days, and then I'll leave."

When she said nothing – he finally glanced at her and saw her enormous eyes watching him.

"I'm sorry for everything," he began – and left the room, leaving her there.

AN HOUR LATER, Elliott was backing out of the driveway, frowning and even more frustrated. Apparently, everyone knew about what was going on between them, which meant that Sarah was talking to Melody, and Melody was talking to her husband - who didn't hold back a thing.

Firefly had pulled Elliott aside almost immediately into a library or den that was in the middle of a remodel, nearly stepping in a tray of paint and looking at him.

"Look," Firefly began. "Some real 'guy talk' between friends?"

"Sure," Elliott retorted, looking at him curiously and a little amused at whatever 'guy talk' he thought he was going to imbue on him. Crossing his arms, he smiled easily. "Go for it."

"Quit thinking with your nuts."

Elliott's mouth dropped open in shock.

"You heard me," Firefly grinned. "Look, I get it. You think your girl is hot, you feel all these sparkly-happy-things in your jeans when you look at her, and you want to hold her, but don't."

"We're not having this conversation..."

"Don't act on it," Firefly interrupted bluntly, and there was something in his eyes that stopped Elliott in his tracks. "Trust me on this. She needs to be the one to reach for you – and you need to hold back until she is ready. If you push her, move too fast, or try too hard – you'll only end up losing her. She needs to be ready, and you've already moved mountains by just getting married. Let her take the next step."

"I need to get back to…"

"Melody was a widow, and we had much of the same problems. The fear, the guilt, the memory of her dead husband, who was my best friend," Firefly said quietly, watching him… and Elliott paused, stunned.

He didn't realize that. Sparky had told him to talk to the other pilot but didn't say why – and now he knew. His newly assigned wingman was smarter than he realized and saw so much.

"How do you actually cross the line?" Elliott asked nervously, feeling embarrassed and a little mortified to be having this discussion with another man.

"Quit thinking about 'the line' and what's in your pants," Firefly grinned. "Be there for her, be her friend, and let it happen naturally between you."

"I'm only here for two more days – and then I'm not coming back because I don't want to bother her."

"Oh, you'll be back, brother. I guarantee it."

Elliott didn't say a word as the other man continued to smile at him.

"Take your time and have fun with your girl today. The children will be fine. Be friends, relax, and just let yourself unwind. Do all the stupid holiday things and just be there with her."

And heard a truck honk, bringing him out of his reverie.

Elliott looked at Sarah's surprised face, hesitated, and then finished backing out of the gravel driveway. It would do neither of them any good if he got into a car accident or did something foolish because he was distracted.

"Sorry," he volunteered sheepishly.

"Are you all right?"

"Yes. Just a simple mistake…" he began and hesitated as he pulled onto the road. "Shall we head to the mall?"

"Sure – or Walmart. They've got a large toy department and…"

"Sounds good," he breathed, realizing that maybe Firefly was right. "Let's get a game to play tonight with the kids after dinner… and a variety of things to put under the tree."

And to his disbelief, he felt Sarah's hand touch his where it lay on the center console that he was using as an armrest. She put her hand over his, lacing their fingers and staring straight ahead as he glanced at her.

"I promised you a hot cocoa too," he volunteered, remembering her request and saw a slight smile touch her lips.

"So you did…"

"This is nice. I like you holding my hand and us being able to talk."

"Me too."

Elliott swallowed nervously, realizing that maybe there was something to what Firefly said. Perhaps the grinning idiot actually knew what he was talking about… and he'd offered to watch the children all day long.

He was going to take him up on that offer – because he intended to make sure today was full of joy and memories for them.

THIRTY MINUTES LATER, Elliott was shoving a lame shopping cart down the aisle, realizing one of the wheels was wobbling horrifically and locking up every few feet, only to hear Sarah's smothered laugh. He looked at her, lifted a brow, and grinned at her, seeing her own wide smile on her face.

"I'm not giving up this cart," he warned, chuckling. "Now,

if I see another empty one in the store – I might swap them out, but this was the last one, so we'll manage."

"I hate how busy it gets at Christmastime here…"

"Yeah, it's pretty packed, so I'm hoping it's not too picked over," he agreed, shoving the offending cart and feeling it wobble before the wheel seized, causing him to curse softly… and heard her laugh again beside him. Just hearing that sweet, feminine laughter made him feel good. "I've got to get my girls a new baby doll – and I was thinking maybe we could get Morgan something cool like a science kit?"

"Really?"

At her word, he stopped and looked at her surprised expression – and melted. She looked so touched, so taken aback, and relieved all at once that it caught him unawares. He took her hand and laid it on his chest, hesitating as Firefly's words replayed in his mind.

"Yeah, 'really'," he said simply – and let go of her hand. He instinctively reached for her like a husband would a wife and was botching the whole friendship-thing.

Only Sarah didn't move.

She stood there, close to him, and looked at him with those gorgeous eyes he knew so well. It took everything to keep from leaning down to try to kiss her as she gazed at him. Gosh, she made his knees weak with just a glance, and he felt her pull her hand from him finally, withdrawing.

"I want to get the children something special. I want them to feel like children, and they've had enough in their young lives, you know?" he said hoarsely… and felt her touch his cheek. Stunned, he looked at her and saw her smile at him, swallowing as he waited.

"Thank you, Elliott," she breathed. "Thank you for being amazing."

"I'm just here with an incredible girl," he countered, using her words and hating the tremor in his voice. "Now, what does my favorite girl want for Christmas?" he teased, trying to brush off the moment and make it more 'friendly' than what he felt.

"I don't know," Sarah said quietly, pulling her hand away and hesitating. "Let's just focus on the kids first, okay?"

"Sounds good," he replied simply, wishing with all of his might that he could read her mind right now.

CHAPTER 18

SARAH

SARAH HAD NEVER ENJOYED Christmas shopping. It was much too crowded, people were too short-tempered, and everything seemed expensive – yet this year felt different. Last year, they barely had a Christmas because it was hard to celebrate after David's passing and with a baby on the way. Somehow, this year, things felt lighter, more alive, like the world was aglow with the lights and sounds of the Season.

Elliott seemed like his old self, laughing and joking around at everything. He'd picked out a baby doll for each girl and a Barbie set, complete with clothes, bottles, and a baby stroller. For Morgan, he bought a geode set that came with a chisel, hammer, and a massive globular rock that was promised to have crystals inside. They selected matching pajamas for all of them at Elliott's request, and fluffy slippers for the children.

"I want to give Morgan a little something special," Elliott began, making an abrupt U-turn in the aisle, walking purposefully in the other direction. "The idea just hit me."

"What are you doing?" she chuckled, following him, and paused when they got to electronics as he yanked up a box excitedly – along with a few others beside it, tossing them in the cart.

"I'm giving him this one before I leave," Elliott said simply – and she looked down to see it was a Polaroid camera, just like what she'd seen at her grandparents' home as a little girl. "I want him to take photos of all of us together in our pajamas, and I think it would be a fun memory for the kids."

Touched, she looked at him in wonder.

He was right.

It would be a fantastic way to let them be children, savor the memories, and have a little fun together as a family. They could take a photo of all of them - or Morgan could take photos of what he wanted, what was important to him, or even allow them to each have a special photograph in their rooms.

Perhaps they'd make a bulletin board for memories she mused and looked at Elliott in wonder. This was a beautiful gift – a thoughtful one.

"I love this idea," she whispered. "Thank you."

"You don't mind?" he hesitated. "You know he's going to be popping out of corners at all times with that camera, right?"

Sarah laughed nervously, nodding and stepped forward to hug him, needing to, right there in the middle of the store. She slid her arms around Elliott's waist and felt him tense as she laid a cheek against his shoulder – only to feel him hug her back.

Feeling his arms around her, holding him close, felt so incredibly amazing and so right. Her mind was screaming guiltily that she was betraying David's memory, yet everything in her was reaching for the person she'd always relied upon as a friend, the man she held close to her heart and mind – Elliott.

Was it so very wrong to want that sense of happiness the three of them used to find hanging out together? Yes, David was gone – but Elliott was right. They were alive. Instead of burying those memories, they needed to hang onto them but not in guilt but rather as a beautiful snapshot of a time that had passed much too soon.

She shivered slightly and felt his breath on her hair as he spoke.

"Hey... this is nothing," he said softly. "It's just me trying to be a half-decent stepdad to an incredible young boy. The children deserve to have holiday memories, and I want them to savor it as long as possible. My dad got me a little cheap camera when I was a kid – and I broke it a month later – so I'm fully expecting the same..."

Sarah chuckled against his shoulder, smiling at the memory he was sharing with her. She didn't even remember the camera, and they had known each other since they were ten, and his father had passed away when he was fifteen.

"I don't remember that," she admitted looking up at him, yet not releasing him from the hug. Her hands were clasped behind his back and his face was so close to hers, smiling tenderly at her.

"Well, duh," he chuckled intimately. "I broke it pretty fast and didn't want my best friend saying, 'I told you so' – again."

She laughed easily, and to her surprise, he pulled her hands from around his back, smiling regretfully.

"Let's get the paper, tape, bows, and other paraphernalia, so we can hide everything... and I promised my girl a hot cocoa. Remember?"

"Yes, you did," she smiled, not wanting the day to be over.

"You also promised to take me to see Christmas lights this evening."

"I promised I would take all of you," he corrected playfully, winking at her. "Which means we need to get this stuff stashed home and wrapped - or hide it really well so we can wrap it all later tonight instead. We can hide it all in our bedroom away from prying eyes."

"Unless..." she whispered, looking up at him with awareness as she tried to take a step forward, reaching for that 'more' he kept hinting at. She saw the flash of awareness in his eyes as his jaw seemed to clench.

"Yes?" he asked huskily, waiting.

"Nothing," she replied, immediately backpedaling and looking away, hearing his heavy sigh.

"We'll wrap them when we get home so the kids have something to shake. It should occupy them for a bit."

"All right," she acknowledged, realizing that she had been so close to suggesting that 'something more' between them – and felt so confused. This was so difficult because of David's memory and how her husband used to be when they were alone, yet Elliott wasn't him.

Elliott had shown he could push his way and obviously wanted her, but he was withdrawing as well, giving her space. It wasn't like she didn't know what would happen between them – she had four children, and that was when it hit her like a ton of bricks.

She stopped walking in the middle of the aisle, lost in thought, as Elliott stepped forward to select a Lego box off the shelf and looked at it. Her mind was whirling, not hearing a thing he was saying at that moment as all the pieces that she struggled with were suddenly snapping together in place, interlocking, and making sense in a way she never imagined.

Each child was different, had to be fed differently, held

differently, had different mannerisms and moods, and she had learned each one. Could it be the same for her marriage?

David had been bold, outgoing, almost to the point he was pushy. He told her he was going to marry her, wanted a big family, and had always taken the lead in their relationship. Yet Elliott was the exact opposite. He was easy-going around her, even-tempered, allowing her to take the lead in all things over the years, just seemingly content to be there – and she saw it even now. When Elliott pushed, pressing her for more, he still withdrew after saying his piece, letting her make the choices for them.

Elliott was right.

David was dead, and she was not - and neither was Elliott.

Somehow, she knew he would wait for her, be there without asking because he always was. Even now, he had stepped forward to care for her, marrying her because he wanted to be at her side always, but was this just a friendship – or was she completely blind to what had been there all along?

Had David seen it? Was that why he'd been jealous? What kind of wife did that make her? She had loved David with everything in her, yet he'd struggled with the idea of having a male friend in her life. She had cared for Elliott as a friend and had told David that several times, but had she been wrong?

No.

She loved David – and what she felt for Elliott, this friendship, was distinctly different. This was comforting, like slipping into a warm bath, knowing you were safe, could relax, and could be your truest self. David had been intense, and whatever this was with Elliott…

She swallowed and looked at him sideways as the answer hit her.

He was her home – and this was also a type of love.

The realization, the shock of it all, left her reeling. It was possible to care for two different people in very different ways, just like her children. They were individuals that deserved to be treasured in very individual ways. She could no more force him to be like someone else than she could be.

She was Sarah— whatever mess that was. That girl had scars that no one would see. She had fears, wishes, hopes, and dreams buried deep down within her. A single light within her had flickered, burned brightly at times, and had seen it nearly extinguished when the sorrow became too much - yet here she was.

A survivor.

And blessed to find someone who treasured her for being herself, despite everything she had been through, experienced, and how she morphed from a girl to a woman, a wife, then a mother, and eventually a widow - and Elliott was still there, waiting.

For her...

Swallowing the lump in her throat, she looked at the miracle nearby – and smiled. She walked to his side and slipped her hand in his.

"I think we have enough for the children," she said quietly. "Let's go."

He didn't say a word and put the box back on the shelf, nodding. Not letting go of her hand, he grasped the front of the buggy and pulled it beside him as they walked together to the front to get in the checkout lines.

"Is everything okay?"

"I think it might be," she admitted and saw the surprise flicker across his face as he smiled back at her silently. Neither said another word as if afraid to disturb this momentary peace they'd found. It didn't feel necessary at that moment, and she took a chance again, wading bravely into a new ocean that she somehow recognized.

She stepped forward into his arms once more, willingly, and hugged him close a second time without prompting and sighed.

Home.

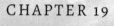

CHAPTER 19

SARAH

PULLING UP TO THE HOUSE, Sarah called in an order for Chinese food to be delivered and knew that they only had so much time to get things wrapped for the children. Elliott was out of the car in a heartbeat, popping the trunk and gathering the bags while she moved to the front door, hanging up the phone, and unlocking it.

"It will be here in about thirty minutes," she volunteered and saw him walking up to the door, both arms laden with bags, and she couldn't help but marvel at the muscles he was displaying, lugging in everything in one trip.

Yeah, she might not have ever considered getting remarried… especially to her best friend, but now looking at him with new eyes?

Her best friend was intensely gorgeous – bordering on 'hot.'

Holding open the door, Elliott murmured 'thanks' as he passed her... and she walked back to the car, peering in the hatch to see if there was anything left, only to see one roll of wrapping paper had fallen out. Chuckling, she rolled her eyes and picked it up, hefting it onto her shoulder like a lumberjack would an ax, and shut the trunk.

As she walked inside the house, she stopped in her tracks, bursting out laughing. It looked like the Walmart toy aisle had exploded in the living room. Every bag had been emptied onto the carpet, the rolls of tape were scattered, along with a bag of bows and curling ribbon, and Elliott stood in the middle of it all, turning around in confusion and looking among the carnage before them.

"Where are the scissors? I know I bought a pair..."

She bopped him on the bum with the tube of wrapping paper playfully – and saw him jump before laughing nervously, his hand cupping his backside. The surprise on his face made something within her warm and happy.

"Don't do that to a guy..." he chuckled easily. "Not unless you mean it."

"There are scissors in the kitchen drawer," she smiled. "You didn't need them, so I fished them out of the cart."

"Sarah, we just bought a lot of stuff we don't need..."

"Exactly."

"But we bought it anyway because it's Christmas."

She walked past him to the kitchen, yanked open the drawer, and brandished two pairs of scissors in her hand as she re-entered the living room, meeting his warm eyes. Kicking off her shoes pointedly, she handed him a pair and tiptoed gingerly among the chaotic mess.

"I like you playing around with me," Elliott volunteered quietly, taking a seat nearby and grabbing the first box. "It's fun. I want things to be fun and light-hearted between us when we are together."

"I just felt like it," she shrugged, trying to play it off slightly, and then looked at him, meeting his smile. "I might do it again. You never know."

"I hope you do."

Both waited, and she looked at the mess, smiling, trying to lighten the mood and distract him.

"Did you really have to scatter everything across the floor?"

"It feels like Christmas when you do," he countered, grinning.

"Is there a method to this madness then?"

"Do you want to work together? I can wrap and you put all the bows, ribbon, and labels on them?"

"Deal," she agreed, moving slightly closer to where the massive bag of bows was located. "You wrap, chuck it toward me, and I'll put the bows on them."

"You got it," he agreed, spreading his legs on the floor and leaning forward to grab another box. She watched as he deftly wrapped a board game that he'd picked up for the children and smiled. He obviously loved games because he'd selected one for each of them – including Henry. He selected a stacking cup game that had little smiley faces on the insides. The chubby sweet baby might be too little for it right now, but he would definitely enjoy holding the brightly colored plastic cups.

He handed her the wrapped box purposefully, moving to the next gift.

"This is Leslie's."

This went on for several minutes, box after box, name after name. She would tie a ribbon around each, putting a bow on them, then taping a nametag to each before sliding it under the tree that had only been put up a day or two before Elliott's arrival.

"Next…" he said simply, tossing a small box in her direction – and she caught it, hesitating, and looked at him in surprise. It was a doll, a soft squishy doll that could not be boxed up.

"Just stick a bow on it?"

"I bought some bags," he admitted, pointing to her left. "Do you want some coffee? Maybe we should take a quick break? Dinner should be here soon, I think."

"Sure," she said, grunting slightly as she leaned for the bags and realized that they would be perfect to hide the dolls inside. She shoved the squishy baby doll inside, yanked the ribbons to close it, and tied them in a double-knot to keep any peeking children out of them, only to see Elliott return a few minutes later as she was on her knees, pushing the bags toward the back of the Christmas tree.

"Do you want to plug it in for a bit?"

"Sure," she replied without glancing at him. Plugging in the tree, she sat back on her knees and smiled at the lights before turning to see him standing there with both cups of coffee. "Perfect," she whispered, getting to her feet and accepting one from him.

They stood there together amidst the chaos as the tinsel glittered and the packages lay under the tree. This was so perfect, so beautiful, that she felt something unfurl within her, sharing this moment with him.

"Thank you for letting me do this," Elliott said softly, taking a sip of his coffee. "I really wanted it to be special for them, you know? Last year was hard because I sure didn't feel like celebrating…"

"Neither did I…"

"But I do now," he finished quietly. "I think all of us need this this year."

"I agree completely."

Elliott sat down on the couch and nervously patted the cushion beside him, inviting her to join him. There was no reason not to – this was only just sitting and nothing else. As she gingerly sat down, she took a sip of her coffee and sighed in happiness.

"Right?" he chuckled quietly. "I don't know if it's the coffee, the coffee maker, the company I am keeping, or the tap water, but the best coffee in the world is right here."

Sarah was touched by his words and looked at him in surprise – only to see him rear back with a look of alarm on his face as he immediately apologized.

"Sorry. I didn't mean to make things uncomfortable."

"No," she whispered, looking at him. "That was really sweet of you – thank you. I appreciate that."

"You're welcome… because it's true."

The doorbell rang, and he immediately jumped up, glancing at her nervously, and then moved to answer it. She watched him make small talk with the driver, yanking out his wallet and tipping him before accepting the plastic bag tied with a knot and shutting the front door.

She rose to help him make their plates, standing beside him in the kitchen as they doled out a little bit on each plate.

"Eggroll?"

"Please."

"Still like hot mustard?"

"Oh yes…" she chuckled and saw his knowing smile as he slid an eggroll out of each bag onto the plate – and handed her a few packets. "Noodles?"

"Always," he quipped, causing the two of them to share a smile as they stood there together. She found herself looking at him more and more, just almost like she needed to absorb and memorize these moments to help fill an emptiness in her. Just being near him made her feel good, complete, alive… and caught his eyes watching her too.

"Hungry?"

"Very," she admitted – and saw him drop an extra

spoonful of General Tso Chicken on her plate atop the noodles. A second later, they each picked up their plates and sat down at the table nearby.

There was a surprising amount of tension she felt in the air or around them, almost like it was tangible. She wished she could read his mind sometimes and knew it was silly. Maybe she was overanalyzing all of this, making too much of it, and...

"Let's eat," he began, picking up his eggroll and not meeting her eyes.

Yeah, it had to be her imagining things, she realized.

They ate in silence, only broken by the sounds of their fork hitting the plate or the fizz of a soda as Elliott opened a can and split it between the two glasses that he'd filled with ice for them. It was a simple meal with a friend, yet it also felt like the most awkward, tense moment. If they were two tectonic plates along a fault, she would bet money there was about to be an earthquake, praying it would be minor, and not decimate everything around her.

"Finished?" he said simply, getting up from his chair and reaching for her plate as she nodded. "I'll wash it up in a bit, but let's finish our coffee and relax before we pick up the kiddos."

"That sounds great," she admitted nervously.

Topping off both cups of coffee, they moved to the living room and sat down on the couch once more, putting a little space between them. She sat at one end and he was at the other. They both sat there quietly, and she saw him start to open his mouth to speak before pausing. He instead took a sip of his coffee and looked away, like he had something to hide.

"You were going to say something," she prompted. "What was it?"

"I was going to ask what you wanted for Christmas this

year," he replied simply, his voice infinitely shy. "I mean, it's our first Christmas as a couple, even if things are strained between us – and I want to do right by you. If things were different, if we dated, I would get you something you know? Did you and David exchange presents? Should we?"

Sarah stood up abruptly – and saw his face pale as he looked up at her in alarm. She put her coffee down on the end table and took his – setting it beside her cup.

"I shouldn't have said it – I'll g-go..." he began hoarsely, looking like he was about to be ill... which hurt her deeply. Had she given him the impression that she wanted him gone?

Instead of flinching or anticipating a flash of pain from the reference to her past, it was surprisingly more like sloughing off a weight that she didn't realize was still there. Christmases *would* be different, life would be different, and she was ready for it. If she was a bird, she was about to leap out into the air, confidently shrugged off all inhibitions because she was safe.

Turning slightly, Sarah sat on Elliott's lap, pinning him in the seat. The look of shock on his face was priceless – and she would have laughed if it wasn't such a sad indication of how broken things might actually be between them.

"What are you d-doing?" he croaked nervously.

Spinning slightly, she adjusted her position and put her feet up on the couch cushion beside him, leaning back against his arm resting on the bolster of the couch before looking at him.

She met his wary eyes, seeing a flicker of hope and fear within those depths as he stared at her and swallowed. His Adam's apple bobbled slightly causing her to smile wryly, realizing that he was just as nervous as she was to mess things up.

"Shouldn't I sit on Santa's lap when he asks what I want for Christmas?" she whispered suggestively, her voice barely a whisper in the stillness of the room. The lights were flickering in the distance, the gifts were almost all wrapped, and it was just them... alone.

"S-Sarah...?"

"I'd like a second chance," she breathed softly, looking at his beautiful eyes and seeing the shock, indecision, and fear in his gaze. "I'd like to tell my new husband without any repercussions just how scared I am that I will disappoint him..."

"You could never disappoint me," he interrupted hoarsely, his eyes searching hers with such openness and longing in his gaze. His arm moved slightly, moving to circle her waist almost in a hug as he put his other hand on her thigh, holding her in place, like he was afraid she'd bolt at his attempt to hold her close.

It felt good to shrug off the last of this shell around her, knowing that he would protect her feelings, support her, and be there for her no matter what. There was no other sensation like it in the world and she was reveling in this new freedom that once seemed so daunting.

"I'd like to tell him how afraid I am that something is... broken... inside of me that can't be fixed," she continued, feeling her eyes sting with emotion as she looked at him, hoping he understood what she was trying to say.

"Nothing is broken in you..."

"Is this normal then?" she asked tearfully. "To miss someone at the same time you desire someone else because I feel like something is wrong with me..."

"I feel like some traitor wanting my best friend's wife..."

"How do you think I feel? David used to be jealous of our friendship, but was it because he saw this? What does that make me?" she hissed emotionally, wiping her eyes. "I want to be happy, but I'm scared I don't deserve it."

"All of this... everything you are saying and feeling... it

makes you normal, Sarah," Elliott said tenderly, moving his hand from her leg and brushing her hair back from her face, tucking it behind her ear. "You are a very loving, giving person, and it's natural to want that same emotion given back to you," he paused and met her eyes, speaking directly to her soul, and his voice cracked with the emotion that was brimming, churning, and fighting to stay hidden... and she saw it.

"I wish you didn't have to go through any of this loss, but I also know that if David was still alive... you wouldn't look twice at me, no matter what you think of yourself right now. You were happy – and I was happy for you. I've always wanted you to be happy," he confessed and smiled sadly before looking away.

Sarah reached for him, touching Elliott's cheek, turning his face back toward her. There, in his eyes, was the truth, making her wonder how she'd ever been so ignorant of the raw and powerful emotions that he'd hidden for so long. A truth that they both knew and buried because it was easier than facing it. It would be hard to explain to the children, friends, and people in town that she'd fallen for her husband's best friend, the children's 'uncle' that actually wasn't... but it was all there before her. There was such love that it gave her the strength to say her deepest, darkest secrets that had been buried for well over a year.

"That's where you are wrong," she breathed softly and heard his breath catch as he stared at her. "I was looking because things weren't so great between us, but not in the way that is easily told because you are two very different people. We were trying to make our marriage work for the children, our commitments, and what we felt for each other – but marriage isn't easy. It's harder than anything you've ever tackled at times. David was sweet and kind. I loved him dearly, and I will always have a piece of him in my heart..."

"But?"

Elliott's voice was achingly hoarse and laden with emotion as she searched his eyes, putting herself on the line. How had she not looked at him, not seen him, or wanted more? What kind of woman was she to marry her best friend a year after her husband died?

"But you are there too... in my heart, and I can't help it," she whispered tearfully, touching his cheek. "Please don't think badly of me or..."

"Never," he promised. "I would never push you, never judge you, and never condemn you for taking a chance at happiness for yourself. If I cannot make you happy someday, then I would hope you would..."

Sarah closed the space between them, effectively silencing him as her lips pressed against his right before she pulled back. It was a brief kiss given innocently to stop the words he was about to speak, but that single gesture opened a floodgate that neither could hold back.

His lips were warm and so different from David's, yet felt so right. It wasn't a passionate kiss but rather a quick movement to stop the indecision, the doubts, the words she didn't want to hear aloud. If they were going to attempt a marriage, she wanted him to double down and fight to hang on, not give up if she was 'unhappy'... but how did you say that when you were barely dipping a toe over the line between them – when it hit her.

You didn't speak – you showed.

Elliott stared at her in awareness, his mouth parting in amazement and wonder. She could see the hope in his eyes, the fear, the avid longing, and he made a slight noise in his throat as he held himself— waiting and afraid. He was still giving her space, and she was done. Mentally, she pirouetted over that line between them in their minds, their hearts, and saw the flare of understanding as they sat there in that split second.

She was already leaning toward him once more, unable to help herself. This was her Elliott, her best friend, her now husband, and she was done fighting all of this between them. Her fingers splayed across his cheek and jaw, holding him close as he moved his hand, sinking it in her hair, pulling her closer to him.

Their eyes met once more as he paused, right before he closed the distance between them in a silent promise. His mouth was soft, tender, and warm. The man kissed her lovingly, taking his time and tasting her. There was no rush between them, no timetable. He was kissing her like a man who would take his time, savoring every moment between them, and she knew.

She wanted him as her husband and in her bed.

Reaching for Elliott, she wanted to wrap her arms around his shoulders that had held so much over the years, silently without question. He'd been the person she'd turned to, the friend that had helped her, her rock when she was broken. As Sarah moved to cling to him, the 'tide' was already turning. She was barely aware that he'd picked her up like she was nothing, creating a thrill that raced along every nerve as he laid her down on the couch cushions beside them especially as he joined her.

Lying there, stretched out along her side, they stared at each other in awareness. There was no doubt in her mind at what he wanted, the fear in their gazes, waiting for this fragile bubble of happiness and solidarity to pop. Both expected something to go wrong because something had always come between them – and they were aware of it now with a shocking clarity.

If it hadn't been the Academy, then it was the distance or something else, or even someone. There were births, deaths, the passage of time, silent fears, all of it, and he'd always been there in the shadows, supporting her every decision because he'd been a part of her soul. They shared a bond that went so deep there was no fighting it anymore. It wasn't just 'friendship' but filled every corner of her in various different ways. He was just her Elliott – and always had been.

"I don't want to pressure you..." he breathed, adjusting slightly and holding himself propped up on an elbow as he looked at her, waiting. There was an inner struggle in his gaze as he stared at her. She saw the wonder, the marvel tinged with a bit of amazement and awe, as he waited.

He always waited for her.

"You're not," she promised.

"Are you sure?" he began hoarsely, his voice trembling. "If we cross this line, everything changes between us. I need you to be sure this is what you want; that you actually want me."

That fearful, whispered statement was enough to solidify her decision. He was still there, still offering yet pulling back, all to make sure she was comfortable taking the next steps.

Sarah touched his cheek, caressing his jaw where he hovered above her, and then pulled him to her in a tender kiss – answering by action, not with words. He made a slight noise in his throat before returning the kiss with his own, murmuring words of love and devotion before he paused, pulling away from her once again.

She opened her eyes, feeling slightly dazed, and a little confused as he sat up and moved away, only to stand up beside the couch where she lay. For a split second, it hit her that he was leaving her there, feeling a wave of fear as she thought he might be pulling back, waiting once more.

But something was different.

His stance, his eyes, his very being... were different. Propping herself on her elbows, she looked at him in surprise – before melting with awareness. He crossed the room, walking toward the family room window to turn the blinds, giving them privacy, before looking back at her.

"You're sure?" he asked once more – and she smiled.

"Let's go to our room," she invited softly, only to see him shake his head negatively. That single motion felt like a splash of cold water on her as she stared at him in shock, until she saw a lazy, contented smile spread across his face as he returned to her, resuming his place beside her on the sofa.

"I want you to know it's me when I make love to you," he whispered tenderly, brushing his nose tenderly against hers and kissing the corner of her lips as he spoke softly. "And that's not going to happen in a bed you once shared with someone else. I know you had a past and would never take that from you – ever."

Sarah touched his cheek, marveling at the man before her. She felt so much love at that moment that it was staggering. Oh, she'd loved David, but this feeling for Elliott was like an abyss in her soul— endless. He pulled her hand from his cheek and kissed her fingertips tenderly, speaking to her.

"You want understanding for Christmas and a second chance? Well, I want a full-sized bed that I, alone, will share with my wife. Just you and me – no shadows of our past, only dreams of a new future. I want to share these stolen moments with you, pour myself into your heart and soul, and cuddle and hold you close all night long as we make love."

He met her eyes, and his smile was everything – specifically stating what he wanted and needed. He obviously felt a sense of wrongness occupying that space, and she was so glad it wasn't just her.

"Until then, I guess it's the couch…" Elliott said in a ho-hum voice, smiling enchantingly as she realized he was teasing her.

"Well, I guess we're going shopping later," she whispered

invitingly, holding his gaze, reaching for the top button of her shirt without looking away. His entire demeanor changed as his eyes heated at seeing that single movement and knowing what was following.

She was ready for him.

For this.

For them…

"We sure are," he affirmed huskily, moving awkwardly as he balanced on one arm, untucking his shirt with the other one. She laughed throatily as she realized he wasn't going to take a chance, leaving her side to change. No, instead, the whole couch shook slightly as he moved awkwardly, yanking his shirt over his head in one smooth motion, mussing up his hair uncaringly. He chuckled and tossed it boldly, landing among the presents on the floor, as they shared a heated look between them.

"Merry Christmas… *husband*," she breathed, touching his cheek and let her fingers dance across his skin as she moved to put her hand on his shoulder, seeing his loving smile so full of joy.

"Merry Christmas, my wife."

CHAPTER 20

SARAH

Lying there on the couch, the two of them sprawled out across the cushions, Sarah couldn't help the smile that seemed to be plastered across her face. Looking toward him where he lay curled at her side, she saw the gentle look of contentment in his eyes as he watched her with so much love.

"You keep looking at me," she whispered nervously.

"I've never seen anything or anyone so beautiful in my life," he replied softly, his finger tracing her jawline and tickling her.

"Ha," she retorted, smiling ruefully at him. "You need your eyes examined, flyboy…"

"I don't think that I do."

"There's stretch marks, cellulite, and I haven't shaved my legs in three days. We probably made cricket sounds for at

least an hour and…" Elliott's delighted laugh had her chuckling along with him as he grinned tenderly at her.

"It was probably closer to ten minutes and more like the
sweet sounds of a saw ripping a log in half…"

"Oh my gosh," she muttered in disbelief, pushing at his
chest as he started laughing wildly again. "Get off of me…"

"I don't think so, Mrs. Trent," he retorted happily, pinning
her hands above her head as he looked down at her. She
wasn't even upset in the slightest if she was being honest. It
was so wonderful to have this sort of playfulness between
them, this friendship mixed with love and laughter. "It's
taken forever to get here – and I don't plan on letting
you go."

Only to have her cell phone ring at that moment where it
lay on the floor among their clothing. They both froze,
looking at each other in awareness.

"The kids…" they uttered in unison.

Elliott shot off the couch and grabbed her phone,
answering it immediately. She couldn't help but stare at his
form as the faint sound of someone speaking came through
the speaker.

"Hey! I said I'd watch them - not adopt them! You know
Bethany taught Betsy to bite? My daughter bit me. What'd
you get me for Christmas, Copperhead? It better be good,
expensive, and rhyme with 'ooze' or 'ear'…"

Elliott laughed easily and glanced at her.

"I'll stop on my way to pick the kids up."

"Don't cheap out on me, flyboy."

"I won't – and thank you," Elliott said quietly. "For
babysitting, for the advice, for your friendship – everything.
I really appreciate it, Firefly."

"It was that good, huh?"

Sarah's mouth dropped open as she realized what the
other pilot was implying and heard Elliott's emphatic 'Yes!' –

before both men started laughing. She stood up and grabbed the phone, only to have him wrestle it away, still chuckling, before he held it to his face once more.

"We'll be there in about an hour or two – and it will be the expensive stuff, I promise," Elliott said bluntly, hanging up the phone as Firefly started mouthing off at him… and smiled at her. "Hi."

"Hi," she repeated, immediately softening. "You know the stores closed twenty minutes ago…"

"Hmm," Elliott whispered, pulling her into his arms and kissed her jaw softly. "Guess we'll go shopping tomorrow, too."

"I don't think Firefly or Melody will babysit again."

"Then perhaps we will see if we can find another sucker over at Flyboys. I keep hearing the guys bragging about that place. I mean, surely things can't be that nice or lucrative over there – can they? I've heard that most of the team that has left Afghanistan went to work for them."

"Sometimes there is more to life than money…" she whispered distractedly as he scooped her up into his arms, depositing her back onto the couch where they'd been cuddling a few moments ago.

"We're going to finish this conversation in a bit…" he said hoarsely, his intent clear as he kissed her tenderly, his words punctuated by each kiss. "I'm kinda… having… issues… concentrating."

"Me too."

"No more talking?" he invited intimately as he joined her, leaning in to kiss her once more.

"I'm done…"

Sᴀʀᴀʜ ᴄᴏᴜʟᴅɴ'ᴛ ᴡɪᴘᴇ the smile off her face despite her blushing furiously as they walked up to the door of the Grainger house. She saw Melody open the front door, waving them in, only to see Firefly step in front of his wife, glaring at Elliott.

"Neither of you is limping… and what's wrong with you, man? Where's my stuff?"

"Sutton!" Melody admonished, laughing knowingly as the couple shared a look before she looked at Sarah. "I'm happy for you both."

"Me too," Firefly grinned. "Oh, and you are soooo welcome, Copperhead."

"Welcome for what?"

"My attempts at explaining why you were late to the kids and what was taking so long," he said simply, grinning proudly as he crossed his arms over his chest. "Morgan! Leslie! Bethany! Let's go. Your new daddy has finished boinking…"

"SUTTON!"

"Melody, can you get little Henry?" Firefly interrupted his outraged and very pregnant wife, grinning and chuckling as Sarah's mouth dropped open in horror. Elliott cursed swiftly beside her, glaring at the man as he clenched his fists, right before Morgan appeared with his sisters directly behind him.

"Hey Uncle Daddy," Bethany volunteered – and Firefly was chortling in sheer delight, slapping his knee.

"Uncle Daddy? She called you 'Uncle Daddy'? Oh my gosh, that's the best thing I've ever heard…"

"Shut up, Firefly," Elliott growled hotly – and Sarah laid a hand on his arm, restraining him. It wouldn't look good to have the two of them end up in a fistfight, not when this couple had been a lifesaver to her for several months now.

"Um, Uncle Elliott?" Leslie said innocently, holding her

doll and looking at the two of them where she stood on the porch near Betsy. "What's 'boinking'?"

"Why did you have to 'slap the meat' – and we're not hungry. We had pizza for dinner. Can we just have roast tomorrow night? I've never heard that before. Mama usually sprinkles stuff on top and puts it in the crockpot. Uncle Firefly told us that mom was doing something different today and…"

Sarah's mouth dropped open in shock as Elliott made a noise in his throat, glaring at the other man, who was dying of laughter and making snorting sounds as he wiped tears from his eyes.

"You think this is funny?"

"ABSOLUTELY HYSTERICAL…" Firefly roared, laughing wildly.

"Uncle Daddy, what is 'stuffing a muffin'?" Bethany asked, tugging on Sarah's hand. "I want a muffin. Can I have raisins with my muffin?"

"Sarah, take the kids to the car – I'm taking Firefly to the woodshed," Elliott snapped hotly, seething visibly before her. She'd never seen him so upset. His fists were clenching and unclenching – and his jaw had a muscle ticking in it, easily seen in the porch light of the older house.

"He doesn't have a woodshed," Morgan volunteered. "They have a henhouse where the chickens lay the eggs, but no woodshed."

"Elliott…"

"Sarah – car – now…"

"Sheesh, Sarah… your guy doesn't have a sense of humor."

"Sutton, leave him alone."

"C'mon, Copperhead… bring it."

She saw this was getting wildly out of control as Firefly was goading Elliott on, pointing at his chin and still laughing at the uncomfortable conversations that they were going to be having with the kids this evening. She stepped forward in front of Elliott as she spoke to the children.

"Boinking, slapping the meat, and stuffing a muffin are all extremely foul terms for something beautiful that happens when a Mommy and Daddy love each other very much," Sarah said simply, taking the lead. "Kids, why don't you get in the car..." and she paused, not looking away from Elliott's eyes.

"These are my friends and they helped me," she began and touched his cheek. "We'll be waiting in the car for you. Do what you need to, say what you need, but this is all things that were going to need to be touched on anyhow. Firefly just forced the conversation that I would rather not have alone."

"Sarah, sometimes they just need to let off steam," Melody volunteered and ushered Betsy back inside. "Sutton, when you are done being a first-class twerp, I'll cut the brownies up."

"It's been a long time since I've gotten into a scrap with someone..." Sutton grinned. "C'mon Copperhead, you got a little bite to you - Eh? Or are you worn out this evening foolin' around?"

Sarah looked at Elliott's eyes, saw the indecision warring in those brown depths and sighed. Guys were so different from girls sometimes, she thought and nodded, leaning up to kiss his cheek as she whispered to him.

"Hit him in the gut so there is no mark – and make sure he doesn't split your lip. I'm going to want to kiss you again later," she breathed softly and stepped back to see Elliott's incredulous smile, right before he chuckled.

"I won't be but two minutes, my love."

"Ten," Firefly corrected from nearby, rubbing his hands together gleefully. "He'll be ten minutes and need a Band-Aid for his widdle, bitty 'boo-boos'..."

"Maybe only thirty seconds…"

Sarah rolled her eyes and walked off toward the car, ushering the children with her as she waved to Melody, who was shrugging in confusion, waving off her husband as the man jogged off toward the side of the house, out of sight excitedly.

"C'mon Inchworm… Copperhead? Puh-lease…"

Sarah heard Firefly still sassing and mouthing off in the distance, taunting her husband – who she knew had a temper to match his hair. "Children, in the car. Now. Let's go…"

"Where's Uncle Elliott?"

"Mama, what is going on?"

"C'mon Copperhead quit stalling and show me what you've…"

"Sometimes guys want to show off a bunch of macho testosterone to each other to make themselves feel better and…"

Pop

Sarah winced openly and finished her statement to the boy who was desperately trying to look behind her as the girls were climbing into the backseat of the car as she held Henry on her hip.

"What was that?" Morgan said bluntly, trying to look around her.

"Testosterone," Sarah replied, not looking over her shoulder… only to hear Firefly groan in the distance while another person, Elliott, was jogging up behind her.

"Okay, kids," Elliott grinned. "Let's go. I feel much, much better."

"Is everything okay?" she asked bluntly, looking back to see Firefly waving cheerfully as he shook his head, obviously rattled, making her shake her own again in confusion.

"Yup. Life is grand," her husband smiled happily and waved to the couple like nothing had ever happened.

"See you tomorrow night for burgers and dogs at Flyboys, Copperhead," Firefly crowed out happily. "And bring my booze!"

"Will do – and thank you, buddy."

Sarah looked between the two of them, saw Melody shrug, and chuckled as the children took their seats and Elliott opened her car door. She moved to get into the vehicle and paused, looking at him.

"You guys are weird."

"And you love me," he countered softly, touching her cheek... and she melted. It was so gently tossed out there between them, almost like he was testing the waters just to make sure this wasn't a fanciful dream they'd shared. She turned her head slightly to kiss his palm and nodded.

"I really do."

AS THEY GOT HOME, the children immediately forgot the entire conversation and line of questioning as they saw the presents. Elliott was carrying Henry in as Morgan, Leslie, and Bethany made a dive for the tree and all the glory of ribbons, bows, and printed paper that gleamed.

"Thank God for small favors..."

"No kidding..."

The two looked at each other and shared a secretive smile of awareness, realizing neither looked forward to the conversation. Elliott leaned toward her, kissing her temple gently as Henry immediately dove for her with his arms extended, making the two of them scramble and chuckle as they adjusted their stance slightly before sharing a brief kiss and hearing silence.

"Uncle Daddy... did you just kiss my Mama?"

That singular high-pitched voice rang out, splitting the silence with an awareness that betrayed the little girl's age. Sure enough, she heard Morgan making gagging sounds, and Leslie bopped him with something creating an audible, hollow 'pop'.

"Spoke too soon," Elliott whispered as his eyes met hers. The two exchanged a brief glance before Sarah turned to look at Bethany.

"Leslie, do not hit your brother with the presents," Sarah began, and Elliott spoke up.

"Yes, Bethany, I did kiss your Mama – because that is how you show love for someone," and Sarah saw the indescribable looks on her children's faces, waiting and bracing herself for more questions.

"And you love me?" Bethany said shyly, putting her finger in her mouth, only to hear Elliott audibly melt in under-standing as he knelt down.

"I love all of you dearly and would happily give any of you a big hug or a kiss," he said quietly, holding open his arms as the girls ran over toward him, kissing him on the cheek. "You are my little 'raisin-ettes'," he chuckled tenderly, smoothing back their hair as he smiled at them and looked up toward her.

"We've all known each other for a long time, since you were each born, and while things have changed... they will also be the , too. I will always love you like your uncle, but now I get to call you daughter – and son," he said, holding out his hand toward Morgan... who hesitated.

"You're my uncle," Morgan said quietly, his face holding so many emotions as the two males looked at each other. "... And my stepdad. My father died."

"You're right," Elliott said without blinking an eye or hesi-tating. "It's a completely different role that I've never held before, so I'm learning it – but I will always be your uncle first... and hopefully your friend."

"Why's Morgan being mean?"

"He's not," Elliott answered openly. "He's sharing how he feels, and that is what we do when we love and trust the people around us. I want Morgan to always be able to say what he feels or thinks to me, knowing that he is safe sharing. I'm not mad because it's true."

"It is?"

Sarah watched the interaction between the family, knowing that Elliott had to be able to handle this, or else the children would never understand or let up. Things had changed, and while Elliott insisted that they defer to her, he was their new father and her husband. David was gone, things were different, and they had to find their places just like she had to.

"Yes. I remember when Morgan was born, his daddy was so proud and was bragging about his son to everyone – including me. I was so happy for your parents because they wanted a baby so much... and I remember coming to see your parents at the hospital."

"What about me?" Bethany said happily.

"And me!" Leslie added.

"They were so happy to have each of you," Elliott smiled, "but those moments will be forever frozen in my mind. What did you have for breakfast yesterday?"

"Huh?" Morgan asked nervously. "Cereal. Why?"

"If there was a new cereal box at the back of the pantry, would you try it... or would you never eat cereal again once you ran out?" Elliott said quietly. "I'm not expecting you to pick one over the other, nor would I ever ask you to. Your father was here first and my best friend. I love my memories with him and will always have them – but I do want to make more memories and have more experience in my life."

Morgan looked at him tearfully, still holding himself stiffly and looking so torn. That wary look was so revealing that Sarah felt tears sting her eyes, and she wanted to go to him but couldn't take this from Elliott or her son. They had to find their way through this 'muck' on their own.

"I would never want you to forget how wonderful your cereal was yesterday morning... but maybe you might grow to like the other cereal someday if you gave it half a chance," Elliott said hoarsely, waving him over. "Because this 'Cheerio' loves you kiddo."

Morgan moved closer, looking at him and his lips twitched as he wiped his eyes, still watching Elliott.

"You are more like 'Frosted Flakes' or 'Fruit Loops'..." the little boy said – and Elliott burst out laughing, along with Leslie, Bethany, and even Sarah. She saw Elliott tug Morgan close, hugging him where he crouched, as Morgan knocked him over, and both girls climbed all over him. Laughing, screaming, and crying out happily as a family.

"Tickle him!"

"Wait a second..."

"Tickle Uncle Daddy!"

"Just Uncle Elliott, Elliott, or Dad... Okay?"

"Get 'em..."

"Who's got fingernails? Ow?"

"I'm gonna smush, Uncle Daddy..."

"Oh, heaven help me..."

And even Henry let out a shriek in her arms, surprising everyone as four faces looked up at them as Sarah looked at the baby.

"Uh oh! Henry wants to get you too!" Bethany shrieked in excitement, going back to 'tickling' – which was actually scratching at Elliott's arm. "Mama, let Henry play!"

"You have to be careful," Sarah warned and knelt beside the snarled knot of limbs that was climbing all over the tackled man who was letting the children play, giving them a safe space to work out everything in them.

"Oh no… someone's got me," Elliott called out as Morgan and Leslie teamed up to tickle his side – making him laugh loudly as Henry let out another shriek. They shared a look, and Sarah smiled at him, realizing just how good life was going to be between the five of them.

"Love you…" he said in between laughs.

"Love you too… and rawrrr! Here comes the little monster," she teased, pretending to make the toddler sit on Elliott's tummy, making all the children laugh once more in sheer delight.

A few hours later, when Henry fell asleep, they moved to tuck in the other children together. It was strangely normal and comforting after having been through so very much in the last few years. Leslie made Elliott kiss her doll good night too – which immediately caused Bethany to request her doll get a kiss also. As they pulled the door to, she heard a moment of rustling before silence as the little girls rolled over to go to sleep.

Moving to put Henry in the crib located in Morgan's room, she heard a noise behind her and started slightly as Elliott closed the bedroom door – holding a package in his hand. His eyes met hers as she nodded in understanding.

"Morgan?" Elliott began, perching on the side of the bed as the boy looked at him. Her son's eyes were huge in his surprised face. "I have something for you that I'd like you to open now, while I'm here."

"You do?"

"Yes. When I was a little boy, my father gave me one; and well, I want you to have one too – except don't break it like I did," Elliott laughed softly and she saw Morgan's nervous smile. "If you do, life still goes on, but it makes it really hard to freeze those memories… if you don't have this."

Morgan looked at Elliott – and immediately tore into the box, looking at him in amazement.

"You got me... a camera?"

"I want you to be able to take photos of special moments, things that mean a lot to you, and we'll pick you up an album to save the photos in – so you can look at them anytime you want to."

"Can you... show me how to use it?"

Sarah pretended to adjust the blanket on Henry as she listened with her back toward the two of them, trying to give them their privacy as they whispered to each other.

"Of course. We have to stick together – which is why when your mama was going to have the baby, or we needed to go do some Christmas shopping - we called Firefly."

"He's nice."

"Yes, he is... because he's a Flyboy – just like you."

"Me?"

"Yup. Would you like to go flying with me tomorrow? I could show you the ropes and..."

"Really?"

"You betcha. My dad used to let me hold the steering wheel when the road was empty – and I think you might be able to do the same in the plane."

"I could fly?"

"Together, with me, yes..."

"Do you mind, Mama?" Morgan asked, and Sarah looked over her shoulder, immediately deferring to Elliott.

"Your stepfather invited you – which means it's okay with me. I follow his judgment and trust him without question," she said softly, meeting Elliott's eyes and feeling a little nervous about her son flying – but she also knew he would keep Morgan safe.

"Let's load your film and then get some rest," Elliott smiled. "We've got a big and exciting day tomorrow."

Sarah heard a couple of clicks and then a whirring sound as it loaded, listening.

"Now, don't touch this button until you are ready. The picture will come out here, and you have to let it develop, but you look through this little square and..."

She saw a flash, turning immediately.

"Whoops," Elliott said innocently, grinning... and heard Morgan's laughter as he covered his mouth with his hands, giggling.

"What are you two doing?" she retorted, realizing that the duo was up to no good.

"Nothing," – and Elliott tucked the photo into his shirt pocket before winking at the little boy, handing him the camera. "Here you go – and you can take a few photos from the air tomorrow if you want."

"W-Will you take a picture with me?"

"I would be honored... but we should let Mama take it so we are actually in the photo and it's not your mother's buns again."

Morgan giggled – and Sarah rolled her eyes at Elliott as he wagged his eyebrows at her, handing her the camera.

"You're awful."

"You love me."

"I really do..."

She saw Elliott turn slightly, and his eyes widened as Morgan threw his arms around his neck, nearly choking him as the child hugged him tightly. Both smiling faces were easy to see in the viewer as she clicked the button, prompting the flash and whirr of the camera as the photo slid out the front panel. She gave it to Morgan and put the camera on the dresser before glancing at the two guys waiting for the photo to develop – and knew the exact moment it did.

Morgan looked up at Elliott, smiling.

"I think that's the best picture I've ever seen," Elliott

began, and Morgan nodded, beaming. "When I call from Afghanistan to say 'Hello,' you'll have something to look at – which means I need someone to take our photo as a family so I can have all of you with me overseas."

"Oh really?"

"Yup. It's a tradition of airmen to keep a photo in your cockpit, your helmet, or your locker, and the photo I have is of your mom, dad, and me when we were in high school," Elliott began, and Sarah gasped in awareness, remembering that day. "We were leaving school and had someone take our picture together – all of us – and I still have it. This is why I wanted to get you a camera, so you have these moments that can never go away."

Her son nodded tearfully, hugging him once more.

"I love you, kiddo – just like I loved your daddy," Elliott said softly, closing his eyes and holding Morgan for several moments before whispering to him. "Let's be friends from here and keep trying to figure out our way, okay? You've always been my little buddy – and I don't ever want that to change."

"I love you, Uncle Elliott."

"Love you too. Now, get some sleep. My copilot needs to be fresh for flight tomorrow."

Elliott stood and smiled tenderly at the boy before ruffling his hair, causing Morgan to laugh again as he nodded and lay down.

"Good night, kiddo."

"Good night."

Elliott turned and took Sarah's hand in his as they left the bedroom – and immediately pulled her into theirs, chuckling knowingly as he turned to kiss her.

"You don't want to make sure they are asleep before we start this?"

"The door is locked…"

"I didn't know you kept that picture of all of us…"

"Yup," he admitted, untucking her shirt and pulling her close to him. "I love that picture of us. It was an easier time because the memories got me through some really tough spots. I always knew I had two people that would look out for me."

"That's how I felt too," she admitted, cradling his head on her shoulder as he kissed her neck, feeling things intensify between them. "Elliott, I thought you didn't want to be in here to…"

"I said I wanted a new bed," he whispered huskily. "I never claimed that I didn't want to…" his voice trailed off suggestively as she shivered in awareness and anticipation.

"True. But…?"

"How about I wash your back, then your front, and then we'll have two locks between us and the kids – and technically, it's not the bed," he invited softly against her skin as she laughed, wrapping her arms around his shoulders as he scooped her up into his arms, heading for the bathroom nearby. "Gosh, I love you, Sarah… and it's going to kill me to leave you in two days."

"Don't think about it," she begged, dotting kisses on his cheeks, his forehead, and his lips as he set her on the counter in the bathroom and paused… pressing his forehead to hers.

"I can't stop thinking of it because my home is here… with you."

"We'll be waiting," she promised, touching his cheek.

"There's so much I want to do," he admitted, touching her hand and holding it against his face. "I want to do all the normal stuff, like take the kids trick-or-treating, go to PTA meetings, make glitter posters at the last second for school projects, help Morgan with Cub Scouts or T-Ball and…"

"He's not in those things," she chuckled softly and met his eyes, hesitating and realizing it wasn't what he was saying,

191

but the meaning behind them. He wanted to be an active parent and part of the family, and knew that when he left, it would be difficult.

"But he could be," Elliott whispered. "I want you all to have every chance to do whatever you want – and you aren't a one-woman army. I want to be your partner, your spouse, and their stepfather."

"You are," she stressed emotionally.

"I know, I've got just a lot more that I want to do - and never enough time to do it," he admitted and let out a little snort of laughter. "I want to yell 'I'm going to Disney World' and for us to take the kids to meet the princesses or Mickey Mouse."

"Oh mercy…" she chuckled, seeing his smile as his eyes crinkled at the corners in joy.

"C'mon Sarah, it could be so much fun. Just think of how much we would have loved to have gone when we were little. We could get those bride and groom ears, get the kids each a Mickey hat, eat candied apples until we are sick, ride everything that they are tall enough to go on…"

"Except the teacups," she interjected quickly, causing him to laugh in awareness. She always had a sensitive stomach and would get ill easily.

"Except the teacups, my love," he promised, tenderly, as he lifted her hair off of her shoulder, his eyes taking in everything before looking back at her again.

"So, here we are… alone," she whispered invitingly, "and the water isn't warming up yet."

"I should correct that," he flirted. "Don't you move."

She watched him turn toward the bathtub in the small room as the water turned on and sighed in awareness as he turned to look back at her. No words were needed as their gazes locked. He stepped close to her once more and smiled.

"Is the good shampoo under the counter?"

"No."

"Good…"

"Why?"

"I want to wash your hair, breathe in your scent, and lose myself in your arms while the water washes over us – together. I need something to remember when I'm gone…" he begged as he captured her lips – and made good on his suggestions moments later.

CHAPTER 21

COPPERHEAD

"WELL, well, well... Look at what we've got here, fellas – a bow-legged copperhead," came a loud drawl followed by several good-natured laughs from the men exiting the building as they pulled up. He knew the teasing was toeing the line, but Elliott was so blasted happy he really didn't care.

"Uncle Daddy?" Bethany asked in his arms, whispering in his ear as he carried her forward. "What's a copperhead?"

Morgan was looking around in wide-eyed wonder as Leslie spotted Betsy and was already running forward. Sarah was getting Henry out of his car seat, and it looked like a lot of the activity was already in motion. There were full-sized folding chairs all at the end of the runway – along with a handful of smaller, children's sized folding chairs in bright colors.

"Copperhead is my nickname at work," he smiled

tenderly and kissed her on the cheek before tickling her tummy. "Cause I'm gonna getcha!"

… And the little girl let out an excited shriek of joy, nearly piercing his eardrum before hugging him tightly. Elliott walked toward Sarah, who was joining him, as they started forward.

"Hey there, Mrs. Trent," Firefly teased, smiling. "Lookin' good, you two."

"It's in the wagon, just pop the hatch and grab the bags," Elliott volunteered, grinning. "Top shelf, brother."

"You are a good man," Firefly boomed, jumping forward and shaking his hand before patting him on the back. "And we'll keep the 'Uncle Daddy' stuff between us."

"It's growing on me…"

"Look, Redneck-Heaven, you cannot out 'hick' my favorite Hick, Armadillo. It's just not done. The man eats squirrels and fried frogs with X-Ray. Don't sink that low, okay?"

"Ugh," Elliott grimaced and shivered – before both men burst out laughing.

"What the heck, Copperhead? Why is Rattler not in uniform?" Alpo hollered, grinning – holding a child-sized T-shirt up, and Elliott smiled.

"Who?" Morgan said, looking back at him.

"I think he means you," Elliott smiled and saw the boy's eyes widen even further. "Hey, Alpo, can I borrow one of the planes for a few minutes?"

"Of course – but Rattler has to be in uniform."

"Go get your T-shirt," Elliott encouraged – and Morgan didn't have to be told a second time. The boy scrambled so fast across the runway that he nearly tripped to get at the other man. Alpo knelt and tugged it over Morgan's head before writing his name on a sticker and putting it across his chest. The man turned Morgan around, who put his fists on his skinny hips and puffed up his little chest.

"I'm Rattler," Morgan announced. "That's my call sign, Mama."

"A fierce one too..." Sarah said tenderly and looked at Elliott. "Let me take Bethany to see the bananas. Glory said she was making magical snacks for the kids and making banana pops – with raisins."

"Raisins?" Bethany perked up immediately, scrambling and trying to climb down from Elliott's arms. He set the little girl down, relieved she wasn't jealous of him taking Morgan up, and kissed Sarah tenderly.

"Don't you want to go?" Elliott asked quickly.

"Motion sickness," Sarah reminded him and smiled. "That's why I try to drive when we go out."

"Ahhh. Someday, but not today."

"No, today, let it be you and Morgan."

"We won't be gone but for just a few minutes – and I promise he'll be safe."

"I already knew that," she smiled and nodded. "Have fun – and we'll have a seat saved for you."

Elliott jogged over to where Morgan was talking with Alpo and Thumper, catching part of what they were saying.

"I hear your daddy is a fierce pilot..."

"You pay attention to him and what he's doing – and someday you'll be flying these planes..."

"Really?"

"Oh yes. We can teach you, or you can go to school later on and let the Air Force teach you how to do it. Your daddy flies a jet that can blast through the sound barrier in..."

"Rattler," Elliott began, smiling. "You ready, buddy? We don't want to lose the light, or else you can't wave to everyone below us."

"Oh gosh, really, Daddy?" Morgan choked out in excitement, his eyes flashing with joy; whereas Elliott nearly came unglued. The little boy who'd been so argumentative, so wary, so nervous about him being more than an 'uncle' – had slipped and called him 'Daddy.'

It wasn't in the cards, nor did he ever want to pressure them to address him a certain way – he just wanted the chance to be the father that he knew David could have been if his friend had been given the chance. Family was everything to the three of them – and still was, no matter what. He would uphold those ideals, that sense of family, and love them like they were his own because they were and always had been, as nephews and nieces and were now sons and daughters.

"Yup," Elliott smiled, touching Morgan's head and beaming at him. "C'mon, co-pilot. Let's watch the sunset from the best seat in the house."

"Copperhead?" Thumper said suddenly. "When do you fly out?"

"Tomorrow morning."

"Can we talk before you leave tonight – alone?"

Elliott saw the two men look at each other and smile, nodding. He wasn't sure what was going on and hesitated.

"It's all good, brother," Alpo grinned. "Go have fun, and we'll discuss an opportunity later away from little ears."

"Me?" Morgan interjected – causing all three to laugh in awareness.

"Yes," Elliott grinned and nudged him closer to the hangar.

"Take Cessna 5739," Alpo hollered from behind him. "She's fueled and ready to go."

Elliott approached the plane and saw the keys were in the ignition, realizing that someone had planned to take this plane up – or assumed he would. Morgan was climbing inside within record time, looking around at everything in awe. The Cessna was an older plane, very dated, but it would still function for what they used it here for. It certainly wasn't his Falcon, but nothing would be either. His Falcon was a powerful beast that would tear through the skies, if he would let it. Whereas this little airplane would putter along and purr like a tiny kitten.

He went through the preflight check quickly, knowing Morgan was getting antsy inside. The boy had on his headphones and was pretending he was in the midst of a dogfight, slamming the yoke to-and-fro just like any young, imaginative boy would.

Climbing inside, Morgan scrambled into his seat and beamed at him.

"Ready for take-off!"

"Buckle up, copilot," he instructed and leaned over to adjust Morgan's buckle and his headphone, and handed him the radio. "I need you to announce our departure," he began, and Morgan was already grabbing for the radio – and he quickly pulled it away.

"Listen…" he paused, smiling and knowing the boy was eager. "You have to do it right, so you need to say 'Cessna 5739' and introduce yourself – then ask if you are okay to take off – all right? Let's practice one time together."

"Okay," Morgan agreed, nodding with wide eyes as he looked at him. "Cessna 7539…"

"Cessna 5739," Elliott corrected tenderly. "That's our plane, and we want to identify ourselves."

"Cessna 5739, this is Morg-ah-*Rattler*…" Morgan hesitated, and Elliott nodded, causing the boy's smile to grow even wider in awareness. He chuckled as Morgan finished and praised him.

"Great job, Rattler," he said, ruffling his hair and straightening his headphones. "Keep this close so I can hear you, okay? – Now, call us in, co-pilot."

Morgan clicked the radio and began to speak, loudly and excitedly.

"Cessna 5739, this is Rattler... are we okay to take-off?"

Elliott really wasn't sure if anyone would respond because everyone was sitting in the chairs, talking, and he could see the grill smoking in the distance, only to hear a response.

"Rattler..." A voice crackled loudly, and he recognized Alpo, realizing that the man must have gone inside the moment they headed for the plane. "You are clear for take-off, pilot. Enjoy your flight."

"Oh, we will!" Morgan yelped happily and then slid the radio back onto its metal hook, practically wriggling in his seat from excitement. "I'm gonna tell my friends at school that I got to fly a plane with my new dad, and this is going to be so cool."

"Did you bring your camera?"

"Ohhh no," Morgan began, looking distraught.

"Here," Elliott said simply – handing him his cell phone. "Take your photos when you want, and we'll send them to Walgreens so you can take printouts to show your buddies."

"It's okay?"

"Absolutely, it's okay – I mean, what good is flying if you can't look super-cool about it... in fact," Elliott leaned sideways, and Morgan held the phone back out to him. He held it up and moved to take a selfie of the two of them. Morgan grinned widely, his big crooked teeth in front were almost too big for his mouth, and the boy held up two fingers, beaming.

"Oh, hang on..." Elliott grinned and slipped a pair of aviator sunglasses on the boy – before posing again. They both held up two fingers, making peace signs, before taking the photo and handing the phone to Morgan again. "There, you gotta show them what a cool guy you are."

"Whose glasses are those?"

"Have no clue," Elliott shrugged as the two males looked at each other – and started laughing. "Let's go, Rattler."

"Let's do this!" Morgan growled fiercely, smiling like never before.

Adjusting the throttle, he talked gently, explaining some of what he was doing, and pointed to the controls, not wanting the boy to be afraid, and then quickly took off. He didn't want to chance getting anywhere close to the end of the runway where Sarah and the children were.

As they lifted off, he heard Morgan's screech of excitement and winced as it pierced his ears painfully, but he understood. The first time he flew in a plane with someone, it was exhilarating, and he'd nearly disgraced his flight suit. His instructor had rolled the plane several times and took him straight up, nearly causing him to pass out. He'd held on, didn't vomit, and it was the one time that he'd truly stood out from the crowd on his own, earning him the call sign.

"You'll do okay, Copperhead," his instructor had laughed. "I never expected this out of you – and you just snuck up out of nowhere, didn't you."

Focusing on the plane, he leveled them out and turned to look at Morgan's awestruck face as the boy pressed his face against the window excitedly.

"Oh man, look at how tiny everything is…"

"Pretty cool, huh…"

"The coolest!"

"You want to steer the plane?"

Morgan's awestruck gaze turned to him in shock.

"Can I?"

"As long as you don't wobble the yoke like you were when I got in the plane," Elliott warned, grinning. "We'll crash. If you are in a jet, thousands and thousands of feet in the air, you might be able to get away with that – but if you do it here, we could damage something or crash."

"Oh, maybe I shouldn't."

"Watch me, Morgan," Elliott instructed tenderly. "Just put your hands on the yoke and hold it steady like me. See this circle here? You want to keep the line as close to this line as you can – this line is the horizon. If you keep us on there, then we fly straight. If you push in, we go down…" and Elliott did so, showing the boy. "If you turn…"

The entire plane rolled to the side, and he saw Morgan's frightened gaze as he held on before quickly straightening it up.

"But if you hold her steady, it will be a smooth flight, and I promise – nothing is going to happen that we can't fix together. Go ahead, Morgan, and I'll take a photo of you flying the plane. Maybe we can get Mama to hang it up on the fridge or the wall."

"Are you sure?"

"Absolutely. This is your first flight, young man – and a first flight with your new stepdad is a moment you don't forget," he smiled. "I love you, kiddo – and I promise nothing is going to happen or hurt you."

"Love you too."

Morgan put his little hands on the yoke and set the phone in the seat so Elliott could take a photo of him, and Elliott smiled, taking his hands off the other yoke slowly before holding them up as the boy smiled brilliantly.

"I'm doing it! I'm flying, Dad!"

"Yes, you sure are!"

"Oh my gosh, I'm really flying the plane – HURRY AND TAKE MY PHOTO!" Morgan ordered in a rushed voice, causing Elliott to laugh happily. He picked up the phone and took a photo – as well as a video.

"Hey, look, Sarah," he spoke, recording. "Morgan is such a

great pilot and he's flying the plane all by himself. Look at my side," he moved the camera from his empty yoke over to Morgan – who immediately waved. "Say hi to your Mom and sisters, Rattler. You're on camera, and I'm recording this."

"Hey Mama, Hi Bethany, Leslie, and Henry... this is so cool – cooler than those dumb dolls and..."

"Let's be nice," Elliott interrupted, fighting to keep from rolling his eyes and laughing at the boy who was obviously at 'that' age.

"This is really neat, and Daddy is teaching me how to do this. Dad, can we do this again when you come back?"

"Absolutely. We can do this whenever I am home, and you want to go up."

"Really?"

"You betcha – it's the perk of being a flyboy, son... and you are one, which is why you have the shirt and a cool call sign."

"You hear that? Rattler is a flyboy!" Morgan announced and paled as they hit a pocket of air, causing the plane to sag physically. "I'm done, Daddy!"

"All right," Elliott chuckled, ending the recording and taking control of the plane again while Morgan held the phone, taking photos and asking more questions. It was a great moment for the two of them to share and as the sun started to descend, he smiled at the talkative child's voice, who hadn't paused yet to take a breath.

"And look at this, I mean, just look at the orange trees. I don't think I've ever seen a sunset like this where it colors everything orangey-red, Daddy. Even the roofs over there, you see 'em, waaaay over there are orangish-black like a jack-o-lantern, and the runway looks almost like a river... oh, what's that glowy stuff? Is that where Mama and the others are waiting? Are you hungry, I'm kinda hungry. I wonder what we are eating. I'm hoping it's not raisins because I'm kinda sick of…"

"Hey, Morgan?" Elliott interrupted gently, smiling.

"Yeah?"

"How about we land and get some dinner – and we can sit with the pilots. You can tell them all about your first flight, eh?"

"Oh yes! I would love that."

"Then let's do it, buddy – want to help me land the Cessna?"

"I won't break it?"

"No. I promise. I'll do most of the work, and we can control it together, okay?"

Five minutes later, they were on the ground and Morgan was practically climbing all over him in a hurry to get out of the plane and talk to everyone else. He hugged Elliott tightly, squeezing his neck, and gave him a kiss on the cheek before darting out of the plane and running off. Thank goodness Elliott had already turned off the engine because the boy ran right by the propeller, giving it a high five, like it was nothing, causing him to wince with awareness as he laughed.

Oh, to be so young, he thought tenderly, realizing Morgan was just a little boy who'd been through way too much.

Getting out of the plane, he pulled the keys from the ignition and shoved them in his pocket, intending to put them in Alpo's hand. He didn't want Morgan to think they could fly the plane on their own. Spotting Sarah, nodding happily as Morgan stood before her, holding Henry in her lap, regaling everyone within earshot of his piloting skills.

"It was soooo cool," Morgan was saying. "I went like this… and like this…" he continued, turning his body as he held his hands in front of him.

"Oh my goodness," a woman with dark hair said, her eyes

shining as she smiled at Morgan, waving him over. "My name is Meredith, and this is my husband, Handsy, who is also a pilot. Come tell me all about your flight, Rattler. You are about my son's age, had he lived, and I want to hear all about what you thought of flying the plane."

As Elliott sat down between Sarah and Firefly, the other man leaned toward him, whispering.

"Handsy left Ghazni before your time – and their son was stillborn. Those two will probably keep Morgan occupied the rest of the evening because of losing Aaron. The boy oughtta sleep well tonight."

"Oh, mercy, I had no idea," Sarah exclaimed in a hushed whisper, looking horrified.

"Yeah, they used to not talk about Aaron at all, and it was a real thorn in their side, but things are slowly healing," Firefly admitted. "All of us have been through the wringer in one way or another. One person's hell is another's heaven, you know?"

Elliott reached over and took Sarah's hand in his as they shared a silent look. She had been through so much, more than any one person should have to deal with – and he was aware of how many struggles she'd survived. When you put it down to basics, they were very lucky to have each other and a family. The children were healthy, they had a roof over their heads, an income that provided food and clothing, and they had each other despite the miles that would come between them.

He pulled her hand to his lips and kissed her knuckles tenderly, murmuring 'Love you' against her skin, seeing her knowing eyes meet his... and nodded. They had always thought alike, got along, and could read each other, having been friends for so long.

Again – another miracle, he realized, suddenly wanting to be closer and alone during these last few hours they had before he flew out. Turning toward her, he saw her eyes watching him and both leaned toward each other.

"Shall we go home early?" he whispered tenderly.

"I was just going to ask you if you minded…"

"Sounds like eight is a great time for the kids to go to bed."

"I was thinking seven," she smiled shyly at him – and he felt it straight to the tip of his boots. "But you are right about eight o'clock."

"What if I like your number better?" he chuckled tenderly, kissing her hand again. "Happy wife… happy life?"

Her throaty laugh was everything – and he was here for it. That was a sound he heard in his sleep, felt in his soul, and would haunt him for the immeasurable days to come before he could return to her.

"Have I mentioned how crazy I am about you?" he whispered in a hushed voice.

"I love you too…" Firefly chimed in and kissed him directly on the forehead – causing a roar of laughter around them as Elliott grimaced, wiping his face with his T-shirt… only to catch Sarah looking at his waist where he'd yanked up the material.

"We're leaving in an hour," she breathed, staring into his eyes.

"Say the word, and we're out," he promised – and ducked as Firefly bent over the chair and hugged him.

"Thank you for my stuff, bro… and I'm glad you are happy."

"Get off of me," Elliott grinned, laughing aloud. "You smell like what I bought."

"Because I opened what you bought – and you should go check out the red cooler under the table… and talk to Thumper while you are over there."

"About?"

"About an opportunity."

TWENTY MINUTES LATER, Elliott was staring at Thumper and Alpo standing before him in confusion and shock. Leave the Air Force and come work for Flyboys? Both men had their arms crossed over their chests in almost a mirror image of each other – yet smiling.

"You're serious?"

"Very."

"And this is an… option?" Elliott began, not wanting to insult anyone. "This pays the bills and there's enough work for everyone?"

"Nobody is going to be a millionaire," Thumper admitted. "But we take the profits at the end of the year and divide it up fairly. We take ten percent to reinvest it in the company and put another ten percent into an emergency fund for the planes before divvying the remainder between all of us as a yearly bonus. Your paycheck will be what you need Harley to schedule for you – and we are dabbling into longer charter flights. Nobody is rich, but we are home with our families and…"

"I have a family of six – including me," he whispered in a hushed voice, looking at them. "We have four kids and…"

"I know, and it's a lot to think about," Thumper admitted. "You need to think about the pros and cons, there are the insurance expenses, you'll need a plane, but we can help you with all of this, and…"

"It would be a change," Alpo began. "But nobody is going to let you flounder or suffer. If you need help watching the kids, we'll do it. We've taken meals to each other when someone is sick. Armadillo wanted a play-ground in the backyard for Luke – and we all showed up to put one in. Ricochet needed a bathroom added to the house and while I wasn't allowed to touch the tools, I could supervise."

"Annoy…" Firefly coughed loudly, walking past them, and patted Elliott on the shoulder. "It'll be okay – if it's what you want. Let me tell you, the steak at home is ten times better than what you get served over there – even if it's on clearance at the I. G. A. grocery store."

"I need to think about it and talk to Sarah," he whispered, floored.

"Yes, you should."

"If you decide to make a move, email me and give me your departure date. We'll get everything else lined up on our end. There will be a ton of paperwork the first week, but we'll have you up in the air in no time…" Thumper offered and handed him a business card. "I still check my Air Force email, but this is easier. Both Harley and I have access to it and will respond quickly."

"The big ol' nerds have everything linked," Alpo grinned.

"You do, too," Thumper chuckled gruffly, looking at his brother-in-law. "Don't even try to hide how wrapped-up you are in your wife and kids."

"Me? I'm hiding nothing…"

"We know!" came several voices, causing them all to laugh in awareness.

"The offer is there, brother," Thumper said simply, extending his hand and Elliott shook it gratefully – accepting the business card.

"I appreciate it."

"A month or a year, it doesn't matter – just remember that you have a security blanket should the time arise."

"Thank you again."

"Of course – why don't you head home with your family before your flight tomorrow?" Thumper said, smiling. "I know I would rather be with them than sitting around the fire with the bunch of us."

"I think I'll take you up on that," Elliott chuckled and took the good-natured ribbing from the friends as they teased him about what he hoped would happen at home. He loved Sarah and wanted to spend as much time as possible showing her, but first, they needed to wear out the kids and tuck them into bed.

CHAPTER 22

SARAH

"We're leaving," Elliott said simply, meeting her eyes and giving her a look that was warm enough to melt rock into lava. "I'll gather the kids; you take Henry toward the car."

"Are you sure?"

"Yes… and we need to talk."

"Is there a problem?"

"Nope!" several of the guys chimed in around them, causing her to look around in awareness as she saw their smiling faces. "Nothing but opportunities and chances."

"I'll give you all the details at home, and then we'll talk about it. Trust me, nothing is wrong."

"All right," she agreed and said her goodbyes to her friends.

"I'll call you tomorrow to check on you," Melody promised. "Maybe we can get coffee together or…"

"We'll figure out something – all of us," Mary interjected, smiling and waving happily from nearby. "Safe travels, Copperhead."

… And Sarah heard multiple goodbyes as they were waved off.

She saw Elliott playfully picking up Bethany and Leslie as Morgan danced around him happily, the four of them talking together secretively… and she smiled. He was such a good person to take them under his wing and love them like his own. It was obvious, and she was truly blessed to come out of such a tragedy like this. Things could have been so different, so hard, yet he stepped in and offered a hand, pulling them up so they could keep 'walking' on this path together, all of them as a family.

Fastening Henry in his car seat, the baby looked at her and frowned, causing her to laugh in awareness. He was starting to get such a vibrant and fun personality as he grew, reminding her of Morgan when he was little.

"My sweet roly-poly boy… you be good for just a bit, and we'll get you back out of the seat," she spoke, as the children started to climb into the station wagon. Morgan flipped over his seat to take the makeshift seat in the back as both girls climbed in beside Henry's car seat. The kids were growing, and she was going to need a minivan or three-row SUV at this rate.

"All righty, let's move out, team…" Elliott bent over, leaning into the car and meeting her eyes as he quickly helped the children buckle in.

"Mama, Daddy said we could make a fort and go camping in our bedroom!" Bethany volunteered excitedly. "He's going to help us build it with the sheets."

"Oh, he is?"

Elliott grinned at her – and winked, causing her to laugh in awareness. He was trying to get the kids tired so they could be alone. What a sneaky man with a one-track mind, she mused happily as she moved to sit in the car. It wasn't ten minutes before they were pulling up to the house, and the kids were climbing out excitedly.

"Mama, can I get the door?" Morgan asked, rushing to her side.

"Sure," she smiled, handing him her key ring and holding up the house key. She watched as he raced up to the front door with excitement, his sisters directly behind him, as Elliott paused for a moment beside her.

"Camping?"

"It will occupy them and wear them out," he smiled. "I want the children to remember these times and take some photos… and after they fall asleep?"

"Uh huh…"

"We can talk."

"Suuure," she drawled knowingly and heard his delighted chuckle. "We'll talk about things, I suppose."

"We can talk while that happens," he smiled, winking.

"I knew it…"

"Oh, come on," he laughed, tugging her sideways to kiss her tenderly. "Is it so terrible for you, my love?"

"Never," she admitted and pressed her forehead to his. "I'm just not ready to say goodbye."

"And that is part of what I want to talk about."

"Mama! Daddy! C'mon…" the kids were hollering from the front door – and both looked toward them, realizing they'd already stripped the sheets from one of the beds.

"Duty calls," Elliott smiled at her, quickly kissing her pertly on the lips.

She got Henry out of his seat, and the baby was wriggling because of all the excitement going on around them. Elliott was playing with the children as they darted around the house, gathering 'magical items' for their campout.

"An acorn!" he exclaimed – and all three children ran out into the backyard as fast as their legs could carry them, returning not a moment later – each with an acorn from under the tree.

"Pillows!" and all three ran to gather their pillows.

This went on for several moments until the children started to realize they didn't need a wooden spoon to go camping.

"Uncle Daddy, why do we need a wooden spoon?"

"Oh," Elliott chuckled, looking so innocent and surprised. "I suppose you don't. Do we need your dolly?"

"Yes!"

"No!" Morgan chimed in.

"Camera?"

"Yes!" Morgan exclaimed – and the girls began to jump around screaming excitedly.

"Take my picture! I want a picture!"

"Let's get the tent set up and then we can take them inside," and Sarah listened to the chaos, smiling happily at her family while she fed Henry for a little bit before giving him some cereal for the night.

"Mamaaaaa…"

"Oh Mama…?"

"You've got to say it louder in case she's busy with your brother."

"Mamaaaaa, c'mere…"

Sarah chuckled, realizing she was being summoned to join them. She quickly stopped feeding Henry, straightening up her clothing before joining them. Henry was fussing slightly at being interrupted, but she cradled him and spoke to him.

"C'mon sweetie, your siblings are calling…"

As she slowly entered Morgan's room, she saw the sheets strung from the bunk above Morgan's bed down to Henry's crib, fastened with knots. Another blanket formed a wall to the 'fort' and was held with a few clothespins... and she saw feet sticking out.

"Where are they, Henry?" she said playfully and heard several hushed giggles before a flash of Morgan's camera, followed by Elliott's 'shhh'. As she lifted the sheet, she saw the children were all lying on a nest of pillows and blankets, their heads in a circle with Elliott's – and he was holding aloft his cell phone, taking a photo.

"Get in here," Elliott smiled, patting a pillow beside him. "We're waiting for the two of you."

"Mama, put Henry by me!"

"And me!"

"This is... something," Sarah chuckled, setting down Henry, who immediately began to kick excitedly and waved his arms as Bethany kissed him. The baby let out a shriek of happiness and made a cooing sound that caused all of them to stop in surprise.

"I think he likes the tent," Morgan volunteered.

"I think you are right," Elliott smiled, reaching up over his head toward the boy and touching his forehead affection-ately – causing Morgan to smile broadly. "You'll have to set this up for everyone when I'm at work, okay? Get your mama to help you tie the knots."

"I promise."

"That's my copilot..." Elliott began thickly, and she knew he was also realizing that the evening was coming to an end much too quickly.

"Scootch over," she ordered, trying to distract him, and she heard the kids laughing as she got down onto the cush-ions and felt his arm pulling her close. Smiling at him, she met his eyes and saw how close he was to her, realizing that he must have moved over a little as well the moment he saw she was joining him.

"Hey, pretty mama…"

"Hey yourself, flyboy…" she whispered tenderly, reaching over to touch his face and felt him kiss the inside of her wrist. "We are camping?"

"We're dreaming," Morgan interjected.

"Oh, we are? What are we dreaming about?"

"What it would be like to go camping for real…"

"Maybe we can do it next year or so," Elliott said simply, surprising her. "I think we need Henry to be a little bigger so he's easier for us to keep an eye on. Right now, he's little, and we have to be very careful with him."

"No smushing."

"Exactly, no smushing, Bethany."

"Oh my gosh," Sarah chuckled nervously and heard Leslie's laugh along with Henry's. "This might be getting a little out of hand."

"Kids, what is the first rule of camping?" Elliott prompted, not looking away from her.

"Nobody gets hurt, or we are done for the night."

"And the second rule?"

"When Mama says we're done – no arguing," all three chimed in, and Leslie paused. "Are we finished?"

"Not yet," Sarah smiled and silently mouthed a 'Thank you' to Elliott, who replied, 'You're welcome'.

"I heard Morgan had a camera, and I saw a flash," she began, smiling at the kids above her in the circle. "Can I see the photo?"

A finger-smudged polaroid was passed around and she chuckled as the kids were sticking out their tongues, being children, and even Elliott was there in the corner, sticking out his tongue.

"My, my, that should go on the fridge."

"It's pretty good – isn't it, Mama?"

"Yes, Morgan- you have a… a gift."

"Let's take one with all of us," Elliott said, holding aloft his cell phone. "Y'all scoot forward carefully and watch Henry." The children began to wriggle slightly, and all their heads were close together in the frame. It was adorable, sweet, innocent, and she met her husband's eyes. The smile he gave her was everything in the camera.

"I love you," she breathed as a chorus of 'love you, mamas' surrounded them, only to hear his response.

"You are my everything."

"And me?"

"Me too?"

"Can I be an 'everything,' Uncle Daddy?"

And heard the click of his phone a few times, realizing he had taken several photos before replying.

"You all are my everything!" he teased, reaching for the children and tickling them. "Watch Henry! Careful…" Only to have Bethany and Leslie scramble up, crawling over her, and plopping down on Elliott.

"Ooof!" he grunted, making the girls laugh as Morgan moved slightly over next to Henry, imparting his brotherly wisdom in hushed words she caught as Elliott nudged her side, both of them listening.

"Henry, girls are weird and gross. You just stick with me, and we'll be the cool guys. I can be Rattler when we fly with Daddy, and you can be Viper. Daddy's call sign is Copperhead, so you can't have that – but you and me? We'll be partners in everything, just stick with me."

Sarah smiled at Elliott – who leaned forward to kiss the tip of her nose.

"It's going to be all right, just like I promised you."

"So it is," she admitted tenderly and didn't look away from his eyes. "Kids, time for bed."

The two lovers didn't look away from each other among the frustrated groans from the children, punctuated by an

'*Aww Mom!*' followed quickly by the '*Please can we stay up a little longer?*' begging.

"Five minutes," she smiled and saw Elliott's playful pout, teasing her silently. He got up and scooped up Henry, making the baby giggle before extending a hand toward her.

"Five minutes," he repeated and mocked in a deep voice like the Terminator, "We'll be back."

As they walked into the kitchen, Elliott accidentally brushed against her, bumping her into the counter and causing her to laugh, knowing exactly what he was doing.

"Goodness Henry, terrible steering there, buddy-boy. Mama isn't the highchair where you get your 'nummys'," Elliott laughed, putting the baby in the seat and buckling him before winking at her and dropping a kiss on her shoulder playfully. "That's where Daddy does though..."

"Elliott!" she hissed, shushing him and laughing.

"That's right, buddy," he continued speaking to the baby, who was cooing happily back at him as if they were holding a conversation. "Yes, sir. Are you going to be the man of the house and take care of Mommy while I'm gone? Hey, Viper? And how cool of a call sign is that from your brother, eh? Are we talking, buddy? Can you answer me, little man?"

Henry cooed loudly as Elliott smiled, looking up at her as she handed him the bowl.

"You want to try?"

"Is that okay?"

"Be my guest..."

She laid a hand on Elliott's shoulder as he scooped up a tiny bit of cereal and milk mixture, watching him as he gently fed it to Henry. The coos of happiness became gurgles for a second before Henry realized he was being fed, and then the 'om-nom-noms' started.

And Elliott laughed tenderly.

"Oh gosh, children are so beautiful," he whispered openly,

his voice full of emotion. She looked at his profile, hesitating because she already had four children, but that was with David. Did he want a child someday? What would that be like? He was gone almost all the time. Did she even dare comment or bring it up?

"We're reaaaady!" came the announcement from the bedrooms, indicating that the children were ready to be tucked in. Elliott looked up at her and smiled, nodding.

"Here, let's trade for a moment…"

Nodding silently, she moved to finish feeding Henry and wiped his mouth a few moments later, hearing Elliott 'tag' off with her.

"Y'all be good and go to bed. Your mama will be right in, okay?"

Sarah got up, patting Henry on the back as he held his head up, looking around before belching loudly in her ear. She chuckled and moved to the farthest room to give the girls kisses, tucking them in – even kissing the dolls as requested, before turning off the lights. As she walked into Morgan's room, he was already yawning loudly in his bed as she kissed his temple.

"Great job, flying today. You are growing up so fast."

"I had so much fun, Mama. It was so cool to look at everything from way up high, and I didn't expect Uncle Elliott to let me fly the plane. Is it okay that I called him 'Daddy'?"

"Yes," she smiled softly at him, touching his face. "You are lucky enough to have two wonderful fathers who love you – and he let you fly the plane because he trusts you. You mean a lot to Elliott, and he really cares."

"He's pretty nice."

"Yes, he is."

"Good night, Mama…"

"Good night, sweetheart – school tomorrow morning, so

get some rest," at his obvious groan of frustration, she continued. "You can take some of your pictures so you can tell your friends about your flight."

"Daddy said he was sending them to the store to get printed because I forgot my camera."

"Then he will," she smiled confidently. "We can pick them up tomorrow, and you can take the photos on Tuesday."

"Okay," Morgan grumbled slightly, but it couldn't be helped. The stores would be closed early in the morning, and Sarah hesitated as she heard the front door open and close in a rush.

"What in the...?"

Her phone beeped in her pocket, and she pulled it out, her chest swelling with love for the incredible man who had fallen into her world as she read Elliott's text message.

Going to Walgreens – be right back, love! Morgan is going to have his pictures for tomorrow, I promise.

She turned it around and showed Morgan the screen – who smiled brightly at her.

"He's a pretty good Daddy, Mama..."

"Yes, he is."

Sarah kissed Morgan's hair once more before moving to change Henry's diaper and change his clothes. She kissed his soft cheeks, nuzzled his little nose, and laid him down gently in the bed. All of her children had always been good about bedtime – and Henry was no different. He immediately rolled to his side and popped his thumb in his mouth, giving off a heavy sigh that seemed almost too big for his body.

"Good night, kids..." she whispered – and moved to clean up the bowl of baby cereal in the kitchen, making them some hot tea. As she finished washing the dishes, and wiping down the highchair tray and table – an idea hit her.

Moving quickly, she darted back to her bedroom, carrying several candles from around the house, lining them on the dresser to make it smell nice and inviting in there. She hadn't bought or worn anything she considered sexy in years because having children had sure changed her body. All the pretty items she'd worn when she first married David didn't even fit over her hips or pooch anymore – and had long since been thrown away, but she had a pretty satin slip that stretched, and she wore under a dress for special occasions.

"I am so lame..." she whispered aloud, smoothing the satin over her stomach and wincing at the obvious stretch marks that could be seen, looking like little lines on the material.

She hated them because you could feel a difference in the skin, even though she 'earned' them by delivering four healthy children. There would be no bikinis anymore, no 'slim fit' jeans, and her stomach constantly looked like it had a pooch from being stretched repeatedly over the years.

"Ugh, what does he even see in me..." she asked her reflection and heard a voice behind her.

"His soulmate..."

Elliott's voice caused her to jump nervously as she saw him standing in the once-closed doorway, watching her. She could see the love in his eyes, the admiration in his gaze, and there was an innate bond that just reached for her, feeling something within her reaching back.

"I see the girl I've always known, the friend I supported, and the woman I love more than anything in the world," he began, his voice quiet and full of emotion. "I see you, there in your eyes, and I love how you see me... the person beyond this face, this body."

"Elliott," she whispered shyly, reaching for her robe on the bed.

"Stop," he begged and hesitated. "Don't hide from me further when you are already wearing something. I love looking at you and seeing the transformation that has happened from each miracle. Maybe I'm the messed up one that thinks stretch marks are sexy," he chuckled, walking into the room and closing the door behind him – and holding up a bag. "I got Morgan's photos."

"Thank you," she smiled, feeling a little nervous and emotionally overwhelmed at all of this. "He'll be so happy and couldn't stop talking about the flight you took him on."

"I love that kid," Elliott admitted, taking a step closer to her. "I've always loved the children, and they've always been a part of me – but it's slightly different now."

"I know…"

"Just like I've always loved you…"

Sarah's eyes looked up and met his as he brushed her hair off her shoulder before touching her cheek.

"I would have never crossed this line before," he breathed, not holding back. "I knew and respected your marriage to David – and loved him like a brother. It destroyed me that he died so young, but I knew seeing you with someone else would hurt even more."

"Elliott…"

"I love you," he whispered passionately. "I loved you as a friend and as the woman you are… and it's going to destroy a part of me to leave you tomorrow."

His eyes held hers, searching, as she swallowed in understanding. Tears were already clogging her throat and stinging her eyes, realizing that they were getting to their goodbyes already.

"I love the way your body responds when Henry cries," he said hoarsely. "I think it's incredibly hot. Those stretch marks make my knees weak and bring out something so primal in me that it's shocking. I adore the fact that you are trying to entice me by dressing in this… but you only have to look at me to get that reaction, Sarah."

"I thought you would want something slinky or…"

"You only have to look at me or smile at me," he repeated softly, his thumb caressing her jaw. "You breathe... and I want you."

He leaned down to kiss her – and she paused, putting a hand on his chest. It was almost comical to see his eyes widen in question as she met his gaze.

"Do you want a baby of your own?"

"Do you want a *fifth* baby?" he countered hoarsely.

"I never really expected to have four," she admitted softly, reaching up to touch his face, memorizing it with her fingertips, and then caressing his temple, stroking his hair. "But I would be curious if our child would have your red hair or temperament, what a blend of us would look like, and..."

"I'm going to say something that is probably going to come out very wrong, and I don't intend it to sound that harsh, but..." Elliott interrupted, almost tensing in her arms as she braced herself for what he was about to say.

"I'm not David," he began and hesitated. "I don't want you to ever feel like you must be pregnant every single time I turn around for me to be happy with you in our marriage. I know he loved the children and was proud of them, but a part of me always wondered how you got through it all. Why do you think I used to give you both such a hard time about being pregnant? Having a baby was so tough on you. I've seen that sweaty, exhausted person in the hospital room who looked like they'd been through the wringer. I saw you after each of the kids – including Henry – and you looked like you'd lost a fight with a heavyweight boxing champ..."

They both let out a nervous chuckle of awareness because it was true. She was not at her finest after having a baby. It took her a few days to get to feeling somewhat normal, and after Henry's delivery, it had been hard. She had other children to watch out for; they caught the flu, and she had still been healing mentally from David's death. It was a lot to go through for any person, much less a new mother.

"If we have a baby," he whispered, touching her cheek with the back of his knuckles. "I'm going to be a mess worrying about you. Would I love a child someday – sure – but there's a reason we've been very careful each time we've been intimate."

"A child is a blessing…"

"Oh, I agree wholeheartedly, but not at the expense of you."

Sarah blinked at his sweet words, marveling at the man before her.

"I would love to have a child, to see what we would create," he murmured, his eyes holding hers. "But if something happened and I lost you so soon after we've found each other…?" His voice broke as he looked away.

"It's not worth it," he finished hoarsely.

"And if I wanted another baby?" she asked hesitantly, turning his face back to hers. "What if I had those same questions, same curiosities, wondering what our child would look like…"

"I would give you anything you asked for within reason," he admitted. "But I cannot lose you."

"I'm not going anywhere, Elliott," she smiled tenderly, putting her hand on the back of his neck to pull him back into a kiss – only to feel him hesitate this time.

"Okaaaay…" she drawled, chuckling.

"If we are even discussing another child, we need to talk about money and the future."

"Well, that's incredibly unromantic," she chuckled, pulling away and looking at him, before sitting down on the edge of the bed. "I guess we are talking instead of making love."

"Sarah…"

"No. Let's talk and hash this out because I think it needs

to be said between us. We need to be able to talk, and now is as good a time as any. When you fly out tomorrow, we'll be stuck using calling cards or communicating via email – and sometimes you need to see the other person's face, their body language, so things don't get misconstrued."

"True," he agreed, gingerly sitting down beside her on the bed – and immediately reaching for her hand. He laced his fingers with hers as they sat there silently… waiting.

"Money?" she prompted after a moment.

"They offered me a job at Flyboys," Elliott began bluntly, causing her eyes to widen in shock as she turned to look at him. "But…" he interrupted quickly, "That is why we need to talk – especially if we are discussing another possible child in the future. Morgan will need braces; things can happen, and I have my benefits right now with the military."

"And Flyboys?" she whispered, trying not to get her hopes up because he seemed very wary about the change.

"They said we won't struggle," Elliott hesitated. "I would get paid per hour of flight, but I won't be making what I earn with hazardous duty pay – which is what I get because I'm stationed in Ghazni."

"I have David's life insurance put away in accounts for the children to pay for their college later on, and…"

"As it should be," he interrupted tenderly, lacing his fingers with hers. "His children should be taken care of and I would expect no less – but I will be adding you all to my insurance, adding you to my bank account when I get back, and all of that will make things a little easier. You don't have to work, unless you want to. I would never expect you to work."

"I like my job, and they've been good to me."

"But if I came home and worked at Flyboys – I would need to buy a plane eventually. I've got a large nest egg set aside, but it would dwindle fast and we would probably both need to work in order to maintain this lifestyle for the kids. Insurance is expensive and…"

"Elliott," she interrupted softly, looking at him. "You don't have to convince me, you know. I will go with whatever you choose to do. You've always wanted to fly, and the Academy was your ticket out. I understand that, but I think you are being handed a chance that you never expected, and change is hard."

"It's scary," he whispered under his breath. "I've got a family to watch out for now, and it's not just me."

"I know."

"What would you have me do?"

"Think about it," she said simply. "I can't make the decision for you because it's your life, your career… just like it's my body."

"You're my wife, my family, my life," he countered.

"I am – and none of that changes with whatever course you choose."

"Are you sure?"

She met his worried eyes and saw the fear in his gaze, realizing he truly was torn with what the right thing to do for them all was. He wanted to be perfect and wanted everything to be wonderful, but sometimes that wasn't how life was meant to be.

"Elliott," she began tenderly. "If you chose to stay in, we would still have each other and make family time a priority when you came home. You are loved here, welcomed, and have a home with us all," she whispered tenderly, gathering her thoughts as she spoke. "If you came home and worked at Flyboys, things would be different – yes. We might get on your nerves after a while, but now things are magical. There are going to be other 'trials' to handle, like bills, navigating traffic at the schools, picking up the kids at daycare, demands on our time, maintaining the house, and so much more – but the one difference is that each night, we could be close together as a family."

"I'm still replacing this bed," he muttered under his breath.

"I know," she chuckled. "I understand, but if we were broke and hard up – I would still sleep here soundly with you, holding you close, and we could dream for more together."

"I thought you were going to make this easy…"

"Nope," she chuckled. "I'm going to point out things on each side, and the only person that can decide is the man who is working the job. You might hate working at Flyboys…"

He gave her a sour look that made her chuckle in amusement.

"Or you might get back and get a promotion?"

And again – gave her a flat look.

"Well, I don't know," she exclaimed, laughing, putting her head against his shoulder. "I'm guessing and assuming blindly."

"I know," he replied, kissing her hair. "Thank you for listening."

"Thank you for talking with me about all of this," she countered.

They sat there for several moments, just holding hands and needing to exist around one another. It was like her soul was recharging just being close to Elliott, and she needed as much of him as possible, filling those emotional banks while she could.

"What's on your mind?" he asked softly.

"Babies," she whispered, looking up at his surprised gaze that melted in an instant. "You might not be decided on things, but I am. I was thinking that if I can handle four… what's one more?"

"Are you serious?"

"Very," she chuckled. "I mean, just because we start trying doesn't mean it will happen right away. It could take several months or not at all. You never know, but…"

"Y-You would," Elliott's voice broke as he stared at her, his eyes glistening. It obviously meant more to him than he wanted to let on, and she was glad she brought it up. The man was made to be a father and knew his heart was big enough for all of them. "You want a baby with me?"

"A tiny piece of Trent to grow under my heart…"

"Oh mercy," he whispered huskily, cupping her face in his hands… before chuckling. "We've gotta get a bigger car, my love."

"Funny, I was already thinking that earlier this evening," she laughed tearfully, twining her arms around his shoulders as he kissed her.

CHAPTER 23

COPPERHEAD
Ghazni, Afghanistan

FIRST DAY BACK, and everything was blowing up in Elliott's face, figuratively and literally. They were on their patrol; he was sitting in his Falcon trying to keep his mind in the game and kept looking at the photograph he'd taped to the console of his plane of his new family.

"Reaper... I've picked up..." Outfield's voice was cut off as something reflected out of the corner of Elliott's eye only a split second before another slid past him much too close.

"Outfield – come in?"

"Where'd that come from?"

"I've got surface-to-air..." Copperhead said bluntly on the radio.

"Where? Where?!"

Elliott could see Outfield's plane as it gave a slight wobble just to the northeast of him in the air. There was smoke billowing from somewhere underneath, and he could see a few pieces of paper flying around inside the glass of the cockpit. Something pierced the side of the plane.

"Reaper..." Elliott began and heard Outfield's voice over his own.

"Engine one is gone... crap – engine two..."

"What's going on, Outfield... status report!" Reaper commanded an answer and there was chaos on the radio.

"Smoke, plane's been breached, and..." Elliott tried to speak up loudly and caught Ricochet's attention.

"What do you see?"

"I'm going down – and I'm hit bad..."

"Outfield...?"

"I've got another launch inbound..." Elliott announced, his screen lighting up wildly as Cavalier and Inferno began arguing, causing him to roll his eyes. So much for keeping calm under pressure.

"I'm pegged! Where is he?"

"I don't see anything..."

"My sensors are screaming..."

"Mayday! Mayday! I'm hit..."

Everything was happening so fast, within seconds. Inferno's Falcon was in the direction that Outfield's plane was angling before the oncoming nosedive toward the ground, and the canopy of the plane flew off.

"I've got ejection!" Elliott screamed in warning, interrupting the chaos on the radio.

"BANK LEFT! BANK LEFT!"

"Where is it?"

"YOUR OTHER LEFT, RIPTIDE..." Cavalier snarled angrily.

"We're all gonna get killed out here..."

"Shut up, Banshee..." Reaper was hollering in the coms,

taking control of the situation and belting out orders. "Inferno – MOVE!"

His breath caught as he saw the seat burst into flames as the detonator threw him upward with enough force to cause bodily harm, removing him from the Falcon as quickly as possible. Man, that was not something you did lightly, either. Before his very eyes, a billion-dollar jet was wobbling precariously toward the ground and had the weirdest, slow spin to it as the pilot was flung wildly into the air. He had eyes on Outfield, knowing the man was in the midst of his own private hell right now. Everything had to function correctly, or you were a goner.

If you were lucky, you'd live with a heck of a backache and a migraine. If you were unlucky, well, you might be in a chair the rest of your life or definitely needing physical therapy to repair the spinal damage. You didn't eject unless it was your last option, and they all knew it.

Especially over hostile territory.

"Ricochet, take your entire wing and bank right…"

"SIR!"

"Teflon, hang back and watch my tail," Reaper said bluntly. "I'm descending and looking for…"

"Reaper…"

"Not now, Ricochet!"

"I've got chute deployment, north… northeast in a two o'clock position, sir!" Ricochet interrupted, repeating the exact words that Elliott had just said. Whatever, he thought. There was bigger fish to fry right now and he just needed to make sure it wasn't his own. He needed to make sure Sarah was never made a widow again, and that single thought slammed home his decision in a heartbeat.

"Where'd those missiles come from…?" Elliott barked, needing answers.

"That same direction Outfield is landing," Cavalier interrupted. "I recommend we return to base."

"Agreed."

"Oh man... we're gonna leave him?" Inferno was beyond upset and he could only imagine what was going through the man's mind right now. It bothered him to think of leaving Outfield here, but he couldn't help him, and circling in the air was only going to burn fuel and make them all targets.

"Inferno – your orders are to return your aircraft to base, do you understand? Outfield, if you can hear me – you are inbound toward hostiles. Do you copy? Outfield?"

"What if he's knocked out?"

"What if he's dead?"

"Shut up – and Bubbles is a stupid call sign, newbie!" Panic was screaming angrily, losing his cool almost as much as Inferno. The calm man was living up to his name now, and it was a little alarming as nervous laughter filled the radio.

Everyone was exceedingly close to breaking, both mentally and emotionally.

It wasn't ten minutes later that Elliott was on the ground and already panicking about Sarah. If Outfield was missing, they would be going 'dark' and cutting off communication until he was found – alive or dead. Walking away from his Falcon, he saw the mess before him and paused, stunned.

The squadron was obviously shaken and thinking the worst possible had happened to their friend, their brother. Reaper looked shell-shocked and stood there silently, barely saying a thing.

"Pararescue takes over from here," Reaper said hoarsely.

"Reaper, hey, are you..." Ricochet began as Panic did an about-face, jogging to the edge of the runway and threw up in the sand. Inferno collapsed, hitting his knees, before folding his body and pressing his forehead to the ground – weeping.

"I can't do this again, man…" Inferno sobbed. "I can't…"

"Shut him up," Panic snapped angrily, spitting in the sand before heaving again.

"I can't… It was empty, dude. Greene's casket was empty! Do you remember that?"

Riptide looked at him, as well as several of the others.

"He ejected," Reaper croaked – not looking at any of them. The man's wingman had been shot down, and that was the ultimate for any of them. You protected your wingman with everything in you, and his had just ejected into enemy territory. "I need to report in, give my state-ment, and speak with someone. If you are troubled, Rico-chet, get him to the offices in building two. There's a chaplain or counselors waiting for anyone who will need them."

"Fall back, everyone – now," Ricochet snapped, "Your commanding officer gave you an order."

Nobody moved.

It was like too much had happened, the breach had been too much, too painful. Sometimes, with death, loss, and fear, you crossed the line between alarm to a 'broken' part of the mind where you stopped functioning… and part of the team was there.

There was a special kind of pain knowing you let down your partner – but this had to be hitting the other man hard. Reaper, Panic, and Inferno were here when the last airman was shot down – Jordan 'Mr. Clean' Greene. The man's name was memorialized on a locker that Teflon was now using.

Inferno was an absolute mess, sobbing.

Panic was beside himself. His reaction scared them all the most. The man was no longer angry, vomiting, or respond-ing. Instead, he was sitting there on the pavement, unrespon-sive, with tears streaking down his face, staring brokenly in the distance.

Riptide had sprinted out of there like the hounds of hell were at his heels.

The others were standing there, looking around at each other, shocked, stunned, and not listening to anyone.

"Ricochet," Elliott barked loudly, catching the other man's eyes – and jerked his head to the side in a silent order. Walking over, he grabbed two pairs of arms blindly and began to drag them to the debriefing room so they could all talk.

Ricochet did the same.

Looking sideways, he saw Reaper's eyes on him, and his slow nod of approval.

The team needed to be drawn back together – quickly.

This was just what Elliott did, apparently. He did it for Sarah right after David died, he pulled his own mess together when his mother passed away, and if the worst possible outcome happened today, then he would be there for the team, for his brothers at arms, pulling them all back together once more as a squadron, before having his own nervous breakdown silently.

That night, he went to compose an email to Sarah, knowing it would be a while before it went through – and got everything out of his mind, his heart, and soul.

My love,

I'm back on base – but it's certainly not home.

Home is in your arms, holding you close, and losing myself in your love.

Home is where the kids can wrestle with me.

Home is where I eat eggs spotted with raisins and tuck dolls into bed along with mischievous little girls. Home is where I have a bright and intelligent pair of sons that wrap me completely around their little fingers by simply being there.

You wanted a baby – and everything in me sincerely hopes

*that we made one together before I left. I keep thinking of
holding you close, imagining your soft kisses, your gentle
smiles, and the way you touch me, and I feel so alone out here
with no signs of relief.*

*One of the pilots went down today, and the only thing I
kept thinking was 'I can't make my Sarah a widow again'.*

*Protocol was so far gone out the window that it wasn't even
funny. It was shocking how fast it all fell apart when I saw him
eject. We don't even know if the pilot is alive, dead, or unin-
jured, but I think we might lose one of the other guys today
because of it. I saw what trauma does to a man today – and it's
not pretty. I don't think he's okay and can't say who it was yet.*

*Maybe when you get this email and the communication
lines open back up, I'll try to call, but I think sometimes the
mental injuries are worse than the physical ones.*

*I miss my soulmate and wish you were here to tell me it's
going to be all right.*

Love,

Elliott

Clicking send on the email, a part of him hoped it went
through and saw the instantly red flag showing that it was
pending delivery. Nope, he thought morosely and got up
from his seat. As he walked back into the barracks, he saw
the others were trying to occupy themselves. Inferno was
tossing Outfield's baseball up in the air and catching it,
Teflon was lying there staring at the ceiling. Cavalier was
slumped on the side of his bunk, his head hung low. Scarecrow was on his knees, praying, and this surprised Elliott
because the man used to make fun of Paradox doing that
very thing, and Panic was sitting on his bunk, silently, tears
streaming down his face and rocking slightly to-and-fro.

"Has Panic talked to one of the counselors yet?" Elliott
asked Ricochet, who nodded as his shoulders sagged.

"He has... and Reaper has gone back to get someone to speak to him again. It's not good."

Elliott cursed under his breath.

"I know," Ricochet agreed morosely. "He's been like that for twenty minutes."

"You've got to get him out of here," Elliott hissed quietly, looking at the other man in disbelief. "*That* is not good for anyone's morale in the team. Help me get him to the sanctuary or in one of the offices."

Both men walked over to Panic's bunk, and Elliott felt their eyes on him, watching. He sat down beside the man and touched his arm.

"Brother, hey... it's Copperhead and Ricochet," he whispered softly, trying to be as gentle as possible. "Hey, we are going to the sanctuary and want you to come with us, okay?"

"D-Did they find him?" Panic said in a broken voice. "Who says goodbye when you have nobody? Who do they contact? Where would they send my coffin if it was me?"

"They are working on it, but you need to hang in there, brother..."

"Greene's coffin was empty," he whispered, his eyes darting wildly around the room. "I don't want to do that again. I can't..."

"And you won't," Elliott promised. "Come with us, okay? Let's take a little walk and talk."

He looked up at Ricochet, who looped his arm around the man and pulled him to his feet.

"We've got you," Ricochet said, and Elliott immediately got on the other side, helping guide the man who was still crying and whispering broken phrases, terrified.

They were losing Panic.

HOURS LATER, Elliott was standing alone in the shower, trying to keep from having his own breakdown. It was hard enough to worry about Outfield and what he had to be going through right now, but knowing it could have been him today, and that he could have made Sarah a pregnant widow once again was almost too much – and combined with saying goodbye?

He closed his eyes and leaned into the water, needing to feel better as his mind moved all the pieces silently in his head; a decision for the future taking shape and forming.

CHAPTER 24

SARAH

Just heard from Reaper, team – we've got one down tonight, and they are searching for him.

Keep him in your prayers this evening...

Active-Duty headcount – Riptide, Ricochet, Inferno, Scarecrow, Copperhead, Banshee, Cavalier, Panic, Teflon, Bubbles, Salt, and Jester are all accounted for.

Oh thank you, Jesus... Ricochet is okay?

Yes – no details but yes, Destiny.

Megan – Riptide is fine.

Sarah – Copperhead is fine.

THAT SINGLE TEXT message was the only one that mattered in the entire slew of them that came across her phone. She wasn't expecting to get a text message from the team at Flyboys telling her that one of the pilots was missing – and nearly fainted from the sheer spike of fear that rocketed through her, followed by the wave of relief.

Sarah – Copperhead is fine.

Her hand covered her mouth as she stepped into her bedroom and shut the door, sliding down it and collapsing onto the floor, sobbing. She'd lost one husband in her short life and never expected to face the possibility again. Sure, she knew Elliott was stationed overseas and he'd made mention of hazardous duty pay, but it never really connected in her mind until now.

… And her phone rang.

"Hello?" she wept, not bothering to hide it.

"Hey," came Melody's soft, understanding voice. "I was wondering how you were doing and glad I called. He's okay, hon."

"I know. It's just…"

"Your brain went to the worst possible outcome automatically because that is how we are programmed?"

"Omigosh, yes," she chuckled tearfully, wiping her eyes on her T-shirt. "I mean, when you've had someone show up on your doorstep…"

"Oh, I know only too well," Melody retorted painfully. "Let me tell you, I still see their faces in my sleep, and they are complete strangers to me. I couldn't tell you their names or if they even introduced themselves. I just kept hearing that smoke alarm from my cooking – and those fateful words."

"I was making rolls and keep hearing Chief Griffin's voice…"

"I don't make apple pie anymore."

"I haven't made yeast rolls since."

"That's why I wanted to call because I know that feeling and wanted to check on you."

"I appreciate it. How are you feeling?"

"Massive? Horribly pregnant? Like my curves have curves? If I was a spillway, then the dam is fixing to give… you know the drill," Melody teased, and Sarah chuckled in sympathetic understanding.

"I do. How much longer do you have?"

"Less than a month…"

"The baby will be here before you know it – and if you need me to watch Betsy…?" her voice trailed off knowingly, remembering the woman was there for her with Henry.

"I might take you up on that."

"The offer is always there."

"And if you get worried or scared – call. Don't be a stranger. We might be swamped or overwhelmed in our own little world, but it doesn't mean that we don't understand what is happening in yours. It just means we haven't had a chance to look up yet."

"Same here. I feel bad sometimes because I haven't reached out as much as I probably should have…"

"Girl, you have children, a family, and work full-time. That makes you 'Miracle Mom' already in my book. You are swimming in wonderful things that pull at your free time. It's all good, I promise."

"I appreciate you saying that."

"Keep plodding along, my friend. Do all your normal stuff – including emailing Copperhead. You might not be able to send it right now, but I assure you the moment he can write or call – he will. It will make him feel good to see his inbox with several emails in it."

"Does this ever get any easier?"

"I don't know," Melody said quietly. "Firefly was out of the Air Force by the time we met, and Jordan had died, so I really can't answer."

"Can I ask a personal question?"

"Of course."

"Are y'all able to make ends meet easily with him working at Flyboys? I mean, I just don't see how it can be so lucrative and employ so many people in a small town in the middle of nowhere."

"Oh, I completely understand," Melody chuckled. "First off, they are the only ones doing anything like this in a hundred-mile radius with the most handsome teachers. Next time you go by the school and look at the students, eighty percent of them are women…" Melody grumbled and Sarah laughed in sudden understanding. "Which really chaps my rear, because my husband is quite a flirt. If Sutton wasn't so loving and attentive, I might actually have a reason to be alarmed but the guy has a marshmallow heart that is all mine. I'm serious though, women come for lessons… *and sign up*. Then they tell their friends. Word spreads like wildfire."

"Okay, got it… they've got the market cornered in more ways than one," Sarah teased as Melody continued.

"And… we do okay," her friend admitted. "We have a huge garden; Sutton works part-time because he wants to be home working on projects and plays with Betsy. I work to help pay the bills and get out of the house. We aren't breaking the bank, but if we need something – we can get it without worry."

The two got quiet for a moment before Melody spoke again.

"Is Copperhead thinking about taking a position at Flyboys? Most of the guys work part-time on purpose. I think Harley, Alpo, Thumper, Glory, and Houdini put in the greatest number of hours. Heck, Romeo practically lives splitting his time between Texas and Alaska. Sometimes Dixie goes, and sometimes, she doesn't. Valkyrie is with the kids a lot, and…"

"I get it – and he's on the fence," Sarah admitted. "I want another baby, and I think he's scared of what it could do to the family financially. It's a big change and not one that can be flipped back, you know?"

"Just be supportive in whatever he decides because it wasn't made easily."

"I know…"

"Well, I better let you go, hon. I just wanted to check on you, but I'm trying to freeze some meals before the baby gets here because I'm not eating peanut butter and jelly for days on end if Sutton cooks."

"If Bethany makes it, there will be raisins in your sandwich…" Sarah teased, chuckling.

"Oh yum," Melody said flatly – causing both women to laugh once more.

"Thank you for calling. I feel better."

"Good. Remember to breathe, for this too will pass… like a kidney stone."

"Amen to that, sister."

Getting slowly to her feet, Sarah washed her face and went to check on the children. It was hard because she felt the emptiness of the house physically like a loss. It was as if his ghost was surrounding her, and if she closed her eyes, she could picture him in the room, moving around or smiling at her. She missed Elliott exponentially.

When they had been 'just friends, ' she missed him, but not like this. She'd had her life, had David, and knew he was happy doing what he loved. Things had changed over the years and that feeling of friendship had morphed into so much more.

Elliott had said 'soulmate,' and it was true.

There was a bond there that was deeper than anything she'd had in her life, and she'd loved David dearly, but this was so different and hard to explain. David, she would die for, but Elliott and the children, she would raze the planet if someone threatened them. There would be no hiding from her, and she would fight until her last breath.

THE EMAILS she'd composed suddenly started going through, and she received several from Elliott before her phone rang.

"Hello?"

"Sarah…" her husband sighed audibly, causing her to melt as tears stung her eyes. "I've been dreaming of your voice and miss you something terrible."

"What happened, Elliott?"

"A plane was shot down, and the pilot ejected. It took pararescue three days to recover him, and he's in medical right now getting treated."

"Is he okay?"

"Yeah, but…"

"What?"

"I've been thinking about the Flyboys thing…"

Her heart skidded to a stop in her chest as she listened.

"I'm nervous because I want to take care of my family financially, but that could have been me – you know?" he whispered in a hushed voice. "I kept thinking about you getting a phone call or someone showing up on the doorstep – and that makes you really question what you want to do."

"I know."

"I'm so torn because I want to be a part of the family, be

there for you, but I know we are going to struggle... but, if I stay here – then I'm just a wallet and not a father."

"Elliott, I will support any decision you make."

"Even if it meant you might still need to work for a while?"

"I like my job, so that's no problem."

"And if there's a baby?"

"Then you would be here when our child was born – whereas you might make it if you get a flight early enough."

"We're gonna be broke," he joked emotionally.

"I've been that way before," she teased tearfully. "I would rather be struggling to pay the bills and seeing your smile than to be alone. We can cut costs or..."

"If it's really bad, I could pick up extra flights or look at getting a job with a commercial airline."

"See? There are options to be had, but all of them involve a change only you can decide on."

"I don't even know my release date yet. I just wanted to talk to you."

"I'm glad you did."

"Are the kids close by, or are they asleep?"

"They are in bed. It's nearly eleven o'clock here."

"I figured," he began and hesitated. "I miss tucking them in and cooking in the kitchen with them. I really miss washing your back and sitting on the couch together."

"What else do you miss on the couch, Handsome...?" she teased intimately, trying to make him smile and she grinned as he chuckled knowingly.

"*That!*" he blurted out. "I really miss *that* a lot, my love."

They both laughed for a moment before he spoke once again.

"I'm going to see what they say and get my date to come home – and you are okay with this...?"

"More than okay," she promised, laying a hand over her

heart because this was something she'd hoped he would decide on his own. It had to be his decision because she wanted no regrets for him – ever. "Just keep me posted and let me know what they say or what happens."

"I promise," he vowed tenderly. "My calling card is already counting down, and I'm not ready to hang up."

"I love you, Elliott... and pretty soon we won't have to hang up ever again."

"I know – and I can't wait."

"Me neither."

"Get some rest, my love," he whispered, and before Sarah could reply, the phone line was dead. She flopped back on the pillows on her bed, feeling almost boneless, as she realized that he'd made his decision.

He was coming home, and only something major would sway him in the other direction. He sounded so settled, so relieved, and even joked around with her once he'd gotten it off of his chest, and she couldn't believe the feeling of hope that just hearing he was going to return gave her.

Elliott was coming home permanently.

A WEEK LATER, THAT 'SOMETHING MAJOR' appeared as a blip on her internal radar... well, actually it *hadn't* appeared - and that was the problem.

Sarah missed her period.

"Oh my gosh," she whispered to herself in the mirror as she was brushing her teeth, feeling nausea churn in her stomach with a twinge at the back of her mind. The only time toothpaste bothered her was when she was pregnant. It was a trigger for her during each pregnancy, and she had to switch from mint to cinnamon to keep from vomiting.

Wrapping her robe around her, she came running out of the bathroom and hollering wildly as she texted Melody.

"Y'all get up and get ready, please. Mommy has to make an extra stop this morning," she began and heard the tired grumblings as the children woke up.

> Sorry it's so early – but who is your OBGYN?
>
> Mine retired after Henry…

ARE YOU PREGNANT???

> I think so – and I'm freaking out because Elliott might change his mind about coming home.

Her phone rang a second later.

"Hello?"

"GIRL…" came Melody's shocked voice. "Y'all take 'getting busy' to a whole new level."

"No kidding," Sarah laughed nervously. "Kids, get ready. We need to head out in a bit."

"Have you met Mallory Parr yet? She's one of us and practices where Dr. Bow used to be on the south end…"

"Neither is ringing a bell."

"Well, you'd remember because she's super sweet and nice. Mallory's husband is Paradox, and I bet you just haven't crossed paths yet. I'm going to text her now, and she'll get you in right away. Just tell her we talked, okay? She's my doctor and the best person ever."

"Will she tell anyone? I haven't told Elliott yet and…"

"No, girl. She's a professional – and a sweetheart. She won't say a word, even if she could."

"Oh, thank God…"

"Congratulations," Melody chuckled. "Can I share?"

"Not yet," Sarah laughed. "I need to tell Elliott first, remember?"

"Heads-up, I might be calling you later…"

"Oh?"

"I've had a twinge in my lower back and…"

"Say the word, and I'll get Betsy, my friend. Tell Firefly to breathe, and that's what friends are for."

"You think my labor is starting, too, huh?"

"Mine always started low in my back and wrapped around the front like a period cramp…"

"Or food poisoning – but you haven't had breakfast yet?"

"Precisely," Sarah chuckled. "Call me later, and I'll swing by to get Betsy – until then, try to rest as much as you can."

"Yup. Going back to bed now and turning on the cartoons for Betsy."

"There you go."

As they said 'bye' to each other, Sarah sighed happily. While it scared her to think that this could affect Elliott's decision, she also knew there was no hiding this between them. He would be just as happy, nervous, and excited as she was about having another child, and the children? Well, there would be discussions about who was going to have to share their room and questions once more, just like when she was pregnant with Henry.

"It might be time to finish off the garage or add on to the house because buying a new one isn't going to be in the cards financially for a long while…" she muttered aloud, shaking her head.

"Kids," she called out. "Is everyone up and brushing your teeth? Let's get ready, okay?"

Rushing them out the door twenty minutes later, she was at the office the moment the front door was unlocked by a smiling woman with two buns on her head, making her look almost like a human teddy bear. Sarah did a double take, smiled warily, and nodded.

"Morning," the woman exclaimed happily, waving Sarah inside along with the children. "C'mon in, you can select the cartoons this morning on the waiting room television," she smiled at Bethany, who was clutching her doll in her arms, watching her. "Good morning, Dolly... I'm so glad to meet you."

"Das my dolly..." Bethany muttered and buried her face against Sarah's leg as she stood there with Henry's stroller, where he was fast asleep and drooling. He looked like an angel but he was definitely getting a little personality that reminded her so much of Morgan. Those chubby cheeks would win the hearts of girls far and wide, but it was those big eyes that melted her own.

"Bethany," Sarah whispered. "Be nice," and turned to look at the effervescent woman standing there waving happily at her sleepy children. "I don't have an appointment, and I need to get my son to school, but I kind of need to get seen – quickly. Morgan, please watch your sisters."

"Oh, um, let me see if we have a spot open. Are you okay – well, don't answer that because you are here, and I'm not a doctor. Hang on, and let's look."

She walked behind the counter as the children quickly headed for the television, turning it on and all three sitting in different poses. Morgan sat cross-legged, Bethany plopped down and folded her knees out to the side like usual, while Leslie perched on a chair, utterly fascinated by the cartoon already.

"Look, it's nothing major, but my friend told me to come here and..." Sarah began and saw a dark-haired woman walk up toward them.

"Are you Melody's friend?"

"Yes," Sarah sagged immediately in relief. "You must be Dr. Parr... I know this is crazy, but..."

"No, honey, come on," Dr. Parr invited and waved her hand toward the smiling receptionist to hand her a clipboard. She took it and looked at her, speaking quickly. "Sunny, this is Copperhead's wife, and she's one of us – can you keep an eye on the kids for like five minutes?"

Sarah's eyes looked between the two women as she quickly followed the doctor toward one of the examination rooms, pushing Henry before her in the stroller.

"Who's she married to?"

"Outfield – and Paradox is my husband," the doctor smiled easily. "Relax. You look as nervous as you could be. You might as well consider us all one big extended family, and Melody told me a little bit about what is going on," she began, shutting the door behind Sarah. "How about you tell me?"

"Well, we started trying, and I think I'm pregnant. Wait, she's married to the guy that went missing?"

"Yes. Focus hon, we are squeezing you in this morning. Any signs?"

"Sorry. Yes, nausea this morning, and I haven't started yet."

"Good enough for me," Mallory chuckled, handing her a cup. "Bathroom first, then we'll do bloodwork."

"Yup – I know the drill."

"I bet you do."

Less than five minutes later, Sunny was smoothing down the tape and cotton swab on her arm, looking up at Mallory.

"Boy, it's been busy..." Mallory joked. "Dixie, Melody, Mary, you – everyone seems to be trying, including us. My husband just came home three months ago, and we're trying, but apparently we are not as lucky as you, Mrs. Copperhead."

"Trent," Sarah smiled. "Sarah Trent."

"I know, I'm teasing. I can't tell you how many times I've been called Mrs. Paradox. It's like some of the guys have a complete mind-melt and cannot remember each other's last names without it stitched across their chest, but they sure remember their call signs."

Mallory rolled her eyes.

"Goobers…" she muttered, chuckling. "Now the doctor comes out in me – I want you to take prenatal vitamins immediately, drink plenty of water, eat leafy greens, and fortify everything. Got it? Let me get your labs back, look at them, and we might add in some iron tablets since you mentioned that you had a history of it in the past."

"Yup. Orange juice and iron… got it."

"Sunny – or Mrs. Outfield – will get you scheduled for your first official appointment. We'll do a sonogram, verify everything looks good, and establish a due date officially… but congratulations – and nice to meet you."

"You too."

"Are you going to the bonfire next week?"

"Maybe?" she hedged. "I've got to see how I'm feeling and what I have going – sometimes the kids have stuff they have to do and…"

"Say no more," Mallory chuckled. "I have a three-year-old that is fascinated with gardening, his cat, and camping… not in that order. If I have to sleep in a tent in the backyard one more time, I'm not going to be a happy camper."

"Raisins in my scrambled eggs," Sarah offered, smiling in understanding.

"Exactly."

Walking out of the doctor's office, she couldn't wipe the smile off of her face and apparently it was obvious. As the children climbed into the car, the barrage of questions began.

"Mama, why did we go to see the doctor?"

"Is Henry sick?"

"Is that why we had to wait and watch cartoons with that nice lady?"

"Can I have puff balls in my hair too?"

"Mama, I think I forgot my lunch on the counter…"

"Morgan, how did you forget your lunch?"

"We were in a hurry, and Leslie wouldn't leave me alone…"

"Nuh-uhhhh…"

"Yah-huhhhh…"

"Kids! Please don't start fighting – and no, Henry isn't sick. I went to talk to the doctor about me."

"Are you sick?"

"Do you need some hot tea, Mama? I can get my tea set and…"

"Actually, I'm going to have a baby," Sarah began and saw the eye rolls in the rearview mirror, surprising her. Morgan and Leslie looked at each other in dismay with a hushed 'Told you!' tossed between them.

"Wait a second… now, babies are good things," she sputtered in disbelief and laughed. "What's with all the drama from you two?"

"Where's the baby going to sleep? I already share a room with a baby…"

"Me too…"

"Hey! I'm not a baby anymore. I'm a big girl now…"

"Actually, I need to talk to your dad about it because I was thinking of making a few changes at the house in the next several months in order to make room."

"Really?"

"Yup. Like a bedroom mixed with a playroom or something – but," she quickly stopped everyone's excited exclamations. "But I need to talk to your dad, and it will not happen overnight. I need you to be patient and flexible because we are going to have another little brother or sister

249

eventually…"

"Can I pick the name?" Bethany asked – causing Morgan and Leslie to look at her angrily, obviously beating them to the punch.

"When Dad comes home, we'll all discuss it and talk about it. Right now, it's just in the very early stages, and I need to get two of you to school and two of you to daycare before rushing to work. I really don't need to be late again."

"What about my lunch?"

"Can you buy lunch in the line if I give you a few dollars?"

"Yeah… but I made a special sandwich."

"You can take a special sand – wait… why is it special?"

"Well, Tommy said that I was a wimp and couldn't eat spicy stuff, and I told him he was a doodie-head…"

"Morgan…" she warned, trying not to smile at his version of a curse word.

"And I made a peanut butter and Picante sauce sandwich instead of using the grape jelly…"

"Oh heavens…" Sarah muttered and immediately pulled over in the first parking lot, throwing open her door and leaning out just in time as she puked. She was still buckled, hanging her head as low as possible, as her breakfast decided to come back up. Dragging in several breaths, she hoped her stomach would stop roiling and spasming painfully.

"So much for nausea and morning sickness…" she whispered aloud to herself as the kids yelled at each other behind her.

"You booty-head-Morgan! Look what you did, you made Mama sick…"

"Picante is tomatoes, you dumb boy…"

"Hush-up, ya' big crybaby…"

"I'm not a crybaby! Moooommmm!"

"Y'all," Sarah breathed, spitting a few times before sitting up. "No more discussion – and here is a few dollars,

Morgan," she said quickly, digging in her purse blindly. "No more discussions about food, okay? I just can't right now and I don't want to get sick to my stomach again – and ignore Tommy, okay?"

"But he's mean…"

"Didn't you catch him eating paste last month?"

"Yes."

"Well, that's not spicy either – and the paste is disgusting."

"It tastes awful…"

"Morgan! Do not eat paste or anything else that isn't food-related. I cannot believe we are having this conversation, and I'm going to be late," Sarah breathed, feeling her stomach churn once more before texting her boss.

Stuck in traffic at the school – be there in ten minutes

"Seriously, guys – and girls – we've got to hurry, okay?"

"You're the one that puked everywhere," Morgan muttered – and Sarah's head whipped around as she leaned over the back seat bodily, still buckled in, to look him dead in the eye. It was slightly satisfying to see him shrink back in alarm as his sisters looked on in silent horror. She kind of hoped she had vomit on her chin, just so they never forgot the lesson she was about to give them all – despite the time.

"Sorry, Mama…" he whispered, staring at her with wide eyes.

"Let's not add *'being rude'* to your vocabulary. I'm not rude to you, and you will never be allowed to be rude to me. Got it, *Rattler?*"

The veiled hint did not go unnoticed as Morgan paled.

"Please don't tell Daddy because I want to fly again…"

"Keep that in mind next time you decide to sass me…" she replied openly and looked at him. "Is it going to happen again?"

"No, ma'am."

"Then I won't tell Dad."

251

"Thank you… ma'am."

"Now, buy your lunch, keep the change, and put it in your piggy bank when you get home… and you let me know if Tommy bothers you again. I will handle him, okay?"

"Yes, ma'am."

"Now, can we please go so I'm not late to work?"

All three voices replied in unison.

"Yes, ma'am."

Sarah nodded, turned around, and adjusted her mirror so they couldn't see her smile. She suddenly understood why Elliott had called Morgan out that day when he'd set him on the counter. There was something that just emphasized you were not going to tolerate a certain behavior when you looked them dead in the eyes to get your point across. She remembered seeing him standing there, soap in his mouth, as the two males stared at each other and wondering what had happened, and now she knew.

I'm going to have to tell him about this, and the baby, she mused, pulling into the elementary school and waving at Principal Mitchell and Mrs. Clark standing there talking.

"All right, Leslie, Mrs. Clark is waiting, sweetie… and Morgan - if you have any trouble, tell Mrs. Hody – okay, honey? She's there to make sure you are taken care of. I love you both and will see you this afternoon."

"Love you, Mama…" Leslie said, leaning forward and kissing her cheek.

"Love you, too…" she replied as Morgan did the same – and hugged her neck.

"Sorry, Mom – and it won't happen again."

"I know – and I'm sorry I got upset, but we can talk more tonight, okay?"

"You aren't mad at me?"

"Disappointed, but never mad. I love you and always will."

"I love you too... and would you be mad if I told you that your mouth smelled funny."

"That would be the puke," she said bluntly, nodding. "I'm waiting to get to work because I have a stash of mouthwash in my desk drawer from when I was pregnant with Henry."

Morgan nodded, shivered in disgust, and then waved instead of kissing her – making her laugh as he got out of the car and ran up to the school building. She waved once more and pulled forward to drop Henry and Bethany off at daycare.

It was going to be a long day.

Elliott,

Do you think we can talk when you get a chance? I really need to run something past you and want to hear your voice. I have a few things that are in motion and might affect our plans.

I love you,

Sarah

CHAPTER 25

COPPERHEAD

"YOU'RE KIDDING ME," Reaper said flatly, looking up at Elliott where he stood.

He had already been feeling sick to his stomach, concerned that maybe he was doing the wrong thing, but everything within him said this was right. He had nightmares of Sarah standing beside a grave crying – except it wasn't David, but him. The thought of finally having it all and then having it ripped away from him was not sitting well. Especially after how much he loved being home with her and filling in as a father.

No, this was the right thing to do – for all of them.

"Can you repeat that one more time, Copperhead?"

"Sir," Elliott began and handed over a written letter of resignation to him, laying it on his desk when Reaper didn't touch it. "I looked up my contract online and…"

"Well, you've got half those men beat then because none of them know how to do that," Reaper said flatly, getting up and shutting the office door before plopping down in his chair again. He slammed his shoes onto the corner of the desk, one at a time, creating a loud 'thump-thump' that reverberated against the walls, and put his hands behind his head. "Continue…"

"I looked up my contract and it's expiring in three months. Instead of re-enlisting my commission, I would like to let it lapse."

"Why?"

"Because I have a family back home and…"

"So do I," Reaper interrupted quietly.

"The whole thing with Outfield really hit home, and I can't do that to Sarah," Elliott began. "Not when my wife has already buried one husband. I want to tuck the kids in, bounce a baby on my knee, and…"

"We all do."

The two men looked at each other, and Elliott felt something eerily close to snapping within him. The man had a very stoic, bland expression on his face that bordered on indifference, but his eyes were sharp.

"I am letting my commission lapse, sir," Elliott began again and looked him straight in the face. "I'm not asking your permission. I'm informing you of my intentions."

And Reaper cracked a slight smile.

"You've got some brass on you, Copperhead. Sit down."

"Sir?"

"Sheesh," Reaper muttered, rubbing the back of his neck and sitting up, looking at him. *"I'm not asking… I'm telling,"* he mocked – and laughed. "Goodness, if I had a few in the squadron that would do the same, then I wouldn't be in this pickle."

"…Um, what pickle?" Elliott asked, taking a seat gingerly.

"Cavalier wants my spot, my position."

"Okay?"

"The team hates him."

"He's a bit of a jerk – yes."

"In order for there to be camaraderie and teamwork, the team has to think or act like a team. If he takes my spot, I could see him saying, 'because I said so'…"

"I could, too," Elliott began and winced. "Begging your pardon, but if you are leaving – why do you care?"

"Because this was my team, my home, my brothers when I arrived here," Reaper said simply. "I don't want to feel like I am abandoning them. I want there to be some order, some easy transition, and…"

"And?"

"I was hoping you'd stay," Reaper said quietly, looking at him.

Elliott swallowed in sudden awareness of what his boss, his leader, was saying. This would have been his dream two years ago, even six months ago – but now? Now, he had a family to think of and wanted to be home with Sarah. What horrible timing that Reaper was lining him up for command now.

"I've actually got your change in rank form here," he said quietly, picking it up. "I needed to bump you so that way I could do it again before I left due to 'needs of wartime' clause to get my way."

"What about Ricochet?"

"He's leaving not long after me."

"I'm flattered," Elliott said hoarsely. "I did not make this decision lightly either, but my wife and I have four children…"

"Oh, I know. I talked with Paradox before he left, and he told me you were marrying someone you knew. Sophie, my wife, said that Sarah is a sweetheart, and I'm very happy for the two of you, but…"

"But you want me to lead the team and stay."

Reaper didn't say a word, only looking at him silently.

"I can't," Elliott said quietly. "I'm truly flattered, but…"

"I know."

The two men sat there for several minutes, not saying a word before Reaper sighed heavily.

"What is your take on the team?"

"They are fracturing," Elliott said honestly. "Inferno is a mess, and I'm glad he is flying out with Outfield. He needs to get away and clear his mind."

Reaper nodded, silent.

"Panic is… broken."

"I know," Reaper said in a hushed voice. "I've got something in the works to help him, and I made a few phone calls. I've known Panic for five years, and he arrived here about the same time I did. He's a good man, quiet, trustworthy – but you are right. Something is wrong with him. When Jordan died, it messed up a lot of us, and I think seeing Outfield's plane crash was the straw that broke him."

"I agree."

"Where is he? I haven't seen him today."

"He's getting evaluated."

The other man's tone, body language, and worried look on his face spoke volumes. It didn't take a genius to understand that something was seriously wrong with the quiet pilot who was struggling. Panic's reaction when they'd landed had even alarmed him – which was why he hurriedly got him away from the others. Everyone had moments where they felt broken, but you had to have a safe place to turn, and being surrounded by coworkers watching you have a breakdown wasn't it.

"Oh…"

"Yeah," Reaper muttered and looked at him. "We aren't discussing any of this – got it?"

"I figured as much," Elliott agreed quickly. "Piranha could handle the team – but only if Cavalier wasn't here. I think he would subconsciously undermine her without realizing it."

"Scarecrow?"

"Not leadership material... and something is going on with him."

"Bubbles? Teflon?"

"No sir – neither. If you were choosing from the current team, Cavalier is your person – or Piranha. Both have rank, both are strong, both would do good, but if I had to choose, I would pick Piranha."

"Despite Cavalier and his reaction?"

"Yes," Elliott said bluntly. "Or have a very blunt heart-to-heart with the man off the record."

"I see."

"Three months?"

"Yes, sir."

"Dismissed," Reaper nodded and picked up the sheet of paper from Elliott, looked at it, and slid it into the folder on his desk. He realized that the man actually *did* have his personnel file there and swallowed again nervously, sincerely afraid that maybe he was making a mistake.

Heading down the hallway toward the communications room, he was intent on emailing Sarah and wished it was later in the evening so he could call instead. He was a jumble of nerves – but staying would mean only seeing Sarah occasionally. If he stayed in the Air Force, the entire family would need to be picked up and moved to wherever he got stationed next, and he couldn't do that to the kids. They'd had enough upheaval in their lives already.

Logging in, Elliott saw he had an email from her and

clicked on it immediately, feeling a sinking sensation in his gut as he read.

What things were in motion?

Had something happened back home?

That couldn't be it, because her email that fateful day about David had a completely different tone to it. This was secretive. Like she wanted to say something and couldn't.

He hesitated and felt a bead of sweat run down his back, wondering if she was having second thoughts about him coming home – because the cat was out of the bag already. No, he needed to talk to her and find out what it was – and fought the urge to sprint back toward Reaper's office to get his resignation letter from him. It had taken a lot to make that step, and he didn't want to do it again.

> *Dear Sarah,*
> *Sounds good – I will call your cell phone at nine o'clock your time. I'm not going to lie, you have me a bit worried but I was planning on calling anyhow because I needed to hear your voice.*
> *Love,*
> *Elliott*

SEVERAL HOURS LATER, Elliott walked back into the communications room and saw Inferno was on the phone with someone, his head tucked down and whispering for privacy. Panic was also there, sitting on the phone, and it looked like he was near tears. Without a word, he grabbed a few napkins off the counter where the coffee pot was and handed them to Panic, patting him on the back silently as the other man looked up, nodding gratefully.

"I understand," Panic whispered, nodding… and hung up

the phone as Elliott picked up his own receiver, preparing to dial.

"Are you okay?"

"I hope so," the quiet man began and hesitated, glancing at him. "Thank you, Copperhead... for everything."

"It's nothing," Elliott said warily, setting down the receiver again and watching him.

Something was wrong.

"Panic... are you okay?"

"No," he admitted, looking up and giving a nervous laugh that caused even Inferno to look up in concern. "I'm being discharged and flying out in a few days... that was my ride from the airport."

Elliott didn't know what to say. The man looked bewildered, shell-shocked, and a little relieved all at the same time. He was at least talking without crying now, and starting to resemble a little more of his old self. Plus, how did you say 'sorry' – when he was leaving, too?

Instead, he got to his feet and held out his hand.

"It's been an honor to fly with you, brother," he began hoarsely and saw the understanding, acknowledgment, and shy pride in the other man's face as he shook his hand.

"I should be ashamed... but I'm relieved."

"Why should you be ashamed? There's nothing wrong with putting yourself and your mental well-being first. You've given everything in the line of duty and have the chance to take a break. There is zero shame in that – and anyone who says differently should try walking a mile in any soldier's shoes."

"Amen to that," Cavalier said from the doorway. "'Sup, 'girls'..."

Elliott was about to open his mouth and say something when Inferno beat him to it. The dark-haired man's head was still bent down for privacy, but there was no mistaking who he was addressing with the foul words that came out of his mouth. Panic let out a nervous bark of laughter as Cavalier's eyes grew wide in shock.

"Oh man," Inferno said, wincing and laying a hand on his chest. "Dang, I've got indigestion, Elana – and a bunch of nosy company. Can I call you again on Saturday? I'll wear something sexy for you."

"You are on a phone, knucklehead," Teflon said, sliding into the room and plopping down into the chair right beside Inferno – who glared at him.

"And one more cause of indigestion just decided to sit next to me. Is there no privacy in this world? Sheesh!" Inferno growled hotly and then turned away, speaking on the phone in a cutesy-baby voice. "Have a great day at work. Go sharpen your claws, my little kitten. Right meow."

"Oh, I think I'm gonna barf…"

"Did he just… *meow*?"

"What the heck am I listening to?"

All five men looked at each other at that moment before three of them burst out laughing, Panic looked morose, and Inferno looked livid.

"Just wait until you fall for some chick!" the man snapped, slapping Teflon on the back of the head as he walked past him. "When it happens to you, and she owns your 'stuff' – you'll be making all sorts of stupid kissy faces, calling her dumb nicknames, and doing baby talk, too. Outfield knows – you should see him talking about his wife! The man practically oozes rainbows and glitter."

"*Masculine* glitter," Outfield interjected, walking into the room and smiling. "And shut up, Inferno. You were the one talking about 'bro-code,' or don't you remember?"

"*Arrrghhh…* never mind. All of you are a bunch of smart-alecks!" the man growled, throwing his hands in the air and walking off in sheer frustration. He stormed out into the hallway, yelling 'move!' at someone in the distance before Elliott sat back down in his chair, meeting Cavalier's eyes.

"He realizes that *he* is the smart-alecky one, right?"

"Inferno is just letting off steam," Elliott shrugged, picking up the phone to dial Sarah once more – only to hear Panic speak softly in a hushed whisper of awareness.

"That's not him. Nothing bothers him…"

"What do you mean?" Cavalier began before anyone else could speak, surprising him. That was a good sign of a mentor, and maybe they were all wrong about him taking over after Reaper had left the Air Force. Perhaps this man had what it would take but needed to grow up.

"He's definitely rattled, but this is different… and I've seen him at his worst."

"You mean, 'in the showers'?" Cavalier laughed openly and bumped his knuckles against Teflon's.

Nope, never mind - spoke much too soon, he thought silently, biting the inside of his cheek and trying desperately to ignore them as he dialed Sarah's phone number, picking up on the second ring.

"Hello? Sarah?" – and immediately heard someone mocking him. Glancing up, holding the phone to his head, he heard her soft voice as he snapped angrily at the men around him. "Shut up and find something to do – or get out of here…"

"Elliott?"

"Sorry, love. I'm just surrounded by men acting like children…"

"Hey, it's okay. I'm taking my ten-minute break at work so I've got a little time to talk away from the counter. How are you? How have you been?"

"I should be asking you that… especially with your email. What's going on, Sarah. I don't have long, remember?"

"Elliott," her voice cracked slightly as she spoke his name, and he felt a spike of dread in his chest at her thick voice. Was she crying? "Elliott, we're going to need to remodel the garage."

"What?" he uttered, completely confused. "Remodel the garage? Why? What's wrong with the garage?"

"Well, we're going to need another bedroom in the house."

"Why? I mean, that's fine, but I don't…" he paused mid-sentence and heard her tearful laugh as she realized something had short-circuited in his head. "Sarah, wait, are we… *are we going to have a baby?*"

"Yes," she said emotionally, and he was melting as tears stung his eyes, laughing with her on the phone in exuberant joy.

"Really? Already? You're pregnant and we're going to have a baby together – *you and me?* You know it's probably going to be red-headed, right?" he joked openly, his voice trembling and blindly accepting a paper towel to wipe his eyes as he realized he was crying. His hands were trembling with emotion as he was overcome with the idea. "I'm going to be a daddy… again?"

"Have I mentioned how much I love the fact that you consider the children yours already? I couldn't ask for a better second chance at being happy than sharing my life with you."

"I'm not David…"

"No, you are my very own Elliott," she began, and he heard the tears in her own voice as she spoke. "You are my best friend, my love, and my soulmate. I loved David, but loving you is as different as the children are. Uniquely special and just as precious."

"Okay, if I wasn't utterly crazy about you before… those words just hit me hard," he joked tearfully, feeling his friends patting him on the back and offering their congratulations. "I'm a mess, and it's been a day."

"What's happened?"

"First off, we are definitely remodeling the garage – in three months."

"Oh?"

"I'm getting out and coming home," Elliott said openly, not caring who heard him. He had no secrets and was over-joyed at the fact that he would be there when their child arrived. The chorus of exclamations around him at the jaw-dropping announcement, followed by his own, had to be surprising to the team… but he didn't care.

This moment, this very second, was his entire world – Sarah.

He never imagined or expected Sarah to want a *fifth* child, much less for it to happen so quickly. A part of him assumed maybe this had been just desperation talking because it was right when he was getting ready to leave her side and return to Afghanistan. He was expecting her to say that she wasn't pregnant and that she'd had a second chance to consider things because having another baby was a lot to deal with.

"Oh, Elliott…" she whispered, openly weeping. "I was hoping you would say that and not change your mind. I was so scared to tell you but knew I couldn't hide this."

"Honey," he began, feeling himself falling apart once again. "Don't ever be afraid to tell me something – especially when it's a blessing like this. I'm here for us, our family, no matter how big it gets. I love you – more than anything in the world, and I want to be there when our baby is born."

"I want this too."

"I'm going to take the other job. We can figure out the bills, and we'll make it work somehow. It's going to be okay," he said openly, knowing she was still paying on things from

David's funeral. He'd seen the envelopes on the counter, knowing she would share when she was ready.

"No regrets?" she breathed, and he heard a high-pitched hiccup from her tears, breaking his heart. His sweet girl had always gotten hiccups after crying, making him treasure all over again what a gift this was to know her all these years and finally be able to admit his feelings, his love for her.

"Shhh, my love," he said, not holding back. "No regrets except that I'm not there to celebrate with you. We can celebrate in three months with our whole family. Maybe we'll surprise the girls with some baby doll clothes and…"

"Oh gosh," she muttered, laughing. "Stop or you are going to make me cry again. You are such a sweet man – and the kids already know."

"I'm *your* man – and always will be," he paused. "Is that why you mentioned the remodel? Let me guess, they were already arguing about who has to share a bedroom with the new baby…"

"I love you," she answered, laughing openly.

"I love you too, Sarah," he chuckled, feeling himself tearing up again at the idea of them having their own child, something he never thought would ever happen despite the joy in making it. "Thank you for telling me and I'm so excited."

"Me too."

"My calling card is…" and the line went dead, causing him to sigh in awareness and disgust. He hated calling cards. They were more frustrating than anything. The brief ten minutes of happiness always left him gutted for hours, and today was no different.

Sarah was going to have his baby.

Their baby.

His legacy.

He always assumed the Trent name would die out

because he was the last in his family and when he'd talked with Paradox that fateful day, the man had brought up about her possibly never wanting a fifth child. Four was a lot to handle sometimes and…

"What the heck, dude?" came a voice, causing him to look up and interrupting his thoughts – only to see several smiling faces watching him. "Five kids?"

Inferno was back – and standing among Cavalier, Bubbles, Teflon, Axis, and several others. They were all watching him, standing there and smiling, only to see Scarecrow's smile fade.

Piranha pushed her way through the crowd of guys, muttering 'coming through' several times. Cavalier stepped back, smirking and looking down at the shorter woman who was his wingman.

"Excuse me, miss…" Cavalier taunted, causing Piranha to wink at him, laughing and moving to take a seat at one of the computers.

"Congratulations 'Papa Copperhead,'" she said easily and looked back toward the doorway. "Are y'all just going to stand there, or did I cut the line for the computers?"

"You can do anything you want, Captain," Cavalier drawled, crossing his arms – and Scarecrow muttered something under his breath walking off.

"Well, somebody's a little pissy tonight," Inferno joked.

"You?" Teflon retorted.

"I swear your call sign shoulda been Hillbilly because those front teeth are coming out - *by me* - one of these days…"

"Fellas," Bubbles said quietly. "Please don't start… Panic? Hey Panic, you okay?" The other man disappeared into the hallway after the other pilot who was leaving them tomorrow.

"So you are really leaving?" Piranha said quietly, watching him. "Even though we all know you are up for Reaper's post."

"Oh, I want to hear this," Cavalier said, plopping down in the chair beside Piranha – who rolled her eyes.

"Yes," Elliott began and looked at them both – hard. "Command was a goal, but not anymore. If either of you are trying for it, you both need a wake-up call."

"Excuse me?" she retorted in surprise, staring at him.

"I didn't stutter," Elliott said bluntly, tensing and waiting for the temperamental woman to lash out. "As someone in charge, you better be able to accept people having a difference of opinion or being able to challenge you. Being in charge isn't about leadership – and that is where you both struggle."

"What the…" Cavalier started laughing, sticking his thumb sideways. "You believe this guy?"

"Hush," Piranha said bluntly, not looking away from Elliott. "Continue."

"Leadership is about building a team, creating a bond where people want to follow you… right now, you both are struggling," he said openly, hoping they would actually hear him – and Elliott suddenly understood why Reaper had been talking to him. He understood what was needed.

They didn't.

"You think this is about being the top dog, being in control, or having nobody question you – but being a leader is about growing your team, listening to them, wanting them to succeed, and helping them when they falter. Have either of you asked about Panic? Outfield? Asked why Inferno is in such a bad mood? Do either of you care?" Elliott said painfully, his voice shaking in frustration as he clenched his fists, nearly pleading with the two that stood the best chance to take over.

"A leader trains, helps, mentors… but that only happens if

they listen and respect you – and right now, they don't. They watch you, they stay away from you, and you don't make an effort to get to know any of the other pilots. You make smart remarks, you isolate yourself, and you have the rank. But that's it."

You could have heard a pin drop at that moment.

"I feel sorry for you, because you should understand all of this by now – and you don't. I don't know what is wrong, or broken in your head, but this isn't a one-man... or one-woman show. Those are our brothers, our friends, our wing-men, and a family – and you should want to be a part of that family. That squadron, that team, *deserves* better than you two."

And he heard a slow applause, causing all three heads to turn toward the door only to see Reaper standing there, leaning against the doorframe. The quiet man stood there, looking at Elliott, but spoke to the pair that he'd just been addressing.

"A leader takes others under his wing, lifting them and encouraging them to be better versions of themselves," Reaper said quietly. "You would do well to learn from Copperhead's example – because he is trying to do just that by giving you both some 'tough love.'"

They sat there silently.

Elliott knew that Reaper was waiting to see who would try to argue with him, try to say something different, or challenge what he said. He was testing them – all of them – and knew the man had come to find him to ask him once more to stay.

"Copperhead would make an excellent squadron commander," Reaper said openly and gave him a slow nod. "But an even more impressive father."

Elliott pressed his lips together, swallowing emotionally, as he realized that the man was going to let him go and understood. He was complimenting him before the others while laying the groundwork to see who would excel in the end.

"I wanted to tell you 'Congratulations' when Inferno stopped me in the hall to share the good news. How about a cup of coffee, and we can talk?"

"I would like that, sir."

Reaper looked at Cavalier and Piranha, giving them a sharp nod, and hesitated. He glanced at Elliott once more, then to the two of them, and opened his mouth, paused, and then spoke once more.

"Some of the guys are playing spades in the commissary."

"Thank you, sir," Piranha said quietly, getting to her feet and looking at Elliott, nodding. "And thank you for the advice. I appreciate it."

Cavalier stood and looked at Elliott, gave him a simple nod, and extended his hand. He clasped it and shook his hand – only to meet the other man's eyes.

"Thank you – and I think I needed to hear that. You are right, and I have a lot of things to work on," Cavalier said in a humble voice. "And Reaper's right – you are going to make a helluva father."

"I already have four amazing children," Elliott smiled and nodded. "But thank you, and that means a lot… now go show this man to our brothers – and watch Inferno."

"Why?"

"He cheats at cards," Elliott grinned as Cavalier laughed openly. "Watch his sleeve if he fidgets, or he'll reach down and itch his ankle. He doesn't know that I know, but it's sure funny to watch him try to be slick about it."

Cavalier nodded and started to walk out of the communications room – only to have Reaper stop him, smirking.

"Scarecrow, too. If he coughs, watch him when he tucks his head down to cover his mouth. It's one of his 'tells,'… but let him keep playing because when he thinks he's got the upper hand, he'll spill his guts and talk about his personal life. The guy is worth getting to know better – I promise."

"Thank you, sir."

Elliott smiled, realizing that Reaper looked almost relieved.

"I hope I wasn't speaking out of line."

"Actually, that was perfect," Reaper replied, nodding and chuckling. "You sure I can't talk you into staying?"

"Nope."

"Dang... well, how about that coffee then? Sophie mailed me a box of homemade cookies."

"Now you are talking – and when you get back home, Reaper, we'll have to go have a beer or maybe grab a burger."

"I'd like that – and call me Ryan. We're off of work, right?"

"Elliott... and yeah, we are."

Reaper laid a hand on his shoulder, smiling at him, as they started down the hallway toward the barracks and offices in the distance.

"*Five* kids, really?"

Elliott laughed.

CHAPTER 26

SARAH

"I'M ON MY WAY..." Firefly barked into the phone, almost in a panic and she could hear Melody in the background, snapping at him.

"Will you slow down? This baby isn't going to eject from my hoo-ha, okay?! Seriously – SLOW DOWN NOW!"

"You're leaking on the floorboard!"

"You're about to leak – *from your nose* – if you wreck this car with our daughter in it!"

"Aww Mel..." she heard him say placatingly as a groan was heard in the background. "Sarah – we are on the way with Betsy, and Melody is in labor."

"I kinda got that," Sarah chuckled, trying not to laugh at the panicking man who was going through this for the first time. David had been a nervous wreck and had driven through the streets with his lights and sirens flashing, only for her first delivery to take fourteen hours. They had plenty of time and she was pretty sure Melody did too.

"I'll meet you…" her voice trailed off as she saw head-lights pulling into the driveway. "Oh, you're here?"

The phone clicked, and she walked out the front door, seeing Melody's grimace as she waved from the passenger seat before giving her a silent thumbs-up. Firefly was pulling Betsy out of the car, booster seat and all, carrying the entire thing to the front door.

Betsy looked confused.

Melody looked utterly frustrated.

Firefly was on the edge of panic – and she didn't have the heart to laugh at the entire scene unfolding before her. Instead, she pointed at the concrete, making him set the seat down and grabbed his arm.

"Are you okay to drive?"

"Yeah, why?"

"You seem… stressed."

"I've really got to go get Melody to…"

"Breathe, Firefly," Sarah ordered firmly and saw his worried gaze. "She needs to be able to rely on you right now – so falling apart and panicking is not going to help her… or you."

He nodded, looking like he was ready to vomit on his shoes – and she continued.

"Melody's going to need you to be calm, advocate for her, and comfort her. I guarantee she is worrying about you, Betsy, and the baby. Don't add to her stress – take them from her by being the man she loves."

"I'm good," he said hoarsely, nodding. "I'm cool. This is fine. Everything is fine – a dumpster fire, but it's my dump-ster, and I kinda love it…"

Sarah couldn't help it – she laughed.

Firefly grinned.

"Don't tell Mel I said that… and I'm good."

"Go," she smiled. "Take your time, and Betsy can spend the night here. She'll be just fine – but text me a photo later of the baby."

"You aren't coming up to the hospital?"

"With five children in tow? No – and my car won't seat that many."

"You're gonna have to fix that."

"Tell me about it," she chuckled pointedly. "Now, go – she's giving you the stink eye."

Betsy looked groggy, and Sarah was really glad it was the weekend. She was off work tomorrow, the kids had no school, and nobody had to get up early unless they wanted to. No, it was a perfect time for this to all be happening.

Leaning down, she unbuckled Betsy from the car seat and scooped up the little girl, who immediately hugged her.

"Where's my Daddy?" Betsy yawned.

"Mommy is going to have her baby, and you are going to play with the kids. It will be so much fun, and they are excited to see you," she began, tugging the car seat into the house with one hand while carrying Betsy with the other arm awkwardly. "Can you walk, and we'll go find…"

"LESLIEEEEE…" Betsy let out a shriek, suddenly wide awake as she spotted Leslie, and Bethany wasn't far behind. Henry was now crying from the playpen, and Morgan was sitting on the couch with his dinosaur book, looking quite peeved.

"All right everyone, let's settle down…"

"Did you bring your dolly?"

"Do you want some raisins?"

"My mommy is having a baby…"

"My mommy is going to have a baby too."

"She is? Her belly isn't puffy like my mommy's…"

"Your mama's belly is big like a ball…"

"Great – I'm surrounded and outnumbered," Morgan grumbled in frustration, adjusting his seat and sighing loudly. "Can y'all be quiet?"

"Morgan is a doo-doo head sometimes… just ignore him."

"Leslie, don't say that."

"Doo-doo-head," Bethany immediately began, and Betsy joined in, chanting. "Doo-doo-head, doo-doo-head…"

"MOMMMMMM?!"

"I'm on it, Morgan - girls, stop it – now."

Henry was still crying from his seat in the swing, his lip curled in a downward 'U' and wobbling as fat tears rolled down his cheeks. Sarah looked at the children arguing, her son talking over her as she tried to get the girls to quit chanting and screaming competitively to see who was the loudest.

Morgan stomped off angrily and slammed his door, which only caused Henry to be even more upset. The cries were now wails as the three little girls started laughing at each other, shrieking, and throwing pillows around the room, pretending the floor was lava.

"I must be insane…" Sarah grimaced, realizing that five children felt very overwhelming right now.

Dearest Elliott,

Well, it's been an interesting day to say the least.

Firefly and Melody had a baby girl at three in the morning. Liberty Sutton Grainger was nearly ten pounds but both Mom & Dad are doing well. They texted a photo of the baby. She's beautiful, and they both look so proud. I cannot wait to see our little one!

I'm sipping on my coffee, waiting for the kids to wake up and World War Three to start again. Morgan actually said he was 'outnumbered' last night – and was furious about it, which got me thinking... if we are finishing the garage, how about we make it our own bedroom?

We can put it together like we want and everything would be our own, plus it would give us a chance to spread the children out some. What do you think? It would also split the house and give us a little more privacy – and I'm really liking that idea, Handsome. In fact, the more I think about it, the happier I am with it.

Are you calling this weekend?

I miss your voice.

Love,

Sarah

SARAH'S PHONE rang two hours later, and she already knew who it was.

"Hello?"

"I missed your voice too," Elliott said tenderly. "I was going to call tomorrow, but I figured I would go ahead since I got the sweetest email in the world from my beloved wife."

"Oh yeah?" she chuckled, her very soul sighing in happiness.

"When a man is told by his gorgeous wife that she wants privacy, to fix up their bedroom, and cannot wait to see their baby… yeah, she gets whatever the heck she wants."

Both laughed softly for a moment before Elliott continued.

"I'm serious, my love. Pick out whatever paint you want, if you want wallpaper, a ceiling fan, whatever your heart desires… and I will make it happen."

"Do you think it's a good idea to have the house split like that – or should we remain…"

"No, it was a brilliant thought," he interrupted so fast it made her smile. "I want some time to ourselves, and the kids are going to want space. We can tell them that the toys do not pass the hallway, thus keeping the toys out of the living room."

"I didn't think about that."

"Sexy and smart... eh?"

"Oh yeah," she agreed easily. "I might go look at paint, but I have a few months to pick out something, plus Betsy is still here at the house."

"Can I impress you?"

"You always do..."

"Guess who has three weeks of PTO still on the books..." Elliott drawled, almost flirting as he whispered to her. "This guy, who misses his wife terribly and is coming home in two months instead of three."

"I am seriously impressed," she whispered, feeling her heart thump wildly in her chest in awareness.

"And that's not all."

"I'm not sure how much more I can take."

"I already bought my ticket and fly in at six in the evening. It will be such a shame to get home in time to have dinner, play with the kids, and then quickly tuck them into bed."

"Well, you have this all planned out, don't you?"

"I'm trying, wife," he chuckled. "I'm really trying."

"That sounds like a spectacular plan, and in two more months, I'll be showing..."

"Stop with the dirty talk," he protested hoarsely. "Do you know how much I have been fantasizing about what your body will look like when you are pregnant?"

"You'll get to see it too, flyboy..."

"Oh mercy, Sarah – I seriously love you, woman."

"I'm counting the days 'til you get home."

"Speaking of counting?"

"Yeah, I will not miss these calling cards…" she said flatly. "Cramping my style with you."

"We'll be done soon enough."

They said their goodbyes just as Morgan walked out of his bedroom, rubbing his eyes and looking at her.

"Henry is up and playing in his crib. Do you want me to try getting him?"

Sarah smiled and got up, taking her son's hand.

"Let me show you how to let down the side of his bed, but if you get him out before I am up, then you are responsible for watching him. That means making sure he doesn't get hurt or pick up something off the floor and put it in his mouth. Do you think you are ready?"

"I can do that," he nodded. "He's my brother, and we guys have to stick together."

"I figured you'd say that," she chuckled, hugging him around the shoulders as she ruffled his head.

SARAH SPENT the next few months picking out a few things for their room as well as planning on painting the children's bedrooms once everything was settled. She was so excited, looking so forward to having her husband coming home, that she felt they were setting up housekeeping for the first time together… and realized it kind of was like that for him.

Elliott had always 'lived' out of his duffel bag… but those days were done.

He was coming home.

CHAPTER 27

COPPERHEAD

Thumper,

I spoke with Sarah and already turned in my resignation to Reaper. I am coming home within three months and will need that job you mentioned. Let's start looking for a small plane for me to purchase.

Can you recommend an electrician? I need to get some stuff done at the house right away, and I'm not sure who to call in town.

I appreciate the help, the offer, and the fact that you all have welcomed us into your world with open arms. Thank you for that – because it's made something terrifying, not quite so overwhelming.

Copperhead

TEN WEEKS LATER...

ELLIOTT WAS WALKING down the aisle toward baggage claim and heard a series of voices screaming 'Daddy' in the distance – and nearly stumbled. His nose burned, and his throat instantly had a lump, as he looked up to see Morgan, Leslie, and Bethany standing there, each holding a red, white, or blue balloon. Even Henry had one tied to his wrist to keep him occupied in the stroller. Sarah was standing there, waving happily and crying. Her hand was over her mouth, and he could see the love shining in her eyes.

And melted.

Oh gosh, he was undone when it came to that woman.

He ran down the rest of the walkway, kissing her immediately before kneeling to hug the children. They'd grown so much in that short time, and all he could keep thinking was, 'It's over'. He loved his job in the Air Force and wasn't leaving it with bitterness or hatred – but rather with pride, recognition of the training he'd received, and gratitude for every moment because it brought him *here*.

"Hey…" he chuckled tearfully, looking up at Sarah again as three sets of arms clung to him, hugging him once more. "I missed you all so much."

"We missed you," Sarah choked out, wiping her eyes before laughing. "Sorry. I'm a mess and…"

"You are freakin' beautiful, woman," he interrupted, standing quickly to kiss her as he laid his hand on her stomach. "I love this so much."

"You just wait," she smiled at him, causing his own to widen in awareness.

"Oh yeah?"

"I have plans for you, mister…"

"I can't wait," he whispered intimately – and heard a gagging sound.

"Oh gosh, why are people always making googly eyes at each other and being all kissy? If this is what grown-up people do, it's gross," Morgan grimaced and put his finger in his mouth, gagging.

Elliott and Sarah looked at each other in wide-eyed surprise before bursting out laughing causing Henry to shriek with excitement as he coughed out a fake laugh.

"I think it's nice how Daddy looks at Mommy…"

"You would…"

"Don't be a poo-poo head…"

"Mom told you not to say that, Bethany!"

"Doodie-poodie-poo-poo," the girl mocked, and Elliott couldn't help the laughter that bubbled up from within him as he looked at Sarah – who shrugged.

"Were we ever that little?"

"We didn't know each other yet."

"Doodie-poodie-poo-poo?" he questioned, grinning, before he winked at her. "Man, it sure would be a shame to have to listen to the kids fight and call each other names when I just got home. I was thinking we could get Happy Meals for dinner, but only if they are good. Have they been good for you today, Sarah?"

Elliott fought the urge to look at the kids and held Sarah's gaze as her lips trembled and eyes danced.

"You're a twerp, you know that?" she whispered.

"Oh, I know," he chuckled. "Always have been."

"Yup."

"Have the kids been good?"

"Mama, pleassseeee? – We've been good, and I won't say that again."

"Liar…"

"Shush-up, Morgan!"

"You shush, Bethany!"

"Does it make me a bad dad," he began whispering to her as he held his beloved wife's gaze. "If I want to get Happy Meals anyway – and just go home so we can be alone?"

"Not at all."

"Live to fight another fight – and all that jazz?"

"Exactly," she smiled. "I love you, and I'm so glad you are here."

"Me too," he admitted. "Despite the arguing, there is nowhere else I'd rather be."

"I hope you always think that."

"I always will," he said, lacing his fingers with hers. "Let's go home."

They walked out of the airport together and Elliott pushed the stroller that Henry was sitting in as the children jumped and danced around them, still arguing and bickering slightly, challenging each other. He really didn't want to get upset with them because he'd just come home – and one thing that meant a lot to him was for them to be able to stand up for themselves, to hold their ground, or be able to feel a certain way. He was raised to be strong in his own self-worth and wanted to impart that to the kids, no matter how hard or annoying it could be.

And paused, looking at the station wagon.

"We're getting another car," he said, looking at her. "A second one. We're going to need something bigger and…"

"I know," she smiled. "I found a minivan I really like and told the dealership we'd be by to look at it later this week."

"Why didn't you get it?"

"Because it's a big purchase, and I'm not doing that without talking to you," she hesitated. "We've done nothing but worry about the future, money, what comes next, and such… you think I want to throw a wrench in the works?"

"Sarah – honey – we need something that seats seven."

"Or eight," she muttered under her breath.

"WHAT?!" Elliott sagged against the silver car beside hers as he stared at her stomach. "Are we having…t-twins?"

"No, but I'm not sure I'm ready to be done," she smiled at him shyly and looked at the kids. "Y'all get in your seats and buckle up, please."

"W-What's going on?" he stammered, staring at her as Sarah leaned toward him and whispered in his ear.

"I kinda like making babies with you… and that smile does a number on me. Maybe we'll have two little Trents before we are done having children, okay? I'm on the fence and definitely want to discuss it once more."

And then she licked his earlobe.

His brain shut down in an instant. Elliott had heard of the 'blue screen of death' on computers but just experienced it physically from the simplest touch from his gorgeous wife. She looked at him, and his knees went weak, but hearing her words and having her make advances at him?

He cursed swiftly under his breath.

"You can have whatever you want," he uttered baldly, feeling his heart thumping wildly and his pulse racing just by the look she gave him. "I'll get a second or third job…"

"To pay for that bar of soap, Daddy…" Morgan jeered happily from the car. "I heard that, and I don't think that's an okay word to use."

"It's not," they said in unison – and shared a smile.

"My apologies, Sarah. That was a very bad word to use, and I'll get my bar of soap when I get home."

"Apology accepted," she said politely and leaned toward him once more – as Elliott braced himself. "You can say *and do* it later, Sexy."

Ten minutes later, he wished he owned stock in Ivory soap.

He was standing in the kitchen, leaning over the sink to

keep from gagging. He had the soap in his mouth for nearly five minutes in front of the kids to make a point, and Sarah watched him, her eyes dancing at the self-inflicted torture to make sure the kids didn't repeat the foul word that slipped from him mindlessly.

His wife was the hottest creature in the universe to him – and just seeing that soft, knowing smile, watching her move about the kitchen as she explained to the kids how you weren't supposed to say words like that, was all in support of his decision to stand there with the soap and silently reminding him.

"We don't say words like that... because they are filthy words," she said breathlessly, meeting his eyes. "Such terms are... vulgar, nasty, and... mercy. Is it warm in the house?"

Elliott smiled around the soap bar – and winked at her.

"I think that's enough," she said quietly.

"Nuh-uh," Morgan chimed in knowingly. "He said it two times. Does that mean if I say it – I should say it several times, cause I only get in trouble once?"

Elliott grunted and shook his head, glaring at them firmly.

"Nope," she translated. "You don't say it at all, and your dad is going to suffer through his punishment... *like a bad boy.*"

He leaned over the sink and whimpered audibly, hearing Sarah laugh in awareness. It had been almost four months since they were alone, and he'd already shared that he couldn't wait to see her belly swollen with his child. The thought of rubbing lotion on those sexy stretchmarks had filled his dreams for weeks now.

And heard the timer on the microwave beep.

He spat out the soap, turned, and looked at her.

"All right kids – hop into bed. We've got some work to do tomorrow on a big family project, and I'll need your help."

"Are you sure?" Sarah said innocently, smirking at him.

"Don't even..." he growled, "I'm not putting that soap back in my mouth..." Just as she opened her mouth – he interrupted her.

"And do not say what I think you are about to... please."

She laughed knowingly, scooping up Henry and ushering the kids back to their bedrooms. The moment they were gone, he walked back to the bathroom to brush his teeth and get the soap taste out of his mouth. It wasn't but a few moments when he heard the children calling for him to tuck them in, and loved it.

As he stepped into the hallway, Sarah glided past him and touched his hip, causing him to grab her wrist as he smiled at her.

"You like playing with fire, don't you?" he whispered knowingly.

"Maybe..."

"Sarah..."

"Go tuck them in," she murmured and reached up to trace his jaw before meeting his eyes. "Then come tuck me in..."

"Troublemaker," he breathed, feeling his heart skip a beat. "You just want me to have to stand there with the soap again, don't you?"

"I'd rather you didn't... did I mention I have cocoa butter lotion on my nightstand for my tummy?"

"Arghhh..."

"Go," she chuckled, winking at him. "I'll see you in two."

"At this rate, it's only gonna take twenty seconds," he muttered – and heard her soft laughter wrap around his spine like a caress.

Elliott darted into both bedrooms, hugging, kissing, and listening patiently as possible to each child as they shared with him what was going on in their lives. He was *trying* to listen, *trying* to pay attention, but he could hear Sarah humming softly in the distance – distracting him.

"G'night, Daddy," Bethany finally finished, and he kissed her cheek, pulled up her sheets, and stood up to leave the room – only to smell something. Something sweet…?

He peeked in on Morgan and Henry and moved Henry's scrunchy teether to the side of the crib away from his serene face, marveling at how peaceful the baby was sleeping, before walking into the hallway… and pausing. Looking to the left, he saw Sarah walk past the bedroom door and saw the candle glow in the distance as something snapped in his brain.

Pivoting on his heel, he began to walk, then stride down the long hallway, shoving the bedroom door open and seeing her delighted smile in the distance as she stood there in an Air Force T-shirt and a pair of stretchy shorts. Forget the lingerie, his wife had never been sexier than she was now, seeing that sweet belly poking out from her shirt.

"Ready for your debriefing, flyboy…" she said suggestively – and he was a goner.

Elliott crossed the room in seconds flat. He picked her up and began kissing her, and hesitated – walking back toward the door he'd forgotten to close… only to see Bethany standing there rubbing her eyes.

He set Sarah down and knelt before the little girl whose lip wobbled.

"Hey, my little Raisinette… what's wrong, sweetie?"

"Are you gonna be here when I wake up?"

"Forever and ever," he promised, his heart melting as he glanced up at Sarah whose eyes were glistening with love. "You are stuck with me."

Bethany nodded.

"Can I have another hug?"

"Of course," he chuckled. "I might have two or three hugs

for you," he said, scooping her up and carrying her back to bed. "C'mon and let's get you tucked in because Daddy cannot wait to have his special eggs in the morning."

Bethany giggled as he lay her back down in the bed and tickled her tummy for a brief second before smiling. "You get some rest, and I'll be here in the morning when you wake up – I promise – but you have to promise me something, okay?"

"Okay," she smiled, nodding vehemently.

"No putting your finger in my mouth," he teased – and saw her shy smile widen. "Deal?"

"Deal."

"I love you, Raisinette."

"I love you too, Daddy."

"Good night," he said softly, kissing her forehead and got up only to see Sarah standing there, watching them. Without a word, he moved toward her, cradling her face in his hands and kissed her tenderly... as they both started to walk awkwardly to their room once more, neither wanting to stop.

This time, he shut and locked the door, turning to look at her and smiling.

"Now about that debriefing..." he chuckled intimately. "Is that still on the table?"

"Table, bed, whatever you want," Sarah grinned, winking at him. "But someone promised me a belly rub to say 'hello'..."

"Oh, that's absolutely happening – along with a very intense debriefing."

Both began to laugh at the play on words, welcoming him back home as they held each other, kissing and treasuring this newfound beginning of their lives together before admiring the life growing within her. It wasn't just about the sex but rather sharing of their souls together.

Elliott spent hours rubbing her stomach, talking about

the baby, about what happened with Outfield, his fears for Panic, and the quiet man's reaction. Unburdening his mind and soul, he shared what he thought of the two potential candidates and even discussed the job at Flyboys as Reaper relayed it to him via his friend Valkyrie.

And bless her – Sarah always listened.

She paid attention, talked with him, and made jokes and comments that drew a laugh from him when he needed one so badly. He craved this closeness, this bond between them, because this wasn't just the love of his life – but his best friend and always had been.

He was home.

ELLIOTT AWOKE GROGGILY the next morning to hear someone knocking loudly on the bedroom door, and the front door.

"What the…" he muttered, yanking on his shorts and a t-shirt as Sarah sat up in confusion. "Stay there, my love."

He opened the bedroom door to see four sets of eyes looking up at him in alarm. Morgan had Henry sitting in his lap, Bethany was cradling her dolly, and Leslie was wringing her hands.

"Someone's knocking, and Mama told me not to answer the door unless it was the police. I didn't see a police car when I peeked out the window," Morgan blurted out in alarm.

"You did the right thing, son…" he said openly and touched his head, hearing the banging again. "Wait here with your mama."

Elliott padded toward the front door and saw several shadows on the front porch, glancing around and realizing there was nothing near the door as a weapon. They weren't expecting anyone – but someone was obviously there and banging on the door once more.

Yanking it open, his mouth dropped.

"Awwww yeah, my brother!" Firefly grinned, pointing to his shorts. "You feeling better yet? Limping? Having problems getting around ya' old fart?"

"What are you doing here?" Elliott asked bluntly, looking in shock over the smiling faces as Harley waved in the distance and held up a box of donuts.

"I'm guessing both of your cell phones are off?" she began and Elliott felt something touch his back, only to see Sarah right behind him.

"What's going on?" she whispered, looking concerned.

"You said you needed an electrician and were starting on a project," Thumper began and Glory cut him off, causing the man to roll his eyes as his shoulders slumped in defeat.

"So ol' 'Grumpy-Thumpy' got the crew together, and we're all here to help. We do the wiring, the hammering, painting, mending, chatting…"

"She's good at that," Firefly interjected.

"…The plumbing and…"

"But not Valkyrie," Firefly interrupted again pointedly – only to get slapped on the back of the head by the other pilot.

"One leak does not make your plumbing skills bad."

"Niagara Falls coming from the main valve does," Alpo volunteered – and then ducked behind Thumper.

"Did I mention I brought donuts?" Harley chimed in again, looking overly chipper and smiling brightly.

"You're here to… to help?"

"Yes," Thumper began again – and then stepped forward to put his hand over Glory's mouth as Alpo started to pitch a fit. He spoke over them, looking at Elliott as several around them laughed. "When someone is getting started, we help move or set up a house… but you have one, so what do you need, brother?"

"I need you to let go of my wife!" Alpo bit out angrily – and Thumper did, only to pull his wingman and best friend into a headlock.

"I cannot get a word in or finish a sentence sometimes… no offense, Glory, but I'd like to have my moment just like everyone else. Have my back for two seconds, wingman."

"I've always had your back, but don't test that line with my Glory…"

"Understood."

"You're here for my 'project' – even if you don't know what it was?" Elliott laughed nervously, watching this whole display and trying to put it all together… only to have Leslie push past him.

"Betsy!"

And held open the door, realizing that whatever this was – this was happening. Leslie grabbed her friend's hand and pulled her forward, which started people pouring into the house. He turned to Sarah and bent his head toward her.

"Go get dressed, my love… I think I know what this is."

"What's going on?"

"We're getting our bedroom – today."

Sarah's eyes widened in understanding as she nodded – immediately taking off for their room. Elliott knelt before Morgan and smiled at him.

"How do you feel about getting a bigger bedroom, buddy?"

"Me?"

"Privilege of being the oldest," Elliott smiled, ruffling the boy's hair as he stared at him in shock. "Go pick up all your stuff in your room as fast as you can – you and Henry are getting a surprise."

"We're rearranging the bedrooms?" Alpo asked, biting into a donut.

"Yes," Elliott hesitated.

"What about me?" Leslie chimed in.

"I think everyone is going to have a surprise later today… go pick up your things as fast as you can, okay?"

"Me too?" Bethany asked happily.

"Yes – everyone grab a donut, and let's get moving."

"What do you need from us, Copperhead?" Firefly began – and Elliott reached out to shake the man's hand.

"Congratulations on the baby - now that I'm here to be able to say it," he began and smiled. "Sarah and I want to make the garage into a bedroom. We're moving the boys into our room and rearranging everything, putting up a ceiling fan, and a few small things."

"Window or no window?" Valkyrie said bluntly, standing there with his arms crossed over his chest and zero expression on his face.

"What's easier?"

"It's the same either way."

"Window, please…"

"Done," he barked and clapped his hands. "Copperhead – with me. We're going to Home Depot and buying supplies. Alpo, pull all the nails, patch any holes, and let's prep the walls. Firefly, can you install a ceiling fan?"

"You know it."

"Did you bring a ladder?"

"Always," Firefly grinned. "I'm getting used to this stuff."

"Harley, can you handle helping the kids?"

"Of course."

"Houdini, Paradox, Sparky, Ghost, X-Ray… let's dismantle the furniture and empty the rooms so we can paint – I'm assuming we are painting?"

"Yes," Sarah said behind him, surprising Elliott as he

stood and smiled at his wife. He'd told her to do what she wanted – and obviously, she'd already started prepping for this. "I've got several gallons of paint, rollers, and trays ready."

"Then let's get at it," Elliott smiled and hesitated. "Not you, though. Sarah, you need to get out of the house if we are doing construction, painting, or there are fumes. I'm not taking any chances. When the kids have their toys picked up – go spend the day with them somewhere, my love. Take them to the park or anywhere else."

He saw her open her mouth to argue before shutting it.

"Uh-huh," he chuckled. "You know I'm right."

"Hush."

"Have a great time, and we'll handle this."

"How about I rub your back tonight?"

"You're on..." he smiled tenderly and kissed the tip of her nose before holding her gaze. "I really love you, and I'm so glad to be here right now."

"I'm glad you are too."

"Okay, okay," Alpo interrupted, chuckling. "I'm happy that you are both happy – but let's get moving, eh?"

Elliott grinned as he winked at her, before scooping up Henry as he was making his way across the living room carpet to touch Glory's sequined sneakers.

"C'mon little man," he said, scooping up the toddler and blowing raspberries on his cheeks before handing Henry to Sarah. "Mama is taking you out for the day."

"Text me later?"

"I promise."

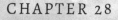

CHAPTER 28

SARAH

SARAH SPENT the day with the children doing all sorts of things. She took Elliott's suggestion and went to the park for a bit, then took them for Happy Meals at McDonald's so they could continue to play… and then went to Walmart. They browsed the aisles, looking at lamps, linens, and wall décor, and each of the children picked out a poster for their room. There was such excitement, so many questions that it was staggering.

And the text messages!

Her phone was blowing up all day long. Text after text, sometimes three or four, from different people, all asking questions about different things – and some of them had her concerned.

Carpet, tile, wood, or are you throwing down a large area rug?

Where?

The Ga-room...

What?

You know... the garage room?

Ohhh – um, whatever is easiest. I mean, it's just a floor to walk on.

Gotcha. I get to pick. Cool!

Wait! What did Elliott say?

Hello?

Helloooo?

Hey Mama-Trentie-poo, the paint you bought was perfect! I love the blue and the swirls it made.

What swirls, Glory?

It's supposed to be a sky blue.

Oh, it's blue and looks so cool – almost like clouds!

Gotta go! Time to paint the girls' room!

Glory – wait – was the blue paint swirled?

Did you mix the paint before you rolled it?

Hello?

Elliott – can you go check the paint? Glory said it had swirls in it

It's fine, my love – I promise.

Okay.

How's it going?

It's going great – but I need to go because we are about to lay the flooring. Alpo said you wanted concrete and you'd put a rug on the floor, but I vetoed that idea. I hope you aren't mad.

He what?

No, I don't want cement floors. I said whatever was easiest.

Okay. We're putting down Pergo so we can walk on it right away.

Thank you

I've always got your back – and always will. You just relax and have some fun today. I'll text you later.

Love you!

Love you too and can I take you up on the backrub tonight?

I'll get some BenGay.

Never thought I'd say this – but I can't wait. LOL.

Hey Sarah – are you okay with custom paint?

More custom than Glory's swirls?

Oh, she told you about that?

Wait – is it really swirled???

Weeeelll... it looks cool – does that help?

Hey Sarah – how mad would you be if I asked you to pick up lamps for your room?

> Sparky, what happened to the ceiling fan I bought?

Um, nothing?

> Why do I need lamps?

Because the sun sets?

> Again – what is wrong with the ceiling fan that is NEW IN THE BOX

I installed it in the wrong bedroom – there! I admitted it!

> Oh.

> I'll get some lamps.

P.S. Your husband is a beast! The man is working hard and gonna be hurting later. I've never seen anyone drive a nail with one hit of the hammer. Between him and Valkyrie, they had the closet built in an hour.

> Closet?

Copperhead said he wanted a walk-in closet for you in the Ga-Room.

> Is everyone calling it a Ga-Room? Hahaha.

YUP!

About seven o'clock, Sarah was worn out, and everyone was fussing. The children were frustrated, tired, bickering like crazy, and she was out of diapers in her diaper bag.

Trying not to snap, she yanked out her phone in the middle of Target and called Elliott.

"Forget this texting garbage…" she muttered and heard him answer.

"Hey Sarah, I was just getting ready to call you…"

"Not snapping – but I need diapers, a stiff drink - *which I cannot have,* and a recliner. I'm coming home whether you are ready or not," she began, rubbing her temple as Bethany began to cry.

"Of course," Elliott began. "I ordered pizzas, and they are on the way. I was just about to call because I think we are finished. All the windows are open to air out the house and I can't wait to see your reaction. We're having everyone over next weekend, and I'm making ribs as a 'Thank you' because this is really something."

"Sounds great. I just need about twenty-four hours of sleep, and I'll be back to my normal self."

"C'mon home, my love… and I'll make sure your recliner is empty."

FIFTEEN MINUTES LATER, Henry was crying in the car, Bethany was sound asleep in her booster seat, Leslie was staring out the window in a daze, and even Morgan was looking like he was about five minutes from falling asleep. Everyone was beat from the busy and exciting day, but Sarah couldn't help her exclamation as she pulled up in front of the house.

"What in the world…"

"Mama, is this the right house?"

"Where's the garage door?"

"What's that big thingie in the truck?"

"The garage door," she whispered in wonder and amazement as the front door opened and a very exhausted Elliott walked toward the car. Morgan was out of the vehicle in seconds, followed by Leslie, running toward the house to look at the changes.

Opening the car door, she smiled at Elliott.

"You've been busy, mister…"

"Happy wife, happy life," he chuckled, but she could hear the fatigue in his voice as he opened Bethany's door, unbuckled her, and scooped up the sleeping girl in his arms. "Hey my little Raisinette, you want to see your new room and have some pizza before bed?"

"My… room?"

Sarah's heart melted at seeing the duo, and she plucked Henry from his car seat, causing the tears to stop as he was freed from his restraints. "Let's get you inside, change your diaper, and feed you too, little man…"

As she walked into the house, she could smell the paint faintly mixed with scents of sawdust in the air. There were people everywhere, looking just as worn out as she felt, and she saw their smiles as they waved while chewing silently.

"Thank you for all your help today. If the facelift of the garage door is any indication, y'all worked your rear ends off," she began, just a bit overwhelmed as she heard Morgan's exclamation of delight.

"I get the big room? Hey! I've got a cool boy's bathroom, too? Oh my gosh, there's a plane on my wall that has my name on it?!"

"What's he talking about," she smiled. "What plane?"

"That would be a little something…" Mary waved and gave her a thumbs-up but before she could say anything else, Leslie was shrieking incoherently and crying.

Startled, she began down the hallway and paused at the door. Her daughter was staring at the wall, pointing, and she expected to see a massive spider or something, only to see a doll house lovingly painted by hand that was almost as tall as she was. There were windows painted with the blue paint, and pale green walls – the same green she'd chosen for one of the bedrooms. Someone, Mary, had taken the paint and added a touching element obviously to each of the children's bedrooms without asking or being prompted.

"M-Mama... my room is p-pink," Leslie cried, her lip wobbling.

"A pretty girl deserves a pretty room," Elliott said from behind Sarah – and she looked up at him, feeling her heart skip a beat at the pride and love in his eyes. Without a word, he kissed Sarah's lips tenderly and turned to walk Bethany down the hallway to the other room – where she heard more excitement.

"I get... butterflies?"

Leslie's eyes widened in comprehension as she looked at the room.

"I get my own room and don't have to share it?"

"It would seem so..." Sarah chuckled, smiling, as the little girl darted into the other room, screeching in delight. Her daughters were talking back and forth about their new discoveries before darting to Morgan's room.

And Sarah followed, amazed that so much had been done so quickly out of the goodness of their hearts. Looking at Elliott, she smiled.

"Ribs – and whatever else they want."

"Right?" he chuckled. "This would have taken me weeks by myself."

"I can't believe all of this," she admitted, marveling that Morgan's room was indeed painted with the pale blue paint, but there were swirls in it... but those swirls had been added by Mary along with an airplane that said 'Rattler' on the side. The boys' beds were set up, along with a carpeted playmat that looked like a city to play cars on.

Sarah quickly changed Henry's diaper as she listened to her son, regaling everyone with his excitement.

"This is the best!" Morgan exclaimed. "And I have my own plane!"

"Yes, you do. Go tell everyone 'thank you' and grab some pizza," she instructed, and the boy was out of the room in a flash.

"I forgot all the bags in the trunk of the car," she said quietly, turning to Elliott. "You and your friends have done miracles."

"That's what I said, and they kept insisting that it was nothing and that we take care of each other," he chuckled. "Just a heads-up, we are on 'dry goods duty' and need to make a box full of cans and other items for the next pilot moving into town."

"I'd be happy to," she chuckled. "Is that what they do?"

"Yup. They help each other move, get settled, make updates to the houses, and do you know Ricochet had a bathroom added to his house? I mean, it's crazy what they do for each other – and when they say 'Flyboys family'... they really mean it."

She set Henry down, who immediately started crying again. The poor boy was so exhausted. This time, Elliott picked him up and put him on his shoulder, kissing his temple and rocking him slightly. She reached out, cupping Elliott's neck, and pulled him close, kissing him tenderly.

"Thank you for loving me," she whispered, pressing her forehead to his as the pair stood close together in the doorway of Morgan's room. "I never imagined how beautiful things would be between us."

"Aren't you curious about our room?" he smiled softly. "Let's feed the kids, get them tucked in, and I'll give you the grand tour."

"Is that what you are calling it?" she flirted and heard his laugh as he kissed her once more before nudging her forward to join in the pizza that was being devoured in record time. Entering the living room, she saw Melody walking in to join them with Liberty in her arms and Betsy at her side.

"Ohhhh my goodness," Sarah crooned, unable to help herself as she smoothed back the baby's pale apricot-colored hair before looking at Elliott. Just seeing that head of hair made her wonder if their own child would have his coloring. She sincerely hoped so. "Liberty is so beautiful."

"We're going to call her Libby for short," Melody smiled tenderly at her husband nearby. "We both wanted to honor Jordan, giving her a patriotic name as well as honoring her Daddy."

"Poor kid," Firefly joked, but his proud voice said otherwise.

"Liberty Sutton Grainger is a mouthful," Elliott teased, chuckling.

"Better than Copperhead…"

"I'm not naming my kid Copperhead…"

"Nah, you'll probably do something mundane and normal."

"Probably," Elliott and Sarah said in unison before looking at each other in surprise and laughing at how similarly they behaved.

"Show me around really quickly," Melody encouraged and nodded to the baby. "I've got about a half hour before feeding time again for this little one, and I'm sure you all want to settle in."

"On that note," Thumper said, getting to his feet with Harley. "Let's go pick up Samantha from Marisol so we can get her tucked into bed."

"Yup," Alpo added, getting to his feet. "We're heading out

too. We don't want to wear out our welcome with Sophie and she's got her hands full with the twins."

Everyone was getting to their feet and making their 'goodbyes' as she thanked each one of them openly, grateful for all of this kindness. Ten minutes later, even the Grainger family had left. Morgan was finishing his pizza, Elliott was feeding Henry a jar of squash, and she was tucking in the girls, who were already falling asleep. As she walked out of Leslie's new bedroom, she nearly collided with Morgan who was running down the hallway, tossing a brief 'Sorry Mom!' behind him. She followed him into his room and saw him brushing his teeth before he leaped into bed.

"This is so cool," Morgan grinned.

"It's a young man's room, isn't it?"

"It's awesome."

"I'm glad you are happy. We'll put your poster up tomorrow."

"Can I say something?" her son asked, and she hesitated, moving to sit on the side of his bed, nodding easily. Elliott walked in with Henry, changing him into pajamas. "I know Dad died, but I'm kinda glad Uncle Elliott is here and now my Daddy too. Is that okay?"

Sarah smiled tenderly at her son, seeing the worry in his eyes, and realized he was still healing just like the rest of them. She smoothed back his hair, leaned down to kiss the tip of his nose, and spoke.

"You know, that's the beautiful thing about being a wonderful person. You can love so many people in different ways, and each is just as precious as the next one. You don't ever have to feel bad for loving more than one person because that love is as individual as the person. I loved your Daddy and always will; but I loved your uncle as my best friend first, long before I ever fell in love with him and agreed to marry him. It's kinda like cake," she smiled and heard Morgan's laugh.

"I like cake – a lot. Your daddy was the best kind of birthday cake with all the flowers and gobs of frosting, but your uncle was also cake – we'll just call him pudding cake, okay?"

"You hear that," Elliott joked, coming to sit behind Sarah and leaning over to tickle the boy. "I'm pudding cake."

"But sometimes, you want something different."

Elliott gave a wide-eyed stare to Morgan, causing the boy to laugh once more, followed by a hushed 'uh oh...' that had her rolling her eyes as the two obviously were playing along and 'feeding' off each other.

"So you take a chance and discover that carrot cake is your favorite now," she teased, turning to rub Elliott's head and ruffling his ruddy, wavy hair. "You'll never turn away a chance to have that cake, knowing it is the best and never going to fail to impress you."

"What am I?" Morgan prompted.

"You are my favorite cheesecake," she chuckled. "Smooth, sweet, and something to celebrate."

"I love cheesecake."

"I love you," she countered, kissing his cheek. "Now get some sleep."

"Good night, Mama," Morgan began and then grinned, chuckling mischievously. "Good night... Carrot Cake!"

"Ohhh, you stinker," Elliott played, hugging the boy and blowing raspberries on his neck, making him laugh as he tickled him. "You quit that, and we both know you are my new wingman..."

"Yeah," Morgan was laughing, smiling from ear to ear, "Yeah, I am, Daddy. I love you."

"I love you too. Get some rest."

"Yes, sir."

Elliott checked the baby monitor by Henry's crib and pulled the door to, following Sarah as she stepped into the hallway. He took her hand and gave her a tender smile as he tugged her forward.

"Are you ready for what's behind the next door?"

"Are you teasing or being serious?"

"A little of both?"

"Hmm…"

"Maybe I should have you close your eyes?"

"Maybe we should just go look at the new bedroom together because I've been very patient already," she said knowingly, smirking at him.

"Ooooh," he mocked. "Does going to the bedroom with me make you feel impatient? How impatient are you?"

"Elliott…" she laughed as he hugged her close, kissing her temple, and guided her toward the 'garage' door, which was sporting a new doorknob.

"You changed the knob?"

"Uh yeah," he retorted softly. "I want it to lock from the inside and keep everyone out, not the interior of the house, keeping us in our room."

"Oh!" she exclaimed, chuckling nervously. "I didn't think about that."

"Give your man a little credit," he teased. "I love details and the fact that you notice them."

And he reached past her, opening the door for her before flipping on the light switch. She blinked several times, marveling at the transformation before her. Gone were the weathered walls that had nail holes over the years and wooden utility shelves that were really now useless. She had sold David's tools at a garage sale, trying to earn money, knowing she would never use them.

The change was nothing short of a miracle.

The steps down to the garage had been finished off, now

butted up against a wall that once had been open. Stunned, she looked at Elliott.

"You closed off the washer and dryer?"

"I thought it would make it feel more like a bedroom – and it gave us a big walk-in closet attached to it."

"Oh, Elliott…" she whispered, touched by his thoughtfulness. It would be wonderful to have it separated from the room but in a convenient location where she could hang up the clothes out of the dryer, walk a few feet, and hang them in the closet. He'd walled off the entire end of the garage to form this room and it fit so well, like it had been made or designed this way. Opening the door, she peered inside and saw he'd moved all their things, their clothes, and it was already prepped for them both.

Turning, she looked back at the room and saw the two windows flanking the bed – and covered her mouth, gasping as she saw the floor. He had indeed put down Pergo wood flooring, but the bed had also been replaced. The nightstands were there, her dresser, the photos she'd had hung on the walls of her bedroom, but in the corner was a bassinet, a floor lamp, and a rocking chair.

"When did…" she said tearfully, looking around the room.

"The guys told me to take Valkyries truck to grab lunch – so I grabbed a few more things while I was out," he admitted and hesitated. "You don't mind, do you?"

"No… never."

"I just wanted you to have a quiet place to be alone with our baby and…"

"Elliott, you don't have to explain," she whispered emotionally, looking at him and touching his face. "I love that we have a space, a haven, just for us. If you want to rock the baby, you can. If I want to feed our child and talk to you,

I can. We have privacy and can be alone together instead of me going off on my own."

He swallowed and laid his hand on her stomach, his eyes widening as the baby kicked in response, almost as if it was aware that Daddy was close by.

"I'm so in love with our room… because it's ours."

"Me too," he whispered, searching her eyes. "Just when I thought life couldn't get any better, you've given me everything."

"Not yet," she smiled tremulously, laying her hand on his where it rested on her stomach as he leaned forward to kiss her softly. "…But I understand what you mean."

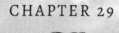

CHAPTER 29

COPPERHEAD
Several months later…

ELLIOTT WATCHED Sarah's expression tighten once more as her whole being tensed as they were watching Frozen with the children. Leslie and Bethany were singing 'Let it Go' at the top of their lungs, dancing in their little pajamas, and twirling their dolls – much to Morgan's frustration as he looked up, glaring at his sisters after being hit with the doll a second time.

"Watch it…"

"Your brother is right. Be careful," Elliott volunteered sportingly. "Henry is sitting right beside you both and if someone gets hurt, the movie is getting turned off."

"But Daddy, I'm Elsa…"

"I'm Anna!" Bethany yelped happily, jumping up and down.

And Sarah made a noise, stiffening again – and this time she looked at him pointedly. Her lips were pressed together as she gave him a sharp nod, causing a bolt of panic to run down his spine.

"Really?"

"Nahhhh…" she grunted almost angrily, glaring at him. "I'm faking."

Elliott cursed – winced as three of the four children looked at him.

"I'll get the soap, Dad… sheesh," Morgan said, rolling his eyes – only to have Sarah chuckle as she moved her hand to hold her stomach. That single move was the only true sign of pain.

"Forget the soap – y'all get your 'go' bags," he ordered without hesitation, dialing Firefly immediately. The other pilot picked up on the second ring.

"Is it time?"

"Yup."

"Need me to come over or…"

"Nope – I'm going to drop them off…" – and saw Sarah shake her head in a panicked motion.

"Now," she grunted, and Elliott dropped the phone. Scrambling, he picked it up and looked at her as he spoke.

"I think we need someone closer, she's not really happy right now…"

"Ya' think?" Firefly laughed openly. "Melody said she was going to wax my – well, never mind. Remember, all the threats melt away once that baby is born or at least I hope so. Call Sophie – she's closest."

"On it," – and hung up, dialing once more, before yelling out over his shoulder. "KIDS, LET'S GO!"

"Well, I'm not your kid," Sophie chuckled. "And I no longer have my right eardrum, but I gather the baby is coming?"

"Yes – can I…"

"I'll be waiting," she interrupted.

"Oh, thank you," he rasped and moved to scoop up Henry as Sarah was already getting to her feet slowly. He felt so bad for her because she was hunched over, holding her stomach and breathing methodically.

How had she hidden this from him – and how long had this been going on?

"Everyone in the car…" he ordered as the kids came flying down the hallway, their little duffel bag in hand. He was so relieved that they had finally broken down and got a second vehicle because the minivan was going to be a blessing now, hauling all of them.

"Wait here, and I'll be right back," Elliott ordered and saw Sarah give him a thumbs-up as she bent over again, this time in the middle of the living room on her slow progression to the front door.

The kids were climbing into the van as he buckled Henry in – and ran back to the door to get Sarah. She was still struggling, making noises between pinched lips and looking at him for help. He could see the silent plea in her eyes and melted.

"I've got you," he whispered – and scooped her up, just to carry her the twenty feet to the car quickly… only to feel something wet on his arm as she let out an unholy moan.

"Sarah?"

"Water… broke… go…"

Setting her in the seat, he ran to get in the driver's seat.

"Everyone buckled?"

"Yessss," came the chorus of voices.

Putting the van in reverse, he drove to Sophie's house quickly and bless her – she was already waddling toward the car doors to help him. The woman was due in a few more months as well.

"Y'all go inside," Sophie said. "Ben is watching Sesame Street."

"Thank you, Soph…" Elliott began, and she smiled.

"Go – get moving. Good luck, Sarah!"

As he pulled out of the drive, he made a U-turn to get back to the main road that would take them toward Tyler. Crossing the bridge, something changed and Sarah was slapping his arm in alarm.

"What?!"

"Baaaaby…" she moaned, her eyes pinched shut, and he watched in disbelief as she reclined her seat back, putting a foot on the dash.

"WHOA – WHAT?! THE BABY IS COMING NOW?"

Elliott drove over a curb into the parking lot of the Dairy Queen – already dialing 9-1-1 as he slammed the car into park and heard his beloved wife groaning in pain, panting, and struggling.

"Elliott…Oh gosh, Elliott…" she whimpered, and he exited the car, coming to her side.

"I'm here, hon. I'm right here," he said blankly. He was there all right – and had never given birth to a baby, nor had he any clue how to help her. He'd seen it on television but the idea of actually attempting this with his first child was waving enough red flags in his mind to be its own parade.

"9-1-1, how can I help you?"

"Yes, my name is Elliott Trent, and my wife is having our baby – right now – in the Dairy Queen parking lot. I need help!" he ordered and heard the placating voice trying to tell him to stay calm, but that was a struggle.

Understatement. Of. The. Year.

"Sir, I need you to tell me if you see the head…"

"Of what?"

"The baby…"

"No. It's in her… OHHHH, you mean, um, yeah, hold

on…" Elliott stuttered numbly, realizing that he had to keep it together so he could help her. "Sarah, babe, I've got to check something okay – and it's not exactly gonna be romantic."

Both the 9-1-1 operator and Sarah let out a pained laugh as she gave him a sharp nod of awareness.

"Need… to… push…" Sarah grunted.

"She said she needs to push," he repeated and lifted his wife's skirt, and his eyes nearly popped out of his head at the same time he flinched. There was a reason women gave birth, and men didn't. That was a sight he would never unsee. "Yep. I can see the head."

"Okay, EMS is on the way, but the baby is crowning."

"Yes."

"I need you to tell her not to push… but you need to be ready to catch the baby."

"Me?"

"Yes, Mr. Trent. That baby is coming if you can see the head."

"Sarah, she said 'don't push'…"

Elliott felt someone shove him aside, and he saw two fire-fighters standing in his place, one of them with his hands up his wife's dress.

"HEY…" he said automatically, and then it hit him that they were there to help. "I could see the head," he volunteered.

"You were squatting like a catcher at a baseball game, I kinda figured, buddy. What's your name – and what's hers?"

"Elliott and Sarah…"

"All right, Elliott – you are about to be a daddy. Sarah? Sarah, can you hear me? I'm Colton, and this knucklehead is Lance. We're with the Ember Creek fire department, and it's okay to push if you need to. We're gonna help you and then take you to the hospital."

"Shouldn't she go now?"

"Well, Elliott, considering I'm holding your baby's head in my hands. I'd rather not drive right now," Colton said quietly, focusing on Sarah. "Ma'am, I want you to give me a good push 'cause this little fella is coming... okay?"

Sarah was grunting and breathing – reaching blindly to her side, and Elliott climbed into the van, coming to her other side.

"I'm here," he promised. "I've got you, and you are doing beautifully."

"Is this your first child or..."

"Fifth."

"Ahhh... well, I see why it's coming fast like this, and she's doing so well. You are a pro, aren't you?" Colton praised, and Elliott looked down to see the bluish tinge to his child's face, nearly breaking him. "Sarah, I want you to give me all you've got, okay?"

She nodded erratically and bore down, shaking and straining so hard that he couldn't help but stare as the baby slipped out of her body in one rush.

"Lance..." Colton began – and shoved a bulb-looking thing in the child's mouth before turning it over and laying it on Sarah. Within seconds, the baby was crying angrily and turning a ruddy color. The wave of relief was overwhelming as Elliott met his wife's eyes and felt himself break, giving her a tearful smile as his lips trembled.

"Plumbing is on the outside," one of the firemen joked, patting Elliott on the shoulder as the other fireman between Sarah's legs chuckled before looking at them both. "You've got a boy."

"Oh gosh," Elliott whispered tearfully, laughing. "I was so nervous I didn't even look. Did you hear that, my love? We've got a boy..."

"He's beautiful, Elliott," Sarah wept, smiling up at him. "Look, he's got your red hair and…"

"I think she's happy he's a ginger…"

"Jeez, Lance, seriously?"

"No, he's right," Elliott laughed. "I've been called one all my life. He's so beautiful…"

"The work isn't over though, is it, Sarah?" Colton said, grabbing his radio and speaking swiftly in what sounded like code. Elliott didn't question it, though, because he knew his own language from flying in the Air Force. Here, this man was the professional, and in the skies, it was his turn.

"Nope," she chuckled as the other firefighter returned with a paramedic beside him.

"Sorry, Colton, I got stuck on the scene."

"Meh, I'm getting pretty good at this."

"What have we got…?"

"Early thirties, no complications, baby was presenting, delivery, and now I'm going to turn her over to you since you've got the stretcher waiting," Colton chuckled.

"All right, little mama… we are going to take a ride in the ambulance to Tyler Memorial to get you and your son checked out. These two men are going to move you over, so all you need to do is hang on to that little guy as soon as I put this blanket over you."

Elliott watched, feeling helpless, and climbed out of the car, following them to the ambulance – only to have the woman stop him.

"I know you are nervous, but they are going to be okay. Why don't you follow us so they don't tow your car off later." He nodded numbly as he heard his cell phone going off in the distance from the open passenger side door of the van.

"Elliott?"

He turned, hearing Sarah's voice centering him almost

immediately as everything within him focused on her in an instant. All the fears, distractions, and chaos around him melted away as he met her eyes.

"I'm fine," she smiled openly. "This is just a precaution, and I'll see you in a minute at the emergency room... Daddy."

He smiled at her tearfully and nodded, realizing she was trying to reassure him of the miracle of what he'd just seen, sharing it was all right, and trying to comfort him like he'd done for her so many times in the past.

"I'll see you soon."

THREE HOURS LATER, phone calls fielded, questions answered, and all the paperwork handled, his beloved Sarah was finally being settled into a hospital room for the night just for observation. Their son was breathtakingly beautiful in a way he never imagined. The sweet sweep of that tiny button nose, those little lips that kept working as he dreamed, and a swath of deep reddish hair that looked almost copper was brushed and covered with a tiny blue and white cap.

His son.

Elliott wasn't sure his heart could be any fuller. He had a beautiful wife, four adorable children who had him completely wrapped around their little fingers, and now, a child he never imagined would ever be conceived was here before him like a tiny cherub.

"When did I become such a troll?" she muttered, trying to smooth her hair and straighten her hospital gown.

"You look breathtakingly beautiful," he confessed, not holding back. "I don't think I could love you more than I do right now."

"That's because of our little man..." she smiled tenderly –

and Elliott couldn't resist. He picked up the baby out of the bassinet, just staring down at his peaceful expression as he let out a little sigh that seemed almost too big for his body.

"I know," he whispered playfully at the baby, looking at her as he dropped a kiss on the infant's forehead. "I feel that same way when I look at your mama, Colton. My whole heart and soul sigh in contentment just seeing her smile."

"Is Colton Elliott Trent okay?" she asked softly. "You don't mind?"

"Are you kidding?" he chuckled. "I wasn't exactly in the right frame of mind to play 'catch' with my son's head. I'm grateful they showed up – and I like the name. Strong, powerful, and slightly different. I want all of our children to be their own person, their own individual selves…"

"Me too."

The baby let out another massive sigh that sounded almost like a coo, and Elliott just melted, feeling tears sting his eyes as he smiled at Sarah once more.

"I never imagined any of this would be possible," he whispered, not caring that he was on the edge of weeping like some emotional ninny. "I've always wanted so much more in my life. I wanted to touch the sky, to make you happy as a friend, and to love you as my wife…"

"And now?"

"I'm just overwhelmed," he admitted. "I didn't think I could love someone more than I love you – but I look at Colton… and it's there. He's three hours old, and I would give our boy anything."

"It's called being a parent," she chuckled.

"Does that make me a bad person if this feeling is stronger? I mean, I sincerely love the children and would do anything for them, but this is staggering," he whispered painfully.

"You are the best person in the world – and there is

something so visceral in holding your child. I understand completely. You are such a good father with the children already, but when it's yours, something else is there too. I get it. I only request that you love them all the same – please – for me."

"Oh, Sarah," he breathed, his heart aching as they discussed something so personal, so private, and so deep between them. "I have always loved the children, and nothing will change that."

"I know," she smiled, her eyes glistening. "I didn't imagine it would, but I'm sure that will come up at some point because kids will be kids."

"And our kids are sharp as tacks," he chuckled. "Man, I remember Morgan telling me that '*I couldn't tell him what to do.*. I saw red but realized that our boy needed a safe place to get his feelings out there, and I wanted to be that. I want them to feel like home is the place where they can be accepted and loved, no matter what – because that is what any father would do."

He sniffed emotionally.

"They may not be my children, but they are *my children*, Sarah…"

"Man, you are sexy when you play the 'Dad-card'…" she teased, trying to break up the emotional moment with laughter – and it worked. He chuckled, embarrassed, and kissed Colton on the forehead once more before laying the baby in her arms.

"You sure make beautiful babies, Mrs. Trent," he whispered, kissing her tenderly as she turned her face up to meet him.

"Wanna do this again next year?"

Both chuckled softly as he pressed his forehead to hers, gently rubbing her nose with his before kissing her once more.

"Maybe?"

"Let's just go ahead with 'yeah,'" Sarah flirted with him, leaning up to kiss him again. "Have I mentioned that I'm crazy about you?"

"I love you – always have and always will," he smiled.

EPILOGUE

Ten years later

ELLIOTT STOOD THERE PROUDLY, adjusting Morgan's tie and focusing on it just so he didn't break down sobbing. No, that could come much later, and he'd willingly turn over his man-card to Sarah, just so she could make him laugh and pull him back together.

"How does it look?" Morgan asked, and Elliott met his eyes, hearing that waver of insecurity.

"You look incredible," he began and felt something within him splinter as he saw his son's eyes. "You've grown into quite a young man and I couldn't be prouder of you right now."

"Really?"

"You remind me so much of your father, God rest his soul, and I see so much of David and your mother in you … but somehow, someway, I do believe I see a little bit of me in there, too."

"Probably all the soap over the years," Morgan retorted, laughing tearfully.

"Probably," Elliott agreed – and hugged him tightly, before clearing his throat and straightening their suits once more. "Gotta get the mushy stuff out of the way and put on our manly pants, right?"

"Right."

"I love you, kid… and you are going to do great things," he said bluntly, cradling his head with his palm, staring at him and marveling at the fact that Morgan was actually an inch taller than him. Gosh, he was a good-looking kid, and he hadn't been joking about how proud he was of him.

One of the admissions officers at the Air Force Academy had even commented on 'it must be something in the water, because we are getting a lot of applicants from East Texas now.'

Morgan being one of them.

He was so proud of him, so proud of all the children and how they were growing, changing and becoming their own person. Morgan was graduating high school today and flying to the Academy early next week – following him around was Libby Grainger who obviously was sporting a crush on the young man – much to Henry's frustration. Ben Merrick, Sophie and Reaper's son, was already there – along with Toby Saxon.

Leslie was captain of the track team and best friends with India Tarrant, Romeo's daughter, despite their age differences. The two were 'thick as thieves' and into everything, whereas Bethany was the exact opposite. His sweet Raisinette was maturing into a shy young lady who loved to bake and wanted to be a chef. She worked part-time with Dixie at the café on the weekends, saving up to buy herself a *blue beetle with pretty eyelashes.*

Henry was incredibly bright, played euphonium in the

marching band, and competed in the academic teams, having won several medals and scholarships already. The boy was incredibly brilliant, decisive, and he had taken a shine to Inferno's wife, asking questions about the legal system and how to become a judge… all while silently pining for Libby.

"Are you guys ready?" Sarah said, knocking at the same time she opened the door. "They are lining up the students for graduation and looking for you Morgan."

"We were discussing man stuff," Elliott said gruffly and gave Morgan a sharp nod, who turned to Sarah and said with a bland expression.

"Man stuff, Mom… don't ask."

"I won't," Sarah chuckled, meeting his eyes. "Well, when you are done discussing 'man stuff' – Colton and Jenna found us some seats with the Graingers and Saxons."

"I better go with Mom so she doesn't start blubbering and crying," Elliott bragged, yanking several paper towels out of the holder mounted on the wall nearby. "For her…"

"Of course, Dad."

"Love you, kid… knock 'em dead, Rattler."

"You know it."

He touched his son's shoulder, nodded curtly, and moved to join Sarah as Morgan scooted past them, jogging down the hallway to line up, his ribbons, academic cords, and graduation gown bouncing with each step.

"Man stuff, huh?" Sarah whispered, lacing her fingers with his as she leaned into his arm, looking up at him tenderly.

"Shush…" he chuckled, leaning down to kiss her. "Is Colton still fidgeting?"

"Yeah, he's miserable in his cast."

"I told him not to take the skateboard down the steps of the high school. He's lucky it was his arm and not his neck."

"And you need to talk to Jenna."

"Oh?"

"Yup," Sarah said primly, giving him a sinking sensation in his gut. "Apparently, your daughter decided to write a foul word on Colton's cast…"

Elliott cursed.

"Yup – that's the one," she chuckled. "So I figured you can have that talk with her, enjoy your Ivory soap bars together, and figure out a way to cover that word on his arm before school on Monday… *Daddy*," she taunted.

"Have I mentioned how much I love you – and how sexy you look today?"

"You aren't getting out of this one, Copperhead."

"Sheesh, tough crowd."

"Must be those Trent genes because…"

"Oh, don't you even start, woman…" he laughed openly, releasing her hand and pulling her into his arms. "I love you, and I remember a certain young girl who was always into some sort of mischief or another."

"And what happened to that girl, hmm?"

"She married her soulmate and lived happily ever after," he said tenderly.

"Lucky girl…" acknowledged softly, gazing up at him with so much love and affection that his heart turned over in his chest in awareness.

"Lucky guy…" he countered, kissing her tenderly, his thumb brushing across her cheek and marveling at the sense of belonging that he felt at her side.

AFTERWORD

 GAHHHH!

I **loved** Copperhead's story!

It's always hard to 'destroy' a person's life in your head, but I wanted their bond to be a little deeper than 'just friends' - I wanted him to be everything to her, to support her, and to be her 'rock'.

My husband came to ask me what I was laughing about as I typed 'Uncle Daddy' - so I can only imagine Firefly's reaction. LOL!

… And Melody.

What better person to discuss losing a spouse, than for someone who had gone through it. When I was outlining and thinking about this book, I wanted to 'place' a few key players in different locations - but when Copperhead was talking with Sparky, I knew there needed to be a referral to another person in order to tie them to Flyboys.

Let's face it, we love it when the team gets together. The text messages kill me and I wish y'all could hear the banter back and forth that I hear in my mind… or at least, I hope it's as vibrant to you as it is to me.

Liberty... what a perfect name for Firefly's daughter! Thank you, Abby.

Josie... Thank you, Stephanie! Loved it!

And Panic? Our boy is going to get his own story, but in a different series. His book is called **In Love with A Rascal** - and I cannot wait for him to 'find' his place, his new home, and slowly begin to heal from his trauma.

I'm currently working on Inferno - and oh man, it's quite fun. Elana is wicked smart and clever... we get to see characters from Flirt's Battalion again *(Colton & Lance are part of the other truck where Justin is the captain)* Soooo much goodness!

Now - who takes over after Reaper?

I'm on the fence about who will take over the Squadron, have a few ideas, a few twists, but I really want to know your opinion - and will be sharing more in my Newsletter.

So if you haven't subscribed... now would be a good time. LOL.

XOXO,

Ginny

Ginny Sterling Newsletter
(You get a free book!)

IN LOVE WITH A RASCAL - PANIC'S STORY

Xander '*Panic*' Isaacs was always cool under pressure. His call sign had been a joke among the other pilots because nothing fazed him, until now. When even the bravest among the team shatters under pressure, they give a chance to one broken Flyboy to pick up the pieces in Wyoming.

Lyndsey was a forensic scientist who is to testify for a trial and needed a safe place to hide, completely off the grid. When the chief of police pulls a few strings, he whisks her off to a farm in the middle of nowhere, and she suddenly finds herself sharing a cabin with the most gorgeous man... with quirks.

Xander hardly spoke to anyone, kept odd hours, and avoided her at every turn. How are you supposed to hold a conversation with someone who runs away from you despite their close quarters?

And what happens when you finally catch him?

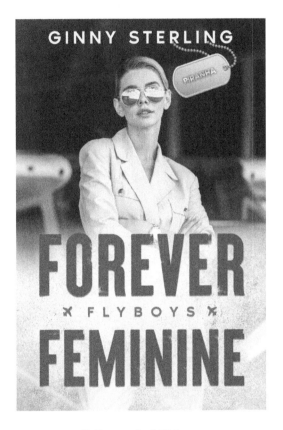

Follow my lead, Flyboy...

Captain Stephanie *'Piranha'* Ely had fought for every
commendation and honor that she'd received her entire life – and
wasn't about to let anyone take that from her. She volunteered for
this assignment, knowing it would guarantee a spot in command...
and had no clue just how much resolve it was actually going to take
– especially when it came to Scarecrow.

Copy that – I'm on your tail...

Joey *'Scarecrow'* Charlton didn't have a care in the world. No commitments, no strings attached back home, and zero drive to do anything else. Eat, sleep, and fly... that was his mantra – or at least it was until Stephanie walked in the room.

Can two complete opposites find a middle ground that is stable enough to build a relationship on... or will the desert sands swirling around them destroy it all?

Healing Hearts Series

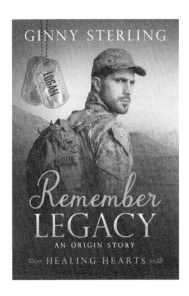

If you love heartwarming, tough guys who fall in love unexpectedly – this is the series for you!

These standalone sweet, clean romances follow a team of soldiers that were once stationed in Afghanistan, bound by friendship.

Opposites attract, soulmates find each other at their lowest points, and friends become lovers across the miles.

HOTSHOTS

GINNY STERLING

HOTSHOTS takes you on a thrilling global adventure with fearless pilots - and the women who adore them. Emotions run high as daring souls embark on relationships they never imagined amidst the skies.

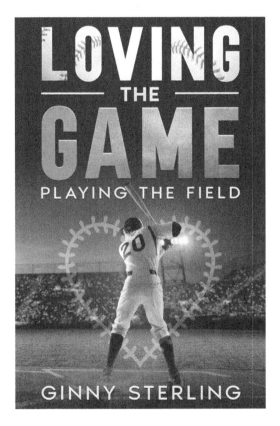

He's baseball's biggest heartthrob

... and she cleans toilets.

Drake Walker had it all – females, fame, and fortune but none of it
was real. The money could disappear, the attention could wane
overnight, and all the women that surrounded him were only there
for one thing – to be able to say they were dating an All-Star
baseball player.

It was a pathetic, lonely life, and he was ready for a change.

Steffi was shocked to see the baseball player barge into her world in the most inconspicuous of places ever – a public bathroom. Now, with a plunger for a scepter, and a dustpan for a shield, the unexpected 'Team' emerges victorious from pursuit... only to make a bargain neither could have ever imagined.

A *(very fake)* relationship.

Every girl dreams of a luxurious life, a handsome prince professing his love, and a kingdom at her feet, but her *'diamond'* had bases, her *'love story'* was full of foul balls, and her *'prince'* was the one wearing white (pants).

What do you do when falling in love isn't quite the fairytale you expected?

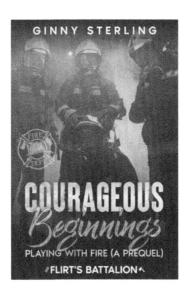

Flirt's Battalion Sweet Romance Series

EMBER CREEK, TEXAS

"I volunteered the entire team, so make sure that your Friday is clear of any activities or events. This is non-negotiable, team, and I really need your help with this charity event. The other shift will be covering for us, and they go up on the auction block this Saturday..." Chief Carpenter said openly, putting his hands on his hips, looking over the table at them.

They'd just gotten back from a roaring blaze that had engulfed a mobile home on the outside of town, and all Kyle could smell was smoke so heavy he could taste it.

It was everywhere, seeping from the pores of his skin and in his clothes, and each of the men at the table reeked of sweat. In fact, several of them had matted down hair that was strange looking because of their thermal gear and helmets.

Hat-hair, he mused, shoveling another bite in his mouth.

"This isn't bordering on harassment or some other rule? I

mean, I've never heard of any job condoning this, and while I know it's for charity... still," Justin began nervously. "I mean, are there guidelines to this... mess?"

"Huh?" Kyle said distractedly, reaching for a slice of cornbread. "What'd the chief say?"

"Weren't you paying attention?" Austin hissed behind his hand. "Dude, this is exciting – and scary!"

"Honestly? Noooo... I'm hungry and we just got back from a run. I can actually smell the chili and the woodsmoke together. It's not half bad," Kyle said chewing noisily, before blowing his nose and wincing at the smoke-filled residue he left in the napkin.

"You're disgusting."

"Hey, at least I didn't do like Austin did last week..."

"Ugh, don't remind me!" Chase muttered.

"You didn't catch any of what the chief just said?" Justin muttered, frowning and kicking Kyle under the table that they were all sitting at.

"I heard him say *'You guys can eat while you listen'*... so I'm eating," Kyle whined, shoveling in a massive bite. "And listening. I'm listening, too. Can you pass the butter?"

"What about the listening part?" Chase uttered. "With them big ol' ears you should have..."

"I just said..." Kyle choked out openly, chewing with his mouth full and talking at the same time, trying to keep anything from falling out.

Man, whoever made the chili this morning – it was fantastic! he thought wildly, stirring his bowl and reaching for the package of cheese once again.

"Did you have something you wanted to add, Rimes?" Fire chief Reese Carpenter said quietly, in a voice that brooked no argument.

It was said that the chief never yelled, never raised his voice, and commanded respect from his team easily by being in the thick of things with them – and treating them like equals. He liked Chief Carpenter – even if he set him on edge sometimes. The man just had a way of looking right through you…

"No sir!" Kyle said immediately, swallowing his food noisily before smiling and nodding. "I think it's a great idea."

"Good – you're going to be first," Chief Carpenter said openly, pointing at each man. "Marks, you're second…"

"Awww man… seriously?" Chase whined immediately, rolling his eyes. "Charity… it's for charity. You are not a piece of meat to be ogled… it's not a date. Charity auction, donating time, not anything else… relax and don't make this weirder than it already is."

Chase hesitated – and then spoke up.

"Do we really have to do this?"

"Yes," the chief said quietly, walking around the table as the men looked at each other in alarm, some in confusion, and Chase looked decidedly uncomfortable as Justin turned a weird shade of greenish-white under his tan.

Kyle's eyes grew wide as Chase slid down even further into his seat, looking almost despondent at the announcement.

What exactly did he get volunteered for – and why would Chase Marks be worried about being ogled like a piece of meat? he wondered silently.

"Olivera, you are third."

"Does this count as a blind date? I can check that off my bucket list of strange new things to experience…" Austin grinned and rubbed his hands together. "I do love me some fine Texas women, and I will happily go up on the auction block. Do I have to wear a shirt? Can I show off my muscles? I can oil my abs up and…"

"Blind date? What? *Wait* – I think I *really* missed some-thing…" Kyle choked on the bite he'd just taken, spewing little pieces of cornbread – which everyone picked up off the table and threw at him at once.

"Dailey... you're fourth..."

"Sir, respectfully, can I just volunteer my time? I'm still reeling and going through recovery from my divorce... and I'd rather not be auctioned off for a dinner date."

"When the person bids on you, you are welcome to discuss your evening plans with the person. They will be made aware ahead of time of the rules and what lines not to cross. No kissing, touching, harassing, no sexual misconduct..."

"WHAT?" Kyle choked again, his eyes bugging out of his skull at the strange conversation that he was suddenly a part of.

This time, Austin slapped him hard on the back several times while Chase threw a paper towel at him, landing in his bowl of chili.

"Pennington... you're fifth. I will even participate and volunteer as the sixth person on the auction block, so that gives them plenty of chance to reach their financial goals for the charity event."

"Whoaaaa boy..." Andy grinned, looking at Chase and saluting him. "I might get my sister to come bid, just so Carpenter can come be my housemaid for the day."

"I'm not wearing the costume unless there is a reserve on the auction – and it will cost you, kiddo," the chief grinned... causing several of the men to laugh openly while Kyle looked around in disbelief.

The men started talking around him in a flurry, passing the bag of shredded cheese, the plastic container of chopped onion, and the tote of sour cream around the table, while Kyle was trying to comprehend what had just happened...

The chief leaned down and clapped a hand on Kyle's

shoulder, speaking softly beside his head in a hushed whisper.

"Thanks for your support, Rimes. I wasn't sure you had it in you, but really appreciate you stepping up to the plate and backing me. According to the Battalion chief, this barely squeaked by for approval, and I think it's going to do really well."

"Sir?" Kyle said, without moving. "Begging your pardon… but what exactly are we doing?"

"We are doing a charity auction for a *'Date with the Firemen of the First Battalion'* – and our entire team is going to be auctioned off to the highest bidder for a date…"

"We are?"

"Yep…" Chief Carpenter laughed. "Just be glad you aren't on the other team."

"Why is that?"

"Let's just say, it involves a photoshoot…"

This time, it was the rest of the team that nearly did a spit-take all at once as they looked up in horror. It was one thing to have to spend time with someone you barely knew, calling it a date for the sake of charity… but photography meant evidence – and they had all seen the firefighter calendars that people ogled all the time.

Kyle couldn't imagine any of them posing nearly naked with suspenders and a helmet for charity… well, maybe Austin?

He'd gouge his eyes out with a Bic pen first…

"That's right – the other truck is making calendars and auctioning them off for some lucky lady to be in the photo _with_ them."

"We got the better end of the deal," Chase said openly, his eyes wide. "My ex would absolutely nail me to the wall and show the judge that for evidence…"

"No kidding," Justin agreed quickly, frowning. "I don't

need any help with that foaming-at-the-mouth attorney that Lauren sicced on me..."

"Ah – so Honey and Lauren have the same lawyer?" Chase joked.

"She rides a broom in the night sky and cackles when she wins a case?"

"That's her!"

Austin, Kyle, and Andy just looked at each other with wide eyes as Chief Carpenter shook his head, walking off with his hands clasped behind his back.

"Are your ex-wives really that bad?"

"YES," both men said emphatically.

"I'm never getting married," Kyle muttered openly, scooping up the last of his chili with his spoon.

"No kidding..." Austin agreed. "I don't need the headache, the heartache, or pants-ache in my trousers. Women are bitter teases and extreme man-haters. There isn't a girl out there that is worth the trouble or drama she causes."

"That's why you date around and live life for yourself," Andy grinned. "It's cheaper. You are generally happier. There's no one to nag you, whine about you having one too many beers, or complaining that you spend too much time at the station..."

"Hear, hear," Chase muttered.

Attention: MVA – motor vehicle accident...

The announcement carried on, along with a bell ringing in the distance calling them all into motion.

Sure enough, the men were flying into their positions, throwing on their protective clothing. It was almost comical to watch, because shoes were being kicked off onto the floor and flying around them, as they started dressing.

"Grab your bunker gear and packs..."

Kyle ran, grabbed his bunker gear, and threw it down on the ground, kicking off his shoes quickly and leaving them where they lay as he stepped into his boots. He grabbed his pants, hiking them up over his trousers he was wearing, and donned his weighted jacket before making sure everything was fastened appropriately.

Checking his tank and the lights on his mask, he heard Chase start yelling for the 'round up'…

"Let's go! Let's go! Let's go!" Chase hollered, waving his hand quickly in the air in a circle.

Justin was already climbing into the driver's seat and the massive rig flared to life as the lights started spinning wildly.

Kyle knew he had seconds to hop on, because Justin would not wait for anyone to dawdle… and you did NOT want Chief Carpenter to find that you were left behind.

"Round it up fellas and let's get moving…"

Kyle leaped onto the truck and into his seat only seconds before the vehicle started lumbering forward and the siren began wailing in the air around him.

"Rock and Roooooll…" Austin and Andy crowed happily, angling their chins to the air, and howling like a couple of playful mutts as the rest of them laughed.

It was showtime!

Friday afternoon…

Kyle was sweating buckets – and it had nothing to do with the temperature of this strangely warm, yet beautiful November afternoon. No, he was nervous, and with good reason. They had all loaded up on one of the smaller fire trucks to make sure to make a 'good show' for the sake of charity…

Before they left, the captain literally inspected each of them, instantly making him wary. He didn't, *shouldn't*, have anyone to impress – and the fact that he was told to tuck in his t-shirt once again… before they were all told to get their hefty, insulated jackets – to make a good show for the people attending the auction.

Listening in disbelief, he realized that this 'auction' was literally going to be an actual meat-market of men for all sorts of women to ogle and bid on. Chase was right! They were going to be ogled like pieces of meat!

He was going to be going on a date with some strange woman, all for the sake of charity.

"I need an adult…" Kyle whispered openly, swallowing nervously.

"You <u>are</u> the adult, dipstick…" Chase whispered loudly, grinning nervously, and sweating almost as much as Kyle was.

The temperature was perfect, and the sun was beating down on them, keeping the chill from the air despite the fact it was late in the year.

"God help us all…" Justin muttered, shaking his head and rubbing the back of his neck nervously.

"Seriously, I don't think I want to do this," Kyle whispered, looking down the line of firemen standing there in the sun wearing their heavy yellow jackets and helmets… and Austin, his partner, wasn't helping things in the slightest.

The outrageous man was posing for the crowd, grinning and smiling, right before slipping off his jacket, causing a group of ogling women to gather near them where they were lined up.

"Awww yeah, this is gonna be great!" Austin crowed happily. "Check this out!"

He flexed his biceps and kissed each one playfully, causing Justin to put his head down in his hands again in annoyance as the chief laughed from where he stood at the end of the line. Every man hesitated and looked down the line to gawk at the stoic man that led them, who was always so quiet.

"See?" Austin jeered happily, elbowing the two men closest to him – Justin and Chase, the two divorcees. "If Carpenter can loosen up and have some fun? Then you two spaz's should be able to as well. I mean, seriously?! It's a beautiful day, there's a breeze, we are off work…" and Austin's voice got louder, working the crowd as he stepped forward and jerked off his uniform shirt, much to Kyle's horror. "… And all these fine women are here to support a good cause – am I right, Ladies?"

A rowdy, boisterous thunder of appreciation swelled around them as Austin flexed again and showed off his tanned six pack, his tattoo, and then openly smiled, shaking hands with the women and kissing knuckles repeatedly.

Yep. The playboy could certainly work a crowd.

"Someone's gotta stop him," Kyle whispered in a hushed panic. "They're gonna expect us *all* to act like *that*…"

"Then *someone's* gonna be really disappointed, aren't they?" Chase muttered.

"No kidding…" Justin agreed.

Austin ripped… literally RIPPED… his t-shirt off of himself, causing several women to scream in excitement – and Kyle nearly died as he realized he screamed aloud as well, but in horror.

Like a girl.

What was his partner even doing?

"I can't do this!" Kyle balked, feeling faint and definitely disturbed at the fiasco that was about to happen. "Chief! Chief! H-Hey – s-someone g-get Carpenter for me… I c-can't do this!"

His voice was breaking and croaking like a boy going

through puberty – and he was thinking of his own pasty skin, if they put him standing next to Andy or Austin. Someone was going to laugh or chase him off the pergola where the auctioneer was...

"Alright... Alright... Alright! My lovely, esteemed ladies of Ember Creek – are you ready to play with fire? Are we having some fun yet? Just look at these fine specimens we have here today..."

"Not yet... but getting there, Mayor Winstead!"

"Right? You've got some flamboyant young men that are eager to get this auction started... and let's hear it for the Flirt's Battalion!"

"First..." Kyle hissed, mortified. "*First* Street battalion... not Flirt's!"

The mayor actually ignored him... and picked up a gavel to bang it on the small podium that she was standing at.

"We're here today to raise funds for the children's home, and every dollar spent is being donated one hundred percent to Sister Agatha's loving care. It will help pay for school clothes, supplies, bicycles, and computers for the children, bringing so much joy and support to our beloved community – that is supported so wonderfully by our wonderful fire chief Reese Carpenter and the Flirt's Battalion..."

"FIRST!" Kyle hissed, correcting her again. "You've got a typo, lady..."

Then Andy and Austin took their places, returning to the line, and Kyle listened in disbelief as he realized that the auction was beginning. He felt several sets of hands shove him up the steps, stumbling, as he walked forward, looking distinctly uncomfortable.

"Now ladies... remember this is for charity, and we have some pesky rules for this proceeding. Now, he might be a very handsome man, but remember this is for one evening with this young firefighter," the mayor smiled – and immediately Kyle felt a shiver of dread run down his spine.

"This fine, *fine* gentleman of the *Flirt's* Battalion…"

"FIRST…" he hissed again, pointedly. "She meant to say *First* Street Battalion Firehouse…"

"I think 'Flirt' fits so much better…" a woman called out happily, waving her wallet… causing Kyle's eyes to pop out of his head as he saw that it was Mrs. Kendall, who called them weekly needing 'assistance'.

It was the same call every single time.

Mrs. Kendall claimed that she'd fallen and couldn't get up – and specifically asked if Kyle was working that day. They would drive out and Kyle would have to endure the teasing of his coworkers, as he walked in to find her sprawled in various stages of undress, picking her up off the floor, and then suddenly?

She would have a miraculous recovery… asking him if he wanted coffee.

The guys always teased him about Mrs. Kendall – who was the same age as his grandmother Mae… and played bingo with the woman on Sundays at the Catholic church on Main Street.

"Hi Kyle…" she waved happily, wobbling her fingers at him, and making him feel cheap, sordid, and uncomfortable in that moment. He'd seen more of this woman than he would ever care to, and had requested that the team tell Mrs. Kendall that he was scheduled 'off' when she called.

"Hello, Mrs. K-Kendall," Kyle said nervously, hating the way his voice stuttered, and he could feel his cheeks heating up.

"Ruthie, you behave now, young lady…" the mayor laughed, causing several in the crowd to chuckle with delight – as Kyle wished the floor would open beneath him.

Maybe lightning would strike the pergola and they would have to evacuate?

In that moment, he was sincerely grateful that he wasn't having to pose for photos like Team Two... because he knew exactly who would mortgage their house or sell a kidney to be in some scantily clad firemen's calendar photograph with him.

Mrs. Kendall.

Kyle swallowed nervously and scanned the crowd as he listened vaguely to the mayor speak.

"This strapping young man is good with his hands..."

"What?" Kyle whispered, realizing how she was twisting the small paragraph they had to write about themselves. "I do carpentry, work on my truck, and am able do small tasks around the house, like painting and electrical work."

"He's *sooo* good with his big, strong hands and can really work a tool..."

"Oh my gosh," Kyle gaped, staring at her in shock and dismay as several people started to whoop excitedly, making his face turn even redder than it already was.

"He's the one that holds the hose, ladies..." the mayor teased playfully. "Charity, remember ladies?"

"I'm on the nozzle team," Kyle squawked, protesting. "I'm a nozzle firefighter, Mrs. Mayor. You're painting a terrible picture of me..."

"TWENTY-FIVE DOLLARS!" a voice called out.

"What?" Kyle said, whipping his head around to see who had bid.

"Make him take off that jacket so we can see his muscles..." a woman cried from the back of the crowd.

"Noooo," he grimaced, clenching it around him protectively.

"Take off your jacket, young man," the mayor urged pointedly under her breath. "It's for charity."

"Charity begins at home," he hissed back, glaring at her. "Why don't you make a donation and get me off this auction block!"

The mayor glared at him and slammed down the gavel to get their attention, causing everyone to look at her – including Kyle.

"Ladies, he said he's not taking off his jacket or anything else unless you get serious about the bidding…"

"I never said that!" Kyle balked.

"FIFTY!"

"SEVENTY-FIVE!"

"Do I hear a hundred?" the mayor asked openly, smiling happily.

"NOOOO?!" he yelped in shock, realizing this was getting completely out of control quickly every time he opened his mouth.

"ONE HUNDRED!" a woman said from the front row, not looking at Kyle, and her face was almost as ruddy with embarrassment as his was.

Her short cropped brown hair ended at her chin, and she was standing there looking like she'd just come from a funeral, wearing all black and dressed modestly despite the warmth of the day.

"There we go…" the mayor encouraged. "Did I mention that this young man, Kyle Rimes, is right at home getting on his hands and knees easily…"

"I scuttle up the fire engine's ladder, sheesh woman! Where did you get all of that?" Kyle hissed, looking at the crowd. "I know this is for charity – and I'm happy to partici-pate, but I'm… *this*… this isn't what you are thinking, ladies…"

"Is he married?" someone yelled out – and the mayor looked at him.

"No," Kyle muttered, knowing that despite what he said, he had lost this fight long before it ever started. "I'm single."

"Do you do woodwork or paint things?" the woman with the short hair asked nervously, catching his attention again as a ripple went through the crowd at his words. He was getting a mental picture of himself having to work around a house, shirtless, wearing a blond wig and tossing his hair like some cover of an old romance book cover model.

"Yeah, I'm pretty good with a circular saw and a jig…" Kyle admitted, swallowing hard as he tried to avoid looking at Mrs. Kendall who was literally fanning herself, made eye contact with him, and then pointed openly at Kyle… mouthing at him.

'You're mine, sweet Kyle'.

Kyle cringed, crossing himself openly.

"TWO HUNDRED!" a voice cried out – and he saw the woman with the short hair had bid again, still refusing to look at him.

"What?!"

"Take off your jacket, mister…" the mayor hissed angrily.

"Look – I'll throw in two hundred to end the stupid auction right now," Kyle said angrily, feeling nausea roll in his stomach at the thought of Mrs. Kendall possibly winning him. The old woman was a terror, and he was afraid she would really cross the line this time! "Get me off this auction block and stop this insanity. I'm not exactly what you are wanting up here…"

"SOLD!" the mayor hollered, banging her gavel noisily. "Mr. Kyle Rimes of the Flirt's Battalion…

"First Street!" Kyle interrupted pointedly.

"… Is yours for one entire twenty-four-hour period, Miss Reyna Mattingly," the mayor continued speaking, smiling at the crowd – and grabbing Kyle by the arm before he walked away.

"Mr. Rimes – you owe the charity two hundred dollars, remember?"

He glared at her, feeling practically man-handled and discomforted as he realized that his time had just been auctioned off like a haunch of meat to a butcher.

Nodding, he dug out his wallet and quickly handed over everything he'd withdrawn from the ATM the day before, intending to get a few things for an apartment he was hoping to lease very soon, that now would just have to wait until next payday…

"Can I have a list of the stupid rules for this farce?" he muttered – and was handed a sheet of paper with the details lined out for him. "Thanks."

"Thank *you*, Mr. Rimes…" the mayor said in a saccharine voice. "Ms. Mattingly? If you'll pay the cashier – there is a small picnic bench where you can discuss your upcoming 'date'…

"Meeting," Kyle corrected as the woman walked up.

"Meeting," the winner of the auction agreed coolly, still not looking at him as she dug out her wallet and paid the cashier. "I'll need a receipt for taxes – please, and thank you."

"Of course, Miss Mattingly."

"Thanks, Dolly…"

The woman turned and looked at him, spinning carefully as to not dig her heels into the grass – and he felt something move within him as he realized she had the most beautiful turquoise eyes he'd ever seen.

"You can paint?" she asked candidly.

"Yeah?"

"Wonderful," she began, and held out her hand in a businesslike manner. "I need your help – and quite a bit of painting done."

"You don't want to go on a date?"

"No," she said nervously, her hand remaining out as she

waited for him to take it. "I need help with my café – and I can't do it alone."

"But we are _not_ dating…?" he reiterated, arching an eyebrow, feeling slightly disappointed and a little relieved that he was off the hook. He could definitely do manual labor, but a part of him kind of wished that maybe she wasn't so disinterested… because she was really pretty.

"One date doesn't make people _'dating'_, you know… besides, it really makes things quite sordid, if I've paid for your company. Don't you think?"

"So, this _is_ a date?"

"No, Mr. Rimes… this is me, hiring you, to help me with some manual labor."

"Is that code for something?" he asked warily, thinking of his partner Austin immediately. Austin was always throwing out things that had a different meaning – and frankly? So did Andy. Those two men spoke an entirely different language sometimes.

"The mayor twisted stuff, so are you doing the same thing? Is _manual labor_ code for some weird, kinky thing that I'm too dumb or naïve to understand?"

The woman, Miss Mattingly, smiled nervously, and her cheeks reddened even more than he thought possible as she held his gaze.

"No. Manual labor is just that: manual labor," she replied. "You are going to work with your hands - painting."

Kyle nodded and listened distractedly as the crowd suddenly roared in delight as the auction continued in the distance, and he gave the elusive Miss Mattingly his phone number and accepted her business card.

"Text me when you have a day off this next week, and we'll get this out of the way, okay?" the woman said bluntly. "Now, if you'll excuse me? I'm late for a meeting…"

Kyle stared as she walked off. She was crossing the street,

heading into the bank at the corner of Main and State Street, leaving him more curious and mystified than before at seeing her – and her reaction to his questions.

She looked almost like she was as bothered as he was regarding the auction, and the fact that she'd just purchased his time and company.

… And he was fascinated.

ABOUT THE AUTHOR

Ginny Sterling is a Texas transplant living in Kentucky. She spends her free time (Ha!) writing, quilting, and spending time with her husband and two children. Ginny can be reached on Facebook, Instagram, Twitter or via email at GinnySterlingBooks@gmail.com

Subscribe now to my Newsletter for updates

Made in the USA
Las Vegas, NV
06 October 2024

96360063R00215